P9-BYY-630

Praise for #1 *New York Times* bestselling author Debbie Macomber

"Debbie Macomber has a gift for evoking the emotions that are at the heart of the genre's popularity."

—*Publishers Weekly*

"With first-class author Debbie Macomber, it's quite simple—she gives readers an exceptional, unforgettable story every time, and her books are always, always keepers!"

—*ReaderToReader.com*

"Macomber is a master storyteller."

—*RT Book Reviews*

Praise for *New York Times* bestselling author RaeAnne Thayne

"RaeAnne Thayne is quickly becoming one of my favorite authors.… Once you start reading, you aren't going to be able to stop."

—*Fresh Fiction* on *Snow Angel Cove*

"A sweet and touching story about two people who, despite the pain of their shared history, find their way back to each other."

—*RT Book Reviews* on *A Cold Creek Reunion*

Debbie Macomber is a number one *New York Times* and *USA TODAY* bestselling author. Her books include *1225 Christmas Tree Lane, 1105 Yakima Street, A Turn in the Road, Hannah's List* and *Debbie Macomber's Christmas Cookbook,* as well as *Twenty Wishes, Summer on Blossom Street* and *Call Me Mrs. Miracle.* She has become a leading voice in women's fiction worldwide and her work has appeared on every major bestseller list, including those of the *New York Times, USA TODAY, Publishers Weekly* and *Entertainment Weekly.* She is a multiple award winner, and won the 2005 Quill Award for Best Romance. There are more than 170 million copies of her books in print. Two of her MIRA Books Christmas titles have been made into Hallmark Channel Original Movies, and the Hallmark Channel has launched a series based on her bestselling Cedar Cove stories. For more information on Debbie and her books, visit her website, debbiemacomber.com.

RaeAnne Thayne finds inspiration in the beautiful northern Utah mountains, where the *New York Times* and *USA TODAY* bestselling author lives with her husband and three children. Her books have won numerous honors, including RITA® Award nominations from Romance Writers of America and a Career Achievement Award from *RT Book Review*s. RaeAnne loves to hear from readers and can be contacted through her website, raeannethayne.com.

#1 *New York Times* Bestselling Author

DEBBIE MACOMBER

DENIM AND DIAMONDS

HARLEQUIN® BESTSELLING AUTHOR COLLECTION

ISBN-13: 978-0-373-01039-4

Denim and Diamonds
Copyright © 2016 by Harlequin Books S.A.

The publisher acknowledges the copyright holders
of the individual works as follows:

Denim and Diamonds
Copyright © 1989 by Debbie Macomber

A Cold Creek Reunion
Copyright © 2012 by RaeAnne Thayne

Recycling programs
for this product may
not exist in your area.

Printed in U.S.A.

CONTENTS

DENIM AND DIAMONDS

Debbie Macomber

To Karen Macomber, sister, dear friend
and downtown Seattle explorer

Prologue

Dusk had settled; it was the end of another cold, harsh winter day in Red Springs, Wyoming. Chase Brown felt the chill of the north wind all the way through his bones as he rode Firepower, his chestnut gelding. He'd spent the better part of the afternoon searching for three heifers who'd gotten separated from the main part of his herd. He'd found the trio a little while earlier and bullied them back to where they belonged.

That tactic might work with cattle, but from experience, Chase knew it wouldn't work with Letty. She should be here, in Wyoming. With him. Four years had passed since she'd taken off for Hollywood on some fool dream of becoming a singing star. Four years! As far as Chase was concerned, that was three years too long.

Chase had loved Letty from the time she was a teenager. And she'd loved him. He'd spent all those lazy afternoons with her on the hillside, chewing on a blade of grass, talking, soaking up the warmth of the sun, and he knew she felt something deep and abiding for him. Letty had been innocent and Chase had sworn she would stay that way until they were married. Although it'd been hard not to make love to her the way he'd wanted. But Chase was a patient man, and he was convinced a lifetime with Letty was worth the wait.

When she'd graduated from high school, Chase had come to her with a diamond ring. He'd wanted her to share his vision of Spring Valley, have children with him to fill the emptiness that had been such a large part of his life since his father's death. Letty had looked up at him, tears glistening in her deep blue eyes, and whispered that she loved him more than she'd thought she'd ever love anyone. She'd begged him to come to California with her. But Chase couldn't leave his ranch and Red Springs any more than Letty could stay. So she'd gone after her dreams.

Letting her go had been the most difficult thing he'd ever had to do. Everyone in the county knew Letty Ellison was a gifted singer. Chase couldn't deny she had talent, lots of it. She'd often talked of becoming a professional singer, but Chase hadn't believed she'd choose that path over the one he was offering. She'd kissed him before she left, with all the innocence of her youth, and pleaded with him one more time to come with her. She'd had some ridiculous idea that he could become her manager. The only thing Chase had ever wanted to manage was Spring Valley, his ranch. With ambition clouding her eyes, she'd turned away from him and headed for the city lights.

That scene had played in Chase's mind a thousand

times in the past few years. When he slipped the diamond back inside his pocket four years earlier, he'd known it would be impossible to forget her. Someday she'd return, and when she did, he'd be waiting. She hadn't asked him to, but there was only one woman for him, and that was Letty Ellison.

Chase wouldn't have been able to tolerate her leaving if he hadn't believed she *would* return. The way he figured it, she'd be back within a year. All he had to do was show a little patience. If she hadn't found those glittering diamonds she was searching for within that time, then surely she'd come home.

But four long years had passed and Letty still hadn't returned.

The wind picked up as Chase approached the barnyard. He paused on the hill and noticed Letty's brother's beloved Ford truck parked outside the barn. A rush of adrenaline shot through Chase, accelerating his heartbeat. Involuntarily his hands tightened on Firepower's reins. Lonny had news, news that couldn't be relayed over the phone. Chase galloped into the yard.

"Evening, Chase," Lonny muttered as he climbed out of the truck.

"Lonny." He touched the brim of his hat with gloved fingers. "What brings you out?"

"It's about Letty."

The chill that had nipped at Chase earlier couldn't compare to the biting cold that sliced through him now. He eased himself out of the saddle, anxiety making the inside of his mouth feel dry.

"I thought you should know," Lonny continued, his expression uneasy. He kicked at a clod of dirt with the toe of his boot. "She called a couple of hours ago."

Lonny wouldn't look him in the eye, and that bothered Chase. Letty's brother had always shot from the hip.

"The best way to say this is straight out," Lonny said, his jaw clenched. "Letty's pregnant and the man isn't going to marry her. Apparently he's already married, and he never bothered to let her know."

If someone had slammed a fist into Chase's gut it wouldn't have produced the reaction Lonny's words did. He reeled back two steps before he caught himself. The pain was unlike anything he'd ever experienced.

"What's she going to do?" he managed to ask.

Lonny shrugged. "From what she said, she plans on keeping the baby."

"Is she coming home?"

"No."

Chase's eyes narrowed.

"I tried to talk some sense into her, believe me, but it didn't do a bit of good. She seems more determined than ever to stay in California." Lonny opened the door to his truck, looking guilty and angry at once. "Mom and Dad raised her better than this. I thank God they're both gone. I swear it would've killed Mom."

"I appreciate you telling me," Chase said after a lengthy pause. It took him that long to reclaim a grip on his chaotic emotions.

"I figured you had a right to know."

Chase nodded. He stood where he was, his boots planted in the frozen dirt until Lonny drove off into the fading sunlight. Firepower craned his neck toward the barn, toward warmth and a well-deserved dinner of oats and alfalfa. The gelding's action caught Chase's attention. He turned, reached for the saddle horn and in one smooth movement remounted the bay.

Firepower knew Chase well, and sensing his mood, the gelding galloped at a dead run. Still Chase pushed him on, farther and farther for what seemed like hours, until both man and horse were panting and exhausted. When the animal stopped, Chase wasn't surprised the unplanned route had led him to the hillside where he'd spent so many pleasant afternoons with Letty. Every inch of his land was familiar to him, but none more than those few acres.

His chest heaving with exertion, Chase climbed off Firepower and stood on the crest of the hill as the wind gusted against him. His lungs hurt and he dragged in several deep breaths, struggling to gain control of himself. Pain choked off his breath, dominated his thoughts. Nothing eased the terrible ache inside him.

He groaned and threw back his head with an anguish so intense it could no longer be held inside. His piercing shout filled the night as he buckled, fell to his knees and covered his face with both hands.

Then Chase Brown did something he hadn't done in fifteen years.

He wept.

Chapter 1

Five years later

Letty Ellison was home. She hadn't been back to Red Springs in more than nine years, and she was astonished by how little the town had changed. She'd been determined to come home a star; it hadn't happened. Swallowing her pride and returning to the town, the ranch, without having achieved her big dream was one thing. But to show up on her brother's doorstep, throw her arms around him and casually announce she could be dying was another.

As a matter of fact, Letty had gotten pretty philosophical about death. The hole in her heart had been small enough to go undetected most of her life, but it was there, and unless she had the necessary surgery, it would soon be lights out, belly up, buy the farm, kick the bucket or whatever else people said when they were about to die.

The physicians had made her lack of options abundantly clear when she was pregnant with Cricket, her daughter. If her heart defect hadn't been discovered then and had remained undetected, her doctor had assured her she'd be dead before she reached thirty.

And so Letty had come home. Home to Wyoming. Home to the Bar E Ranch. Home to face whatever lay before her. Life or death.

In her dreams, Letty had often imagined her triumphant return. She saw herself riding through town sitting in the back of a red convertible, dressed in a strapless gown, holding bouquets of red roses. The high school band would lead the procession. Naturally the good people of Red Springs would be lining Main Street, hoping to get a look at her. Being the amiable soul she was, Letty would give out autographs and speak kindly to people she hardly remembered.

Her actual return had been quite different from what she'd envisioned. Lonny had met her at the Rock Springs Airport when she'd arrived with Cricket the evening before. It really had been wonderful to see her older brother. Unexpected tears had filled her eyes as they hugged. Lonny might be a onetime rodeo champ and now a hard-bitten rancher, but he was the only living relative she and Cricket had. And if anything were to happen to her, she hoped her brother would love and care for Cricket with the same dedication Letty herself had. So far, she hadn't told him about her condition, and she didn't know when she would. When the time felt right, she supposed.

Sunlight filtered in through the curtain, and drawing in a deep breath, Letty sat up in bed and examined her old bedroom. So little had changed in the past nine years. The lace doily decorating the old bureau was the same one that had been there when she was growing up. The photograph of her and her pony hung on the wall. How Letty had loved old Nellie. Even her bed was covered with the same quilted spread that had been there when she was eighteen, the one her mother had made.

Nothing had changed and yet everything was different. Because *she* was different.

The innocent girl who'd once slept in this room was gone forever. Instead Letty was now a woman who'd become disenchanted with dreams and disillusioned by life. She could never go back to the guileless teen she'd been, but she wouldn't give up the woman she'd become, either.

With that thought in mind, she folded back the covers and climbed out of bed. Her first night home, and she'd slept soundly. *She* might not be the same, but the sense of welcome she felt in this old house was.

Checking in the smallest bedroom across the hall, Letty found her daughter still asleep, her faded yellow "blankey" clutched protectively against her chest. Letty and Cricket had arrived exhausted. With little more than a hug from Lonny, she and her daughter had fallen into bed. Letty had promised Lonny they'd talk later.

Dressing quickly, she walked down the stairs and was surprised to discover her brother sitting at the kitchen table, waiting for her.

"I was beginning to wonder if you'd ever wake up," he said, grinning. The years had been good to Lonny. He'd always been handsome—as dozens of young women had noticed while he was on the rodeo circuit. He'd quit eight years ago, when his father got sick, and had dedicated himself to the Bar E ever since. Still, Letty couldn't understand why he'd stayed single all this time. Then again, she could. Lonny, like Chase Brown, their neighbor, lived for his land and his precious herd of cattle. That was what their whole lives revolved around. Lonny wasn't married because he hadn't met a woman he considered an asset to the Bar E.

"How come you aren't out rounding up cattle or repairing fences or whatever it is you do in the mornings?" she teased, smiling at him.

"I wanted to welcome you home properly."

After pouring herself a cup of coffee, Letty walked to the table, leaned over and kissed his sun-bronzed cheek. "It's great to be back."

Letty meant that. Her pride had kept her away all these years. How silly that seemed now, how pointless and stubborn not to admit her name wasn't going to light up any marquee, when she'd lived and breathed that knowledge each and every day in California. Letty had talent; she'd known that when she left the Bar E nine years ago. It was the blind ambition and ruthless drive she'd lacked. Oh, there'd been brief periods of promise and limited success. She'd sung radio commercials and done some backup work for a couple of rising stars, but she'd long ago given up the hope of ever making it big herself. At one time, becoming a singer had meant the world to her. Now it meant practically nothing.

Lonny reached for her fingers. "It's good to have you home, sis. You've been away too long."

She sat across from him, holding her coffee mug with both hands, and gazed down at the old Formica tabletop. In nine years, Lonny hadn't replaced a single piece of furniture.

It wasn't easy to admit, but Letty needed to say it. "I should've come back before now." She thought it was best to let him know this before she told him about her heart.

"Yeah," Lonny said evenly. "I wanted you back when Mom died."

"It was too soon then. I'd been in California less than two years."

It hurt Letty to think about losing her mother. Maren Ellison's death had been sudden. Although Maren had begged her not to leave Red Springs, she was a large part of the reason Letty had gone. Her mother had had talent, too. She'd been an artist whose skill had lain dormant while she wasted away on a ranch, unappreciated and unfulfilled. All her life, Letty had heard her mother talk about painting in oils someday. But that day had never come. Then, when everyone had least expected it, Maren had died—less than a year after her husband. In each case, Letty had flown in for the funerals, then returned to California the next morning.

"What are your plans now?" Lonny asked, watching her closely.

Letty's immediate future involved dealing with social workers, filling out volumes of forms and having a dozen doctors examine her to tell her what she already knew. Heart surgery didn't come cheap. "The first thing I thought I'd do was clean the house," she said, deliberately misunderstanding him.

A guilty look appeared on her brother's face and Letty chuckled softly.

"I suppose the place is a real mess." Lonny glanced furtively around. "I've let things go around here for the past few years. When you phoned and said you were coming, I picked up what I could. You've probably guessed I'm not much of a housekeeper."

"I don't expect you to be when you're dealing with several hundred head of cattle."

Lonny seemed surprised by her understanding. He stood and grabbed his hat, adjusting it on his head. "How long do you plan to stay?"

Letty shrugged. "I'm not sure yet. Is my being here a problem?"

"Not in the least," Lonny rushed to assure her. "Stay as long as you like. I welcome the company—and decent meals for a change. If you want, I can see about finding you a job in town."

"I don't think there's much call for a failed singer in Red Springs, is there?"

"I thought you said you'd worked as a secretary."

"I did, part-time, and as a temp." In order to have flexible hours, she'd done what she'd had to in order to survive, but in following her dream she'd missed out on health insurance benefits.

"There ought to be something for you, then. I'll ask around."

"Don't," Letty said urgently. "Not yet, anyway." After the surgery would be soon enough to locate employment. For the time being, she had to concentrate on making arrangements with the appropriate authorities. She should probably tell Lonny about her heart condition, she decided reluctantly, but it was too much to hit him with right away. There'd be plenty of time later, after the arrangements had been made. No point in upsetting him now. Besides, she wanted him to become acquainted with Cricket before he found out she'd be listing him as her daughter's guardian.

"Relax for a while," Lonny said. "Take a vacation. There's no need for you to work if you don't want to."

"Thanks, I appreciate that."

"What are brothers for?" he joked, and drained his coffee. "I should get busy," he said, rinsing his cup and setting it on the kitchen counter. "I should've gotten started hours ago, but I wanted to talk to you first."

"What time will you be back?"

Lonny's eyes widened, as though he didn't understand. "Five or so, I guess. Why?"

"I just wanted to know when to plan dinner."

"Six should be fine."

Letty stood, her arms wrapped protectively around her waist. One question had been burning in her mind from the minute she'd pulled into the yard. One she needed to ask, but whose answer she feared. She tentatively broached the subject. "Will you be seeing Chase?"

"I do most days."

"Does he know I'm back?"

Lonny's fingers gripped the back door handle. "He knows," he said without looking at her.

Letty nodded and she curled her hands into fists. "Is he...married?"

Lonny shook his head. "Nope, and I don't imagine he ever will be, either." He hesitated before adding, "Chase is a lot different now from the guy you used to know. I hope you're not expecting anything from him, because you're headed for a big disappointment if you are. You'll know what I mean once you see him."

A short silence followed while Letty considered her brother's words. "You needn't worry that I've come home expecting things to be the way they were between Chase and me. If he's different...that's fine. We've all changed."

Lonny nodded and was gone.

The house was quiet after her brother left. His warning about Chase seemed to taunt her. The Chase Brown she knew was gentle, kind, good. When Letty was seventeen he'd been the only one who really understood her dreams. Although it had broken his heart, he'd loved her enough to encourage her to seek her destiny. Chase had loved her more than anyone before or since.

And she'd thrown his love away.

"Mommy, you were gone when I woke up." Looking forlorn, five-year-old Cricket stood in the doorway of the kitchen, her yellow blanket clutched in her hand and dragging on the faded red linoleum floor.

"I was just downstairs," Letty said, holding out her arms to the youngster, who ran eagerly to her mother, climbing onto Letty's lap.

"I'm hungry."

"I'll bet you are." Letty brushed the dark hair away from her daughter's face and kissed her forehead. "I was talking to Uncle Lonny this morning."

Cricket stared up at her with deep blue eyes that were a reflection of her own. She'd inherited little in the way of looks from her father. The dark hair and blue eyes were Ellison family traits. On rare occasions, Letty would see traces of Jason in their child, but not often. She tried not to think about him or their disastrous affair. He was out of her life and she wanted no part of him—except for Christina Maren, her Cricket.

"You know what I thought we'd do today?" Letty said.

"After breakfast?"

"After breakfast." She smiled. "I thought we'd clean house and bake a pie for Uncle Lonny."

"Apple pie," Cricket announced with a firm nod.

"I'm sure apple pie's his favorite."

"Mine, too."

Together they cooked oatmeal. Cricket insisted on helping by setting the table and getting the milk from the refrigerator.

As soon as they'd finished, Letty mopped the floor and washed the cupboards. Lonny's declaration about not being much of a housekeeper had been an understatement. He'd done the bare minimum for years, and the house was badly in need of a thorough cleaning. Usually, physical activity quickly wore Letty out and she became breathless and light-headed. But this morning she was filled with an enthusiasm that provided her with energy.

By noon, however, she was exhausted. At nap time, Letty lay down with Cricket, and didn't wake until early afternoon, when the sound of male voices drifted up the stairs. She realized almost immediately that Chase Brown was with her brother.

Running a brush through her short curly hair, Letty composed herself for the coming confrontation with Chase and walked calmly down the stairs.

He and her brother were sitting at the table, drinking coffee.

Lonny glanced up when she entered the room, but Chase looked away from her. Her brother had made a point of telling her that Chase was different, and she could see the truth of his words. Chase's dark hair had become streaked with gray in her absence. Deep crevices marked his forehead and grooved the sides of his mouth. In nine years he'd aged twenty, Letty thought with a stab of regret. Part of her longed to wrap her arms around him the way she had so many years before. She yearned to bury her head in his shoulder and weep for the pain she'd caused him.

But she knew she couldn't.

"Hello, Chase," she said softly, walking over to the stove and reaching for the coffeepot.

"Letty." He lowered his head in greeting, but kept his eyes averted.

"It's good to see you again."

He didn't answer that; instead he returned his attention to her brother. "I was thinking about separating part of the herd, driving them a mile or so south. Of course, that'd mean hauling the feed a lot farther, but I believe the benefits will outweigh that inconvenience."

"I think you're going to a lot of effort for nothing," Lonny said, frowning.

Letty pulled out a chair and sat across from Chase. He could only ignore her for so long. Still his gaze skirted hers, and he did his utmost to avoid looking at her.

"Who are you?"

Letty turned to the doorway, where Cricket was standing, blanket held tightly in her hand.

"Cricket, this is Uncle Lonny's neighbor, Mr. Brown."

"I'm Cricket," she said, grinning cheerfully.

"Hello." Chase spoke in a gruff unfriendly tone, obviously doing his best to disregard the little girl in the same manner he chose to overlook her mother.

A small cry of protest rose in Letty's throat. Chase could be as angry with her as he wanted. The way she figured it, that was his right, but he shouldn't take out his bitterness on an innocent child.

"Your hair's a funny color," Cricket commented, fascinated. "I think it's pretty like that." Her yellow blanket in tow, she marched up to Chase and raised her hand to touch the salt-and-pepper strands that were more pronounced at his temple.

Chase frowned and moved back so there wasn't any chance of her succeeding.

"My mommy and I are going to bake a pie for Uncle Lonny. Do you want some?"

Letty held her breath, waiting for Chase to reply. Something about him appeared to intrigue Cricket. The child couldn't stop staring at him. Her actions seemed to unnerve Chase, who made it obvious that he'd like nothing better than to forget her existence.

"I don't think Mr. Brown is interested in apple pie, sweetheart," Letty said, trying to fill the uncomfortable silence.

"Then we'll make something he does like," Cricket insisted. She reached for Chase's hand and tugged, demanding his attention. "Do you like chocolate chip cookies? I do. And Mommy makes really yummy ones."

For a moment Chase stared at Cricket, and the pain that flashed in his dark eyes went straight through Letty's heart. A split second later he glanced away as though he couldn't bear to continue looking at the child.

"Do you?" Cricket persisted.

Chase nodded, although it was clearly an effort to do so.

"Come on, Mommy," Cricket cried. "I want to make them *now*."

"What about my apple pie?" Lonny said, his eyes twinkling.

Cricket ignored the question, intent on the cookie-making task. She dragged her blanket after her as she started opening and closing the bottom cupboards, searching for bowls and pans. She dutifully brought out two of each and rummaged through the drawers until she located a wooden spoon. Then, as though suddenly finding the blanket cumbersome, the child lifted it from the floor and placed it in Chase's lap.

Letty could hardly believe her eyes. She'd brought Cricket home from the hospital in that yellow blanket and the little girl had slept with it every night of her life since. Rarely would she entrust it to anyone, let alone a stranger.

Chase looked down on the much-loved blanket as if the youngster had deposited a dirty diaper in his lap.

"I'll take it," Letty said, holding out her hands.

Chase gave it to her, and when he did, his cold gaze locked with hers. Letty felt the chill in his eyes all the way through her bones. His bitterness toward her was evident with every breath he drew.

"It would've been better if you'd never come back," he said so softly she had to strain to hear.

She opened her mouth to argue. Even Lonny didn't know the real reason she'd returned to Wyoming. No one did, except her doctor in California. She hadn't meant to come back and disrupt Chase's life—or anyone else's, for that matter. Chase didn't need to spell out that he didn't want anything to do with her. He'd made that clear the minute she'd walked into the kitchen.

"Mommy, hurry," Cricket said. "We have to bake cookies."

"Just a minute, sweetheart." Letty was uncertain how to handle this new problem. She doubted Lonny had chocolate chips in the house, and a trip into town was more than she wanted to tackle that afternoon.

"Cricket…"

Lonny and Chase both stood. "I'm driving on over to Chase's for the rest of the afternoon," Lonny told her. He obviously wasn't accustomed to letting anyone know his whereabouts and did so now only as an afterthought.

"Can I go, too?" Cricket piped up, so eager her blue eyes sparkled with the idea.

Letty wanted her daughter to be comfortable with Lonny, and she would've liked to encourage the two of them to become friends, but the frown that darkened Chase's brow told her now wasn't the time.

"Not today," Letty murmured, looking away from the two men.

Cricket pouted for a few minutes, but didn't argue. It wouldn't have mattered if she had, because Lonny and Chase left without another word.

Dinner was ready and waiting when Lonny returned to the house that evening. Cricket ran to greet him, her pigtails bouncing. "Mommy and me cooked dinner for you!"

Lonny smiled down on her and absently patted her head, then went to the bathroom to wash his hands. Letty watched him and felt a tugging sense of discontent. After years of living alone, Lonny tended not to be as communicative as Letty wanted him to be. This was understandable, but it made her realize how lonely he must be out here on the ranch night after night without anyone to share his life. Ranchers had to be more stubborn than any other breed of male, Letty thought.

To complicate matters, there was the issue of Cricket staying with Lonny while Letty had the surgery. The little girl had never been away from her overnight.

Letty's prognosis for a complete recovery was good,

but there was always the possibility that she wouldn't be coming home from the hospital. Any number of risks had to be considered with this type of operation, and if anything were to happen, Lonny would have to raise Cricket on his own. Letty didn't doubt he'd do so with the greatest of care, but he simply wasn't accustomed to dealing with children.

By the time her brother had finished washing up, dinner was on the table. He gazed down at the ample amount of food and grinned appreciatively. "I can't tell you how long it's been since I've had a home-cooked meal like this. I've missed it."

"What have you been eating?"

He shrugged. "I come up with something or other, but nothing as appetizing as this." He sat down and filled his plate, hardly waiting for Cricket and Letty to join him.

He was buttering his biscuit when he paused and looked at Letty. Slowly he put down the biscuit and placed his knife next to his plate. "Are you okay?" he asked.

"Sure," she answered, smiling weakly. Actually, she wasn't—the day had been exhausting. She'd tried to do too much and she was paying the price, feeling shaky and weak. "What makes you ask?"

"You're pale."

That could be attributed to seeing Chase again, but Letty didn't say so. Their brief meeting had left her feeling melancholy all afternoon. She'd been so young and so foolish, seeking bright lights, utterly convinced that she'd never be satisfied with the lot of a rancher's wife. She'd wanted diamonds, not denim.

"No, I'm fine," she lied as Lonny picked up the biscuit again.

"Mommy couldn't find any chocolate chips," Cricket said, frowning, "so we just baked the apple pie."

Lonny nodded, far more interested in his gravy and biscuits than in conversing with a child.

"I took Cricket out to the barn and showed her the horses," Letty said.

Lonny nodded, then helped himself to seconds on the biscuits. He spread a thick layer of butter on each half.

"I thought maybe later you could let Cricket give them their oats," Letty prompted.

"The barn isn't any place for a little girl," Lonny murmured, dismissing the suggestion with a quick shake of his head.

Cricket looked disappointed and Letty mentally chastised herself for mentioning the idea in front of her daughter. She should've known better.

"Maybe Uncle Lonny will let me ride his horsey?" Cricket asked, her eyes wide and hopeful. "Mommy had a horsey when *she* was a little girl—I saw the picture in her room. I want one, too."

"You have to grow up first," Lonny said brusquely, ending the conversation.

It was on the tip of Letty's tongue to ask Lonny if he'd let Cricket sit in a saddle, but he showed no inclination to form a relationship with her daughter.

Letty was somewhat encouraged when Cricket went in to watch television with Lonny while she finished the dishes. But no more than ten minutes had passed before she heard Cricket burst into tears. A moment later, she came running into the kitchen. She buried her face in

Letty's stomach and wrapped both arms around her, sobbing so hard her shoulders shook.

Lonny followed Cricket into the room, his face a study in guilt and frustration.

"What happened?" Letty asked, stroking her daughter's head.

Lonny threw his hands in the air. "I don't know! I turned on the TV and I was watching the news, when Cricket said she wanted to see cartoons."

"There aren't any on right now," Letty explained.

Cricket sobbed louder, then lifted her head. Tears ran unrestrained down her cheeks. "He said *no,* real mean."

"She started talking to me in the middle of a story about the rodeo championships in Vegas, for Pete's sake." Lonny stabbed his fingers through his hair.

"Cricket, Uncle Lonny didn't mean to upset you," Letty told her. "He was watching his program and you interrupted him, that's all."

"But he said it *mean.*"

"I hardly raised my voice," Lonny came back, obviously perplexed. "Are kids always this sensitive?"

"Not really," Letty assured him. Cricket was normally an easygoing child. Fits of crying were rare and usually the result of being overtired. "It was probably a combination of the flight and a busy day."

Lonny nodded and returned to the living room without speaking to Cricket directly. Letty watched him go with a growing sense of concern. Lonny hadn't been around children in years and didn't have the slightest notion how to deal with a five-year-old. Cricket had felt more of a rapport with Chase than she did her own uncle, and Chase had done everything he could to ignore her.

Letty spent the next few minutes comforting her daughter. After giving Cricket a bath, Letty read her a story and tucked her in for the night. With her hand on the light switch, she acted out a game they'd played since Cricket was two.

"Blow out the light," she whispered.

The child blew with all her might. At that precise moment, Letty flipped the switch.

"Good night, Mommy."

"Night, sweetheart."

Lonny was waiting for her in the living room, still frowning over the incident between him and his niece. "I don't know, Letty," he said, apparently still unsettled. "I don't seem to be worth much in the uncle department."

"Don't worry about it," she said, trying to smile, but her thoughts were troubled. She couldn't schedule the surgery if she wasn't sure Cricket would be comfortable with Lonny.

"I'll try not to upset her again," Lonny said, looking doubtful, "but I don't think I relate well to kids. I've been a bachelor for too long."

Bachelor...

That was it. The solution to her worries. All evening she'd been thinking how lonely her brother was and how he needed someone to share his life. The timing was perfect.

Her gaze flew to her brother and she nearly sighed aloud with relief. What Lonny needed was a wife.

And Letty was determined to find him one.

Fast.

Chapter 2

It wasn't exactly the welcome parade Letty had dreamed about, with the bright red convertible and the high school marching band, but Red Springs's reception was characteristically warm.

"Letty, it's terrific to see you again!"

"Why, Letty Ellison, I thought you were your dear mother. I never realized how much you resemble Maren. I still miss her, you know."

"Glad you're back, Letty. Hope you plan to stay a while."

Letty smiled and shook hands and received so many hugs she was late for the opening hymn at the Methodist church the next Sunday morning.

With Cricket by her side, she slipped silently into a pew and reached for a hymnal. The hymn was a familiar one from her childhood and Letty knew the lyrics well. But even before she opened her mouth to join the others, tears welled up in her eyes. The organ music swirled around her, filling what seemed to be an unending void in her life. It felt so good to be back. So right to be standing in church with her childhood friends and the people she loved.

Attending services here was part of the magnetic pull that had brought her back to Wyoming. This comforting and spiritual experience reminded her that problems were like mountains. There wasn't one she couldn't handle with God's help. Either she'd climb it, pass around it or carve a tunnel through it.

The music continued and Letty reached for a tissue, dabbing at the tears. Her throat had closed up, and that made singing impossible, so she stood with her eyes shut, soaking up the words of the age-old hymn.

Led by instinct, she'd come back to Red Springs, back to the Bar E and the small Methodist church in the heart of town. She was wrapping everything that was important and familiar around her like a homemade quilt on a cold December night.

The organ music faded and Pastor Downey stepped forward to offer a short prayer. As Letty bowed her head, she could feel someone's bold stare. Her unease grew until she felt herself shudder. It was a sensation her mother had often referred to as someone walking over her grave. An involuntary smile tugged at Letty's mouth. That analogy certainly hit close to home. Much too close.

When the prayer was finished, it was all Letty could do not to turn around and find out who was glaring at her. Although she could guess…

"Mommy," Cricket whispered, loudly enough for half the congregation to hear. "The man who likes chocolate chip cookies is here. He's two rows behind us."

Chase. Letty released an inward sigh. Just as she'd

suspected, he was the one challenging her appearance in church, as if her presence would corrupt the good people of this gathering. Letty mused that he'd probably like it if she wore a scarlet A so everyone would know she was a sinner.

Lonny had warned her that Chase was different. And he was. The Chase Brown Letty remembered wasn't judgmental or unkind. He used to be fond of children. Letty recalled that, years ago, when they walked through town, kids would automatically come running to Chase. He usually had coins for the gum-ball machine tucked away in his pocket, which he'd dole out judiciously. Something about him seemed to attract children, and the fact that Cricket had taken to him instantly was proof of his appeal.

An icy hand closed around Letty's heart at the memory. Chase was the type of man who should've married and fathered a houseful of kids. Over the years, she'd hoped he'd done exactly that.

But he hadn't. Instead Chase had turned bitter and hard. Letty was well aware that she'd hurt him terribly. How she regretted that. Chase had loved her, but all he felt for her now was disdain. In years past, he hadn't been able to disguise his love; now, sadly, he had difficulty hiding his dislike.

Letty had seen the wounded look in his eyes when she'd walked into the kitchen the day before. She'd known then that she'd been the one to put it there. If she hadn't been so familiar with him, he might've been able to fool her.

If only she could alter the past....

"Mommy, what's his name again?" Cricket demanded.

"Mr. Brown."

"Can I wave to him?"

"Not now."

"I want to talk to him."

Exasperated, Letty placed her hand on her daughter's shoulder and leaned down to whisper, "Why?"

"Because I bet he has a horse. Uncle Lonny won't let me ride his. Maybe Mr. Brown will."

"Oh, Cricket, I don't think so...."

"Why not?" the little girl pressed.

"We'll talk about this later."

"But I can ask, can't I? Please?"

The elderly couple in front of them turned around to see what all the commotion was about.

"Mommy?" Cricket persisted, clearly running out of patience.

"Yes, fine," Letty agreed hurriedly, against her better judgment.

From that moment on, Cricket started to fidget. Letty had to speak to her twice during the fifteen-minute sermon; during the closing hymn, Cricket turned around to wave at Chase. She could barely wait for the end of the service so she could rush over and ask about his horse.

Letty could feel the dread mounting inside her. Chase didn't want anything to do with Cricket, and Letty hated the thought of him hurting the little girl's feelings. When the final prayer was offered, Letty added a small request of her own.

"Can we leave now?" Cricket said, reaching for her mother's hand and tugging at it as the concluding burst of organ music filled the church.

Letty nodded. Cricket dropped her hand and was off. Letty groaned inwardly and dashed after her.

Standing on the church steps, Letty saw that Chase was walking toward the parking lot when Cricket caught up with him. She must have called his name, because Chase turned around abruptly. Even from that distance, Letty could see his dark frown. Quickening her step, she made her way toward them.

"Good morning, Chase," she greeted him, forcing a smile as she stood beside Cricket.

"Letty." His hat was in his hand and he rotated the brim, as though eager to make his escape, which Letty felt sure he was.

"I asked him already," Cricket blurted out, glancing up at her mother.

From the look Chase was giving Letty, he seemed to believe she'd put Cricket up to this. As if she spent precious time thinking up ways to irritate him!

"Mr. Brown's much too busy, sweetheart," Letty said, struggling to keep her voice even and controlled. "Perhaps you can ride his horse another time."

Cricket nodded and grinned. "That's what he said, too."

Surprised, Letty gazed up at Chase. She was grateful he hadn't been harsh with her daughter. From somewhere deep inside, she dredged up a smile to thank him, but he didn't answer it with one of his own. A fresh sadness settled over Letty. The past would always stand between them and there was nothing Letty could do to change that. She wasn't even sure she should try.

"If you'll excuse me," she said, reaching for Cricket's hand, "there are some people I want to talk to."

"More people?" Cricket whined. "I didn't know there were so many people in the whole world."

"It was nice to see you again, Chase," Letty said, turning away. Not until several minutes later did she realize he hadn't echoed her greeting.

* * *

Chase couldn't get away from the church fast enough. He didn't know why he'd decided to attend services this particular morning. It wasn't as if he made a regular practice of it, although he'd been raised in the church. He supposed that something perverse inside him was interested in knowing if Letty had the guts to show up.

The woman had nerve. Another word that occurred to him was *courage;* it wouldn't be easy to face all those people with an illegitimate daughter holding her hand. That kind of thing might be acceptable in big cities, but people here tended to be more conservative. Outwardly folks would smile, but the gossip would begin soon enough. He suspected that once it did, Letty would pack up her bags and leave again.

He wished she would. One look at her the day she'd arrived and he knew he'd been lying to himself all these years. She was paler than he remembered, but her face was still a perfect oval, her skin creamy and smooth. Her blue eyes were huge and her mouth a lush curve. There was no way he could continue lying to himself. He was still in love with her—and always would be.

He climbed inside his pickup and started the engine viciously. He gripped the steering wheel hard. Who was he trying to kid? He'd spent years waiting for Letty to come back. Telling himself he hated her was nothing more than a futile effort to bolster his pride. He wished there could be someone else for him, but there wasn't; there never would be. Letty was the only woman he'd ever loved, heart and soul. If she couldn't be the one to fill his arms during the night, then they'd remain empty. But there was no reason for Letty ever to know that. The fact was, he'd prefer it if she didn't find out.

Chase Brown might be fool enough to fall in love with the wrong woman, but he knew better than to hand her the weapon that would shred what remained of his pride.

"You must be Lonny's sister," a feminine voice drawled from behind Letty.

Letty finished greeting one of her mother's friends before turning. When she did, she met a statuesque blonde, who looked about thirty. "Yes, I'm Lonny's sister," she said, smiling.

"I'm so happy to meet you. I'm Mary Brandon," the woman continued. "I hope you'll forgive me for being so direct, but I heard someone say your name and thought I'd introduce myself."

"I'm pleased to meet you, Mary." They exchanged quick handshakes as Letty sized up the other woman. Single—and eager. "How do you know Lonny?"

"I work at the hardware store and your brother comes in every now and then. He might have mentioned me?" she asked hopefully. When Letty shook her head, Mary shrugged and gave a nervous laugh. "He stops in and gets whatever he needs and then he's on his way." She paused. "He must be lonely living out on that ranch all by himself. Especially after all those years in the rodeo."

Letty could feel the excitement bubbling up inside her. Mary Brandon definitely looked like wife material to her, and it was obvious the woman was more than casually interested in Lonny. As far as Letty was concerned, there wasn't any better place to find a prospective mate for her brother than in church.

The night before, she'd lain in bed wondering where she'd ever meet someone suitable for Lonny. If he hadn't found anyone in the past few years, there was nothing to guarantee that she could come up with the perfect mate in just a few months. The truth was, she didn't know whether he'd had any serious—or even not-so-serious—relationships during her years away. His rodeo success had certainly been an enticement to plenty of girls, but since he'd retired from the circuit and since their parents had died, her brother had become so single-minded, so dedicated to the ranch, that he'd developed tunnel vision. The Bar E now demanded all his energy and all his time, and consequently his personal life had suffered.

"Your brother seems very nice," Mary was saying.

And eligible, Letty added silently. "He's wonderful, but he works so hard it's difficult for anyone to get to know him."

Mary sent her a look that said she understood that all too well. "He's not seeing anyone regularly, is he?"

"No." But Letty wished he was.

Mary's eyes virtually snapped with excitement. "He hides away on the Bar E and hardly ever socializes. I firmly believe he needs a little fun in his life."

Letty's own eyes were gleaming. "I think you may be right. Listen, Mary, perhaps we should talk..."

Chase was working in the barn when he heard Lonny's truck. He wiped the perspiration off his brow with his forearm.

Lonny walked in and Chase immediately recognized that he was upset. Chase shoved the pitchfork into the hay and leaned against it. "Problems?"

Lonny didn't answer him right away. He couldn't seem to stay in one place. "It's that fool sister of mine."

Chase's hand closed around the pitchfork. Letty had

been on his mind all morning and she was the last person he wanted to discuss. Lonny appeared to be waiting for a response, so Chase gave him one. "I knew she'd be nothing but trouble from the moment you told me she was coming home."

Lonny removed his hat and slapped it against his thigh. "She went to church this morning." He turned to glance in Chase's direction. "Said she saw you there. Actually, it was her kid, Cricket, who mentioned your name. She calls you 'the guy who likes chocolate chip cookies.'" He grinned slightly at that.

"I was there," Chase said tersely.

"At any rate, Letty talked to Mary Brandon afterward."

A smile sprang to Chase's lips. Mary had set her sights on Lonny three months ago, and she wasn't about to let up until she got her man.

"Wipe that smug look off your face, Brown. You're supposed to be my friend."

"I am." He lifted a forkful of hay and tossed it behind him. Lonny had been complaining about the Brandon woman for weeks. Mary had done everything but stand on her head to garner his attention. And a wedding ring.

Lonny stalked aggressively to the other end of the barn, then returned. "Letty's overstepped the bounds this time," he muttered.

"Oh? What did she do?"

"She invited Mary to dinner tomorrow night."

Despite himself, Chase burst out laughing. He turned around to discover his friend glaring at him and stopped abruptly. "You're kidding, I hope?"

"Would I be this upset if I was? She invited that… woman right into my house without even asking me how I felt about it. I told her I had other plans for dinner tomorrow, but she claims she needs me there to cut the meat. Nine years in California and she didn't learn how to cut meat?"

"Well, it seems to me you're stuck having dinner with Mary Brandon." Chase realized he shouldn't find the situation so funny. But he did. Chase wasn't keen on Mary himself. There was something faintly irritating about the woman, something that rubbed him the wrong way. Lonny had the same reaction, although they'd never discussed what it was that annoyed them so much. Chase supposed it was the fact that Mary came on so strong. She was a little too desperate to snare herself a husband.

Brooding, Lonny paced the length of the barn. "I told Letty I was only staying for dinner if you were there, too."

Chase stabbed the pitchfork into the ground. "You did *what?*"

"If I'm going to suffer through an entire dinner with that...that woman, I need another guy to run interference. You can't expect me to sit across the dinner table from those two."

"Three," Chase corrected absently. Lonny hadn't included Cricket.

"Oh, yeah, that's right. Three against one. It's more than any man can handle on his own." He shook his head. "I love my sister, don't get me wrong. I'm glad she decided to come home. She should've done it years ago...but I'm telling you, I like my life exactly as it is. Every time I turn around, Cricket's underfoot asking me questions. I can't even check out the news without her wanting to watch cartoons."

"Maybe you should ask Letty to leave." A part of

Chase—a part he wasn't proud of—prayed that Lonny would. He hadn't had a decent night's sleep since he'd found out she was returning to Red Springs. He worked until he was ready to drop, and still his mind refused to give him the rest he craved. Instead he'd been tormented by resurrected memories he thought he'd buried years before. Like his friend, Chase had created a comfortable niche for himself and he didn't like his peace of mind invaded by Letty Ellison.

"I can't ask her to leave," Lonny said in a burst of impatience. "She's my *sister!*"

Chase shrugged. "Then tell her to uninvite Mary."

"I tried that. Before I knew it, she was reminding me how much Mom enjoyed company. Then she said that since she was moving back to the community, it was only right for her to get to know the new folks in town. At the time it made perfect sense, and a few minutes later, I'd agreed to be there for that stupid dinner. But there's only one way I'll go through with this and that's if you come, too."

"Cancel the dinner, then."

"Chase! How often do I ask you for a favor?"

Chase glared at him.

"All right, *that* kind of favor!"

"I'm sorry, Lonny, but I won't have anything to do with Mary Brandon."

Lonny was quiet for so long that Chase finally turned to meet his narrowed gaze. "Is it Mary or Letty who bothers you?" his friend asked.

Chase tightened his fingers around the pitchfork. "Doesn't matter, because I won't be there."

Letty took an afternoon nap with Cricket, hoping her explanation wouldn't raise Lonny's suspicions. She'd told him she was suffering from the lingering effects of jet lag.

First thing Monday morning, she planned to contact the state social services office. She couldn't put it off any longer. Each day she seemed to grow weaker and tired more easily. The thought of dealing with the state agency filled her with apprehension; accepting charity went against everything in her, but the cost of the surgery was prohibitive. Letty, who'd once been so proud, was forced to accept the generosity of the tax-payers of Wyoming.

Cricket stirred beside her in the bed as Letty drifted into an uneasy sleep. When she awoke, she noticed Cricket's yellow blanket draped haphazardly over her shoulders. Her daughter was gone.

Yawning, she went downstairs to discover Cricket sitting in front of the television. "Uncle Lonny says he doesn't want dinner tonight."

"That's tomorrow night," Lonny shouted from the kitchen. "Chase and I won't be there."

Letty's shoulders sagged with defeat. She didn't understand how one man could be so stubborn. "Why not?"

"Chase flat out refuses to come and I have no intention of sticking around just to cut up a piece of meat for you."

Letty poured herself a cup of coffee. The fact that Chase wouldn't be there shouldn't come as any big shock, but it did, accompanied by a curious pain.

Scowling, she sat down at the square table, bracing her elbows on it. Until that moment, she hadn't realized how much she wanted to settle the past with Chase. She needed to do it before the surgery.

"I said Chase wasn't coming," Lonny told her a second time.

"I heard you—it's all right," she replied, doing her best to reassure her brother with an easy smile that belied the emotion churning inside her. It'd been a mistake to invite Mary Brandon to dinner without consulting Lonny first. In her enthusiasm, Letty had seen the other woman as a gift that had practically fallen into her lap. How was she to know her brother disliked Mary so passionately?

Lonny tensed. "What do you mean, 'all right'? I don't like the look you've got in your eye."

Letty dropped her gaze. "I mean it's perfectly fine if you prefer not to be here tomorrow night for dinner. I thought it might be a way of getting to know some new people in town, but I should've cleared it with you first."

"Yes, you should have."

"Mary seems nice enough," Letty commented, trying once more.

"So did the snake in the Garden of Eden."

Letty chuckled. "Honestly, Lonny, anyone would think you're afraid of the woman."

"This one's got moves that would be the envy of a world heavyweight champion."

"Obviously she hasn't used them, because she's single."

"Oh, no, she's too smart for that," Lonny countered, gesturing with his hands. "She's been saving them up, just for me."

"Oh, Lonny, you're beginning to sound paranoid, but don't worry, I understand. What kind of sister would I be if I insisted you eat Mama's prime rib dinner with the likes of Mary Brandon?"

Lonny's head shot up. "You're cooking Mom's recipe for prime rib?"

She hated to be so manipulative, but if Lonny were to give Mary half a chance, he might change his mind. "You don't mind if I use some of the meat in the freezer, do you?"

"No," he said, and swallowed. "I suppose there'll be plenty of leftovers?"

Letty shrugged. "I can't say, since I'm thawing out a small roast. I hope you understand."

"Sure," Lonny muttered, frowning.

Apparently he understood all too well, because an hour later, her brother announced he probably would be around for dinner the following night, after all.

Monday morning Letty rose early. The coffee had perked and bacon was sizzling in the skillet when Lonny wandered into the kitchen.

"Morning," he said.

"Morning," she returned cheerfully.

Lonny poured himself a cup of coffee and headed for the door, pausing just before he opened it. "I'll be back in a few minutes."

At the sound of a pickup pulling into the yard, Letty glanced out the kitchen window. Her heart sped up at the sight of Chase climbing out of the cab. It was as if those nine years had been wiped away and he'd come for her the way he used to when she was a teenager. He wore jeans and a shirt with a well-worn leather vest. His dark hair curled crisply at his sun-bronzed nape and he needed a haircut. In him, Letty recognized strength and masculinity.

He entered the kitchen without knocking and stopped

short when he saw her. "Letty," he said, sounding shocked.

"Good morning, Chase," she greeted him simply. Unwilling to see the bitterness in his gaze, she didn't look up from the stove. "Lonny's stepped outside for a moment. Pour yourself a cup of coffee."

"No, thanks." Already he'd turned back to the door.

"Chase." Her heart was pounding so hard it felt as though it might leap into her throat. The sooner she cleared the air between them, the better. "Do you have a minute?"

"Not really."

Ignoring his words, she removed the pan from the burner. "At some point in everyone's life—"

"I said I didn't have time, Letty."

"But—"

"If you're figuring to give me some line about how life's done you wrong and how sorry you are about the past, save your breath, because I don't need to hear it."

"Maybe you don't," she said gently, "but I need to say it."

"Then do it in front of a mirror."

"Chase, you're my brother's best friend. It isn't as if we can ignore each other. It's too uncomfortable to pretend nothing's wrong."

"As far as I'm concerned nothing *is* wrong."

"But—"

"Save your breath, Letty," he said again.

Chapter 3

"Mr. Chase," Cricket called excitedly from the foot of the stairs. "You're here!"

Letty turned back to the stove, fighting down anger and indignation. Chase wouldn't so much as listen to her. Fine. If he wanted to pretend there was nothing wrong, then she would give an award-winning performance herself. He wasn't the only one who could be this childish.

The back door opened and Lonny blithely stepped into the kitchen. "You're early, aren't you?" he asked Chase as he refilled his coffee cup.

"No," Chase snapped impatiently. The look he shot Letty said he wouldn't have come in the house at all if he'd known she was up.

Lonny paid no attention to the censure in his neighbor's voice. He pulled out a chair and sat down. "I'm not ready to leave yet. Letty's cooking breakfast."

"Mr. Chase, Mr. Chase, did you bring your horsey?"

"It's Mr. *Brown*," Letty corrected as she brought two plates to the table. Lonny immediately dug into his bacon-and-egg breakfast, but Chase ignored the meal—as though eating anything Letty had made might poison him.

"Answer her," Lonny muttered between bites. "Otherwise she'll drive you nuts."

"I drove my truck over," Chase told Cricket.

"Do you ever bring your horsey to Uncle Lonny's?"

"Sometimes."

"Are you a cowboy?"

"I suppose."

"Wyoming's the Cowboy State," Letty told her daughter.

"Does that mean everyone who lives here has to be a cowboy?"

"Not exactly."

"But close," Lonny said with a grin.

Cricket climbed onto the chair next to Chase's and dragged her yellow blanket with her. She set her elbows on the table and cupped her face in her hands. "Aren't you going to eat?" she asked, studying him intently.

"I had breakfast," he said, pushing the plate toward her.

Cricket didn't need to be asked twice. Kneeling on the chair, she reached across Chase and grabbed his fork. She smiled up at him, her eyes sparkling.

Letty joined the others at the table. Lately her appetite hadn't been good, but she forced herself to eat a piece of toast.

The atmosphere was strained. Letty tried to avoid looking in Chase's direction, but it was impossible to ignore the man. He turned toward her unexpectedly, catching her look and holding it. His eyes were dark and intense. Caught off guard, Letty blushed.

Chase's gaze darted from her eyes to her mouth and stayed there. She longed to turn primly away from him with a shrug of indifference, but she couldn't. Years ago, Letty had loved staring into Chase's eyes. He had the most soulful eyes of any man she'd ever known. She was trapped in the memory of how it used to be with them. At one time, she'd been able to read loving messages in his eyes. But they were cold now, filled with angry sparks that flared briefly before he glanced away.

What little appetite Letty had was gone, and she put her toast back on the plate and shoved it aside. "Would it be all right if I took the truck this morning?" she asked her brother, surprised by the quaver in her voice. She wished she could ignore Chase altogether, but that was impossible. He refused to deal with the past and she couldn't make him talk to her. As far as Letty could tell, he preferred to simply overlook her presence. Only he seemed to find that as difficult as she found ignoring him. That went a long way toward raising her spirits.

"Where are you going?"

"I thought I'd do a little shopping for dinner tonight." It was true, but only half the reason she needed his truck. She had to drive to Rock Springs, which was fifty miles west of Red Springs, so she could talk to the social services people there about her eligibility for Medicaid.

"That's right—Mary Brandon's coming to dinner, isn't she?" Lonny asked, evidently disturbed by the thought.

It was a mistake to have mentioned the evening meal, because her brother frowned the instant he said Mary's name. "I suppose I won't be needing the truck," he said, scowling.

"I appreciate it. Thanks," Letty said brightly.

Her brother shrugged.

"Are you coming to dinner with Mommy's friend?" Cricket asked Chase.

"No," he said brusquely.

"How come?"

"Because he's smart, that's why," Lonny answered, then stood abruptly. He reached for his hat, settled it on his head and didn't look back.

Within seconds, both men were gone.

"You'll need to complete these forms," the woman behind the desk told Letty, handing her several sheets.

The intake clerk looked frazzled and overburdened. It was well past noon, and Letty guessed the woman hadn't had a coffee break all morning and was probably late for her lunch. The clerk briefly read over the letter from the physician Letty had been seeing in California, and made a copy of it to attach to Letty's file.

"Once you're done with those forms, please bring them back to me," she said.

"Of course," Letty told her.

Bored, Cricket had slipped her arms around her mother's waist and was pressing her head against Letty's stomach.

"If you have any questions, feel free to ask," the worker said.

"None right now. Thank you for all your help." Letty stood, Cricket still holding on.

For the first time since Letty had entered the government office, the young woman smiled.

Letty took the sheets and sat at a table in a large lobby. One by one, she answered the myriad questions. Before she'd be eligible for Wyoming's medical assistance program, she'd have to be accepted into the Supplemental Security Income program offered through the federal government. It was a humiliating fact of life, but proud, independent Letty Ellison was about to go on welfare.

Tears blurred her eyes as she filled in the first sheet. She stopped long enough to wipe them away before they spilled onto the papers. She had no idea what she'd tell Lonny once the government checks started arriving. Especially since he seemed so confident he could find her some kind of employment in town.

"When can we leave?" Cricket said, close to her mother's ear.

"Soon." Letty was writing as fast as she could, eager to escape, too.

"I don't like it here," Cricket whispered.

"I don't, either," Letty whispered back. But she was grateful the service existed; otherwise she didn't know what she would've done.

Cricket fell asleep in the truck during the hour's drive home. Letty was thankful for the silence because it gave her a chance to think through the immediate problems that faced her. She could no longer delay seeing a physician, and eventually she'd have to tell Lonny about her heart condition. She hadn't intended to keep it a secret, but there was no need to worry him until everything was settled with the Medicaid people. Once she'd completed all the paperwork, been examined by a variety of knowledgeable doctors so they could tell her what she already knew, then she'd be free to explain the situation to Lonny.

Until then, she would keep this problem to herself.

"Letty!" Lonny cried from the top of the stairs. "Do I have to dress for dinner?"

"Please," she answered sweetly, basting the rib roast before sliding it back in the oven for a few more minutes.

"A tie, too?" he asked without enthusiasm.

"A nice sweater would do."

"I don't own a 'nice' sweater," he shouted back.

A couple of muffled curses followed, but Letty chose to ignore them. At least she knew what to get her brother next Christmas.

Lonny had been in a bad temper from the minute he'd walked in the door an hour earlier, and Letty could see that this evening was headed for disaster.

"Mommy!" Cricket's pigtails were flying as she raced into the kitchen. "Your friend's here."

"Oh." Letty quickly removed the oven mitt and glanced at her watch. Mary was a good ten minutes early and Letty needed every second of that time. The table wasn't set, and the roast was still in the oven.

"Mary, it's good to see you." Letty greeted her with a smile as she rushed into the living room.

Mary walked into the Ellison home, her eyes curious as she examined the living room furniture. "It's good to be here. I brought some fresh-baked rolls for Lonny."

"How thoughtful." Letty moved into the center of the room. "I'm running a little behind, so if you'll excuse me for a minute?"

"Of course."

"Make yourself comfortable," Letty called over her shoulder as she hurried back to the kitchen. She looked around, wondering which task to finish first. After she'd returned from Rock Springs that afternoon and done the shopping, she'd taken a nap with Cricket. Now she regretted having wasted that time. The whole meal felt so disorganized and with Lonny's attitude, well—

"This is a lovely watercolor in here," Mary called in to her. "Who painted it?"

"My mother. She was an artist," Letty answered, taking the salad out of the refrigerator. She grabbed silverware and napkins on her way into the dining room. "Cricket, would you set the table for me?"

"Okay," the youngster agreed willingly.

Mary stood in the room, hands behind her back as she studied the painting of a lush field of wildflowers. "Your mother certainly had an eye for color, didn't she?"

"Mom was very talented," Letty replied wistfully.

"Did she paint any of the others?" Mary asked, gesturing around the living room.

"No…actually, this is the only painting we have of hers."

"She gave the others away?"

"Not exactly," Letty admitted, feeling a flash of resentment. With all her mother's obligations on the ranch, plus helping Dad when she could during the last few years of his life, there hadn't been time for her to work on what she'd loved most, which was her art. Letty's mother had lived a hard life. The land had drained her energy. Letty had been a silent witness to what had happened to her mother and swore it wouldn't be repeated in her own life. Yet here she was, back in Wyoming. Back on the Bar E, and grateful she had a home.

"How come we're eating in the dining room?" Lonny muttered irritably as he came downstairs. He buried his hands in his pockets and made an obvious effort to ignore Mary, who stood no more than five feet away.

"You know Mary, don't you?" Letty asked pointedly.

Lonny nodded in the other woman's direction, but managed to do so without actually looking at her.

"Hello, Lonny," Mary cooed. "It's a real pleasure to see you again. I brought you some rolls—hot from the oven."

"Mary brought over some homemade dinner rolls," Letty reiterated, resisting the urge to kick her brother in the shin.

"Looks like those rolls came from the Red Springs Bakery to me," he muttered, pulling out a chair and sitting down.

Letty half expected him to grab his knife and fork, pound the table with them and chant, *Dinner, dinner, dinner.* If he couldn't discourage Mary by being rude, he'd probably try the more advanced "caveman" approach.

"Well, yes, I did pick up the rolls there," Mary said, clearly flustered. "I didn't have time after work to bake."

"Naturally, you wouldn't have," Letty responded mildly, shooting her brother a heated glare.

Cricket scooted past the two women and handed her uncle a plate. "Anything else, Mommy?"

Letty quickly checked the table to see what was needed. "Glasses," she mumbled, rushing back into the kitchen. While she was there, she took the peas off the burner. The vegetable had been an expensive addition to the meal, but Letty had bought them at the market in town, remembering how much Lonny loved fresh peas. He deserved some reward for being such a good sport—or so she'd thought earlier.

Cricket finished setting the table and Letty brought out the rest of their dinner. She smiled as she joined the others. Her brother had made a tactical error when he'd chosen to sit down first. Mary had immediately taken the chair closest to him. She gazed at him with wide adoring eyes while Lonny did his best to ignore her.

As Letty had predicted earlier, the meal was a disaster, and the tension in the air was thick. Letty made several attempts at conversation, which Mary leaped upon, but the minute either of them tried to include Lonny, the subject died. It was all Letty could do to keep from kicking her brother under the table. Mary didn't linger after the meal.

"Don't ever do that to me again," Lonny grumbled as soon as Letty was back from escorting Mary to the front door.

She sank down in the chair beside him and closed her eyes, exhausted. She didn't have the energy to argue with her brother. If he was looking for an apology, she'd give him one. "I'm sorry, Lonny. I was only trying to help."

"Help what? Ruin my life?"

"No!" Letty said, her eyes flying open. "You need someone."

"Who says?"

"I do."

"Did you ever stop to think that's a bit presumptuous on your part? You're gone nine years and then you waltz home, look around and decide what you can change."

"Lonny, I said I was sorry."

He was silent for a lengthy moment, then he sighed. "I didn't mean to shout."

"I know you didn't." Letty was so tired she didn't know how she was going to manage the dishes. One meal, and she'd used every pan in the house. Cricket was clearing the table for her and she was so grateful she kissed her daughter's forehead.

Lonny dawdled over his coffee, eyes downcast. "What makes you think I need someone?" he asked quietly.

"It seems so lonely out here. I assumed—incorrectly, it appears—that you'd be happier if there was someone to share your life with. You're a handsome man, Lonny, and there are plenty of women who'd like to be your wife."

One corner of his mouth edged up at that. "I intend to marry someday. I just haven't gotten around to it, that's all."

"Well, for heaven's sake, what are you waiting for?" Letty teased. "You're thirty-four and you're not getting any younger."

"I'm not exactly ready for social security."

Letty smiled. "Mary's nice—"

"Aw, come off it, Letty. I don't like that woman. How many times do I have to tell you that?"

"—but I understand why she isn't your type," Letty finished, undaunted.

"You do?"

She nodded. "Mary needs a man who'd be willing to spend a lot of time and money keeping her entertained. She wouldn't make a good rancher's wife."

"I knew that the minute I met her," Lonny grumbled. "I just didn't know how to put it in words." He mulled over his thoughts, then added, "Look at the way she let you and Cricket do all the work getting dinner on the table. She didn't help once. That wouldn't sit well with most folks."

"She was company." Letty felt an obligation to defend Mary. After all, she hadn't *asked* the other woman to help with the meal, although she would've appreciated it. Besides, Lonny didn't have a lot of room to talk; he'd waited to be served just like Mary had.

"Company, my foot," Lonny countered. "Could you see Mom or any other woman you know sitting around making idle chatter while everyone else is working around her?"

Letty had to ackowledge that was true.

"Did you notice how she wanted everyone to think she'd made those rolls herself?"

Letty had noticed, but she didn't consider that such a terrible thing.

Lonny reached into the middle of the table for a carrot stick, chewing on it with a frown. "A wife," he murmured. "I agree that a woman would take more interest in the house than I have in the past few years." He crunched down on the carrot again. "I have to admit it's been rather nice having my meals cooked and my laundry folded. Those are a couple of jobs I can live without."

Letty practically swallowed her tongue to keep from commenting.

"I think you might be right, Letty. A wife would come in handy."

"You could always hire a housekeeper," Letty said sarcastically, irritated by his attitude and unable to refrain from saying something after all.

"What are you so irked about? You're the one who suggested I get married in the first place."

"From the way you're talking, you seem to think of a wife as a hired hand who'll clean house and cook your meals. You don't want a *wife*. You're looking for a servant. A woman has to get more out of a relationship than that."

Lonny snorted. "I thought you females need to be needed. For crying out loud, what else is there to a marriage but cooking and cleaning and regular sex?"

Letty glared at her brother, stood and picked up their coffee cups. "Lonny, I was wrong. Do some woman the ultimate favor and stay single."

With that she walked out of the dining room.

"So how did dinner go?" Chase asked his friend the following morning.

Lonny's response was little more than a grunt.

"That bad?"

"Worse."

Although his friend wouldn't appreciate it, Chase had gotten a good laugh over this dinner date of Lonny's with the gal from the hardware store. "Is Letty going to set you up with that Brandon woman again?"

"Not while I'm breathing, she won't."

Chase chuckled and loosened the reins on Firepower. Mary Brandon was about as subtle as a jackhammer. She'd done everything but throw herself at Lonny's feet, and she probably would've done that if she'd thought it would do any good. Chase wanted to blame Letty for getting Lonny into this mess, but the Brandon woman was wily and had likely manipulated the invitation out of Letty. Unfortunately Lonny was the one who'd suffered the consequences.

Chase smiled, content. Riding the range in May, looking for newborn calves, was one of his favorite chores as a rancher. All creation seemed to be bursting out, fresh and alive. The trees were budding and the wind was warm and carried the sweet scent of wildflowers with it. He liked the ranch best after it rained;

everything felt so pure then and the land seemed to glisten.

"That sister of yours is determined to find you a wife, isn't she?" Chase teased, still smiling. "She hasn't been back two weeks and she's matchmaking to beat the band. Before you know it, she'll have you married off. I only hope you get some say in whatever woman Letty chooses."

"Letty doesn't mean any harm."

"Neither did Lizzy Borden."

When Lonny didn't respond with the appropriate chuckle, Chase glanced in his friend's direction. "You look worried. What's wrong?"

"It's Letty."

"What about her?"

"Does she seem any different to you?"

Chase shrugged, hating the sudden concern that surged through him. The only thing he wanted to feel for Letty was apathy, or at best the faint stirring of remembrance one had about a casual acquaintance. As it was, his heart, his head—every part of him—went into overdrive whenever Lonny brought his sister into the conversation.

"How do you mean—different?" Chase asked.

"I don't know for sure." He hesitated and pushed his hat farther back on his head. "It's crazy, but she takes naps every afternoon. And I mean *every* afternoon. At first she said it was jet lag."

"So she sleeps a lot. Big deal," Chase responded, struggling to sound disinterested.

"Hey, Chase, you know my sister as well as I do. Can you picture Letty, who was always a ball of energy, taking naps in the middle of the day?"

Chase couldn't, but he didn't say so.

"Another thing," Lonny said as he loosely held his gelding's reins, "Letty's always been a neat freak. Remember how she used to drive me crazy with the way everything had to be just so?"

Chase nodded.

"She left the dinner dishes in the sink all night. I found her putting them in the dishwasher this morning, claiming she'd been too tired to bother after Mary left. Mary was gone by seven-thirty!"

"So she's a little tired," Chase muttered. "Let her sleep if it makes her happy."

"It's more than that," Lonny continued. "She doesn't sing anymore—not a note. For nine years she fought tooth and nail to make it in the entertainment business, and now it's as if…as if she never had a voice. She hasn't even touched the piano since she's been home—at least not when I was there to hear her." Lonny frowned. "It's like the song's gone out of her life."

Chase didn't want to talk about Letty and he didn't want to think about her. In an effort to change the subject he said, "Old man Wilber was by the other day."

Lonny shook his head. "I suppose he was after those same acres again."

"Every year he asks me if I'd be willing to sell that strip of land." Some people knew it was spring when the flowers started to bloom. Chase could tell when Henry Wilber approached him about a narrow strip of land that bordered their property line. It wasn't the land that interested Wilber as much as the water. Nothing on this earth would convince Chase to sell that land. Spring Valley Ranch had been in his family for nearly eighty years and each generation had held on to those acres through good times and bad. Ranching wasn't exactly making Chase a millionaire, but he would die before he sold off a single inch of his inheritance.

"You'd be a fool to let it go," Lonny said.

No one needed to tell Chase that. "I wonder when he'll give up asking."

"Knowing old man Wilber," Lonny said with a chuckle, "I'd say never."

"Are you going to plant any avocados?" Cricket asked as Letty spaded the rich soil that had once been her mother's garden. Lonny had protested, but he'd tilled a large section close to the house for her and Cricket to plant. Now Letty was eager to get her hands in the earth.

"Avocados won't grow in Wyoming, Cricket. The climate isn't mild enough."

"What about oranges?"

"Not those, either."

"What *does* grow in Wyoming?" she asked indignantly. "Cowboys?"

Letty smiled as she used the sturdy fork to turn the soil.

"Mommy, look! Chase is here…on his horsey." Cricket took off, running as fast as her stubby legs would carry her. Her reaction was the same whenever Chase appeared.

Letty stuck the spading fork in the soft ground and reluctantly followed her daughter. By the time she got to the yard, Chase had climbed down from the saddle and dropped the reins. Cricket stood awestruck on the steps leading to the back porch, her mouth agape, her eyes wide.

"Hello, Chase," Letty said softly.

He looked at her and frowned. "Didn't that old straw hat used to belong to your mother?"

Letty nodded. "She wore it when she worked in the garden. I found it the other day." Chase made no further comment, although Letty was sure he'd wanted to say something more.

Eagerly Cricket bounded down the steps to stand beside her mother. Her small hand crept into Letty's, holding on tightly. "I didn't know horsies were so big and *pretty*," she breathed.

"Firepower's special," Letty explained. Chase had raised the bay from a yearling, and had worked with him for long, patient hours.

"You said you wanted to see Firepower," Chase said, a bit gruffly. "I haven't got all day, so if you want a ride it's got to be now."

"I can ride him? Oh, Mommy, can I really?"

Letty's blood roared in her ears. She opened her mouth to tell Chase she wasn't about to set her daughter on a horse of that size.

Before she could voice her objection, however, Chase quieted her fears. "She'll be riding with me." With that he swung himself onto the horse and reached down to hoist Cricket into the saddle with him.

As if she'd been born to ride, Cricket sat in front of Chase on the huge animal without revealing the least bit of fear. "Look at me!" she shouted, grinning widely. "I'm riding a horsey! I'm riding a horsey!"

Even Chase was smiling at such unabashed enthusiasm. "I'll take her around the yard a couple of times," he told Letty before kicking gently at Firepower's sides. The bay obediently trotted around in a circle.

"Can we go over there?" Cricket pointed to some undistinguishable location in the distance.

"Cricket," Letty said, clamping the straw hat onto

her head and squinting up. "Chase is a busy man. He hasn't got time to run you all over the countryside."

"Hold on," Chase responded, taking the reins in both hands and heading in the direction Cricket had indicated.

"Chase," Letty cried, running after him. "She's just a little girl. Please be careful."

He didn't answer her, and not knowing what to expect, Letty trailed them to the end of the long drive. When she reached it, she was breathless and light-headed. It took her several minutes to walk back to the house. She was certain anyone watching her would assume she was drunk. Entering the kitchen, Letty grabbed her prescription bottle—hidden from Lonny in a cupboard—and swallowed a couple of capsules without water.

Not wanting to raise unnecessary alarm, she went back to the garden, but had to sit on an old stump until her breathing returned to normal. Apparently her heart had gotten worse since she'd come home. Much worse.

"Mommy, look, no hands," Cricket called out, her arms raised high in the air as Firepower trotted back into the yard.

Smiling, Letty stood and reached for the spading fork.

"Don't try to pretend you were working," Chase muttered, frowning at her. "We saw you sitting in the sun. What's the matter, Letty? Did the easy life in California make you lazy?"

Once more Chase was baiting her. And once more Letty let the comment slide. "It must have," she said and looked away.

Chapter 4

Chase awoke just before dawn. He lay on his back, listening to the birds chirping outside his half-opened window. Normally their singing would have cheered him, but not this morning. He'd slept poorly, his mind preoccupied with Letty. Everything Lonny had said the week before about her not being herself had bounced around in his brain for most of the night.

Something *was* different about Letty, but not in the way Chase would have assumed. He'd expected the years in California to transform her in a more obvious way, making her worldly and cynical. To his surprise, he'd discovered that in several instances she seemed very much like the naive young woman who'd left nine years earlier to follow a dream. But the changes were there, lots of them, complex and subtle, when he'd expected them to be simple and glaring. Perhaps what troubled Chase was his deep inner feeling that something was genuinely wrong with her. But try as he might, he couldn't pinpoint what it was. That disturbed him the most.

Sitting on the edge of the bed, Chase rubbed his hands over his face and glanced outside. The cloudless dawn sky was a luminous shade of gray. The air smelled crisp and clean as Wyoming offered another perfect spring morning.

Chase dressed in his jeans and a Western shirt. Downstairs, he didn't bother to fix himself a cup of coffee; instead he walked outside, climbed into his pickup and headed over to the Bar E.

Only it wasn't Lonny who drew him there.

The lights were on in the kitchen when Chase pulled into the yard. He didn't knock, but stepped directly into the large family kitchen. Letty was at the stove, the way he knew she would be. She turned when he walked in the door.

"Morning, Chase," she said with a smile.

"Morning." Without another word, he walked over to the cupboard and got himself a mug. Standing next to her, he poured his own coffee.

"Lonny's taking care of the horses," she told him, as if she needed to explain where her brother was.

Briefly Chase wondered how she would've responded if he'd said it wasn't Lonny he'd come to see.

"Cricket talked nonstop for hours about riding Firepower. It was the thrill of her life. Thank you for being so kind to her, Chase."

Chase held back a short derisive laugh. He hadn't planned to let Cricket anywhere near his gelding. His intention all along had been to avoid Letty's daughter entirely. To Chase's way of thinking, the less he had to do with the child the better.

Ignoring Cricket was the only thing he could do, because every time he looked at that sweet little girl, he felt nothing but pain. Not a faint flicker of discomfort, but a deep wrenching pain like nothing he'd ever experienced. Cricket represented everything about Letty that he wanted to forget. He couldn't even glance at the child without remembering that Letty had given herself to another man, and the sense of betrayal cut him to the bone.

Naturally Cricket was innocent of the circumstances surrounding her birth, and Chase would never do anything to deliberately hurt the little girl, but he couldn't help feeling what he did. Yet he'd given her a ride on Firepower the day before, and despite everything, he'd enjoyed himself.

If the truth be known, the ride had come about accidentally. Chase had been on the ridge above the Bar E fence line when he saw two faint dots silhouetted against the landscape, far in the distance. Almost immediately he'd realized it was Letty and her daughter, working outside. From that moment on, Chase hadn't been able to stay away. He'd hurried down the hill, but once he was in the yard, he had to come up with some logical reason for showing up in the middle of the day. Giving Cricket a chance to see Firepower had seemed solid enough at the time.

"Would you like a waffle?" Letty asked, breaking into his musings.

"No, thanks."

Letty nodded and turned around. "I don't know why

Cricket's taken to you the way she has. She gets excited every time someone mentions your name. I'm afraid you've made a friend for life, whether you like it or not."

Chase made a noncommittal noise.

"I can't thank you enough for bringing Firepower over," Letty continued. "It meant a lot to me."

"I didn't do it for you," he said bluntly, watching her, almost wanting her to come back at him with some snappy retort. The calm way in which Letty swallowed his barbs troubled him more than anything else.

As he'd suspected, Letty didn't respond. Instead she brought butter and syrup to the table, avoiding his gaze.

The Letty Ellison he remembered had been feisty and fearless. She wouldn't have tolerated impatience or tactlessness from anyone, least of all him.

"This coffee tastes like it came out of a sewer," he said rudely, setting his cup down hard on the table.

The coffee was fine, but he wanted to test Letty's reactions. In years past, she would've flared right back at him, giving as good as she got. Nine years ago, Letty would've told him what he could do with that cup of coffee if he didn't like the taste of it.

She looked up, her face expressionless. "I'll make another pot."

Chase was stunned. "Forget it," he said quickly, not knowing what else to say. She glanced at him, her eyes large and shadowed in her pale face.

"But you just said there's something wrong with the coffee."

Chase was speechless. He watched her, his thoughts confused.

What had happened to his dauntless Letty?

* * *

Letty was working in the garden, carefully planting rows of corn, when her brother's pickup truck came barreling down the drive. When he slammed on the brakes, jumped out of the cab and slammed the door, Letty got up and left the seed bag behind. Her brother was obviously angry about something.

"Lonny?" she asked quietly. "What's wrong?"

"Of all the stupid, idiotic, crazy women in the world, why did I have to run into *this* one?"

"What woman?" Letty asked.

Lonny thrust his index finger under Letty's nose. "She—she's going to pay for this," he stammered in his fury. "There's no way I'm letting her get away with what she did."

"Lonny, settle down and tell me what happened."

"There!" he shouted, his voice so filled with indignation it shook.

He was pointing at the front of the pickup. Letty studied it, but didn't see anything amiss. "What?"

"Here," he said, directing her attention to a nearly indistinguishable dent in the bumper of his ten-year-old vehicle.

The entire truck was full of nicks and dents. When a rancher drove a vehicle for as many years as Lonny had, it collected its share of battle scars. It needed a new left fender, and a new paint job all the way around wouldn't have hurt, either. As far as Letty could tell, Lonny's truck was on its last legs, as it were—or, more appropriately, tires.

"Oh, you mean *that* tiny dent," she said, satisfied she'd found the one he was referring to.

"Tiny dent!" he shouted. "That...woman nearly cost me a year off my life."

"Tell me what happened," Letty demanded a second time. She couldn't remember ever seeing her brother this agitated.

"She ran a stop sign. Claimed she didn't see it. What kind of idiot misses a stop sign, for Pete's sake?"

"Did she slam into you?"

"Not exactly. I managed to avoid a collision, but in the process I hit the pole."

"What pole?"

"The one holding up the stop sign, of course."

"Oh." Letty didn't mean to appear dense, but Lonny was so angry, he wasn't explaining himself clearly.

He groaned in frustration. "Then, ever so sweetly, she climbs out of her car, tells me how sorry she is and asks if there's any damage."

Letty rolled her eyes. She didn't know what her brother expected, but as far as Letty could see, Lonny was being completely unreasonable.

"Right away I could see what she'd done, and I pointed it out to her. But that's not the worst of it," he insisted. "She took one look at my truck and said there were so many dents in it, she couldn't possibly know which one our *minor* accident had caused."

In Letty's opinion the other driver was absolutely right, but saying as much could prove dangerous. "Then what?" she asked cautiously.

"We exchanged a few words," he admitted, kicking the dirt and avoiding Letty's gaze. "She said my truck was a pile of junk." Lonny walked all the way around it before he continued, his eyes flashing. "There's no way I'm going to let some *teacher* insult me like that."

"I'm sure her insurance will take care of it," Letty said calmly.

"Damn straight it will." He slapped his hat back on his head. "You know what else she did? She tried to buy me off!" he declared righteously. "Right there in the middle of the street, in broad daylight, in front of God and man. Now I ask you, do I look like the kind of guy who can be bribed?"

At Letty's questioning look, her irate brother continued. "She offered me fifty bucks."

"I take it you refused."

"You bet I refused," he shouted. "There's two or three hundred dollars' damage here. Probably a lot more."

Letty bent to examine the bumper again. It looked like a fifty-dollar dent to her, but she wasn't about to say so. It did seem, however, that Lonny was protesting much too long and loud over a silly dent. Whoever this woman was, she'd certainly gained his attention. A teacher, he'd said.

"I've got her license number right here." Lonny yanked a small piece of paper from his shirt pocket and carefully unfolded it. "Joy Fuller's lucky I'm not going to report her to the police."

"Joy Fuller," Letty cried, taking the paper away from him. "I know who she is."

That stopped Lonny short. "How?" he asked suspiciously.

"She plays the organ at church on Sundays, and as you obviously know, she teaches at the elementary school. Second grade, I think."

Lonny shot a look toward the cloudless sky. "Do the good people of Red Springs realize the kind of woman they're exposing their children to? Someone should tell the school board."

"You've been standing in the sun too long. Come inside and have some lunch," Letty offered.

"I'm too mad to think about eating. You go ahead without me." With that he strode toward the barn.

Letty went into the house, and after pouring herself a glass of iced tea, she reached for the church directory and dialed Joy Fuller's number.

Joy answered brusquely on the first ring. "Yes," she snapped.

"Joy, it's Letty Ellison."

"Letty, I'm sorry, but your brother is the rudest… most arrogant, unreasonable man I've ever encountered."

"I can't tell you how sorry I am about this," Letty said, but she had the feeling Joy hadn't even heard her.

"I made a simple mistake and he wouldn't be satisfied with anything less than blood."

"Can you tell me what happened?" She was hoping Joy would be a little more composed than Lonny, but she was beginning to have her doubts.

"I'm sure my version is nothing like your brother's," Joy said, her voice raised. "It's simple, really. I ran the stop sign between Oak and Spruce. Frankly, I don't go that way often and I simply forgot it was there."

Letty knew the intersection. A huge weeping willow partially obscured the sign. There'd been a piece in the weekly paper about how the tree should be trimmed before a collision occurred.

"I was more than willing to admit the entire incident was my fault," Joy went on. "But I couldn't even tell which dent I'd caused, and when I said as much, your brother started acting like a crazy man."

"I don't know what's wrong with Lonny," Letty confessed. "I've never seen him like this."

"Well, I'd say it has something to do with the fact that I turned him down the last time he asked me out."

"*What?* This is the first I've heard of it. You and my brother had a…relationship?"

Joy gave an unladylike snort. "I wouldn't dignify it with that name. He and I… He— Oh, Letty, never mind. It's all history. Back to this so-called accident…" She drew in an audible breath. "I told him I'd contact my insurance company, but to hear him tell it, he figures it'll take at least two thousand dollars to repair all the damage I caused."

That was ridiculous. "I'm sure he didn't mean it—"

"Oh, he meant it, all right," Joy interrupted. "Personally, I'd rather have the insurance people deal with him, anyway. I never want to see your arrogant, ill-tempered, bronc-busting brother again."

Letty didn't blame her, but she had the feeling that in Joy Fuller, her brother had met his match.

At four o'clock, Lonny came into the house, and his mood had apparently improved, because he sent Letty a shy smile and said, "Don't worry about making me dinner tonight. I'm going into town."

"Oh?" Letty said, looking up from folding laundry.

"Chase and I are going out to eat."

She smiled. "Have a good time. You deserve a break."

"I just hope that Fuller woman isn't on the streets."

Letty raised her eyebrows. "Really?"

"Yeah, really," he snapped. "She's a menace."

"Honestly, Lonny, are you still mad about that… silly incident?"

"I sure am. It isn't safe for man or beast with someone like her behind the wheel."

"I do believe you protest too much. Could it be that you're attracted to Joy? *Still* attracted?"

Eyes narrowed, he stalked off, then turned back around and muttered, "I was *never* attracted to her. We might've seen each other a few times but it didn't work out. How could it? She's humorless, full of herself and…and she's a city slicker. From the West Coast, the big metropolis of Seattle, no less."

"I've heard it's a nice place," Letty said mildly.

Lonny did not consider that worthy of comment, and Letty couldn't help smiling.

His bathwater was running when he returned several minutes later, his shirt unbuttoned. "What about you, Letty?"

"What do you mean?" she asked absently, lifting the laundry basket onto the table. The fresh, clean scent of sun-dried towels made the extra effort of hanging them on the line worth it.

"What are you doing tonight?"

"Nothing much." She planned to do what she did every Saturday night. Watch a little television, polish her nails and read.

Her brother pulled out a chair, turned it around and straddled it. "From the minute you got home, you've been talking about marrying me off. That's the reason you invited that Brandon woman over for dinner. You admitted it yourself."

"A mistake that won't be repeated," she assured him, fluffing a thick towel.

"But you said I need a woman."

"A wife, Lonny. There's a difference."

"I've been thinking about what you said, and you might be right. But what about you?"

Letty found the task of folding bath towels vitally important. "I don't understand."

"When are you going to get married?"

Never, her mind flashed spontaneously.

"Letty?"

She shrugged, preferring to avoid the issue and knowing it was impossible. "Someday...maybe."

"You're not getting any younger."

Letty supposed she had that coming. Lonny's words were an echo of her own earlier ones to him. Now she was paying the penalty for her miserable attempt at matchmaking. However, giving Lonny a few pat answers wasn't going to work, any more than it had worked with her. "Frankly, I'm not sure I'll ever marry," she murmured, keeping her gaze lowered.

"Did... Cricket's father hurt you that much?"

Purposely she glanced behind her and asked stiffly, "Isn't your bathwater going to run over?"

"I doubt it. Answer me, Letty."

"I have no intention of discussing what happened with Jason. It's in the past and best forgotten."

Lonny was silent for a moment. "You're so different now. I'm your brother—I care about you—and it bothers me to see you like this. No man is worth this kind of pain."

"Lonny, please." She held the towels against her stomach. "If I'm different it isn't because of what happened between me and Jason. It's...other things."

"What other things?" Lonny asked, his eyes filled with concern.

That was one question Letty couldn't answer. At least not yet. So she sidestepped it. "Jason taught me an extremely valuable lesson. Oh, it was painful at the time, don't misunderstand me, but he gave me Cricket, and she's my joy. I can only be grateful to Jason for my daughter."

"But don't you hate him for the way he deceived you and then deserted you?"

"No," she admitted reluctantly, uncertain her brother would understand. "Not anymore. What possible good would that do?"

Apparently absorbed in thought, Lonny rubbed his hand along the back of his neck. Finally he said, "I don't know, I suppose I want him to suffer for what he put you through. Some guy I've never even seen got you pregnant and walked away from you when you needed him most. It disgusts me to see him get off scot-free after the way he treated you."

Unexpected tears pooled in Letty's eyes at the protectiveness she saw in her brother. She blinked them away, and when she could speak evenly again, she murmured, "If there's anything I learned in all those years away from home, it's that there's an order to life. Eventually everything rights itself. I don't need revenge, because sooner or later, as the old adage says, what goes around, comes around."

"How can you be so calm about it, though?"

"Take your bath, Lonny," she said with a quick laugh. She shoved a freshly folded towel at him. "You're driving me crazy. And you say *Cricket* asks a lot of questions."

* * *

Chase arrived a couple of hours later, stepping gingerly into the kitchen. He completely avoided looking at or speaking to Letty, who was busy preparing her and Cricket's dinner. He walked past Letty, but was waylaid by Cricket, who was coloring in her book at the dining room table.

Chase seemed somewhat short with the child, Letty noted, but Cricket had a minimum of ten important questions Chase needed to answer regarding Firepower. The five-year-old didn't seem to mind that Chase was a little abrupt. Apparently her hero could do no wrong.

Soon enough Lonny appeared. He opened a can of beer, and Letty listened to her brother relate his hair-raising encounter with "the Fuller woman" at the stop sign in town as if he were lucky to have escaped with his life.

The two men were in the living room while Letty stayed in the kitchen. Chase obviously wanted to keep his distance, and that was just as well. He'd gone out of his way to irritate her lately and she'd tolerated about all she could. Doing battle with Chase now would only deplete her energy. She'd tried to square things with him once, and he'd made his feelings abundantly clear. For now, Letty could do nothing but accept the situation.

"Where do you think we should eat?" Lonny asked, coming into the kitchen to deposit his empty beer can.

"Billy's Steak House?" Chase called out from the living room. "I'm in the mood for a thick sirloin."

Letty remembered that Chase had always liked his meat rare.

"How about going to the tavern afterward?" Lonny suggested. "Let's see if there's any action to be had."

Letty didn't hear the response, but whatever it was caused the two men to laugh like a couple of rambunctious teenagers. Amused, Letty smiled faintly and placed the cookie sheet with frozen fish sticks in the oven.

It wasn't until later, while Letty was clearing away the dinner dishes, that the impact of their conversation really hit her. The "action" they were looking for at the Roundup Tavern involved women.... Although she wouldn't admit it to Lonny—and he'd never admit it himself—she suspected he might be hoping Joy Fuller would show up.

But Chase—what woman was *he* looking for? Would anyone do, so long as she wasn't Letty? Would their encounter go beyond a few dances and a few drinks?

Tight-lipped, Letty marched into the living room and threw herself down on the overstuffed chair. Cricket was playing with her dolls on the carpet and Letty pushed the buttons on the remote control with a vengeance. Unable to watch the sitcom she usually enjoyed, she turned off the set and placed a hand over her face. Closing her eyes was a mistake.

Instantly she imagined Chase in the arms of a beautiful woman, a sexy one, moving suggestively against him.

"Oh, no," Letty cried, bolting upright.

"Mommy?"

Letty's pulse started to roar in her ears, drowning out reason. She looked at Cricket, playing so contentedly, and announced curtly, "It's time for bed."

"Already?"

"Yes... Remember, we have church in the morning," she said.

"Will Chase be there?"

"I... I don't know." If he was, she'd...she'd ignore him the way he'd ignored her.

Several hours later, Cricket was in bed asleep and Letty lay in her own bed, staring sightlessly into the dark. Her fury, irrational though it might be, multiplied with every passing minute. When she could stand it no longer, Letty hurried down the stairs and sat in the living room without turning on any lights.

She wasn't there long before she heard a vehicle coming up the drive. The back door opened and the two men stumbled into the house.

"Sh-h-h," she heard Chase whisper loudly, "you'll wake Letty."

"God forbid." Lonny's slurred words were followed by a husky laugh.

"You needn't worry, I'm already awake," Letty said righteously as she stood in the doorway from the dining room into the kitchen. She flipped on the light and took one look at her brother, who was leaning heavily against Chase, one arm draped across his neighbor's neck, and snapped, "You're drunk."

Lonny stabbed a finger in her direction. "Nothing gets past you, does it?"

"I'll get him upstairs for you," Chase said, half dragging Lonny across the kitchen.

Lonny's mood was jovial and he attempted to sing some ditty, off-key, the words barely recognizable. Chase shushed him a second time, reminding him that Cricket was asleep even if Letty wasn't, but his warning went unheeded.

Letty led the way, trudging up the stairs, arms folded. She threw open Lonny's bedroom door and turned on the light.

Once inside, Lonny stumbled and fell across the bed, glaring up at the ceiling. Letty moved into the room and, with some effort, removed his boots.

Chase got a quilt from the closet and unfolded it across his friend. "He'll probably sleep for the rest of the night."

"I'm sure he will," Letty said tightly. She left Lonny's bedroom and hurried down the stairs. She was pacing the kitchen when Chase joined her.

"What's the matter with you?" he asked, frowning.

"How dare you bring my brother home in that condition," she demanded, turning on him.

"You wanted me to leave him in town? Drunk?"

If he'd revealed the slightest amount of guilt or contrition, Letty might've been able to let him go without another word. But he stood in front of her, and all she could see was the imagined woman in that bar. The one he'd danced with...and kissed and—

Fury surged up inside her, blocking out sanity. All week he'd been baiting her, wanting to hurt her for the pain she'd caused him. Tonight he'd succeeded.

"I hate you," she sobbed, lunging at him.

He grabbed her wrists and held them at her sides. "Letty, what's gotten into you?"

She squirmed and twisted in his arms, frantically trying to free herself, but she was trapped.

"Letty?"

She looked up at him, her face streaked with tears she didn't care to explain, her shoulders heaving with emotion.

"You're angry because Lonny's drunk?" he whispered.

"No," she cried, struggling again. "You went to that bar. You think I don't know what you did but—"

"*What* are you talking about?"

"You went to the Roundup to…to pick up some woman!"

Chase frowned, then shook his head. "Letty, no!"

"Don't lie to me…don't!"

"Oh, Letty," he murmured. Then he leaned down to settle his mouth over hers.

The last thing Letty wanted at that moment was his touch or his kiss. She meant to brace her hands against his chest and use her strength to push him away. Instead her hands inched upward until she was clasping his shoulders. The anger that had consumed her seconds before was dissolving in a firestorm of desire, bringing to life a part of her that had lain dormant from the moment she'd left Chase Brown's arms nine years before.

Chapter 5

Chase kissed her again and again while his hands roved up and down the curve of her spine as though he couldn't get enough of her.

His touch began to soothe the pain and disappointment that had come into her life in their long years apart. She was completely vulnerable to him in that moment. She *wanted* him.

And Chase wanted her.

"Letty..."

Whatever he'd intended to say was lost when his mouth covered hers with a hungry groan. Letty's lips parted in eager response.

She'd been back in Red Springs for several weeks, but she wasn't truly home until Chase had taken her in his arms and kissed her. Now that she was with him, a peace settled over her. Whatever lay before her, life or death, she was ready, suffused with the serenity his embrace offered. Returning to this small town and the Bar E were only a tiny part of what made it so important to come home for her surgery. Her love for Chase had been the real draw; it was what had pulled her back, and for the first time she was willing to acknowledge it.

Letty burrowed her fingers into his hair, her eyes shut, her head thrown back. Neither she nor Chase spoke. They held on to each other as though they were afraid to let go.

A sigh eased from Letty as Chase lifted his head and tenderly kissed her lips. He brought her even closer and deepened his probing kiss until Letty was sure her knees were about to buckle. Then his mouth abandoned hers to explore the hollow of her throat.

Tears welled in her eyes, then ran unheeded down her cheeks. Chase pressed endless kisses over her face until she forgot everything but the love she'd stored in her heart for him.

When she was certain nothing could bring her any more pleasure than his kiss, he lowered his hand to her breast—

"Mommy!"

Cricket's voice, coming from the top of the stairs, penetrated the fog of Letty's desire. Chase apparently hadn't heard her, and Letty had to murmur a protest and gently push him aside.

"Yes, darling, what's wrong?" Her voice sounded weak even to her own ears as she responded to her daughter.

Chase stumbled back and raised a hand to his face, as if he'd been suddenly awakened from a dream. Letty longed to go to him, but she couldn't.

"Uncle Lonny keeps singing and he woke me up!" Cricket cried.

"I'll be right there." Letty prayed Chase understood that she couldn't ignore her daughter.

"Mommy!" Cricket called more loudly. "Please hurry. Uncle Lonny sings terrible!"

"Just a minute." She retied her robe, her hands shaking. "Chase—"

"This isn't the time to do any talking," he said gruffly.

"But there's so much we need to discuss." She whisked the curls away from her face. "Don't you think so?"

"Not now."

"But—"

"Go take care of Cricket," he said and turned away.

Letty's heart was heavy as she started for the stairs. A dim light illuminated the top where Cricket was standing, fingers plugging her ears.

In the background, Letty heard her brother's drunken rendition of "Puff the Magic Dragon." Another noise blended with the first, as Chase opened the kitchen door and walked out of the house.

The next morning, Letty moved around downstairs as quietly as possible in an effort not to wake her brother. From everything she'd seen of him the night before, Lonny was going to have one heck of a hangover.

The coffee was perking merrily in the kitchen as Letty brushed Cricket's long hair while the child stood patiently in the bathroom.

"Was Uncle Lonny sick last night?" Cricket asked.

"I don't think so." Letty couldn't remember hearing him get out of bed during the night.

"He sounded sick when he was singing."

"I suppose he did at that," Letty murmured. "Or sickly, anyway." She finished tying the bright red ribbons in Cricket's hair and returned to the kitchen for a cup of coffee. To her astonishment, Lonny was sitting at the table, neatly dressed in a suit and tie.

"Lonny!"

"Morning," he greeted her.

Although his eyes were somewhat bloodshot, Lonny didn't look bad. In fact, he acted as though he'd gone sedately to bed at nine or ten o'clock.

Letty eyed him warily, unsure what to make of him. Only a few hours earlier he'd been decidedly drunk— but maybe not as drunk as she'd assumed. And Chase hadn't seemed inebriated at all.

"How are you feeling?" she asked, studying him carefully.

"Wonderful."

Obviously his escapades of the night before hadn't done him any harm. Unexpectedly he stood, then reached for his Bible, wiping the dust off the leather binding.

"Well, are you two coming to church with me or not?" he asked.

Letty was so shocked it took her a moment to respond. "Yes…of course."

It wasn't until they'd pulled into the church parking lot that Letty understood her brother's newly formed desire for religion. He was attending the morning service not because of any real longing to worship. He'd come hoping to see Joy Fuller again. The thought surprised Letty as much as it pleased her. Red Springs's second-grade teacher had managed to reignite her brother's interest. That made Letty smile. From the little Letty knew of the church organist, Joy would never fit Lonny's definition of the dutiful wife.

The congregation had begun to file through the wide doors. "I want to sit near the front," Lonny told Letty, looking around.

"If you don't mind, I'd prefer to sit near the back," Letty said. "In case Cricket gets restless."

"She'll be good today, won't you, cupcake?"

The child nodded, clearly eager for her uncle's approval. Lonny took her small hand in his and, disregarding Letty's wishes, marched up the center aisle.

Groaning inwardly, Letty followed her brother. At least his choice of seats gave Letty the opportunity to scan the church for any sign of Chase. Her quick survey told her he'd decided against attending services this morning, which was a relief.

Letty had been dreading their next encounter, yet at the same time she was eager to talk to him again. She felt both frightened and excited by their rekindled desire for each other. But he'd left her so brusquely the night before that she wasn't sure what to expect. So much would depend on his reaction to her. Then she'd know what he was feeling—if he regretted kissing her or if he felt the same excitement she did.

Organ music resounded through the church, and once they were settled in their pew, Letty picked up a hymnal. Lonny sang in his loudest voice, staring intently at Joy as she played the organ. Letty resisted the urge to remind him that his behavior bordered on rude.

When Joy faltered over a couple of notes, Lonny smiled with smug satisfaction. Letty moaned inwardly. So *this* was her brother's game!

"Mommy," Cricket whispered, standing backward on the pew and looking at the crowd. "Chase is here."

Letty's grip on the hymnal tightened. "That's nice, sweetheart."

"Can I go sit with him?"

"Not now."

"Later?"

"No."

"How come?"

"Cricket," Letty pleaded. "Sit down and be quiet."

"But I like Chase and I want to sit with him."

"Maybe next week," she said in a low voice.

"Can I ask him after the pastor's done talking at everybody?"

Letty nodded, willing to agree to just about anything by then. The next time her brother insisted on sitting in the front pew, he would do so alone.

No worship service had ever seemed to take longer. Cricket fidgeted during the entire hour, eager to run and talk to Chase. Lonny wasn't much better. He continued to stare at Joy and did everything but make faces at her to distract the poor woman. Before the service was half over, Letty felt like giving him a good, hard shake. Even as a young girl, she'd never seen her older brother behave more childishly. The only reason he'd come to church was to make poor Joy as uncomfortable as he possibly could.

By the time Letty was outside the church, Cricket had already found Chase. From his stiff posture, Letty knew he'd planned on escaping without talking to her and the last thing he'd wanted was to be confronted by Cricket. Letty's heart swelled with fresh pain. So this was how he felt.

He regretted everything.

Letty hastened to her daughter's side and took her small hand. "Uncle Lonny's waiting for us at the truck," she said, her eyes skirting Chase.

"But I haven't asked Chase if I can sit with him next week."

"I'm sure he has other friends he'd prefer to sit with," Letty answered, hiding her impatience.

"I can answer for myself." Chase's voice was clipped and unfriendly. "As it happens, Cricket, I think your mother's right. It would be best if you sat with her in church."

"Can't you sit in the same row as us?"

"No."

"Why not?"

Chase didn't say anything for an awkward moment, but when he did, he looked past Letty. "Because I'd rather not."

"Okay," Cricket said, apparently accepting that without a problem.

"It's time to go," Letty said tersely. Only a few hours earlier, Chase had held her in his arms, kissed her and loved her with a gentleness that had fired her senses back to life. And in the light of a new day, he'd told her as plainly as if he'd shouted it from the church steps that it had all been a mistake, that nothing had changed and he didn't want anything to do with her.

After all the hurt she'd suffered in California, Letty thought she was immune to this kind of pain. In the span of a few minutes Chase had taught her otherwise.

Cricket raced ahead of Letty to Lonny's truck and climbed inside. For his part, her brother seemed to be taking his time about getting back to the ranch. He talked to a couple of men, then finally joined Cricket and Letty.

"We're ready anytime you are," Letty said from inside the truck.

"In a minute," he returned absently, glancing around before he got in.

Letty realized Lonny was waiting for Joy to make an appearance. The parking lot was nearly deserted now. There were only three other cars left, and Lonny had parked next to one of them, a PT Cruiser. Letty had no trouble figuring out that it belonged to Joy.

Lonny was sitting in the truck, with the window down, his elbow resting on the frame, apparently content to laze away in the sunshine while he waited.

"Lonny?" Letty pressed. "Can we please go?" After the way he'd behaved in church, Letty had every intention of having a serious discussion with her brother, but she preferred to do it when Cricket wasn't around to listen. She'd also prefer not to witness another embarrassing skirmish between him and Joy Fuller.

"It'll only be another minute."

He was right; the church door opened and Joy came out. She hesitated when she saw Lonny's pickup beside her car.

"What are you going to say to her?" Letty whispered angrily.

"Oh, nothing much," Lonny murmured back, clearly distracted. When Joy approached her car, Lonny got out of the pickup and leaned indolently against the side, bracing one foot on the fender.

"I wouldn't do that if I were you," Joy said scathingly.

She was nearly as tall as Lonny, her dark hair styled so it fell in waves around her face. Her cheeks were a rosy hue and Letty couldn't help wondering if confronting Lonny again was why they were so flushed.

"Do what?" Lonny demanded.

"Put your foot on that truck. You might damage your priceless antique."

"I'll have you know, this truck isn't even ten years old!"

Joy feigned shock, opening her eyes wide while she held her hand against her chest. "Is that so? I could've sworn you claimed otherwise only yesterday. But, then, it seems you have a problem keeping your facts straight."

"You were impossible to talk to yesterday, and I can see today isn't going to be any better."

"Impossible?" Joy echoed. "Me? *You* were the one jumping up and down and acting like an idiot."

"Me?" Lonny tilted back his head and forced a loud laugh. "That's a good one."

Joy ignored him and continued to her car.

Lonny dropped his foot and yanked open the truck door. "I thought we might be able to settle our differences, but you're being completely unreasonable."

"Perhaps I am, but at least I don't throw temper tantrums in the middle of the street."

"Yeah, but *I* know how to drive."

"Based on *what?* Taking that...that unsafe rattletrap on a public road should be an indictable offense!"

"Rattletrap? *Unsafe?*" Lonny slapped his hat against his thigh. "Just who do you think you are, talking to me like that?"

"If you don't like the way I talk, Mr. Rodeo Star, then stay away from me."

"It'll be my pleasure."

Suddenly, Lonny couldn't seem to get out of the parking lot fast enough. He gripped the steering wheel as if he was driving in the Indy 500.

"Lonny," Letty ordered, "slow down."

When he reached the end of the street, he drove off as if the very fires of hell were licking at his heels.

"Lonny!" Letty cried a second time. If he continued to drive in this manner, she'd walk home. "You're driving like a maniac. Stop the truck this minute!"

"Didn't I tell you that woman's a living, breathing menace?" he snapped, but he reduced his speed. To his credit, he looked surprised by how fast he'd been traveling. "I swear she drives me over the edge."

"Then do as she says and stay away from her," Letty advised, shaking her head in wonder. But she doubted he would.

He ignored her comment. "Did you see the way she laid into me?"

"Lonny, you provoked her."

"Then you didn't see things the way they happened," he muttered, shooting Letty a look of indignation. "I was only trying to be friendly."

Her brother was as unreasonable as he'd claimed Joy was. "I like Joy and I think you were rude to her this morning," Letty returned primly.

"When?"

"Oh, honestly! The only reason you came to church was to intimidate her into making a mistake while she was playing the organ. When you succeeded, I thought you were going to stand up and cheer."

Lonny cast her a frown that said Letty should consider counseling. "You're totally wrong, little sister."

Letty rolled her eyes. "Have you figured out *why* you feel so strongly?"

"Because she needs to be put in her place, that's why!"

"And you think you're the one to do it?"

"Damn right! I'm not about to let any woman get away with the things she said to me."

"Calling this truck an antique or—" she grinned "—a rattletrap...well, they don't exactly sound like fighting words to me."

Lonny turned into the long dusty drive leading to the house. "You women really stick together, don't you?" he asked bitterly. "No matter how stupid you act."

"Stupid?"

He pulled the truck into his usual spot. "Yeah. Like the fact that Joy Fuller doesn't know how to drive and then blames me. And what about you? You're the perfect example, taking off on some fool dream. Chase should never have let you go."

"It wasn't up to Chase to stop me or not. He couldn't have, anyway—no one could. I wasn't going to end up like Mom, stuck out here in no-man's-land, working so hard... Why, she was little more than a slave."

Lonny's eyes widened as he turned to her. "That's the way you see Mom?"

"You mean you don't?" How could her brother be so blind? Their mother had worked herself into an early grave, sacrificing her talent and her dreams for a few head of cattle and an unforgiving land.

"Of course I don't! Mom had a good life here. She loved the ranch and everything about it."

"You're so oblivious you can't see the truth, can you?

Mom hated it here, only she wasn't honest enough to admit it, not even to herself."

"And you hate it, too?" he asked, his voice dangerously quiet.

"I did."

Lonny climbed out of the pickup and slammed the door. "No one asked you to come back, Letty. You could turn around and go straight back to California." With that he stormed into the house.

Fueled by her anger, Letty stayed in the truck, tears streaming down her face. She and Lonny had both been furious and the conversation had quickly gotten out of control. She should never have said the things she did. And Lonny shouldn't have, either. Now wasn't the time to deal with the past.

"Mommy?" Cricket leaned against her mother, obviously confused and a little frightened. "Why was Uncle Lonny shouting at you?"

"He was angry, honey."

"You were shouting at him, too."

"I know." She climbed out of the cab and helped Cricket clamber down. They walked into the house, and Lonny glared at her. She glared right back, surprised by how heated her response to him remained. In an effort to avoid continuing their argument, Letty went upstairs and changed her clothes. She settled Cricket with her activity book and crayons, then went outside and grabbed the hoe. Venting her frustration in the garden was bound to help. Once they'd both cooled down, they could discuss the matter rationally.

Lonny left soon afterward, barreling down the driveway as if he couldn't get away from her fast enough.

She was happy to see him go.

* * *

Chase felt as though his world had been knocked off its axis and he was struggling with some unknown force to right it again.

Letty was to blame for this. A part of him yearned to take Letty in his arms, love her, care for her and make up to her for the pain and disappointment she'd suffered. Yet something powerful within him wouldn't allow him to do it. He found himself saying and doing things he'd never intended.

Telling her he preferred not to sit beside her daughter in church was a prime example. The only reason he even attended was to be close to Letty. He rarely listened to the sermons. Instead, he sat and pretended Letty was the one sitting next to him. He thought about what it would be like to hear her lovely voice again as she sang. He imagined how it would feel to hold her hand while the pastor spoke.

Cricket had provided him with the perfect excuse to do those things. His pride wouldn't have suffered, and he'd be doing something to appease the kid. No one needed to know that being with Letty was what he'd wanted all along.

Yet he'd rejected the child's request flat out. And he'd been equally unwilling to talk to Letty last night. Chase didn't know how to explain his own actions. He was behaving like an idiot.

On second thought, his actions made perfect sense. He was protecting himself, and with good reason. He figured that if Letty really planned to make a life for herself in Red Springs, she'd be doing something about finding a decent job and settling down. She hadn't done that. Every piece of evidence pointed in the direction of her leaving again. She behaved as if this was an extended vacation and once she'd rested, she'd be on her way. Other than the garden she'd planted, he couldn't see any sign of permanence.

Chase couldn't allow his emotions to get involved with Letty a second time. He hadn't fully healed from the first. It wasn't that simple, however. He loved her, and frankly, he doubted he'd ever stop.

Rubbing his face, Chase drew in a deep, shuddering breath. He hadn't meant to touch her the night before, but her outrage, her eyes shooting sparks, had reminded him of the old Letty. The Letty who'd been naive, perhaps, but confident and self-assured, certain of her own opinions. He'd forgotten that he'd promised himself he'd never touch her again. One kiss and he'd been lost....

Even now, hours later, the memory of the way she'd melted in his embrace had the power to arouse him. He pushed it out of his mind. The best thing to do was forget it ever happened.

He went outside and got into the truck, deciding he'd go into town and do some shopping. Perhaps keeping busy would ease the ache in his heart.

Still confused, Chase wondered if he'd feel differently if Letty had made more of an effort to acknowledge their kisses. Cricket had come running up to him after the church service and Letty wouldn't even meet his eye. Obviously the memory of their encounter embarrassed her.

That pleased him.

And it infuriated him.

If Letty was disconcerted by their kissing, it said she didn't often let men touch her like that—which made him glad. The thought of another man making love to her was enough to produce a fireball of resentment in the pit of his stomach.

But her actions that morning also infuriated him, because she so obviously regretted what they'd done. While he'd spent the night dreaming of holding her and kissing her, she'd apparently been filled with remorse. Maybe she thought he wasn't good enough for her.

Telephone poles whizzed past him as he considered that bleak possibility.

A flash of red caught his attention. He looked again. It was Cricket, standing alone at the end of the Bar E driveway, crying. She was wearing the same dress she'd worn at church.

Chase stepped on his brakes and quickly backed up. When he reached the little girl, she looked up and immediately started running to him.

"Chase…oh, Mr. Chase!"

"Cricket," he said sternly, climbing out of the truck, angry with Letty for being so irresponsible. "What are you doing here? Where's your mother?"

Sobbing, the little girl ran and hugged his waist. "Uncle Lonny and Mommy shouted at each other. Then Uncle Lonny left and Mommy went outside. Now she's sleeping in the garden and I can't wake her up."

Chapter 6

Letty sat on the porch steps, rubbing her eyes. Her knees felt weak and her eyes stubbornly refused to focus. It had been through sheer force of will that she'd made it from the garden to the back steps. She trembled with fear and alarm. Although she'd called for Cricket, the little girl was nowhere in the house or garden. Letty had to find her daughter despite the waves of nausea and weakness.

The last thing Letty remembered clearly was standing in the garden, shoveling for all she was worth, weeding because she was furious with Lonny and equally upset with herself for being drawn into such a pointless argument.

"Cricket," Letty called out again, shocked by how unsteady her voice sounded. Her daughter had been standing beside her only a few minutes before. Now she was gone.

The roar of an approaching truck was nearly deafening. Letty didn't have the strength to get up, so she sat there and waited. Whoever it was would have to come to her.

"Letty?"

"Mommy! Mommy!"

Chase leaped out of the pickup and quickly covered the space that separated them. Cricket was directly behind him, her face wet and streaked with tears.

Confused, Letty glanced up at them. She had no idea how Cricket had come to be with Chase. Even more surprising was the way he looked, as though he was ill himself. His face was gray, set and determined, but she couldn't understand why.

"What happened?" Chase demanded.

For a long moment her mind refused to function. "I... I think I fainted."

"Fainted?"

"I must have." She wiped her forehead, forcing a smile. By sheer resolve, she started to stand, but before she was fully on her feet, Chase had scooped her up in his arms.

"Chase," she protested. "Put me down... I'm perfectly all right."

"Like hell you are."

He seemed furious, as if she'd purposely fainted in a ploy to gain his sympathy. That added to her frustration and she tried to get free. Her efforts, however, were futile; Chase merely tightened his grip.

Cricket ran ahead of him and opened the back door. "Is Mommy sick?"

"Yes," Chase answered, his mouth a white line of

impatience. He didn't so much as look at Letty as he strode through the house.

"I'm fine, sweetheart," Letty countered, trying to reassure her daughter, who ran beside Chase, intently studying her mother. Cricket looked so worried and frightened, which only distressed Letty more.

Chase gently deposited Letty on the sofa, then knelt beside her, his gaze roaming her face, inspecting her for any injury. Reluctantly, as if he was still annoyed, he brought his hand to her forehead. "You're not feverish," he announced.

"Of course I'm not," she shot back, awkwardly rising to an upright position. If everyone would give her a few minutes alone and some breathing room, she'd feel better. "I'm fine. I was weeding the garden, and next thing I knew I was on the ground. Obviously I got too much sun."

Cricket knelt on the carpet. "I couldn't wake you up," she murmured, her blue eyes round, her face shiny with tears.

Letty reached out to hug her. "I'm sorry I scared you, honey."

"Did you hit your head?" Chase asked.

"I don't think so." Tentatively she touched the back of her skull. As far as she could tell, there wasn't even a lump to suggest she'd hit anything besides the soft dirt.

"Cricket, go get your mother a glass of water."

The child took off running as if Chase's request was a matter of life and death.

"How did Cricket ever find you?" Letty asked, frowning. Her daughter wouldn't have known the way to Chase's ranch, and even if she had, it was several minutes away by car.

"I saw her on the road."

"The road," Letty repeated, horrified. "She got that far?"

"She was in a panic, and with Lonny gone, she didn't know what else to do."

Letty stared at Chase. "I'm grateful you stopped. Thank you."

Cricket charged into the living room with the glass of water, which was only partially full. Letty assumed the other half had spilled. She planted a soft kiss on her daughter's cheek as a thank-you.

"I think your mother could use a blanket, too," Chase murmured. His mouth was set and obstinate, but for what reason Letty could only speculate. It was unreasonable for him to be angry with her because she'd fainted!

Once more Cricket raced out of the room.

Chase continued to frown at Letty. He seemed to think that if he did that long enough, he'd discover why she'd taken ill. She boldly met his look and did her best to reassure him with a smile, but obviously failed.

Chase closed his eyes, and when he opened them again, the agony that briefly fluttered into his gaze was a shock. He turned away from her as if he couldn't bear to have her look at him.

"Letty, I didn't know what to think when I found Cricket," he said, and dragged a breath between clenched teeth. "For all I knew you could have been dead."

Motivated by something other than reason, Letty raised her hand to his face, running the tips of her fingers along his tense jaw. "Would you have cared?" she whispered.

"Yes," he cried. "I don't want to, but heaven help me, I do."

He reached for her, kissing her awkwardly, then hungrily, his mouth roving from one side of her face to the other, brushing against her eyes, her cheek, her ears and finally her throat.

They were interrupted by Cricket, who dashed into the room.

"I brought Mommy a blankey," Cricket said. She edged her way between Letty and Chase and draped her yellow knit blanket across Letty's lap.

"Thank you, sweetheart."

Chase rose and paced the floor in front of the sofa. "I'm calling Doc Hanley."

Letty was overcome with panic. She'd purposely avoided the physician, who'd been seeing her family for as long as she could remember. Although she trusted Doc Hanley implicitly, he wasn't a heart specialist, and if she was seen going in and out of his office on a regular basis there might be talk that would filter back to Lonny or Chase and cause them concern.

"Chase," she said, "calling Doc Hanley isn't necessary. I was in the sun too long—that's all. I should've known better."

"You're in the sun every day. Something's wrong. I want you to see a doctor."

"All right," she agreed, thinking fast. "I'll make an appointment, if you want, but I can't today—none of the offices are open."

"I'll drive you to the hospital," he insisted.

"The nearest hospital's an hour from here."

"I don't care."

"Chase, please, I'm a little unsettled, but basically

I'm fine. What I need more than anything is some rest. The last thing I want to do is sit in a hot, stuffy truck and ride all the way into Rock Springs so some doctor can tell me I got too much sun."

Chase paced back and forth, clearly undecided.

"I'll just go upstairs and lie down. It's about time for Cricket's nap, anyway," Letty said calmly, although her heart was racing. She really did feel terrible. Dizzy. Disoriented. Nauseous.

Chase wasn't pleased about Letty's proposal, but nodded. "I'll stay here in case you need me later."

"That really isn't necessary," she said again.

He turned and glared at her. "Don't argue with me. I'm not in the mood."

That was obvious. With some effort, although she struggled to conceal it, Letty stood and walked up the stairs. Chase followed her as though he suspected she might not make it. Letty was exhausted by the time she entered her bedroom.

"I'll take a nap and feel totally refreshed in a couple of hours. You wait and see."

"Right," Chase said tersely. As soon as she was lying down, he left.

Letty sat across the desk from Dr. Faraday the next afternoon. He'd wanted to talk to her after the examination.

"I haven't received your records from your physician in California yet, but I'm expecting them any day," he said.

Letty nodded, making an effort to disguise her uneasiness. As she'd promised Chase, she'd contacted the heart specialist in Rock Springs first thing Monday morning. She'd seen Dr. Faraday the week before and he'd asked that she come in right away. His brooding look troubled her.

"Generally speaking, how are you?"

"Fine." That was a slight exaggeration, but other than being excessively tired and the one fainting spell, she *had* felt healthy most of the time.

Dr. Faraday nodded and made a notation in her file. It was all Letty could do not to stand up and try to read what he'd written. He was a large man, his face dominated by a bushy mustache that reminded Letty of an umbrella. His eyes were piercing, and Letty doubted that much got past him.

"The results from the tests we did last week are in, and I've had a chance to review them. My opinion is that we shouldn't delay surgery much longer. I'll confer with my colleague, Dr. Frederickson, and make my report to the state. I'm going to ask that they put a rush on their approval."

Letty nodded and watched as he lifted his prescription pad from the corner of his desk. "I want you to start taking these pills right away."

"Okay," Letty agreed. "How long will I be in the hospital, Doctor?" Although she tried to appear calm, Letty was frightened. She'd never felt more alone. Her sense of humor, which had helped her earlier, seemed to have deserted her.

"You should plan on being in the hospital and then the convalescent center for up to two weeks," he replied absently, writing out a second prescription.

"Two weeks?" Letty cried. That was far longer than she'd expected.

His eyes met hers. "Is that a problem?"

"Not…exactly." It seemed foolish now, but Letty had automatically assumed that Lonny would be able to watch Cricket for her. He'd be happy to do that, she was confident, if her hospital stay was going to be only a few days. Even with the responsibilities of the ranch, he'd have found a way to look after the five-year-old, maybe hiring a part-time babysitter. True, it would have been an inconvenience for him, but Lonny was family. But two weeks was too long for Letty to even consider asking him.

Lonny and Cricket were just beginning to find their footing with each other. Cricket had accepted him, and Lonny seemed to think that as kids went, his niece was all right. Letty smiled to herself—she didn't want to do anything that would threaten their budding relationship.

A list of people who could possibly watch Cricket flashed through Letty's mind. There were several older women from church who'd been her mother's friends, women Letty would feel comfortable asking. Any one of them would take excellent care of her daughter. Whoever Letty found would have her hands full, though. Cricket had never spent much time away from Letty.

"I'd like you to make an appointment for Thursday," Dr. Faraday said, adding a couple of notes to her file. "See my receptionist before you leave and she'll give you a time."

Letty nodded, chewing on her lower lip. She wondered what she was going to say to Lonny about needing the truck again so soon.

Cricket was waiting for her in the hallway outside Dr. Faraday's office. She sat next to the receptionist and was busy coloring in her activity book. The child looked up and smiled when Letty came out. She placed her crayons neatly back in the box, closed her book and crawled down from the chair, hurrying to Letty's side.

Letty made her appointment for later in the week, then she and Cricket headed for the parking lot.

It was during the long drive home that Letty decided to broach the subject of their being separated.

"Cricket, Mommy may have to go away for a few days."

"Can I go with you?"

"Not this time. Uncle Lonny will be busy with the ranch, so you won't be able to stay with him, either."

Cricket shrugged.

Letty didn't think she'd mind not staying with Lonny. Her brother still hadn't come to appreciate the finer points of watching cartoons.

"Do you remember Mrs. Martin from church?" Letty asked. "She was my mommy's good friend." Dorothy Martin was a dear soul, although she'd aged considerably since her husband's death. Letty knew her mother's friend would agree to care for Cricket until Letty was able to do so herself.

"Does Mrs. Martin have gray hair and sing as bad as Uncle Lonny?"

"That's the one. I was thinking you could stay with her while I'm away."

"Don't want to." Cricket rejected Mrs. Martin without further comment.

"I see." Letty sighed. There were other choices, of course, but they were all women Cricket had met only briefly.

"What about—"

Cricket didn't allow her to finish.

"If you're going away and I can't go with you, then I

want to stay with Chase. I bet he'd let me ride Firepower again, and we could make chocolate chip cookies."

Letty should've guessed Chase would be her first choice.

"He'd read me stories like you do and let me blow out the lights at bedtime," Cricket continued. "We'd have lots of fun together. I like Chase better than anyone 'cept you." She paused, then added as extra incentive, "We could sit in church together and everything."

A tight knot formed in Letty's throat. In making her decision to return to Red Springs, she could never have predicted that Cricket would take such a strong and instant liking to Chase Brown.

"Mommy, could I?"

"I'm afraid Chase has to work on his ranch the same way Uncle Lonny does."

"Oh." Cricket sighed in disappointment.

"Think of all the people we've met since we came to live with Uncle Lonny," Letty suggested. "Who do you like best other than Chase?"

Cricket seemed to need time to mull over the question. She crossed her legs and tugged at one pigtail, winding the dark hair around her index finger as she considered this important decision.

"I like the lady who plays the organ second-best."

Joy Fuller was the perfect choice, although Letty was certain Lonny wouldn't take Cricket's preference sitting down. "I like Ms. Fuller, too," she told her daughter. "I'll talk to her. But my going away isn't for sure yet, honey, so there's no need to say anything to anyone. Okay?"

"Is it a surprise?"

"Yes." Letty's fingers tightened on the steering

wheel. She hated to mislead Cricket, but she couldn't have her daughter announce to Chase or her brother that she was going away and leaving Cricket behind.

"Oh, goody. I won't tell anyone," she said, pretending to zip her mouth closed.

"It's so nice to see you, Letty," Joy said as she stood in the doorway of her small rental house. "You, too, Cricket." A smile lit up Joy's face. "Your phone call came as a pleasant surprise."

Cricket followed Letty inside.

"I made some iced tea. Would you like some?"

"Please." Letty sat in the compact living room; as always, Cricket was at her side.

"Cricket, I have some Play-Doh in the kitchen if you'd like to play with that. My second-graders still enjoy it. I've also got some juice just for you."

Cricket looked to her mother and Letty nodded. The child trotted into the kitchen after Joy. Letty could hear them chatting, and although it was difficult to stay where she was, she did so the two of them could become better acquainted.

Joy returned a few minutes later with frosty glasses of iced tea. She set one in front of Letty, then took the chair opposite her.

"Cricket certainly is a well-behaved child. You must be very proud of her."

"Thank you, I am." Letty's gaze fell to her fingers, which were tightly clenched on the glass of iced tea. "I take it you and Lonny have come to some sort of agreement?"

Joy sighed, her shoulders rising reflexively, then sagging with defeat. "To be honest, I think it's best if he and I don't have anything to do with each other. I don't know what it is about your brother that irritates me so much. I mean, last fall we seemed to get along okay. But—and I'm sorry to say this, Letty—he's just so *arrogant.* He acted like I was supposed to be really impressed that he was a rodeo champion back in the day. *And* he kept calling me a hopeless city slicker because I'm from Seattle." She shook her head. "Now we can't even talk civilly to each other."

Letty doubted Joy would believe her if she claimed Lonny was still attracted to her. The problem was that he was fighting it so hard.

"You may find this difficult to believe," she said, "but Lonny's normally a calm, in-control type of guy. I swear to you, Joy, I've never seen him behave the way he has lately."

"I've known him for almost a year, but I had no idea he was that kind of hothead."

"Trust me, he usually isn't."

"He phoned me last Sunday."

At Letty's obvious surprise, Joy continued, eyes just managing to avoid her guest. "He started in about his stupid truck again. Then he mentioned something about an argument with you and how that was my fault—and then apparently you fainted, but he didn't really explain. Anyway, I hung up on him." She glanced over at Letty. "What happened to you? He sounded upset."

"He was, but mostly he was angry with himself. We got into an argument—which was *not* your fault—and, well, we both said things we didn't mean and immediately regretted. I went outside to work in the garden and… I don't know," she murmured. "The sun must've bothered me, because the next thing I knew, I'd fainted."

"Oh, Letty! Are you all right?"

"I am, thanks." Letty realized she was beginning to get good at exaggerating the state of her health.

"Did you see a doctor?"

"Yes. Everything's under control, so don't worry."

Cricket wandered in from the kitchen with a miniature cookie sheet holding several flat Play-Doh circles. "Mommy, I'm baking chocolate chip cookies for Chase."

"Good, sweetheart. Will you bake me some, too?"

The child nodded, then smiled shyly up at Joy. "Did you ask her, Mommy?"

"Not yet."

Letty's gaze followed Cricket back into the kitchen. She could feel Joy's curiosity, and wished she'd been able to lead into the subject of Cricket's staying with her a little more naturally.

"There's a possibility I'll need to be away for a week or two in the near future," she said, holding the glass with both hands. "Unfortunately I won't be able to take Cricket with me, and I doubt Lonny could watch her for that length of time."

"I wouldn't trust your brother to care for Cricket's *dolls,*" Joy said stiffly, then looked embarrassed.

"Don't worry, I don't think I'd feel any differently toward my brother if I were in your shoes," Letty said, understanding her friend's feelings.

"As you were saying?" Joy prompted, obviously disturbed that the subject of Lonny had crept into the conversation.

"Yes," Letty said, and straightened. This wasn't easy; it was a lot to ask of someone she'd only known for a little while. "As I explained, I may have to go away for a couple of weeks, and since I can't leave Cricket with my brother, I'm looking for someone she could stay with while I'm gone."

Joy didn't hesitate for a second. "I'd be more than happy to keep her for you. But there's one problem. I've still got three more weeks of school. I wouldn't be able to take her until the first week of June. Would you need to leave before then?"

"No... I'd make sure of that." For the first time, Letty felt the urge to tell someone about her condition. It would be so good to share this burden with someone she considered a friend, someone who'd calm and reassure her. Someone she trusted.

But Joy was a recent friend, and it seemed wrong to shift the burden onto her shoulders. And if Lonny somehow discovered Letty's secret, he'd be justifiably angry that she'd confided her troubles in someone she barely knew and not her own flesh and blood.

"Letty..."

She looked up then and realized her thoughts had consumed her to the point that she'd missed whatever Joy had been saying. "I'm sorry," she said, turning toward her.

"I was just suggesting that perhaps you could leave Cricket with me for an afternoon soon—give us the opportunity to get better acquainted. That way she won't feel so lost while you're away."

"That would be wonderful."

As if knowing the adults had been discussing her, Cricket came into the living room. "Your chocolate chip cookies are almost cooked, Mommy."

"Thank you, sweetheart. I'm in the mood for something chocolate."

"Me, too," Joy agreed, smiling.

"Mommy will share with you," Cricket stated confidently. "She *loves* chocolate."

All three laughed.

"Since Cricket's doing so well, why don't you leave her here for an hour or two?"

Letty stood. "Cricket?" She looked at her daughter, wanting to be sure the child felt comfortable enough to be here alone with Joy.

"I have to stay," Cricket said. "My cookies aren't finished cooking yet."

"I'd be delighted with the company," Joy said so sincerely Letty couldn't doubt her words. "I haven't got anything planned for the next hour or so, and since you're already here, it would save you a trip into town later on."

"All right," Letty said, not knowing exactly where she'd go to kill time. Of course, she could drive back to the Bar E, but there was nothing for her there. She reached for her purse. "I'll be back...soon."

"Take your time," Joy said, walking her to the door. Cricket came, too, and kissed Letty goodbye with such calm acceptance it tugged at her heart.

Once inside her brother's battered pickup, she drove aimlessly through town. That was when she decided to visit the town cemetery. No doubt her parents' graves had been neglected over the years. The thought saddened her and yet filled her with purpose.

She parked outside the gates and ambled over the green lawn until she arrived at their grave sites. To her surprise they were well maintained. Lonny had obviously been out here recently.

Standing silent, feeling oppressed by an overwhelming sense of loss, Letty bowed her head. Tears gathered in her eyes, but Letty wiped them aside; she hadn't come here to weep. Her visit had been an impromptu one, although the emotions were churning inside her.

"Hi, Daddy," she whispered. "Hi, Mom. I'm back... I tried California, but it didn't work out. I never knew there were so many talented singers in the world." She paused, as though they'd have some comment to make, but there was only silence. "Lonny welcomed me home. He didn't have to, but he did. I suppose you know about my heart...that's what finally convinced me I had to be here."

She waited, not expecting a voice of authority to rain down from the heavens, yet needing something...except she didn't know what.

"What's it like...on the other side?" Letty realized that even asking such a question as if they could answer was preposterous, but after her visit with Dr. Faraday, she'd entertained serious doubts that she'd ever recover. "Don't worry, I don't actually think you're going to tell me. Anyway, I always did like surprises."

Despite her melancholy, Letty smiled. She knelt beside the tombstones and reverently ran the tips of her fingers over the names and dates engraved in the marble. Blunt facts that said so little about their lives and those who'd loved them so deeply.

"I went to the doctor today," she whispered, her voice cracking. "I'm scared, Mom. Remember how you used to comfort me when I was a little girl? I wish I could crawl into your lap now and hear you tell me that everything's going to be all right." With the back of her hand she dashed away the tears that slid unrestrained down her cheeks.

"There's so much I want to live for now, so many things I want to experience." She remembered how she'd joked and kidded with the California doctors about her condition. But the surgery was imminent, and Letty wasn't laughing anymore.

"Mom. Dad." She straightened, coming to her feet. "I know you loved me—never once did I doubt that—and I loved you with all my heart…damaged though it is," she said with a hysterical laugh. "I wish you were with me now… I need you both so much."

Letty waited a couple of minutes, staring down at the graves of the two people who'd shaped and guided her life with such tender care. A tranquillity came to her then, a deep inner knowledge that if it had been humanly possible, her mother would have thrown both arms around her, hugged her close and given her the assurance she craved.

"I need someone," Letty admitted openly. Her burden was becoming almost more than she could bear. "Could you send me a friend?" she whispered. "Someone I can talk to who'll understand?" Names slipped in and out of her mind. The pastor was a good choice. Dorothy Martin was another.

"Letty?"

At the sound of her name, she turned and looked into Chase's eyes.

Chapter 7

"I saw Lonny's pickup on the road," Chase said, glancing over his shoulder. His hat was tipped back on his head as he studied her, his expression severe. "What are you doing here, Letty?"

She looked down at her parents' graves as a warm, gentle breeze blew over her. "I came to talk to Mom and Dad."

Her answer didn't seem to please him and he frowned. "Where's Cricket?"

"She's with Joy Fuller."

"Joy Fuller." He repeated the name slowly. "Lonny's Joy Fuller?"

"One and the same."

A sudden smile appeared on his face. "Lonny's certainly taken a dislike to that woman, although he was pretty keen on her for a while there."

"Lonny's making an utter fool of himself," Letty said.

"That's easy enough to do," Chase returned grimly.

His face tightened. "Did you make an appointment with the doctor like you promised?"

Letty nodded. She'd hoped to avoid the subject, but she should've known Chase wouldn't allow that.

"And?" he barked impatiently. "Did you see him?"

"This afternoon." She would've thought that would satisfy him, but apparently it didn't. If anything, his frown grew darker.

"What did he say?"

"Not to vent my anger in the hot sun," she told him flippantly, then regretted responding to Chase's concern in such a glib manner. He was a friend, perhaps the best she'd ever had, and instead of answering him in an offhand way, Letty should be grateful for his thoughtfulness. Only minutes before she'd been praying for someone with whom she could share her burdens, and then Chase had appeared like someone out of a dream.

He could, in every sense, be the answer to her prayer.

"Chase," she said, moving between the headstones, unsure how to broach the difficult subject. "Have you thought very much about death?"

"No," he said curtly.

Strangely stung by his sharp reaction, she continued strolling, her hands behind her back. "I've thought about it a lot lately," she said, hoping he'd ask her why.

"That's sick, Letty."

"I don't think so," she said, carefully measuring each word. "Death, like birth, is a natural part of life. It's sunrise and sunset, just the way the song says."

"Is that the reason you're wandering among the tombstones like...like some vampire?"

It took her several minutes to swallow a furious response. Did she need to hit this man over the head before he realized what she was trying to tell him? "Oh, Chase, that's a mean thing to say."

"Do you often stroll through graveyards as if they're park grounds?" he asked, his voice clipped. "Or is this a recent pastime?"

"Recent," she said, smiling at him. She hoped he understood that no matter how much he goaded her, she wasn't going to react to his anger.

"Then may I suggest you snap out of whatever trance you're in and join the land of the living? There's a whole world out there just waiting to be explored."

"But the world isn't always a friendly place. Bad things happen every day. No one said life's fair. I wish it was, believe me, but it isn't."

"Stop talking like that. Wake up, Letty!" He stepped toward her as if he'd experienced a sudden urge to shake her, but if that was the case, he restrained himself.

"I'm awake," she returned calmly, yearning for him to understand that she loved life, but was powerless to control her own destiny. She felt a deep need to prepare him for her vulnerability to death. Now if only he'd listen.

"It's really very lovely here, don't you think?" she asked. "The air is crisp and clear, and there's the faint scent of sage mingled with the wildflowers. Can't you smell it?"

"No."

Letty ignored his lack of appreciation. "The sky is lovely today. So blue... When it's this bright I sometimes think it's actually going to touch the earth." She paused, waiting for Chase to make some kind of response, but he remained resolutely silent. "Those huge white clouds resemble Spanish galleons sailing across the seas, don't they?"

"I suppose."

Her linked hands behind her back, she wandered down a short hill. Chase continued to walk with her, but the silence between them was uneasy. Just when Letty felt the courage building inside her to mention the surgery, he spoke.

"You lied to me, Letty."

His words were stark. Surprised, she turned to him and met his gaze. It was oddly impassive, as if her supposed deceit didn't matter to him, as though he'd come to expect such things from her.

"When?" she demanded.

"Just now. I phoned Doc Hanley's office and they said you hadn't so much as called. You're a liar—on top of everything else."

Letty's breath caught painfully in her throat. The words to prove him wrong burned on her lips. "You don't have any right to check up on me." She took a deep breath. "Nevertheless, I didn't lie to you. I never have. But I'm not going to argue with you, if that's what you're looking for."

"Are you saying Doc Hanley's office lied?"

"I'm not going to discuss this. Believe what you want." She quickened her steps as she turned and headed toward the wrought-iron gates at the cemetery entrance. He followed her until they stood next to the trucks.

"Letty?"

She looked at him. Anger kindled in his eyes like tiny white flames, but Letty was too hurt to appease him with an explanation. She'd wanted to reveal a deep part of herself to this man because she trusted and loved him. She couldn't now. His accusation had ruined what she'd wanted to share.

He reached out and clasped her shoulders. "I need to know. Did you or did you not lie to me?"

The scorn was gone from his eyes, replaced with a pain that melted her own.

"No... I did see a doctor, I swear to you." She held her head at a proud angle, her gaze unwavering, but when she spoke, her voice cracked.

His eyes drifted closed as if he didn't know what to believe anymore. Whatever he was thinking, he didn't say. Instead he pulled her firmly into his embrace and settled his mouth on hers.

A tingling current traveled down her body at his touch. Letty whimpered—angry, hurt, excited, pleased. Still kissing her, Chase let his hands slide down to caress her back, tugging her against him. Her body was already aflame and trembling with need.

Chase held her tightly as he slipped one hand up to tangle in her short curls. His actions were slow, hesitant, as if he was desperately trying to stop himself from kissing her.

"Letty..." he moaned, his breath featherlight against her upturned face. "You make me want you...."

She bowed her head. The desire she felt for him was equally ravenous.

Chase dragged in a heavy breath and expelled it loudly. "I don't want to feel the things I do."

"I know." It was heady knowledge, and Letty took delight in it. She moved against him, craving the feel of his arms around her.

Chase groaned. His mouth found hers once more and he kissed her tentatively, as if he didn't really want to be touching her again, but couldn't help himself. This increased Letty's reckless sensation of power.

He slid his hands up her arms and gripped her shoulders. Letty shyly moved her body against him; unfortunately the loving torment wasn't his alone, and she halted abruptly at the intense heat that surged through her.

A car drove past them, sounding its horn.

Letty had forgotten that they were standing on the edge of the road. Groaning with embarrassment, she buried her face against his heaving chest. Chase's heart felt like a hammer beating against her, matching her own excited pulse.

"Listen to me, Letty," he whispered.

He held her head between his hands and gently lifted her face upward, his breath warm and moist against her own.

"I want you more than I've ever wanted a woman in my life. You want me, too, don't you?"

For a moment she was tempted to deny everything, but she couldn't.

"Don't you?" he demanded. His hands, which were holding her face, were now possessive. His eyes, which had so recently been clouded with passion, were now sharp and insistent.

Letty opened her mouth to reply, but some part of her refused to acknowledge the truth. Her fear was that Chase would find a way to use it against her. He didn't trust her; he'd told her that himself. Desire couldn't be confused with love—at least not between them.

"Don't you?" he questioned a second time.

Knowing he wouldn't free her until she gave him an answer, Letty nodded once.

The instant she did, he released her. "That's all I wanted to know." With that he turned and walked away.

For the three days after her confrontation with Chase, Letty managed to avoid him. When she knew he'd be over at the house, she made a point of being elsewhere.

Her thoughts were in chaos, her emotions so muddled and confused that she didn't know what to think or feel toward him anymore.

Apparently Chase was just as perplexed as she was, because he seemed to be avoiding her with the same fervor. Normally he stopped by the house several mornings a week. Not once since they'd met in the cemetery had he shown up for breakfast. Letty was grateful.

She cracked three eggs in a bowl and started whipping them. Lonny was due back in the house any minute and she wanted to have his meal ready when he arrived. Since her argument with her brother, he'd gone out of his way to let her know he appreciated her presence. He appeared to regret their angry exchange as much as Letty did.

The back door opened, and Lonny stepped inside and hung his hat on the peg next to the door. "Looks like we're in for some rain."

"My garden could use it," Letty said absently as she poured the eggs into the heated frying pan, stirring them while they cooked. "Do you want one piece of toast or two?"

"Two."

She put the bread in the toaster. Her back was to her brother when she spoke. "Do you have any plans for today?"

"Nothing out of the ordinary."

She nodded. "I thought you were supposed to see the insurance adjuster about having the fender on your truck repaired."

"It isn't worth the bother," Lonny said, walking to the stove to refill his coffee cup.

"But I thought—"

Lonny had made such a fuss over that minuscule dent in his truck that Letty had assumed he'd want to have it fixed, if for no other reason than to irritate Joy.

"I decided against it," he answered shortly.

"I see." Letty didn't, but that was neither here nor there. She'd given up trying to figure him out when it came to his relationship with Joy Fuller.

"I hate it when you say that," he muttered.

"Say what?" Letty asked, puzzled.

"'I see' in that prim voice, as if you know exactly what I'm thinking."

"Oh."

"There," he cried, slamming down his coffee cup. "You did it again."

"I'm sorry, Lonny. I didn't mean anything by it." She dished up his eggs, buttered the toast and brought his plate to the table.

He glanced at her apologetically when she set his breakfast in front of him, picked up his fork, then hesitated. "If I turn in a claim against Joy, her insurance rates will go up. Right?"

Letty would've thought that would be the least of her brother's concerns. "That's true. She'd probably be willing to pay you something instead. Come to think of it, didn't she offer you fifty dollars to forget the whole thing?"

Lonny's eyes flared briefly. "Yes, she did."

"I'm sure Joy would be happy to give you the money if you'd prefer to handle the situation that way. She wants to be as fair as she can. After all, she admitted from the first that the accident was her fault."

"What else could she do?"

Letty didn't respond.

"I don't dare contact her, though," Lonny said, his voice low.

As she sat down across from him, Letty saw that he hadn't taken a single bite of his eggs. "Why not?"

He sighed and looked away, clearly uncomfortable. "The last time I tried to call her she hung up."

"You shouldn't have blamed her for our argument. That was a ridiculous thing to do. Ridiculous and unfair."

A lengthy pause followed. "I know," Lonny admitted. "I was lashing out at her because I was furious with myself. I was feeling bad enough about saying the things I did to you. Then I found out you fainted soon afterward and I felt like a real jerk. The truth is, I had every intention of apologizing when I got back to the house. But you were upstairs sleeping and Chase was sitting here, madder than anything. He nearly flayed me alive. I guess I was looking for a scapegoat, and since Joy was indirectly involved, I called her."

"Joy wasn't involved at all! Directly *or* indirectly. You just wanted an excuse to call her."

He didn't acknowledge Letty's last comment, but said, "I wish I hadn't done it."

"Not only that," she went on as though he hadn't spoken, "Chase had no right to be angry with you."

"Well, he thought he did." Lonny paused. "Sometimes I wonder about you and Chase. You two have been avoiding each other all week. I mention your name and he gets defensive. I mention him to you and you change the subject. The fact is, I thought that once you got home and settled down, you and Chase might get married."

At those words, Letty did exactly what Lonny said she would. She changed the subject. "Since you won't be taking the truck in for body work, someone needs to tell Joy. Would you like me to talk to her for you?"

Lonny shrugged. "I suppose."

"What do you want me to say?"

Lonny shrugged again. "I don't know. I guess you can say I'm willing to drop the whole insurance thing. She doesn't need to worry about giving me that fifty dollars, either—I don't want her money."

Letty ran one finger along the rim of her coffee cup. "Anything else?"

Her brother hesitated. "I guess it wouldn't do any harm to tell her I said I might've overreacted just a bit the day of the accident, and being the sensitive kind of guy I am, I regret how I behaved.... This, of course, all depends on how receptive she is to my apology."

"Naturally," Letty said, feigning a sympathetic look. "But I'm sure Joy will accept your apology." Letty wasn't at all certain that was true, but she wanted to reassure her brother, who was making great leaps in improving his attitude toward her friend.

Digging his fork into his scrambled eggs, Lonny snorted softly. "Now *that's* something I doubt. Knowing that woman the way I do, I'll bet Joy Fuller demands an apology written in blood. But this is the best she's going to get. You tell her that for me, will you?"

"Be glad to," Letty said.

Lonny took a huge bite of his breakfast, as if he'd suddenly realized how hungry he was. He picked up a piece of toast with one hand and waved it at Letty. "You might even tell her I think she does a good job at church with the organ. But play that part by ear, if you know what I mean. Don't make it sound like I'm buttering her up for anything."

"Right."

"Do you want the truck today?"

"Please." Letty had another doctor's appointment and was leading up to that request herself.

Lonny stood up and carried his plate to the sink. "I'll talk to you this afternoon, then." He put on his hat, adjusted it a couple of times, then turned to Letty and smiled. "You might follow your own advice, you know."

"What are you talking about?"

"You and Chase. I don't know what's going on, but I have a feeling that a word or two from you would patch everything up. Since I'm doing the honorable thing with Joy, I'd think you could do the same with Chase."

With that announcement he was gone.

Letty sat at the table, both hands around the warm coffee mug, while she mulled over Lonny's suggestion. She didn't know what to say to Chase, or how to talk to him anymore.

More than a week had passed since Chase had seen Letty. Each day his mood worsened. Each day he grew more irritable and short-tempered. Even Firepower, who had always sensed his mood and adjusted his own temperament, seemed to be losing patience with him. Chase didn't blame the gelding; he was getting to the point where he hated himself.

Something had to be done.

The day Chase had found Letty wandering through the cemetery, he'd been driving around looking for her. She'd promised him on Sunday that she'd see Doc Hanley. Somehow, he hadn't believed she'd do it. Chase had been furious when he discovered she hadn't seen the doctor. It'd taken him close to an hour to locate Letty.

When he did, he'd had to exercise considerable restraint not to blast her for her lack of common sense. She'd fainted, for crying out loud! A healthy person didn't just up and faint. Something was wrong.

But before Chase could say a word, Letty had started in with that macabre conversation about death and dying. His temper hadn't improved with her choice of subject matter. The old Letty had been too full of life even to contemplate death. It was only afterward, when she was in his arms, that Chase discovered the vibrant woman he'd always known. Only when he was kissing her that she seemed to snap out of whatever trance she was in.

It was as though Letty was half-alive these days. She met his taunts with a smile, refused to argue with him even when he provoked her. Nothing had brought a response from her, with the exception of his kisses.

Chase couldn't take any more of this. He was going to talk to her and find out what had happened to change her from the lively, spirited woman he used to know. And he didn't plan to leave until he had an answer.

When he pulled into the yard, Cricket was the only one he saw. The child was sitting on the porch steps, looking bored and unhappy. She brightened as soon as he came into view.

"Chase!" she called and jumped to her feet.

She ran toward him with an eagerness that grabbed his heart. He didn't know why Cricket liked him so much. He'd done nothing to deserve her devotion. She was so pleased, so excited, whenever she saw him that her warm welcome couldn't help but make him feel... good.

"I'm glad you're here," she told him cheerfully.

"Hello, Cricket. It's nice to see you, too."

She slipped her small hand into his and smiled up at him. "It's been ages and *ages* since you came over to see us. I missed you a whole bunch."

"I know."

"Where've you been all this time? Mommy said I wasn't supposed to ask Uncle Lonny about you any-more, but I was afraid I wouldn't see you again. You weren't in church on Sunday."

"I've been...busy."

The child sighed. "That's what Mommy said." Then, as though suddenly remembering something important, Cricket tore into the house, returning a moment later with a picture that had been colored in with the utmost care. "This is from my book. I made it for you," she announced proudly. "It's a picture of a horsey."

"Thank you, sweetheart." He examined the picture, then carefully folded it and put it in his shirt pocket.

"I made it 'cause you're my friend and you let me ride Firepower."

He patted her head. "Where's your mother?"

"She had to go to Rock Springs."

"Who's watching you?"

Cricket pouted. "Uncle Lonny, but he's not very good at it. He fell asleep in front of the TV, and when I changed the channel, he got mad and told me to leave it 'cause he was watching it. But he had his eyes closed. How can you watch TV with your eyes closed?"

She didn't seem to expect an answer, but plopped herself down and braced her elbows on her knees, her small hands framing her face.

Chase sat down next to her. "Is that why you're sit-ting out here all by yourself?"

Cricket nodded. "Mommy says I'll have lots of friends to play with when I go to kindergarten, but that's not for months and months."

"I'm sure she's right."

"But you're my friend and so is Firepower. I like Firepower, even if he's a really big horse. Mommy said I could have a horsey someday. Like she did when she was little."

He smiled at the child, fighting down an emotion he couldn't identify, one that kept bobbing to the surface of his mind. He remembered Letty when she was only a few years older than Cricket. They had the same color hair, the same eyes and that same stubborn streak, which Chase swore was a mile wide.

"My pony's going to be the best pony *ever*," Cricket prattled on, clearly content to have him sitting beside her, satisfied that he was her friend.

It hit Chase then, with an impact so powerful he could hardly breathe. His heart seemed to constrict, burning within his chest. The vague emotion he'd been feeling was unmistakable now. Strong and unmistakable. He loved this little girl. He didn't *want* to love Cricket, didn't want to experience this tenderness, but the child was Letty's daughter. And he loved Letty. In the last few weeks he'd been forced to admit that nine long years hadn't altered his feelings toward her.

"Chase—" Lonny stepped outside and joined them on the back porch. "When did you get here?"

"A few minutes ago." He had trouble finding his voice. "I came over to talk to Letty, but she's not here."

"No, she left a couple of hours ago." He checked his watch, frowning as he did. "I don't know what time to expect her back."

"Did she say where she was going?"

Lonny glanced away, his look uncomfortable. "I have no idea what's going on with that woman. I wish I did."

"What do you mean?" Chase knew his friend well enough to realize Lonny was more than a little disturbed.

"She's been needing the truck all week. She's always got some errand or another. I don't need it that much myself, so I don't mind. But then yesterday I noticed she's been putting a lot of miles on it. I asked her why, but she got so defensive and closemouthed we nearly had another fight."

"So did you find out where she's going?"

"Rock Springs," Lonny said shortly. "At least, that's what she claims."

"Why? What's in Rock Springs?"

Lonny shrugged. "She never did say."

"Mommy goes to see a man," Cricket interjected brightly. "He looks like the one on TV with the mustache."

"The one on TV with the mustache," Lonny repeated, exchanging a blank stare with Chase. "Who knows what she means by that?"

"He's real nice, too," Cricket went on to explain patiently. "But he doesn't talk to me. He just talks to Mommy. Sometimes they go in a room together and I have to wait outside, but that's all right 'cause I work in my book."

Lonny's face tensed as he looked at Chase again. "I'm sure that isn't the way it sounds," he murmured.

"Why should I care what she does," Chase lied. "I don't feel a thing for her. I haven't in years."

"Right," Lonny returned sarcastically. "The problem is, you never could lie worth a damn."

Chapter 8

The arrival of Letty's first welfare check had a curious effect on her. She brought in the mail, sat down at the kitchen table and carefully examined the plain beige envelope. Tears filled her eyes, then crept silently down her face. Once she'd been so proud, so independent, and now she was little more than a charity case, living off the generosity of taxpayers.

Lonny came in the back door and wiped his feet on the braided rug. "Mail here?" he asked impatiently.

Her brother had been irritated with her for the past couple of weeks without ever letting her know exactly why. Letty realized his displeasure was connected to her trips into Rock Springs, and her secrecy about them, but he didn't mention them again. Although he hadn't said a word, she could feel his annoyance every time they were together. More than once over the past few days, Letty had toyed with the idea of telling Lonny about her heart condition, but whenever she thought of approaching him, he'd look at her with narrow, disapproving eyes.

Without waiting for her to respond, Lonny walked over to the table and sorted through the bills, flyers and junk mail.

Letty stood and turned away from him. She wiped her cheeks, praying that if he did notice her tears he wouldn't comment.

"Mommy!" Cricket crashed through the back door, her voice high with excitement. "Chase is here on Firepower and he's got another horsey with him. Come and look." She was out the door again in an instant.

Letty smiled, tucked the government check in her pocket and followed her daughter outside. Sure enough, Chase was riding down the hillside on his gelding, holding the reins of a second horse, a small brown-and-white pinto trotting obediently behind the bay.

"Chase! Chase!" Cricket stood on the top step, jumping up and down and frantically waving both arms.

Chase slowed his pace once he reached the yard. Lonny joined his sister, trying to hide a smile. Bemused, Letty stared at him. The last time she could remember seeing him with a silly grin like that, she'd been ten years old and he was suffering through his first teenage crush.

Unable to wait a second longer, Cricket ran out to greet her friend. Smiling down at the child, Chase lowered his arms and hoisted her into the saddle beside him. Letty had lost count of the times Chase had "just happened" to stop by with Firepower in the past few weeks. Cricket got as excited as a game show winner whenever he was around. He'd taken her riding more than once. He was so patient with the five-year-old, so gentle. The only time Chase had truly laughed in Letty's presence was when he was with her daughter—and Cricket treasured every moment with her hero.

In contrast, Letty's relationship with Chase had deteriorated to the point that they'd become, at best, mere acquaintances. Chase went out of his way to avoid talking to her. It was as if their last meeting in the cemetery, several weeks before, had killed whatever love there'd ever been between them.

Letty watched from the porch as Chase slid out of the saddle and onto the ground, then lifted Cricket down. He wore the same kind of silly grin as Lonny, looking exceptionally pleased with himself.

"Well, what do you think?" Lonny asked, rocking back on his heels, hands in his pockets. He seemed almost as excited as Cricket.

"About what?" Letty felt as if everyone except her was in on some big secret.

Lonny glanced at her. "Chase bought the pony for Cricket."

"What?" Letty exploded.

"It's a surprise," Lonny whispered.

"You're telling me! Didn't it cross his mind—or yours—to discuss the matter with *me?* I'm her mother... I should have some say in this decision, don't you think?"

For the first time, Lonny revealed signs of uneasiness. "Actually, Chase did bring up the subject with me, and I'm the one who told him it was okay. After all, I'll be responsible for feeding it and paying the vet's bills, for that matter. I assumed you'd be as thrilled as Cricket."

"I am, but I wish one of you had thought to ask me first. It's...it's common courtesy."

"You're not going to make a federal case out of this, are you?" Lonny asked, his gaze accusing. "Chase is just doing something nice for her."

"I know," she sighed. But that wasn't the issue.

Chase and Cricket were standing next to the pony when Letty approached them in the yard. Apparently Chase had just told her daughter the pony now belonged to her, because Cricket threw her arms around Chase's neck, shouting with glee. Laughing, Chase twirled her in a circle, holding her by the waist. Cricket's short legs flew out and she looked like a tiny top spinning around and around.

Letty felt like an outsider in this touching scene, although she made an effort to smile and act pleased. Perhaps Cricket sensed Letty's feelings, because as soon as she was back on the ground, she hurried to her mother's side and hugged her tightly.

"Mommy, did you see Jennybird? That's the name of my very own pony."

Chase walked over and placed his hands on the little girl's shoulders. "You don't object, do you?" he asked Letty.

How could she? "Of course not. It's very thoughtful of you, Chase." She gazed down at her daughter and restrained herself from telling him she wished he'd consulted her beforehand. "Did you thank him, sweetheart?"

"Oh, yes, a hundred million, zillion times."

Letty turned back to the porch, fearing that if she stood there any longer, watching the two of them, she'd start to weep. The emotions she felt disturbed her. Crazy as it seemed, the most prominent one bordered on jealousy. How she yearned for Chase to look at her with the same tenderness he did Cricket. Imagine being envious of her own daughter!

Chase didn't hide his affection for the child. In the span of a few weeks, the pair had become great friends, and Letty felt excluded, as if she were on the outside looking in. Suddenly she couldn't bear to stand there anymore and pretend everything was fine. As unobtrusively as possible, she walked back to the house. She'd almost reached the door when Chase stopped her.

"Letty?"

She turned to see him standing at the bottom of the steps, a frown furrowing his brow.

"You dropped this." He extended the plain envelope to her.

The instant she realized what it was, Letty was mortified. Chase stood below her, holding out her welfare check, his face distorted with shock and what she was sure must be scorn. When she took the check, his eyes seemed to spark with questions. Before he could ask a single one, she whirled around and raced into the house.

It shouldn't have surprised Letty that she couldn't sleep that night, although she seemed to be the only member of the family with that problem. After all the excitement with Jennybird, Cricket had fallen asleep almost immediately after dinner. Lonny had been snoring softly when Letty had dressed and tiptoed past his bedroom on her way downstairs.

Now she sat under the stars, her knees under her chin, on the hillside where she'd so often met Chase when they were young. Chase had listened to her talk about her dreams and all the wonderful things in store for her. He'd held her close and kissed her and believed in her and with her.

That secure feeling, that sense of being loved, had driven Letty back to this spot now. There'd been no place else for her to go. She felt more alone than ever, more isolated—cut off from the people she loved, who loved her. She was facing the most difficult problem of her life and she was doing it utterly alone.

Letty knew she should be pleased with the unexpected change in Chase's attitude toward Cricket…and she was. It was more than she'd ever expected from him, more than she'd dared to hope. And yet, she longed with all her heart for Chase to love *her*.

But he didn't. That was a fact he'd made abundantly clear.

It was hard to be depressed out here, Letty mused as she studied the spectacular display in the heavens. The stars were like frosty jewels scattered across black velvet. The moon was full and brilliant, a madcap adventurer in a heaven filled with like-minded wanderers.

Despite her low spirits, Letty found she was smiling. So long ago, she'd sat under the same glittering moon, confident that nothing but good things would ever come into her life.

"What are you doing here?"

The crisp voice behind her startled Letty. "Hello, Chase," she said evenly, refusing to turn around. "Are you going to order me off your land?"

Chase had seen Letty approach the hillside from the house. He'd decided the best tactic was to ignore her.

She'd leave soon enough. Only she hadn't. For more than an hour she'd sat under the stars, barely moving. Unable to resist anymore, he'd gone over to the hill, without knowing what he'd say or do.

"Do you want me to leave?" she asked. He hadn't answered her earlier question.

"No," he answered gruffly.

His reply seemed to please her and he felt her tension subside. She relaxed, clasped her bent knees and said, "I haven't seen a night this clear in…forever." Her voice was low and enticing. "The stars look like diamonds, don't they?"

They did, but Chase didn't respond. He shifted his weight restlessly as he stood behind her, gazing up at the heavens, too.

"I remember the last time I sat on this hill with you, but…but that seems a million years ago now."

"It was," he said brusquely.

"That was the night you asked me to marry you."

"We were both young and foolish," he said, striving for a flippant air. He would've liked Letty to believe the ridiculous part had been in *wanting* her for his wife, but the truth was, he'd hoped with everything in him that she'd consent. Despite all the heartbreak, he felt the same way this very moment.

To his surprise, Letty laughed softly. "Now we're both older and wiser, aren't we?"

"I can't speak for anyone but myself." Before he was even conscious of moving, Chase was on the ground, sitting next to her, his legs stretched out in front of him.

"I wish I knew then what I do now," she continued. "If, by some miracle, we were able to turn back the clock to that night, I'd like you to know I'd jump at your proposal."

A shocked silence followed her words. Chase wished he could believe her, but he couldn't.

"You were after diamonds, Letty, and all I had to offer you was denim."

"But the diamonds were here all along," she whispered, staring up at the stars.

Chase closed his eyes to the pain that squeezed his heart. He hadn't been good enough for her then, and he wasn't now. He didn't doubt for an instant that she was waiting to leave Red Springs. When the time came she'd run so fast his head would spin. In fact, he didn't know what was keeping her here now.

The crux of the problem was that he didn't trust Letty. He couldn't—not anymore, not since he'd learned she was seeing some man in Rock Springs. Unfortunately it wasn't easy to stop caring for her. But in all the years he'd cherished Letty, the only thing his love had gotten him had been pain and heartache.

When she'd first come back to Wyoming, he'd carefully allowed himself to hope. He'd dreamed that they'd find a way to turn back time, just as she'd said, and discover a life together. But in the past few weeks she'd proved to him over and over how impossible that was.

Chase's gut twisted with the knowledge. He'd done everything he could to blot her out of his life. In the beginning, when he'd recognized his feelings for Cricket, he'd thought he would fight for Letty's love, show her how things could change. But could they really? All he could offer her was a humble life on a cattle ranch— exactly what he'd offered her nine years ago. Evidently someone else had given her something better. She'd fallen for some bastard in California, someone unworthy of her love, and now, apparently she was doing it again, blatantly meeting another man. Good riddance, then. The guy with the mustache was welcome to her. All Chase wanted was for her to get out of his life, because the pain of having her so close was more than he could stand.

"I think Cricket will remember today as long as she lives," Letty said, blithely unaware of his thoughts. "You've made her the happiest five-year-old in the world."

He didn't say anything; he didn't want to discuss Cricket. The little girl made him vulnerable to Letty. Once he'd lowered his guard, it was as if a dam of love had broken. He didn't know what he'd do when Letty moved away and took the little girl with her.

"She thinks you're the sun and the moon," Letty said in a way that suggested he need not have done a thing for Cricket to worship him.

"She's a sweet kid." That was the most he was willing to admit.

"Jason reminded me of you." She spoke so softly it was difficult to make out her words.

"I beg your pardon?"

"Jason was Cricket's father."

That man was the last person Chase wanted to hear about, but before he could tell Letty so, she continued in a voice filled with pain and remembered humiliation.

"He asked me out for weeks before I finally accepted. I'd written you and asked you to join me in California, and time and again you turned me down."

"You wanted me to be your manager! I'm a rancher. What did I know about the music business?"

"Nothing… I was asking the impossible," she said, her voice level, her words devoid of blame. "It was ridiculous—I realize that now. But I was so lonely for you, so lost."

"Apparently you found some comfort."

She let the gibe pass, although he saw her flinch and knew his words had hit their mark. He said things like that to hurt her, but the curious thing was, *he* suffered, too. He hurt himself as much as he hurt Letty, maybe more.

"He took me to the best restaurants in town, told me everything I wanted to hear. I was so desperate to believe him that a few inconsistencies didn't trouble me. He pretended to be my friend, and I needed one so badly. He seemed to share my dream the way you always had. I couldn't come back to Wyoming a nobody. You understand that, don't you?"

Chase didn't give her an answer and she went on without waiting for one.

"I was still chasing my dreams, but I was so lonely they were losing their appeal.

"I never planned to go so far with Jason, but it happened, and for days afterward I was in shock. I was—"

"Letty, stop, I don't want to hear this." Her relationship with Cricket's father was a part of her life he wanted to remove completely from his mind.

Letty ignored him, her voice shaky but determined. "Soon afterward I found out I was pregnant. I wanted to crawl into a hole and die, but that wasn't the worst part. When I told Jason, he misunderstood… He seemed to think I wanted him to marry me. But I didn't. I told him because, well, because he was Cricket's father. That's when I learned he was married. *Married.* All that time and he'd had a wife."

"Stop, Letty. I'm the last person you should be telling this to. In fact, I don't want to hear any of it," Chase shouted. He clenched his fists in impotent rage, hating the man who'd used and deceived Letty like this.

"It hurts to talk about it, but I feel I have to. I want you to know that—"

"Whatever you have to say doesn't matter anymore."

"But, Chase, it does, because as difficult as you may find this to believe, I've always loved you...as much then as I do now."

"Why didn't you come home when you found out you were pregnant?"

"How could I have? Pregnant and a failure, too. Everyone expected me to make a name for Red Springs. I was so ashamed, so unhappy, and there was nowhere to go."

She turned away and Chase saw her wipe the tears from her eyes. He ached to hold and comfort her, his heart heavy with her grief, but he refused to make himself vulnerable to her again. She spoke of loving him, but she didn't mean it. She couldn't, not when there was someone else in her life.

"What changed your mind?" he asked. "What made you decide to come back now?"

Several minutes passed, far longer than necessary to answer a simple question. Obviously something had happened that had brought her running back to the Bar E when she'd managed to stay away all those years. Something traumatic.

"I suppose it was a matter of accepting defeat," she finally said. "In the years after Cricket's birth, the determination to succeed as a singer left me. I dabbled in the industry, but mainly I did temp work. As the years passed, I couldn't feel ashamed of Cricket. She's the joy of my life."

"But it took you nine years, Letty. *Nine* years."

She looked up at him, her eyes filled with pain, clearly revealed in the moonlight that seemed as bright as day.

The anger was still with him. The senselessness of it all—a dream that had ruined their lives. And for what? "I loved you once," he said starkly, "but I don't now, and I doubt I ever will again. You taught me that the only thing love brings is heartache."

She lowered her head and he saw new tears.

"I could hate you for the things you've done," he said in a low, angry voice.

"I think you do," she whispered.

Chase hadn't known what to expect, but it wasn't this calm, almost humble acceptance of his resentment.

Maybe the proud, confident Letty was gone forever, but he couldn't believe that was true. Every once in a while, he saw flashes of the old Letty. Just enough to give him hope.

"I *don't* hate you, Letty," he murmured in a tormented whisper. "I wish I could, but I can't... I can't."

Chase intended to kiss her once, then release her and send her back to the house. It was late, and they both had to get up early. But their kiss sparked, then caught fire, leaping to sudden brilliance. She sighed, and the sound was so soft, so exciting, that Chase knew he was lost even before he pressed her against the cool, fragrant grass.

Lying down beside her, Chase felt helpless, caught in

a maze of love and desire. He tried to slow his breathing, gain control of his senses, but it was impossible, especially when Letty raised her hand and stroked his shoulders through the fabric of his shirt, then glided her fingers around to his back.

Chase felt engulfed by his love for her, lost, drowning, and it didn't matter, nothing did, except the warm feeling of her beside him, longing for him as desperately as he longed for her.

Again and again he kissed her, and when he paused to collect his senses, she eased her hand around his neck and gently brought his mouth back to hers.

Their need for each other was urgent. Fierce. Chase couldn't get enough of her. He kissed her eyes, her cheeks, her forehead and tenderly nuzzled her throat.

Eventually he released her and she sagged breathlessly against him. No other woman affected him the way Letty did. Why her? Of all the women in the world, why did he have to love *her?* For years she'd rewarded his loyalty with nothing but pain.

But it wasn't distress he was feeling now. The pleasure she brought him was so intense he wanted to cry out with it. He kissed her and her soft, gasping breaths mingled with his own. Chase was shaking and he couldn't seem to stop—shaking with anticipation and desire, shaking with the resolve not to make love to her, not to claim her completely, because once he did, he'd never be able to let her go. He wanted her, but he needed her to love him as much as he loved her. A love that came from their hearts and minds—not just the passionate dictates of their bodies.

His jaw tight with restraint, he closed his hands around hers and gently lifted her away from him.

"Chase?" she whispered, perplexed.

If she was confused, it was nothing compared to the emotions churning inside him. He'd always loved her, still did, yet he was turning her away again, and it was agonizing. She wanted him, and she'd let him know that. But he wouldn't make love to her. Not now.

"Letty...no."

She bowed her head. "You...don't want to make love to me?" she whispered tremulously. "Just one time..."

"No," he told her bluntly. "It wouldn't be enough."

He stroked her hair and kissed her gently. Then he realized the true significance of what she'd said. She only wanted him to love her *one time*. "You're going away, aren't you, Letty?" He felt her tense in his arms before her startled gaze found his.

"Who told you?"

Without responding, he pushed her away from him and stood.

"Chase?"

"No one told me," he said, the love and tenderness he felt evaporating in the heat of her betrayal. "I guessed."

Chapter 9

"What happened with you and Letty last night?" Lonny asked Chase early the next morning. They'd planned on repairing the fence that separated their property lines.

"What's between Letty and me is none of your business."

Lonny paused to consider this while rubbing the side of his jaw. "Normally I'd agree with you, but my sister looked really bad this morning. To be honest, I haven't been particularly pleased with her myself lately."

Lonny followed him to the pile of split cedar fence posts. "When Cricket mentioned Letty meeting some man in Red Springs," he continued, "I was madder 'n anything. But after all the fuss I made about her interfering in my life, I didn't think I had the right to ask her a whole lot of questions."

"Then why start with me now?" After that, Chase ignored his friend and loaded the posts into the back of his pickup. His mood hadn't improved since he'd left Letty only a few hours ago.

"I'm sticking my nose where it doesn't belong because you're the best friend I've got."

"Then let's keep it that way." Chase wiped the perspiration from his brow, then went back to heaving posts, still trying to pretend Lonny hadn't introduced the subject of his sister.

"You're as bad as she is," Lonny shouted.

"Maybe I am."

Lonny jerked on his gloves and walked toward the pile of wood. He pulled one long piece free, balanced it on his shoulder and headed toward the truck.

"I don't think she slept all night," Lonny muttered.

It was difficult for Chase to feel any sympathy when he hadn't, either.

"I got downstairs this morning and she was sitting in the kitchen, staring into space. I swear there were enough damp tissues on that table to insulate the attic."

"What makes you think I had anything to do with Letty crying?"

"Because she more or less told me so—well, less rather than more," Lonny muttered, shaking his head. "She wouldn't say a word at first, mind you—she's as tight-lipped as you are, but harder to reason with, Letty being a woman and all."

"Listen, if your sister wants to shed a few tears, that's her concern. Not mine. Not yours. Understand?"

Lonny tipped back the rim of his hat. "Can't say I do. Look, Chase, I know you're furious at me for butt-ing in, and I don't blame you. But the least you can do is hear me out."

"I'm a busy man, Lonny, and I'd appreciate it if you kept your thoughts to yourself."

Lonny disregarded his suggestion. "Like I said, I don't know what happened between you, but—"

"How many times do I have to tell you? It's none of your business."

"It is if it's hurting my sister," Lonny said darkly. "And she's hurting plenty."

"That's her problem." Chase had to take care of himself, protect his own heart; he couldn't worry about hers, or so he told himself.

"Why don't you talk to her?" Lonny was saying.

"What do you expect me to say? Are you going to tell me that, too? I respect you, Lonny, but I'm telling you right now to butt out. What's between Letty and me doesn't have anything to do with you." It would be a shame to ruin a lifetime friendship because of Letty, but Chase wasn't about to let Lonny Ellison direct his actions toward her.

They worked together for the next few hours without exchanging another word. Neither seemed willing to break the icy silence. They were repairing the fence, replacing the rotting posts with new ones. Normally, a day like that was an opportunity to joke and have a little fun. Today, it seemed, they could barely tolerate each other.

"I'm worried about her," Lonny said when they broke for lunch. He stared at his roast beef sandwich, then took a huge bite, quickly followed by another.

Chase sighed loudly. "Are you back to talking about

Letty again?" Although she hadn't left his mind for an instant, he didn't want to discuss her.

"I can't help it!" Lonny shouted as he leaped to his feet and threw the remains of his lunch on the ground with such force that bits of apple flew in several directions. "Be mad at me if you want, Chase. Knock me down if it'll make you feel better. But I can't let you do this to Letty. She's been hurt enough."

"That isn't my fault!"

"I've never seen her like this—as if all the life's gone out of her. She sits and stares into space with a look that's so pathetic it rips your heart out. Cricket started talking to her this morning and she hardly noticed. You know that's not like Letty."

"She's leaving," Chase shouted, slamming his own lunch against the tree. "Just like she did before—she's walking away. It nearly destroyed me the first time, and I'm not letting her do that to me again."

"Leaving?" Lonny cried. "What do you mean? Did she tell you that herself?"

"Not exactly. I guessed."

"Well, it's news to me. She enrolled Cricket in kindergarten the other day. That doesn't sound like she's planning to move."

"But…" Chase's thoughts were in chaos. He'd assumed that Letty would be leaving; she'd certainly given him that impression. In fact, she'd said so—hadn't she?

"Would it be so difficult to ask her directly?" Lonny said. "We've repaired all the fence we're going to manage today. Come to the house and ask her point-blank. Letty doesn't lie. If she's planning to leave Red Springs, she'll admit it."

Chase expelled his breath forcefully. He might as well ask her, since Lonny wasn't going to quit bugging him until he did. And yet…

"Will you do that, at least?" Lonny urged.

"I…" Indecision tore at Chase. He didn't want any contact with Letty; he was still reeling from their last encounter. But he'd never seen Lonny behave like this. He was obviously worried about Letty. It wasn't typical of Lonny to get involved in another man's business and that alone was a more convincing argument than anything he'd said.

"You're driving me back to the house, aren't you?" Lonny asked matter-of-factly.

"What about Destiny?"

"I'll pick him up later."

Lonny said this casually, as if he often left his horse at Spring Valley. As far as Chase could remember, he'd never done so in all the years they'd been friends and neighbors.

"All right, I'll ask her," Chase agreed, but reluctantly. He'd do it, if for nothing more than to appease Lonny, although Chase wanted this issue with Letty cleared up. From what he remembered, she'd made her intentions obvious. Yet why she'd enrolled Cricket in kindergarten—which was several months away—was beyond him. It didn't make sense.

Lonny muttered something under his breath as he climbed into the cab of the truck.

The first thing Chase noticed when he rolled into the yard at Lonny's place was that his friend's battered pickup was missing. He waited outside while Lonny hurried into the kitchen.

"She's not here," Lonny said when he returned, holding a note. "She's gone into town to see Joy Fuller."

Chase frowned. Now that he'd made the decision to confront Letty, he was disappointed about the delay. "I'll ask her another time," he said.

"No." Lonny had apparently sensed Chase's frustration. "I mean… I don't think it would do any harm to drive to Joy's. I've been wanting to talk to her, anyway, and this business with Letty gives me an excuse."

"You told me it was completely over. What possible reason could you have to talk to her?"

Lonny was already in the truck. Chase couldn't help noticing the color that tinged his face. "I might've been a bit…hasty. She might not have a sense of humor, but if Letty thinks she's okay, maybe I should give her another chance."

"Well, she is cute. But does she want to give *you* another chance?"

Lonny swallowed and glanced out the window. He didn't answer Chase's question—but then, how could he? Whether or not Joy would be willing to get involved with him again was debatable. Chase suspected Lonny was a lot more interested in Joy than he'd let on; he also suspected Joy might not feel quite the same way.

"Take a right at the next corner," Lonny said as they entered town. "Her house is the first one on the left."

Chase parked under the row of elms. "I'll wait here," he said abruptly.

Lonny got out of the truck and hesitated before he shut the door. "That might not be such a good idea."

"Why not?"

"Well, I'm not sure if Joy's going to talk to me. And what about Letty? Don't you want to see her?"

Chase sighed. Now that he'd had time to think about it, running into town to find Letty wasn't that brilliant a plan.

"Come with me, okay?" Lonny said. "That way Joy might not throw me out the second she sees me."

Sighing loudly, Chase left the truck, none too pleased by any of this. He accompanied Lonny to Joy Fuller's door and watched in surprise as Lonny licked his fingertips and smoothed down the sides of his hair before ringing the bell. It was all Chase could do not to comment.

Cricket answered the door. "Hi, Uncle Lonny. Hi, Chase." She whirled around and shouted over her shoulder. "Joy, it's my uncle Lonny and Chase! You remember Chase, don't you? He's my very best friend in the whole world." Then she ran back into the house.

A minute or so passed before Joy came to the door, Cricket on her heels.

"Yes?" she said stiffly.

She wore a frilly apron tied around her waist, and traces of flour dusted her nose. She'd obviously been baking, and knowing Cricket, it was probably chocolate chip cookies.

Lonny jerked the hat from his head. "We were wondering…me and Chase, my neighbor here, if it would be convenient to take a moment of your time."

Chase had never heard his friend more tongue-tied. Lonny made it sound as though they were old-fashioned snake oil salesmen, come to pawn their wares.

"We can't seem to talk to each other without yelling, Mr. Ellison," Joy returned. Her hands were neatly clasped in front of her, and her gaze was focused somewhere in the distance.

"I'd like to talk to Letty," Chase said. The way things were going, it could be another half hour before anyone learned the reason for their visit. Not that he actually knew what his friend planned to say to Joy—or if Lonny had even figured it out himself.

"Mommy's gone," Cricket piped up.

"She left a few minutes ago," Joy explained.

"Did she say where she was going?"

"No...but I'm sure you can catch her if it's important."

"Go, man," Lonny said, poking his elbow into Chase's ribs. "I'll stay here—that is, if Miss Fuller has no objections."

"*Ms*. Fuller," Joy corrected, her eyes narrowing.

"*Ms*. Fuller," Lonny echoed.

"You can stay, but only if you promise you won't insult me in my own home. Because I'm telling you right now, Lonny Ellison, I won't put up with it."

"I'll do my best."

"That may not be good enough," she said ominously.

"Which way did Letty go?" Chase demanded, decidedly impatient with the pair.

"Toward downtown," Joy said, pointing west. "You shouldn't have any trouble finding her. She's driving that piece of junk Mr. Ellison seems so fond of."

For a moment Lonny looked as if he'd swallowed a grapefruit. His face flamed red, he swallowed hard and it was obvious he was doing everything in his power not to let loose with a blistering response. His efforts were promptly rewarded with a smile from Joy.

"Very good, Mr. Ellison. You've passed the test." She stepped aside to let him enter.

"I won't be long," Chase told them.

Lonny repeatedly twisted the brim of his hat. "Take your time," he muttered. "But go!"

Chase didn't need any more incentive and ran toward his pickup. As soon as the engine roared to life, he shifted gears and swerved out into the traffic, such as it was.

Red Springs's main street was lined with small businesses that had diagonal parking in front. Chase could determine at a single glance that Lonny's truck wasn't in sight. He drove the full length of the town and down a couple of side streets, but she wasn't there, either.

Mystified, he parked and stood outside his truck, looking down Main Street in both directions. Where could she possibly have gone?

Letty came out of Dr. Faraday's office and sat in Lonny's truck for several minutes before she started the engine. After waiting all these weeks, after stringing out the medical and financial details of her life as though they were laundry on a clothesline—after all this, she should feel some sort of release knowing that the surgery was finally scheduled.

But she didn't.

Instead she experienced an overwhelming sadness. Tears burned in her eyes, but she held her head high and drove toward the freeway that would take her back to Red Springs. Now that everything had been cleared with the doctor and the state, Letty felt free to explain what was wrong with her to her brother. She'd leave it to him to tell Chase—if he wanted.

Chase. Quickly she cast all thoughts of him aside, knowing they'd only bring her pain.

A few miles out of town, Letty saw another truck in

her rearview mirror, several cars back. Her first reaction was that someone was driving a model similar to the one Chase had.

Not until the truck started weaving in and out of traffic in an effort to catch up with her did Letty realize it *was* Chase's.

Why was he following her? All she could think was that something terrible must have happened... Cricket! Oh, no, it had to be Cricket.

Letty pulled to the side of the road.

Chase was right behind her.

Shutting off the engine, she climbed out and saw him leap from his vehicle and come running toward her.

"Letty. Letty." He wrapped his arms around her, holding her with a tenderness she thought he could no longer feel.

She loosened his grip enough to raise her head. "Is anything wrong with Cricket?" she asked urgently.

He frowned. "No," he said before he kissed her with a thoroughness that left her weak and clinging.

"Then what are you doing here?"

Chase closed his eyes briefly. "That's a long story. Letty, we've got to talk."

She broke free from his embrace. "I don't think we can anymore. Every time we get close to each other, we end up arguing. I know I hurt you, Chase, but I don't know how much longer I can stand being hurt back. After last night, I decided it was best if we didn't see each other again."

"You make us sound as bad as Lonny and Joy."

"Worse."

"It doesn't have to be that way."

"I don't think we're capable of anything else," she whispered. "Not anymore."

His eyes blazed into hers. "Letty, I *know*."

Chase wasn't making any sense. If he knew they were incapable of sustaining a relationship, then why had he been driving like a madman to catch her? Frankly, she wasn't in the mood for this. All she wanted to do was get Cricket and go home.

Chase dropped his arms and paced in front of her. "The day you fainted in the garden, I should've figured it out. For weeks before, Lonny had been telling me how tired you were all the time, how fragile you'd become." He shook his head. "I thought it was because you were depressed and California had spoiled you."

"It did. I'm a soft person, unaccustomed to anything resembling hard work."

Chase ignored her sarcasm. "Then that day in the cemetery…you tried to tell me, didn't you?" But he didn't allow her to answer his question. "You started talking about life and death, and all I could do was get angry with you because I thought you'd lied. I wasn't even listening. If I had been, I would've heard what you were trying to tell me."

Tears blurred her vision as she stood silent and unmoving before him.

"It's the reason you dragged Mary Brandon over to the house for dinner that night, isn't it?" Again he didn't wait for her response. "You figured that if Lonny was married and anything happened to you, Cricket would have a secure home."

"Not exactly," she managed. In the beginning her thoughts had leaned in that direction. But she wasn't the manipulative type, and it had soon become obvious that Lonny wanted nothing to do with her schemes.

Chase placed his hands on her shoulders. "Letty, I saw Dr. Faraday." A hint of a smile brushed the corners of his mouth. "I wanted to go over to the man and hug him."

"Chase, you're still not making any sense."

"Cricket told me that when you came to Rock Springs, you visited a man with a mustache—a man who looked like someone on TV."

"When did she tell you that?"

"Weeks ago. But more damning was that she claimed you went into a room together, and she had to stay outside and wait for you."

"Oh, dear..."

"You can imagine what Lonny and I thought."

"And you believed it?" It seemed that neither Chase nor her brother knew her. Both seemed willing to condemn her on the flimsiest evidence. If she *were* meeting a man, the last person she'd take with her was Cricket. But apparently that thought hadn't so much as entered their minds.

"We didn't know what to believe," Chase answered.

"But you automatically assumed the worst?"

Chase looked properly chagrined. "I know it sounds bad, but there'd been another man in your life before. How was I to know the same thing wasn't happening again?"

"How were you to know?" Letty echoed, slumping against the side of the truck. "How were you to know?" she repeated in a hurt whisper. "What kind of person do you think I am?"

"Letty, I'm sorry."

She covered her eyes and shook her head.

"From the moment you returned, everything's felt wrong. For a while I thought my whole world had been knocked off its axis. Nothing I did seemed to balance it. Today I realized it wasn't my world that was off-kilter, but yours, and I couldn't help feeling the effects."

"You're talking in riddles," she said.

Once more he started pacing, running his fingers through his hair. "Tell me what's wrong. Please. I want to know—I need to know."

"It's my heart," she whispered.

He nodded slowly. "I figured that's what it had to be. Dr. Faraday's specialty was the first thing I noticed when I saw you walk into his office."

"You saw me walk into his office?"

His gaze skirted away from hers. "I followed you to Rock Springs." He continued before she could react. "I'm not proud of that, Letty. Lonny convinced me that you and I needed to talk. After last night, we were both hurting so badly…and I guess I wasn't the best company this morning. Lonny and I went back to the ranch and found your note. From there, we went to Joy's place and she said you'd just left and were heading into town. I drove there and couldn't find you anywhere. That was when I realized you'd probably driven to Rock Springs. If you were meeting a man, I wanted to find out who it was. I had no idea what I'd do—probably nothing—but I had to know."

"So…so you followed me."

He nodded. "And after you walked back to the truck, I went into the office—where I caught sight of the good doctor…and his mustache."

She sighed, shaking her head.

"Letty, you have every reason in the world to be angry. All I can do is apologize."

"No." She met his eyes. "I wanted to tell you. I've kept this secret to myself for so long and there was no one…no one I could tell and I needed—"

"Letty…please, what's wrong with your heart?"

"The doctors discovered a small hole when I was pregnant with Cricket."

"What are they going to do?"

"Surgery."

His face tightened. "When?"

"Dr. Faraday's already scheduled it. I couldn't afford it…. When you saw my first welfare check I wanted to die. I knew what you thought and there wasn't any way to tell you how much I hate being a recipient of… charity."

Chase shut his eyes. "Letty, I failed you—you needed me and I failed you."

"Chase, I'm not going to blame you for that. I've failed you, too."

"I've been so blind, so stupid."

"I've suffered my share of the same afflictions," she said wryly.

"This time I can change things," he said, taking her by the shoulders.

"How?"

"Letty." His fingers were gentle, his eyes tender. "We're getting married."

Chapter 10

"Married," Letty said, repeating the word for the twentieth time in the past hour. Chase sat her down, poured her a cup of coffee and brought it to the kitchen table. Only a few days earlier, he'd thought nothing of watching her do a multitude of chores. Now he was treating her as if she were an invalid. If Letty hadn't been so amused by his change in attitude, she would've found his behavior annoying.

"I'm not arguing with you, Letty Ellison. We're getting married."

"Honestly, Chase, you're being just a little dramatic, don't you think?" She loved him for it, but that didn't alter the facts.

"No!" His face was tormented with guilt. "Why didn't I listen to you? You tried to tell me, and I was so pigheaded, so blind." He knelt in front of her and took both her hands in his, eyes dark and filled with emotion. "You aren't in any condition to fight me on this, Letty, so just do as I ask and don't argue."

"I'm in excellent shape." Chase could be so stubborn, there were times she found it impossible to reason with him. Despite all that, she felt a deep, abiding love for this man. Yet there were a multitude of doubts they hadn't faced or answered.

Chase hadn't said he loved her or even that he cared. But then, Chase always had been a man of few words. When he'd proposed the first time, he'd told her, simply and profoundly, how much he loved her and wanted to build a life with her. That had been the sweetest, most romantic thing she'd ever heard. Letty had supposed that what he'd said that night was going to be all the poetry Chase would ever give her.

"You're scheduled for heart surgery!"

"I'm not on my deathbed yet!"

He went pale at her joke. "Letty, don't even say that."

"What? That I could die? It's been known to happen. But I hope it won't with me. I'm otherwise healthy, and besides, I'm too stubborn to die in a hospital. I'd prefer to do it in my own bed with my grandchildren gathered around me, fighting over who'll get my many jewels." She said this with a hint of dark drama, loving the way Chase's eyes flared with outrage.

In response, he shook his head. "It's not a joking matter."

"I'm going to get excellent care, so don't worry, okay?"

"I'll feel better once I talk to Dr. Faraday myself. But when I do, I'm telling you right now, Letty Ellison, it'll be as your husband."

Letty rolled her eyes. She couldn't believe they were having this discussion. Yet Chase seemed so adamant, so certain that marrying now was the right thing to do. Letty loved him more than ever, but she wasn't nearly as convinced of the need to link their lives through marriage while the surgery still loomed before her. Afterward would be soon enough.

Her reaction seemed to frustrate Chase. "All right, if my words can't persuade you, then perhaps this will." With that he wove his fingers into her hair and brought his lips to hers. The kiss was filled with such tenderness that Letty was left trembling in its aftermath.

Chase appeared equally shaken. His eyes held hers for the longest moment, then he kissed her again. And again—

"Well, isn't this peachy?"

Lonny's harsh tone broke them apart.

"Lonny." Chase's voice sounded odd. He cast a glance at the kitchen clock.

"'I won't be long,'" Lonny mimicked, clearly agitated. "It's been *four* hours, man! Four minutes with that…that woman is more than any guy could endure."

"Where's Cricket?" Letty asked, instantly alarmed.

"With *her.*" He turned to Chase, frowning. "Did you know all women stick together, even the little ones? I told Cricket to come with me, and she ran behind Joy and hid. I couldn't believe my eyes—my own niece!"

Letty sprang to her feet. "I'm going to call Joy and find out where Cricket is."

"How'd you get back here?" Chase asked his friend.

"Walked."

Letty paused in the doorway, anxious to hear more of her brother's reply.

"But it's almost twenty miles into town," she said.

"You're telling me?" Lonny moaned and slumped into a chair. The first thing he did was remove his left boot, getting it off his swollen foot with some difficulty. He released a long sigh as it fell to the floor. Next he flexed his toes.

"What happened?"

"She kicked me out! What do you think happened? Do I look like I'd stroll home for the exercise?" His narrowed eyes accused both Letty and Chase. "I don't suppose you gave me another thought after you dropped me off, did you? Oh, no. You two were so interested in playing kissy face that you conveniently forgot about *me*."

"We're sorry, Lonny," Letty said contritely.

Lonny's gaze shifted from Letty to Chase and back again. "I guess there's no need to ask if you patched things up—that much is obvious." By this time, the second dust-caked boot had hit the floor. Lonny peeled off his socks. "Darn it, I've got blisters on my blisters, thanks to the two of you."

"We're getting married," Chase announced without preamble, his look challenging Letty to defy him.

Lonny's head shot up. "What?"

"Letty and I are getting married," Chase repeated. "And the sooner the better."

Lonny's eyes grew suspicious, and when he spoke his voice was almost a whisper. "You're pregnant again, aren't you?"

Letty burst out laughing. "I wish it was that simple."

"She's got a defective heart," Chase said, omitting the details and not giving Letty the opportunity to explain more fully. "She has to have an operation—major surgery from the sound of it."

"Your heart?" Shocked, Lonny stared at her. "Is that why you fainted that day?"

"Partially."

"Why didn't you tell me?"

"I couldn't. Not until I had everything sorted out with the government, and the surgery was scheduled. You would've worried yourself into a tizzy, and I didn't want to dump my problems on top of all your other responsibilities."

"But…" He frowned, apparently displeased with her response. "I could've helped…or at least been more sympathetic. When I think about the way you've cleaned up around here… You had no business working so hard, planting a garden and doing everything else you have. I wish you'd said something, Letty. I feel like a jerk."

"I didn't tell anyone, Lonny. Please understand."

He wiped the back of his hand over his mouth. "I hope you never keep anything like this from me again."

"Believe me, there were a thousand times I wanted to tell you and couldn't."

"I'm going to arrange for the wedding as soon as possible," Chase cut in. "You don't have any objections, do you, Lonny?" His voice was demanding and inflexible.

"Objections? Me? No…not in the least."

"Honestly, Chase," Letty said, patting her brother's shoulder. "This whole conversation is becoming monotonous, don't you think? I haven't agreed to this yet."

"Call Joy and find out where Cricket is," he told her.

Letty moved to the phone and quickly dialed Joy's number. Her friend answered on the second ring. "Joy, it's Letty. Cricket's with you, right?"

"Yes, of course. I wouldn't let that brother of yours

take her, and frankly, she wouldn't have gone with him, anyway. I'm sorry, Letty. I really am. You're my friend and I adore Cricket, but your brother is one of the most—" She stopped abruptly. "I... I don't think it's necessary to say anything else. Lonny's your brother—you know him better than anyone."

In some ways Letty felt she didn't know Lonny at all. "Joy, whatever happened, I'm sorry."

"It's not your fault. By the way, did Chase ever catch up with you? I didn't think to mention until after he'd gone that you'd said something about a doctor's appointment."

"Yes, he found me. That's the reason it's taken me so long to get back to you. I'm home now, but Chase and I have been talking for the past hour or so. I didn't mean to leave Cricket with you all this time."

"Cricket's been great, so don't worry about that. We had a great time—at least, we did until your brother decided to visit." She paused and Letty heard regret in her voice when she spoke again. "I don't know what it is with the two of us. I seem to bring out the worst in Lonny—I know he does in me."

Letty wished she knew what it was, too. Discussing this situation over the phone made her a little uncomfortable. She needed to see Joy, read her expression and her body language. "I'll leave now to pick up Cricket."

"Don't bother," Joy said. "I was going out on an errand and I'll be happy to drop her off."

"You're sure that isn't a problem?"

"Positive." Joy hesitated again. "Lonny got home all right, didn't he? I mean it *is* a long walk. When I told him to leave, I didn't mean for him to hike the whole way back. I forgot he didn't have the truck. By the time

I realized it, he'd already started down the sidewalk and he ignored me when I called him."

"Yes, he's home, no worse for wear."

"I'll see you in a little while, then," Joy murmured. She sounded guilty, and Letty suspected she was bringing Cricket home hoping she'd get a chance to apologize. Unfortunately, in Lonny's mood, that would be nearly impossible.

Letty replaced the phone, but not before Lonny shouted from the kitchen, "What do you mean, 'no worse for wear'? I've got blisters that would've brought a lesser man to his knees."

"What did you want me to tell her? That you'd dragged yourself in here barely able to move?"

"Letty, I don't think you should raise your voice. It can't be good for your heart." Chase draped his arm around Letty's shoulders, led her back to the table and eased her onto a chair.

"I'm not an invalid!" she shouted, immediately sorry for her outburst. Chase flinched as if she'd attacked him, and in a way she had.

"Please, Letty, we have a lot to discuss. I want the details for this wedding ironed out before I leave." He knelt in front of her again, and she wondered if he expected her to keel over at any moment.

She sighed. Nothing she'd said seemed to have reached Chase.

"I'm taking a bath," Lonny announced. He stuffed his socks inside his boots and picked them up as he limped out of the kitchen.

"Chase, listen to me," Letty pleaded, her hands framing his worried face. "There's no reason for us to marry now. Once the surgery's over and I'm back on my feet, we can discuss it, if you still feel the same."

"Are you turning me down a second time, Letty?"

"Oh, Chase, you know that isn't it. I told you the other night how much I love you. If my feelings for you didn't change in all the years we were apart, they won't in the next few months."

"Letty, you're not thinking clearly."

"It's my heart that's defective, not my brain."

"I'll arrange for the license right away," he continued as if she hadn't spoken. "If you want a church wedding with all the trimmings, we'll arrange for that later."

"Why not bring Pastor Downey to the hospital, and he can administer the last rites while he's there," she returned flippantly.

"Don't say that!"

"If I agree to this, I'll be married in the church— the first time."

"You're not thinking."

"Chase, you're the one who's diving into the deep end here—not me. Give me one solid reason why we should get married now."

"Concern for Cricket ought to be enough."

"What's my daughter got to do with this?"

"She loves me and I love her." His mouth turned up in a smile. "I never guessed I could love her as much as I do. In the beginning, every time I saw her it was like someone had stuck a knife in my heart. One day—" he lowered his gaze to the floor "—I realized that nothing I did was going to keep me from loving that little girl. She's so much a part of you, and I couldn't care about you the way I do and *not* love her."

Hearing him talk about his feelings for Cricket lifted

Letty's sagging spirits. It was the closest he'd come to admitting he loved her.

"More than that, Letty, if something did happen to you, I'd be a better parent than Lonny. Don't you agree?"

Chase was arguably more of a natural, and he had greater patience; to that extent she did agree. "But," she began, "I don't—"

"I know," he said, raising his hand. "You're thinking that you don't have to marry me to make me Cricket's legal guardian, and you're right. But I want you to consider Lonny's pride in all this. If you give me responsibility for Cricket, what's that going to say to your brother? He's your only living relative, and he'd be hurt if he felt you didn't trust him to properly raise your child."

"But nothing's going to happen!" Letty blurted out, knowing she couldn't be completely sure of that.

"But what if the worst *does* happen? If you leave things as they are now, Lonny might have to deal with a grief-stricken five-year-old child. He'd never be able to cope, Letty."

She knew he was right; Lonny would be overwhelmed.

"This situation is much too important to leave everything to fate," he said, closing his argument. "You've got Cricket's future to consider."

"This surgery is a fairly standard procedure." The doctor had told her so himself. Complicated, yes, but not uncommon.

"Yes, but as you said before, things can always go wrong. No matter how slight that chance is, we need to be prepared," Chase murmured.

Letty didn't know what to think. She'd asked Chase

to come up with one good argument and he'd outdone himself. In fact, his preoccupation with morbid possibilities struck her as a bit much, considering that he wouldn't let her make even a slight joke about it. However, she understood what he was doing—and why. There were other areas Chase hadn't stopped to consider, though. If they were married, he'd become liable for the cost of her medical care.

"Chase, this surgery isn't cheap. Dr. Faraday said I could be in the hospital as long as two weeks. The hospital bill alone will run into five figures, and that doesn't include the doctor's fee, convalescent care or the pharmaceutical bills, which will add up to much, much more."

"As my wife, you'll be covered by my health insurance policy."

He said this with such confidence that Letty almost believed him. She desperately wanted to, but she was pretty sure that wouldn't be the case. "In all likelihood, your insurance company would deny the claim since my condition is preexisting."

"I can find that out easily enough. I'll phone my broker and have him check my policy right now." He left and returned five minutes later. "It's just as I thought. As my wife, you'd automatically be included for all benefits, no matter when we found out about your heart condition."

It sounded too good to be true. "Chase... I don't know."

"I'm through with listening to all the reasons we can't get married. The fact is, you've rejected one proposal from me, and we both suffered because of it. I won't let you do it a second time. Now will or won't you marry me?"

"You're *sure* about the insurance?"

"Positive." He crouched in front of her and took both her hands in his. "You're going to marry me, Letty. No more arguments, no more ifs, ands or buts." He grinned at her. "So we're getting married?"

Chase made the question more of a statement. "Yes," she murmured, loving him so much. "But you're taking such a risk…"

His eyes narrowed. "Why?"

"Well, because—" She stopped when Cricket came running through the door and held out her arms to her daughter, who flew into them.

"I'm home." Cricket hugged Letty, then rushed over to Chase and threw her arms around his neck with such enthusiasm it nearly knocked him to the floor.

Letty watched them and realized, above anything else, how right Chase was to be concerned about Cricket's welfare in the unlikely event that something went wrong. She drew in a shaky breath and held it until her lungs ached. She loved Chase, and although he hadn't spelled out his feelings for her, she knew he cared deeply for her and for Cricket.

Joy stood sheepishly near the kitchen door, scanning the area for any sign of Lonny. Letty didn't doubt that if her brother were to make an appearance, Joy would quickly turn a designer shade of red.

"Joy, come in," Letty said, welcoming her friend.

She did, edging a few more feet into the kitchen. "I just wanted to make sure Cricket was safely inside."

"Thanks so much for watching her for me this afternoon," Letty said, smiling broadly. "I appreciate it more than you know."

"It wasn't any problem."

A soft snicker was heard from the direction of the hallway. Lonny stood there, obviously having just gotten out of the shower. His dark hair glistened and his shirt was unbuttoned over his blue jeans. His feet were bare.

Joy stiffened. "The only difficulty was when unexpected company arrived and—"

"Uncle Lonny was yelling at Joy," Cricket whispered to her mother.

"Don't forget to mention the part where she was yelling at me," Lonny said.

"I'd better go." Joy stepped back and gripped the doorknob.

"I'm not stopping you," Lonny said sweetly, swaggering into the room.

"I'm on my way out, *Mr.* Ellison. The less I see of you, the better."

"My feelings exactly."

"Lonny. Joy." Letty gestured at each of them. They were both so stubborn. Every time they were within range of each other, sparks ignited—and, in Letty's opinion, they weren't *just* sparks of anger.

"I'm sorry, Letty, but I cannot tolerate your brother."

Lonny moved closer to Joy and Letty realized why his walk was so unusual. He was doing his utmost not to limp, what with all his blisters. Lonny stopped directly in front of Joy, his arms folded over his bare chest. "The same goes for you—only double."

"Goodbye, Letty, Chase. Goodbye, Cricket." Joy completely ignored Lonny and walked out of the house.

The instant she did, Lonny sat down and started to rub his feet. "Fool woman."

"I won't comment on who's acting like a fool here, brother dearest, but the odds are high that you're in the competition."

Chase sat in the hospital waiting room and picked up a *Time* magazine. He didn't even notice the date until he'd finished three news articles and realized everything he'd read about had happened months ago.

Like the stories in the out-of-date magazine, Chase's life had changed, but the transformation had taken place within a few days, not months.

A week after following Letty into Rock Springs and discovering her secret, he was both a husband and a father. He and Letty had a small wedding at which Pastor Downey had been kind enough to officiate. And now they were facing what could be the most difficult trial of their lives together—her heart surgery.

Setting the magazine aside, Chase wandered outside to the balcony, leaning over the railing as he surveyed the foliage below.

Worry entangled his thoughts and dominated his emotions. And yet a faint smile hovered on his lips. Even when they'd wheeled Letty into the operating room, she'd been joking with the doctors.

A vision of the nurses, clad in surgical green from head to foot, who'd wheeled Letty through the double doors and into the operating room, came back to haunt him. They'd taken Letty from his side, although he'd held her hand as long as possible. Only Chase had seen the momentary look of stark fear, of panic, in her eyes.

But her gaze had found his and her expression became one of reassurance.

She was facing a traumatic experience and she'd wanted to encourage *him*.

Her sweet smile hadn't fooled him, though. Letty was as frightened as he was, perhaps more; she just wouldn't let anyone know it.

She could die in there, and he was powerless to do anything to stop it. The thought of her death made him ache with an agony that was beyond description. Letty had been back in Wyoming for less than two months and already Chase couldn't imagine his life without her. The air on the balcony became stifling. Chase fled.

"Chase!" Lonny came running after him. "What's happened? Where's Letty?"

Chase's eyes were wild as he stared at his brother-in-law. "They took her away twenty minutes ago."

"Hey, are you all right?"

The question buzzed around him like a cloud of mosquitoes, and he shook his head.

"Chase." Lonny clasped his shoulders. "I think you should sit down."

"Cricket?"

"She's fine. Joy's watching her."

Chase nodded, sitting on the edge of the seat, his elbows on his knees, his hands covering his face. Letty had come into his life when he'd least expected her back. She'd offered him love when he'd never thought he'd discover it a second time. Long before, he'd given up the dream of her ever being his wife.

They'd been married less than a day. Only a few hours earlier, Letty had stood before Pastor Downey and vowed to love him—Chase Brown. Her *husband*.

And here she was, her life on the line, and they had yet to have their wedding night.

Chase prayed fate wouldn't be so cruel as to rip her from his arms. He wanted the joy of loving her and being loved by her. The joy of fulfilling his dreams and building happiness with her and Cricket and whatever other children they had. A picture began to form in his mind. Two little boys around the ages of five and six. They stood side by side, the best of friends, each with deep blue eyes like Letty's. Their hair was the same shade as his own when he was about their age.

"She's going to make it," Lonny said. "Do you think my sister's going to give up on life without a fight? You know Letty better than that. Relax, would you? Everything's going to work out."

His friend's words dispelled the vision. Chase wished he shared Lonny's confidence regarding Letty's health. He felt so helpless—all he could do was pray.

Chase stood up abruptly. "I'm going to the chapel," he announced, appreciating it when Lonny chose to stay behind.

The chapel was empty, and Chase was grateful for the privacy. He sat in the back pew and stared straight ahead, not knowing what to say or do that would convince the Almighty to keep Letty safe.

He rotated the brim of his hat between his fingers while his mind fumbled for the words to plead for her life. He wanted so much more than that, more than Letty simply surviving the surgery, and then felt selfish for being so greedy. As the minutes ticked past, he sat and silently poured out his heart, talking as he would to a friend.

Chase had never been a man who could speak eloquently—to God or, for that matter, to Letty or anyone else. He knew she'd been looking for words of love the day he'd proposed to her. He regretted now that he hadn't said them. He'd felt them deep in his heart, but something had kept them buried inside. Fear, he suspected. He'd spoken them once and they hadn't meant enough to keep her in Red Springs. He didn't know if they'd mean enough this time, either.

An eternity passed and he stayed where he was, afraid to face whatever would greet him upon his return. Several people came and went, but he barely noticed them.

The chapel door opened once more and Chase didn't have to turn around to know it was Lonny. Cold fear dampened his brow and he sat immobilized. The longest seconds of his life dragged past before Lonny joined him in the pew.

"The surgery went without a hitch—Letty's going to be just fine," he whispered. "You can see her, but only for a minute."

Chase closed his eyes as the tension drained out of him.

"Did you hear me?"

Chase nodded and turned to his lifelong friend. "Thank God."

The two men embraced and Chase was filled with overwhelming gratitude.

"Be warned, though," Lonny said on their way back to the surgical floor. "Letty's connected to a bunch of tubes and stuff, so don't let it throw you."

Chase nodded.

One of the nurses who'd wheeled his wife into surgery was waiting when Chase returned. She had him dress in sterile surgical garb and instructed him to follow her.

Chase accompanied her into the intensive care unit. Letty was lying on a gurney, perfectly still, and Chase stood by her side. Slowly he bent toward her and saw that her eyes were closed.

"Letty," he whispered. "It's Chase. You're going to be fine."

Chase thought he saw her mouth move in a smile, but he couldn't be sure.

"I love you," he murmured, his voice hoarse with emotion. "I didn't say it before, but I love you—I never stopped. I've lived my life loving you, and nothing will ever change that."

She was pale, so deathly pale, that he felt a sudden sharp fear before he realized the worst of the ordeal was over. The surgery had etched its passing on her lovely face, yet he saw something else, something he hadn't recognized in Letty before. There was a calm strength, a courage that lent him confidence. She was his wife and she'd stand by his side for the rest of their days.

Chase kissed her forehead tenderly before turning to leave.

"I'll see you in the morning," he told her. *And every morning after that,* he thought.

Chapter 11

"Here's some tea," Joy said, carrying a tray into the living room, where Letty was supposed to be resting.

"I'm perfectly capable of getting my own tea, for heaven's sake," Letty mumbled, but when Joy approached, she offered her friend a bright smile. It didn't do any good to complain—and she didn't want to seem ungrateful—although having everyone wait on her was frustrating.

She was reluctant to admit that the most difficult aspect of her recovery was this lengthy convalescence. She'd been released from the hospital two weeks earlier, still very weak; however, she was regaining her strength more and more every day. According to Dr. Faraday, this long period of debility was to be expected. He was pleased with her progress, but Letty found herself becoming increasingly impatient. She yearned to go back to the life she'd just begun with Chase. It was as if their marriage had been put on hold.

They slept in the same bed, lived in the same house, ate the same meals, but they might as well have been brother and sister. Chase seemed to have forgotten that she was his *wife*.

"You're certainly looking good," Joy said as she took the overstuffed chair across from Letty. She poured them each a cup of tea and handed the first one to Letty. Then she picked up her own and sat back.

"I'm feeling good." Her eyes ran lovingly over the room with its polished oak floors, thick braided rug and the old upright piano that had once been hers. The house at Spring Valley had been built years before the one on the Bar E, and Chase had done an excellent job on the upkeep. When she'd been released from the hospital, Chase had brought her to Spring Valley and dutifully carried her over the threshold. But that had been the only husbandly obligation he'd performed the entire time she'd been home.

During her hospital stay, Lonny and Chase had packed her things and Cricket's, and moved them to the house at Spring Valley. Perhaps that had been a mistake, because Letty's frustration mounted as she hungered to become Chase's wife in every way.

She took a sip of the lemon-scented tea, determined to exhibit more patience with herself and everyone else. "I can't thank you enough for all you've done."

Joy had made a point of coming over every afternoon and staying with Letty. Chase had hired an extra man to come over in the early mornings so he could be with her until it was nearly noon. By then she'd showered and dressed and been deposited on the living room couch, where Chase and Cricket made a game of serving her breakfast.

"I've hardly done anything," Joy said, discounting Letty's appreciation. "It's been great getting better acquainted. Cricket is a marvelous little girl, and now that I know you, I understand why. You're a good mother, Letty, but even more important, you're a wonderful person."

"Thank you." Letty smiled softly, touched by Joy's tribute. She'd worked hard to be the right kind of mother, but there were plenty of times when she had her doubts, as any single parent did. Only she wasn't single anymore....

"Speaking of Cricket, where is she?"

"Out visiting her pony," Letty said, and grinned. Cricket thought that marrying Chase had been a brilliant idea. According to her, there wasn't anyone in the whole world who'd make a better daddy. Chase had certainly lived up to her daughter's expectations. He was patient and gentle and kind to a fault. The problem, if it could be termed that, was the way Chase treated *her,* which was no different from the way he treated Cricket. But Letty yearned to be a wife. A real wife.

"What's that?" Joy asked, pointing at a huge box that sat on the floor next to the sofa.

"Lonny brought it over last night. It's some things that belonged to our mother. He thought I might want to sort through them. When Mom died, he packed up her belongings and stuck them in the back bedroom. They've been there ever since."

Joy's eyes fluttered downward at the mention of Lonny's name. Letty picked up on that immediately. "Are you two still not getting along?" she asked, taking a chance, since neither seemed willing to discuss the other.

"Not exactly. Didn't you ask me to write down the

recipe for that meatless lasagna? Well, I brought it along and left it in the kitchen."

From little things Letty had heard Lonny, Chase and Joy drop, her brother had made some effort to fix his relationship with Joy while Letty was in the hospital. Evidently whatever he'd said or done had worked, because the minute she mentioned Joy's name to Lonny he got flustered.

For her part, Joy did everything but stand on her head to change the subject. Letty wished she knew what was going on, but after one miserable attempt to involve herself in her brother's love life, she knew better than to try again.

"Mommy," Cricket cried as she came running into the living room, pigtails skipping. "Jennybird ate an apple out of my hand! Chase showed me how to hold it so she wouldn't bite me." She looped her small arms around Letty's neck and squeezed tight. "When can you come and watch me feed Jennybird?"

"Soon." At least, Letty hoped it would be soon.

"Take your time," Joy said. "There's no reason to push yourself, Letty."

"You're beginning to sound like Chase," Letty said with a grin.

Joy shook her head. "I doubt that. I've never seen a man more worried about anyone. The first few days after the surgery, he slept at the hospital. Lonny finally dragged him home, fed him and insisted he get some rest."

Joy wasn't telling Letty anything she didn't already know. Chase had been wonderful, more than wonderful, from the moment he'd learned about her heart condition. Now, if he'd only start treating her like a wife instead of a roommate....

"I want you to come and see my new bedroom,"

Cricket said, reaching for Joy's hand. "I've got a new bed with a canopy and a new bedspread and a new pillow and everything."

Joy turned to Letty. "Chase again?"

Letty nodded. "He really spoils her."

"He loves her."

"He loves me," Cricket echoed, pointing a finger at her chest. "But that's okay, because I like being spoiled."

Letty sighed. "I know you do, sweetheart, but enough is enough."

Chase had been blunt about the fact that Cricket was his main consideration when he asked Letty to marry him. His point had been a valid one, but Letty couldn't doubt for an instant that Chase loved them both. Although he hadn't said the words, they weren't necessary; he'd shown his feelings for her in a hundred different ways.

"I'd better go take a gander at Cricket's room, and then I should head back into town," Joy said as she stood. "There's a casserole in the refrigerator for dinner."

"Joy!" Letty protested. "You've done enough."

"Shush," Joy said, waving her index finger under Letty's nose. "It was a new recipe, and two were as easy to make as one."

"You're going to have to come up with a better excuse than that, Joy. You've been trying out new recipes all week." Although she chided her friend, Letty was grateful for all the help Joy had given her over the past month. Her visits in the afternoons had brought Chase peace of mind so he could work outside without constantly worrying about Letty. The casseroles and salads Joy contributed for dinner were a help, too.

Chase wouldn't allow Letty to do any of the household chores yet and insisted on preparing their meals himself.

Never in a thousand years would Letty have dreamed that she'd miss doing laundry or dishes. But there was an unexpected joy in performing menial tasks for the people she loved. In the past few weeks, she'd learned some valuable lessons about life. She'd experienced the nearly overwhelming need to do something for someone else instead of being the recipient of everyone else's goodwill.

The house was peaceful and still as Joy followed Cricket up the stairs. When they returned a few minutes later, Cricket was yawning and dragging her blanket behind her.

"I want to sleep with you today, Mommy."

"All right, sweetheart."

Cricket climbed into the chair across from Letty, which Joy had recently vacated, and curled up, wrapping her blanket around her. Letty knew her daughter would be asleep within five minutes.

Watching the child, Letty was grateful that Cricket would be in the morning kindergarten class, since she still seemed to need an afternoon nap.

Joy worked in the kitchen for a few minutes, then paused in the doorway, smiled at Cricket and waved goodbye. Letty heard the back door close as her friend left the house.

In an hour or so Chase would come to check her. Letty cherished these serene moments alone and lay down on the couch to nap, too. A few minutes later she realized she wasn't tired, and feeling good about that, she sat up. The extra time was like an unexpected gift and her gaze fell on the carton her brother had brought. Carefully Letty pried open the lid.

Sorting through her mother's personal things was bound to be a painful task, Letty thought as she lov-

ingly removed each neatly packed item from the cardboard container.

She pulled out a stack of old pattern books and set
those aside. Her mother had loved to sew, often spending a winter evening flipping through these pages, planning new projects. Letty had learned her sewing skills
from Maren, although it had been years since she'd sat
down at a sewing machine.

Sudden tears welled up in Letty's eyes at the memories of her mother. Happy memories of a loving mother
who'd worked much too hard and died far too young.
A twinge of resentment struck her. Maren Ellison had
given her life's blood to the Bar E ranch. It had been her
husband's dream, not hers, and yet her mother had made
the sacrifice.

Letty wiped away her tears and felt a surge of sor-
row over her mother's death, coming so soon after her
father's. Maren had deserved a life so much better than
the one she'd lived.

Once Letty's eyes had cleared enough to continue
her task, she lifted out several large strips of brightly
colored material in odd shapes and sizes and set them
on the sofa. Bits and pieces of projects that had been
carefully planned by her mother and now waited endlessly for completion.

Then Letty withdrew what had apparently been her
mother's last project. With extreme caution, she unfolded the top of a vividly colored quilt, painstakingly
stitched by hand.

Examining the patchwork piece produced a sense
of awe in Letty. She was astonished by the time and
effort invested in the work, and even more astonished
that she recognized several swatches of the material her

mother had used in the quilt. The huge red star at the very center had been created from a piece of leftover fabric from a dress her mother had made for Letty the summer she'd left home. A plaid piece in one corner was from an old Western shirt she'd worn for years. After recognizing one swatch of material after another, Letty realized that her mother must have been making the quilt as a Christmas or birthday gift for her.

Lovingly she ran the tips of her fingers over the cloth as her heart lurched with a sadness that came from deep within. Then it dawned on her that without too much difficulty she'd be able to finish the quilt herself. Everything she needed was right here. The task would be something to look forward to next winter, when the days were short and the nights were Arctic-cold.

After folding the quilt top and placing it back in the box, Letty discovered a sketchbook, tucked against the side of the carton. Her heart soared with excitement as she reverently picked it up. Her mother had loved to draw, and her talent was undeniable.

The first sketch was of a large willow against the backdrop of an evening sky. Letty recognized the tree immediately. Her mother had sketched it from their front porch years ago. The willow had been cut down when Letty was in her early teens, after lightning had struck it.

Letty had often found her mother sketching, but the opportunity to complete any full-scale paintings had been rare. The book contained a handful of sketches, and once more Letty felt a wave of resentment. Maren Ellison had deserved the right to follow her own dreams. She was an artist, a woman who'd loved with a generosity that touched everyone she knew.

"Letty." Chase broke into her thoughts as he hurried

into the house. He paused when he saw Cricket asleep in the chair. "I saw Joy leave," he said, his voice a whisper.

"Chase, there's no need to worry. I can stay by myself for an hour or two."

He nodded, then wiped his forearm over his brow and awkwardly leaned over to brush his lips over her cheek. "I figured I'd drop in and make sure everything's under control."

"It is." His chaste kiss only frustrated Letty. She wanted to shout at him that the time had come for him to act like a married man instead of a saint.

"What's all this?" Chase asked, glancing around her. Letty suspected he only slept three hours a night. He never went to bed at the same time she did, and he was always up before she even stirred. Occasionally, she heard him slip between the sheets, but he stayed so far over on his side of the bed that they didn't even touch.

"A quilt," Letty said, pointing at the cardboard box.

"Is that the box Lonny brought here?"

"Yes. Mom was apparently working on it when she died. She was making it for me." Letty had to swallow the lump in her throat before she could talk again. She turned and pointed to the other things she'd found. "There's some pieces of material in here and pattern books, as well."

"What's this?"

"A sketch pad. Mom was an artist," Letty said proudly.

His eyebrows drew together. "I didn't realize that," he said slowly. He flipped through the book of pencil sketches. "She was very talented."

Chase sounded a little surprised that he hadn't known about her mother's artistic abilities. "Mom was an incredible woman. I don't think anyone ever fully appreciated that—I know I didn't."

Chase stepped closer and massaged Letty's shoulders with tenderness and sympathy. "You still miss her, don't you?"

Letty nodded. Her throat felt thick, and she couldn't express everything she was feeling, all the emotion rising up inside her.

Chase knelt in front of her, his gaze level with hers. He slipped his callused hands around the nape of her neck as he brought her into his arms. Letty rested her head against his shoulder, reveling in his warm embrace. It had been so long since he'd held her and even longer since he'd kissed her...really kissed her.

Raising her head slightly, she ran the moist tip of her tongue along the side of his jaw. He filled her senses. Chase tensed, but still Letty continued her sensual movements, nibbling at his earlobe, taking it into her mouth...

"Letty," he groaned, "no."

"No what?" she asked coyly, already knowing his answer. Her mouth roved where it wanted, while she held his face in her hands, directing him as she wished. She savored the edge of his mouth, teasing him, tantalizing him, until he moaned anew.

"Letty." He brought his hands to her shoulders.

Letty was certain he'd meant to push her away, but before he could, she raised her arms and slid them around his neck. Then she leaned against him. Chase held her there.

"Letty." Her name was a plea.

"Chase, kiss me, please," she whispered. "I've missed you so much."

Slowly, as if uncertain he was doing the right thing, Chase lowered his mouth to touch her parted lips with his. Letty didn't move, didn't breathe, for fear he'd stop. She would've screamed in frustration if he had. His brotherly pecks on the cheeks were worse than no kisses at all; they just made her crave everything she'd been missing. Apparently Chase had been feeling equally deprived, because he settled his mouth over hers with a passion and need that demanded her very breath.

"What's taken you so long?" she asked, her voice urgent.

He answered her with another fiery kiss that robbed her of what little strength she still had. Letty heard a faint moan from deep within his chest.

"Letty...this is ridiculous," he murmured, breaking away, his shoulders heaving.

"What is?" she demanded.

"My kissing you like this."

He thrust his fingers through his hair. His features were dark and angry.

"I'm your *wife,* Chase Brown. Can't a man kiss his wife?"

"Not like this...not when she's— You're recovering from heart surgery." He moved away from her and briefly closed his eyes, as though he needed an extra moment to compose himself. "Besides, Cricket's here."

"I'm your wife," Letty returned, not knowing what else to say.

"You think I need to be reminded of that?" he shot back. He got awkwardly to his feet and grabbed his hat and gloves. "I have to get to work," he said, slamming his hat on top of his head. "I'll be home in a couple of hours."

Letty couldn't have answered him had she tried. She felt like a fool now.

"Do you need anything before I go?" he asked without looking at her.

"No."

He took several steps away from her, stopped abruptly, then turned around. "It's going to be months before we can do—before we can be husband and wife in the full sense," he said grimly. "I think it would be best if we avoided situations like this in the future. Don't you agree?"

Letty shrugged. "I'm sorry," she whispered.

"So am I," he returned grimly and left the house.

"Mommy, I want to learn how to play another song," Cricket called from the living room. She was sitting at the upright piano, her feet crossed and swinging. Letty had taught her "Chopsticks" earlier in the day. She'd been impressed with how easily her daughter had picked it up. Cricket had played it at least twenty times and was eager to master more tunes.

"In a little while," Letty said. She sat at the kitchen table, peeling potatoes for dinner and feeling especially proud of herself for this minor accomplishment. Chase would be surprised and probably a little concerned when he realized what she'd done. But the surgery was several weeks behind her and it was time to take on some of the lighter responsibilities. Preparing dinner was hardly an onerous task; neither was playing the piano with her daughter.

Seeking her mother's full attention, Cricket headed into the kitchen and reached for a peeler and a potato. "I'll help you."

"All right, sweetheart."

The chore took only a few minutes, Letty peeling

four spuds to Cricket's one. Next the child helped her collect the peelings and clean off the table before leading her back into the living room.

"Play something else, Mommy," the little girl insisted, sitting on the bench beside Letty.

Letty's fingers ran lazily up and down the keyboard in a quick exercise. She hadn't touched the piano until after her surgery. Letty supposed there was some psychological reason for this, but she didn't want to analyze it now. Until Cricket's birth, music had dominated her life. But after her daughter's arrival, her life had turned in a different direction. Music had become a way of entertaining herself and occasionally brought her some paying work, although—obviously—*that* was no longer the case.

"Play a song for me," Cricket commanded.

Letty did, smiling as the familiar keys responded to her touch. This piano represented so much love and so many good times. Her mother had recognized Letty's musical gift when she was a child, only a little older than Cricket. Letty had started taking piano lessons in first grade. When she'd learned as much as the local music instructors could teach her, Maren had driven her into Rock Springs every week. A two-hour drive for a half-hour lesson.

"Now show me how to do it like you," Cricket said, completely serious. "I want to play just as good as you."

"Sweetheart, I took lessons for seven years."

"That's okay, 'cause I'm five."

Letty laughed. "Here, I'll play 'Mary Had a Little Lamb' and then you can move your fingers the way I do." Slowly she played the first lines, then dropped her hands on her lap while Cricket perfectly mimicked the simple notes.

"This is fun," Cricket said, beaming with pride.

Ten minutes later, she'd memorized the whole song. With two musical pieces in her repertoire, Cricket was convinced she was possibly the most gifted musical student in the history of Red Springs.

The minute Chase was in the door, Cricket flew to his side. "Chase! Chase, come listen."

"Sweetie, let him wash up first," Letty said with a smile.

"What is it?" Chase asked, his amused gaze shifting from Cricket to Letty, then back to Cricket again.

"It's a surprise," Cricket said, practically jumping up and down with enthusiasm.

"You'd better go listen," Letty told him. "She's been waiting for you to come inside."

Chase washed his hands at the kitchen sink, but hesitated when he saw the panful of peeled potatoes. "Who did this?"

"Mommy and me," Cricket told him impatiently.

"Letty?"

"And I lived to tell about it. I'm feeling stronger every day," she pointed out, "and there's no reason I can't start taking up the slack around here a little more."

"But—"

"Don't argue with me, Chase," she said in what she hoped was a firm voice.

"It hasn't been a month yet," he countered, frowning.

"I feel fine!"

It looked as if he wanted to argue, but he apparently decided not to, probably because Cricket was tugging anxiously at his arm, wanting him to sit down in the living room so he could hear her recital.

Letty followed them and stood back as Cricket directed Chase to his favorite overstuffed chair.

"You stay here," she said.

Once Chase was seated, she walked proudly over to the piano and climbed onto the bench. Then she looked over her shoulder and ceremoniously raised her hands. Lowering them, she put every bit of emotion her five-year-old heart possessed into playing "Chopsticks."

When she'd finished, she slid off the seat, tucked her arm around her middle and bowed. "You're supposed to clap now," she told Chase.

He obliged enthusiastically, and Letty stifled a laugh at how seriously Cricket was taking this.

"For my next number, I'll play—" She stopped abruptly. "I want you to guess."

Letty sat on the armchair, resting her hand on his shoulder. "She's such a ham."

Chase grinned up at her, his eyes twinkling with shared amusement.

"I must have quiet," Cricket grumbled. "You aren't supposed to talk now...."

Once more Cricket gave an Oscar-quality performance.

"Bravo, bravo," Chase shouted when she'd slipped off the piano bench.

Cricket flew to Chase's side and climbed into his lap. "Mommy taught me."

"She seems to have a flair for music," Letty said.

"I'm not as good as Mommy, though." Cricket sighed dramatically. "She can play anything...and she sings pretty, too. She played for me today and we had so much fun."

Letty laughed. "I'm thinking of giving Cricket piano

lessons myself," Letty said, sure that Chase would add his wholehearted approval.

To her surprise, Letty felt him tense beneath her fingers. It was as if all the joy had suddenly and mysteriously disappeared from the room.

"Chase, what's wrong?" Letty whispered.

"Nothing."

"Cricket, go get Chase a glass of iced tea," Letty said. "It's in the refrigerator."

"Okay," the child said, eager as always to do anything for Chase.

As soon as the little girl had left, Letty spoke. "Do you object to Cricket taking piano lessons?"

"Why should I?" he asked, without revealing any emotion. "As you say, she's obviously got talent."

"Yes, but—"

"We both know where she got it from, don't we," he said with a resigned sigh.

"I would think you'd be pleased." Chase had always loved it when she played and sang; now he could barely stand it if she so much as looked at the piano.

"I *am* pleased," he declared. With that, he walked into the kitchen, leaving Letty more perplexed than ever.

For several minutes, Letty sat there numbly while Chase talked to Cricket, praising her efforts.

Letty had thought Chase would be happy, but he clearly wasn't. She didn't understand it.

"Someday," she heard him tell Cricket, his voice full of regret, "you'll play as well as your mother."

Chapter 12

Astride Firepower at the top of a hill overlooking his herd, Chase stared vacantly into the distance. Letty was leaving; he'd known it from the moment he discovered she'd been playing the piano again. The niggling fear had been with him for days, gnawing at his heart.

Marrying her had been a gamble, a big one, but he'd accepted it, grateful for the opportunity to have her and Cricket in his life, even if it was destined to be for a short time. Somehow, he'd find the courage to smile and let her walk away. He'd managed it once and, if he had to, he could do it again.

"Chase."

At the sound of his name, carried softly on the wind, Chase twisted in the saddle, causing the leather to creak. He frowned as he recognized Letty, riding one of his mares, advancing slowly toward him. Her face was lit with a bright smile and she waved, happy and elated. Sadly he shared little of her exhilaration. All he could think about was his certainty that she'd soon be gone.

Letty rode with a natural grace, as if she'd been born to it. Her beauty almost broke his heart.

Chase swallowed, and a sense of dread swelled up inside him. Dread and confusion—the same confusion that being alone with Letty always brought. He wanted her, and yet he had to restrain himself for the sake of her health. He wanted to keep her with him, and yet he'd have to let her go if that was her choice.

Sweat broke out across his upper lip. He hadn't touched Letty from the moment he'd learned of her heart condition. Now she needed to recover from her surgery. It was debatable, however, whether he could continue to resist her much longer. Each day became more taxing than the one before. Just being close to her sapped his strength. Sleeping with her only inches away had become almost impossible and as a result he was constantly tired…as well as frustrated.

Chase drew himself up when she joined him. "What are you doing here?" he asked. He sounded harsher than he'd intended.

"You didn't come back to the house for lunch," she murmured.

"Did it occur to you that I might not be hungry?" He was exhausted and impatient and hated the way he was speaking to her, but he felt himself fighting powerful emotions whenever he was near her.

"I brought you some lunch," Letty said, not reacting to his rudeness. "I thought we…we might have a picnic."

"A picnic?" he echoed with a short sarcastic laugh.

Letty seemed determined to ignore his mood, and

smiled up at him, her eyes gleaming with mischief. "Yes," she said, "a picnic. You work too hard, Chase. It's about time you relaxed a little."

"Where's Cricket?" he asked, his tongue nearly sticking to the roof of his mouth. It was difficult enough keeping his eyes off Letty without having to laze around on some nice, soft grass and pretend he had an appetite. Oh, he was hungry, all right, but it was Letty he needed; only his wife would satisfy his cravings.

"Cricket went into town with Joy," she said, sliding down from the mare. "She's helping Joy get her new classroom ready, although it's questionable how much help she'll actually be. School's only a couple of weeks away, you know."

While she was speaking, Letty emptied the saddlebags. She didn't look back at him as she spread a blanket across the grass, obviously assuming he'd join her without further argument. Next she opened a large brown sack, then knelt and pulled out sandwiches and a thermos.

"Chase?" She looked up at him.

"I… I'm not hungry."

"You don't have to eat if you don't want, but at least take a break."

Reluctantly Chase climbed out of the saddle. It was either that or sit where he was and stare down her blouse.

Despite the fact that Letty had spent weeks inside the house recuperating, her skin was glowing and healthy, Chase noted. Always slender, she'd lost weight and had worked at putting it back on, but he'd never guess it, looking at her now. Her jeans fit snugly, and her lithe, elegant body seemed to call out to him.…

"I made fresh lemonade. Would you like some?" She

interrupted his tortured thoughts, opening the thermos and filling a paper cup, ready to hand it to him.

"No...thanks." Chase felt both awkward and out of place. He moved closer to her, drawn by an invisible cord. He stared at her longingly, then dropped to his knees, simply because standing demanded so much energy.

"The lemonade's cold," she coaxed. As if to prove her point, she took a sip.

The tip of her tongue came out and she licked her lips. Watching that small action, innocent yet sensuous, was like being kicked in the stomach.

"I said I didn't want any," he said gruffly.

They were facing each other, and Letty's gaze found his. Her eyes were wide, hurt and confused. She looked so beautiful.

He realized he should explain that he knew she was planning to go back to California, but his tongue refused to cooperate. Letty continued to peer at him, frowning slightly, as though trying to identify the source of his anger.

At that instant, Chase knew he was going to kiss her and there wasn't a thing he could do to stop himself. The ache to touch her had consumed him for weeks. He reached out for her now, easing her into his embrace. She came willingly, offering no resistance.

"Letty..."

Intuitively she must have known his intent, because she closed her eyes and tilted back her head.

At first, as if testing the limits of his control, Chase merely touched his mouth to hers. The way her fingers curled into his chest told him she was as eager for his touch as he was for hers. He waited, savoring the taste and feel of her in his arms, and when he could deny himself no longer, he deepened the kiss.

With a soft sigh, Letty brought her arms around his neck. Chase's heart was pounding and he pulled back for a moment, breathing in her delectable scent—wildflowers and some clean-smelling floral soap.

He ran his fingers through her hair as he kissed her again. He stopped to breathe, then slowly lowered them both to the ground, lying side by side. Then, he sought her mouth once more. He felt consumed with such need, yet forced himself to go slowly, gently....

Since Letty had returned to Red Springs, Chase had kissed her a number of times. For the past few weeks he'd gone to sleep each night remembering how good she'd felt in his arms. He had treasured the memories, not knowing when he'd be able to hold her and kiss her again. *Soon,* he always promised himself; he'd make love to her soon. Every detail of every time he'd touched her was emblazoned on his mind, and he could think of little else.

Now that she was actually in his arms, he discovered that the anticipation hadn't prepared him for how perfect it would be. The reality outdistanced his memory—and his imagination.

His mouth came down hard on hers, releasing all the tension inside him. Letty's breathing was labored and harsh and her fingers curled more tightly into the fabric of his shirt, then began to relax as she gave herself completely over to his kiss.

Chase was drowning, sinking fast. At first he associated the rumbling in his ears with the thunder of his own heartbeat. It took him a moment to realize it was the sound of an approaching horse.

Chase rolled away from Letty with a groan.

She sat up and looked at him, dazed, hurt, confused.

"Someone's riding toward us," he said tersely.

"Oh."

That one word bespoke frustration and disappointment and a multitude of other emotions that reflected his own. He retrieved his gloves and stood, using his body to shield Letty from any curious onlooker.

Within seconds Lonny trotted into view.

"It's your brother," Chase warned, then added something low and guttural that wasn't meant for her ears. His friend had quite the sense of timing.

Chase saw Letty turn away and busy herself with laying out their lunch.

As Lonny rode up, pulling on his horse's reins, Chase glared at him.

More than a little chagrined, Lonny muttered, "Am I interrupting something?"

"Of course not," Letty said, sounding unlike herself. She kept her back to him, making a task of unfolding napkins and unwrapping sandwiches.

Chase contradicted her words with a scowl. The last person he wanted to see was Lonny. To his credit, his brother-in-law looked as if he wanted to find a hole to hide in, but that didn't help now.

"Actually, I was looking for Letty," Lonny explained, after clearing his throat. "I wanted to talk to her about... something. I stopped at the house, but there wasn't anyone around. Your new guy, Mel, was working in the barn and he told me she'd come out here. I guess, uh, I should've figured it out."

"It would've been appreciated," Chase muttered savagely.

"I brought lunch out to Chase," Letty said.

Chase marveled that she could recover so quickly.

"There's plenty if you'd care to join us," she said.

"You might as well," Chase said, confirming the invitation. The moment had been ruined and he doubted they'd be able to recapture it.

Lonny's gaze traveled from one to the other. "Another time," he said, turning his horse. "I'll talk to you later, sis."

Letty nodded, and Lonny rode off.

"You should go back to the house yourself," Chase said without meeting her eyes.

It wasn't until Letty had repacked the saddlebags and ridden after her brother that Chase could breathe normally again.

Lonny was waiting for Letty when she trotted into the yard on Chase's mare. His expression was sheepish, she saw as he helped her down from the saddle, although she was more than capable of doing it on her own.

"I'm sorry, Letty," he mumbled. Hot color circled his ears. "I should've thought before I went traipsing out there looking for you."

"It's all right," she said, offering him a gracious smile. There was no point in telling him he'd interrupted a scene she'd been plotting for days. Actually, her time with Chase told her several things, and all of them excited her. He was going crazy with desire for her. He wanted her as much as she wanted him.

"*You* may be willing to forgive me, but I don't think Chase is going to be nearly as generous."

"Don't worry about it," she returned absently. Her brother had foiled Plan A, but Plan B would go into action that very evening.

"Come on in and I'll get you a glass of lemonade."

"I could use one," Lonny said, obediently following his sister into the kitchen.

Letty could see that something was troubling her brother, and whatever it was appeared to be serious. His eyes seemed clouded and stubbornly refused to meet hers.

"What did you want to talk to me about?"

He sat down at the scarred oak table. Removing his hat, he set it on the chair beside him. "Do you remember when you first came home you invited Mary Brandon over to the house?"

Letty wasn't likely to forget it; the evening had been a catastrophe.

"You seemed to think I needed a wife," Lonny continued.

"Yes…mainly because you'd become consumed by the ranch. Your rodeo days are over—"

"My glory days," he said with a self-conscious laugh.

"You quit because you had to come back to the Bar E when Dad got sick. Now you're so wrapped up in the ranch, all your energy's channeled in that one direction."

He nodded, agreeing with her, which surprised Letty.

"The way I see it, Lonny, you work too hard. You've given up—been forced to give up—too much. You've grown so…short-tempered. In my arrogant way I saw you as lonely and decided to do something about it." She was nervous about her next remark but made it anyway. "I was afraid this place was going to suck the life out of you, like I thought it had with Mom."

"Are you still on that kick?" he asked, suddenly angry. Then he sighed, a sound of resignation.

"We had a big fight over this once, and I swore I

wouldn't mention it again, but honestly, Letty, you're seeing Mom as some kind of martyr. She loved the ranch...she loved Wyoming."

"I know," Letty answered quietly.

"Then why are you arguing with me about it?"

Letty ignored the question, deciding that discretion was well-advised at the moment. "It came to me after I sorted through the carton of her things that you brought over," she said, toying with her glass. "I studied the quilt Mom was making and realized that her talent *wasn't* wasted. She just transferred it to another form—quilting. At first I was surprised that she hadn't used the sewing machine to join the squares. Every stitch in that quilt top was made by hand, every single one of them."

"I think she felt there was more of herself in it that way," Lonny suggested.

Letty smiled in agreement. "I'm going to finish it this winter. I'll do the actual quilting—and I'll do it by hand, just like she did."

"It's going to be beautiful," Lonny said. "Really beautiful."

Letty nodded. "The blending of colors, the design— it all spells out how much love and skill Mom put into it. When I decided to leave Red Springs after high school, I went because I didn't want to end up like Mom, and now I realize I couldn't strive toward a finer goal."

Lonny frowned again. "I don't understand. You left for California because you didn't want to be a rancher's wife, and yet you married Chase...."

"I know. But I love Chase. I always have. It wasn't being a rancher's wife that I objected to so much. Yes, the life is hard. But the rewards are plentiful. I knew that nine years ago, and I know it even more profoundly now. My biggest fear was that I'd end up dedicating my life to ranching like Mom did and never achieve my own dreams."

"But Mom was happy. I never once heard her complain. I guess that's why I took such offense when you made it sound as if she'd wasted her life. Nothing could be farther from the truth."

"I know that now," Letty murmured. "But I didn't understand it for a long time. What upset me most was that I felt she could never paint the way she wanted to. There was always something else that needed her attention, some other project that demanded her time. It wasn't until I saw the quilt that I understood.... She sketched for her own enjoyment, but the other things she made were for the people she loved. The quilt she was working on when she died was for me, and it's taught me perhaps the most valuable lesson of my life."

Lonny's face relaxed into a smile. "I'm glad, Letty. In the back of my mind I had the feeling that once you'd recuperated from the surgery, you'd get restless. But you won't, will you?"

"You've got to be kidding," she said with a laugh. "I'm a married woman, you know." She twisted the diamond wedding band around her finger. "My place is here, with Chase. I plan to spend the rest of my life with him."

"I'm glad to hear that," he said again, his relief evident.

"We got off the subject, didn't we?" she said apologetically. "You wanted to talk to me." He hadn't told her why, but she could guess....

"Yes.... Well, it has to do with..." He hesitated, as

if saying Joy Fuller's name would somehow conjure her up.

"Joy?" Letty asked.

Lonny nodded.

"What about her?"

In response, Lonny jerked his fingers through his hair and glared at the ceiling. "I'm telling you, Letty, no one's more shocked by this than me. I've discovered that I like her. I…mean I *really* like her. The fact is, I can't stop thinking about Joy, but every time I try to talk to her, I say something stupid, and before I know it, we're arguing."

Letty bent her head to show she understood. She'd witnessed more than one of her brother's clashes with Joy.

"We don't just argue like normal civilized people," Lonny continued. "She can make me so angry I don't even know what I'm saying anymore."

Letty lowered her eyes, afraid her smile would annoy her brother, especially since he'd come to her for help. Except that, at the moment, she didn't feel qualified to offer him any advice.

"The worst part is," he went on, "I was in town this morning, and I heard that Joy's agreed to go out with Glen Brewster. The thought of her dating another man has me all twisted up inside."

"Glen Brewster?" That surprised Letty. "Isn't he the guy who manages the grocery store?"

"One and the same," Lonny confirmed, scowling. "Can you imagine her going out with someone like Glen? He's all wrong for her!"

"Have you asked Joy out yourself?"

The way the color streaked his face told Letty what

she needed to know. "I don't think I should answer that." He lifted his eyes piteously. "I want to take her out, but everyone's working against me."

"Everyone?"

He cleared his throat. "No, not everyone. I guess I'm my own worst enemy—I know that sounds crazy. I mean, it's not like I haven't had girlfriends before. But she's different from the girls I met on the rodeo circuit." He stared down at the newly waxed kitchen floor. "All I want you to do is tell me what a woman wants from a man. A woman like Joy. If I know that, then maybe I can do something right—for once."

The door slammed in the distance. Lonny's gaze flew up to meet Letty's. "Joy?"

"Probably."

"Oh, great," he groaned.

"Don't panic."

"Me?" he asked with a short, sarcastic laugh. "Why should I do that? The woman's told me in no uncertain terms that she never wants to see me again. Her last words to me were—and I quote—'take a flying leap into the nearest cow pile.'"

"What did you say to her, for heaven's sake?"

He shrugged, looking uncomfortable. "I'd better not repeat it."

"Oh, Lonny! Don't you ever learn? She's not one of your buckle bunnies—but you already know that. Maybe if you'd quit insulting her, you'd be able to have a civil conversation."

"I've decided something," he said. "I don't know how or when, but I'm going to marry her." The words had no sooner left his lips than the screen door opened.

Cricket came flying into the kitchen, bursting to tell

her mother about all her adventures with Joy at the school. She started speaking so fast that the words ran together. "I-saw-my-classroom-and-I-got-to-meet-Mrs.-Webber...and I sat in a real desk and everything!"

Joy followed Cricket into the kitchen, but stopped abruptly when she saw Lonny. The expression on her face suggested that if he said one word to her—one word—she'd leave.

As if taking his cue, Lonny reached for his hat and stood. "I'd better get back to work. Good talking to you, Letty," he said stiffly. His gaze skipped from his sister to Joy, and he inclined his head politely. "Hello, *Ms.* Fuller."

"*Mr.* Ellison." Joy dipped her head, too, ever so slightly.

They gave each other a wide berth as Lonny stalked out of the kitchen. Before he opened the screen door, he sent a pleading glance at Letty, but she wasn't sure what he expected her to do.

Chase didn't come in for dinner, but that didn't surprise Letty. He'd avoided her so much lately that she rarely saw him in the evenings anymore. Even Cricket had commented on it. She obviously missed him, although he made an effort to work with her and Jenny-bird, the pony.

The house was dark, and Cricket had been asleep for hours, when Letty heard the back door open. Judging by the muffled sounds Chase was making, she knew he was in the kitchen, washing up. Next he would shower.

Some nights he came directly to bed; others he'd sit in front of the TV, delaying the time before he joined her. In the mornings he'd be gone before she woke. Letty didn't know any man who worked as physically hard as Chase did on so little rest.

"You're later than usual tonight," she said, standing barefoot in the kitchen doorway.

He didn't turn around when he spoke. "There's lots to do this time of year."

"Yes, I know," she answered, willing to accept his lame excuse. "I didn't get much of a chance to talk to you this afternoon."

"What did Lonny want?"

So he was going to change the subject. Fine, she'd let him. "Joy problems," she told him.

Chase nodded, opened the refrigerator and took out a carton of milk. He poured himself a glass, then drank it down in one long swallow.

"Would you like me to run you a bath?"

"I'd rather take a shower." Reluctantly he turned to face her.

This was the moment Letty had been waiting for. She'd planned it all night. The kitchen remained dark; the only source of light was the moon, which cast flickering shadows over the wall. Letty was leaning against the doorjamb, her hands behind her back. Her nightgown had been selected with care, a frothy see-through piece of chiffon that covered her from head to foot, yet revealed everything.

Letty knew she'd achieved the desired effect when the glass Chase was holding slipped from his hand and dropped to the floor. By some miracle it didn't shatter. Chase bent over to retrieve it, and even standing several yards away, Letty could see that his fingers were trembling.

"I saw Dr. Faraday this morning," she told him, keeping her voice low and seductive. "He gave me a clean bill of health."

"Congratulations."

"I think this calls for a little celebration, don't you?"

"Celebration?"

"I'm your wife, Chase, but you seem to have conveniently forgotten that fact. There's no reason we should wait any longer."

"Wait?" He was beginning to sound like an echo.

Letty prayed for calm.

Before she could say anything else, he added abruptly, "I've been out on the range for the past twelve hours. I'm dirty and tired and badly in need of some hot water."

"I've been patient all this time. A few more minutes won't kill me." She'd never thought it would come to this, but she was going to have to seduce her own husband. So be it. She was hardly an expert in the techniques of seduction, but instinct was directing her behavior—instinct and love.

"Letty, I'm not in the mood. As I said, I'm tired and—"

"You were in the mood this afternoon," she whispered, deliberately moistening her lips with the tip of her tongue.

He ground out her name, his hands clenched at his sides. "Perhaps you should go back to bed."

"Back to bed?" She straightened, hands on her hips. "You were supposed to take one look at me and be overcome with passion!"

"I was?"

He was silently laughing at her, proving she'd done an excellent job of making a fool of herself. Tears sprang to her eyes. Before the surgery and directly afterward,

Chase had been the model husband—loving, gentle, concerned. He couldn't seem to spend enough time with her. Lately just the opposite was true. The man who stood across from her now wasn't the same man she'd married, and she didn't understand what had changed him.

Chase stood where he was, feet planted apart, as if he expected her to defy him.

Without another word, Letty turned and left. Tears blurred her vision as she walked into their room and sank down on the edge of the bed. Covering her face with both hands, she sat there, her thoughts whirling, gathering momentum, until she lost track of time.

"Letty."

She vaulted to her feet and wiped her face. "Don't you *Letty* me, you...you arrogant cowboy." That was the worst thing she could come up with on short notice.

He was fresh from the shower, wearing nothing more than a towel around his waist.

"I had all these romantic plans for seducing you—and...and you made me feel I'm about as appealing as an old steer. So you want to live like brother and sister? Fine. Two can play this game, fellow." She pulled the chiffon nightie over her head and yanked open a drawer, grabbing an old flannel gown and donning that. When she'd finished, she whirled around to face him.

To her chagrin, Chase took one look at her and burst out laughing.

Chapter 13

"Don't you *dare* laugh at me," Letty cried, her voice trembling.

"I'm not," he told her. The humor had evaporated as if it had never been. What he'd told her earlier about being tired was true; he'd worked himself to the point of exhaustion. But he'd have to be a crazy man to reject the very thing he wanted most. Letty had come to him, demolished every excuse not to hold and kiss her, and like an idiot he'd told her to go back to bed. Who did he think he was? A man of steel? He wasn't kidding anyone, least of all himself.

Silently he walked around the end of the bed toward her.

For every step Chase advanced, Letty took one away from him, until the backs of her knees were pressed against the mattress and there was nowhere else to go.

Chase met her gaze, needing her love and her warmth so badly he was shaking with it.

Ever so gently he brought his hands up to frame her face. He stroked away the moisture on her cheeks, wanting to erase each tear and beg her forgiveness for having hurt her. Slowly, he slid his hands down the sides of her neck until they settled on her shoulders.

"Nothing in my life has been as good as these past months with you and Cricket," he told her, although the admission cost him dearly. He hadn't wanted to tie her to him with words and emotional bonds. If she stayed, he wanted it to be of her own free will, not because she felt trapped or obliged.

"I can't alter the past," he whispered. "I don't have any control of the future. But we have now...tonight."

"Then why did you...laugh at me?"

"Because I'm a fool. I need you, Letty, so much it frightens me." He heard the husky emotion in his voice, but didn't regret exposing his longing to her. "If I can only have you for a little while, I think we should take advantage of this time, don't you?"

He didn't give her an opportunity to respond, but urged her toward him and placed his mouth on hers, kissing her over and over until her sweet responsive body was molded against him. He'd dreamed of holding Letty like this, pliable and soft in his arms, but once again reality exceeded his imagination.

"I was beginning to believe you hated me," she whimpered against his mouth. Then, clinging to him, she resumed their kiss.

"Let's take this off," he said a moment later, tugging at the flannel gown. With a reluctance that excited him all the more, Letty stepped out of his arms just far enough to let him pull the gown over her head and discard it.

"Oh, Letty," he groaned, looking at her, heaving a sigh of appreciation. "You're so beautiful." He felt humble seeing her like this. Her beauty, so striking, was revealed only to him, and his knees went weak.

"The scar?" Her eyes were lowered.

The red line that ran the length of her sternum would fade in the years to come. But Chase viewed it as a badge of courage. He leaned forward and kissed it, gently, lovingly, breathing her name.

"Oh, Chase, I thought…maybe you found me ugly and that's why…you wouldn't touch me."

"No," he said. "Never."

"But you *didn't* touch me. For weeks and weeks you stayed on your side of the bed, until…until I thought I'd go crazy."

"I couldn't be near you and not want you," he admitted hoarsely. "I had to wait until Dr. Faraday said it was okay." If those weeks had been difficult for Letty, they'd been doubly so for him.

"Do you want to touch me now?"

He nodded. From the moment they'd discarded her gown, Chase hadn't been able to take his eyes off her.

"Yes. I want to hold you for the rest of my life."

"Please love me, Chase." Her low, seductive voice was all the encouragement he needed. He eased her onto the bed, securing her there with his body. He had to taste her, had to experience all the pleasure she'd so unselfishly offered him earlier.

Their lovemaking was everything he could've hoped for—everything he *had* hoped for. She welcomed him readily and he was awed by her generosity, lost in her love.

Afterward, Chase lay beside Letty and gathered her in his arms. As he felt the sweat that slid down her face, felt the heavy exhaustion that claimed his limbs, he wondered how he'd been able to resist her for so long.

Letty woke at dawn, still in Chase's arms. She felt utterly content—and excited. Plan B hadn't worked out exactly the way she'd thought it would, but it had certainly produced the desired effect. She felt like sitting up and throwing her arms in the air and shouting for sheer joy. She was a wife!

"Morning," Chase whispered.

He didn't look at her, as if he half expected her to be embarrassed by the intimacies they'd shared the night before. Letty's exhilarated thoughts came to an abrupt halt. Had she said or done something a married woman shouldn't?

She was about to voice her fears when her husband turned to her, bracing his arms on either side of her head. She met his eyes, unsure of what he was asking. Slowly he lowered his mouth to hers, kissing her with a hungry need that surprised as much as delighted her.

"How long do we have before Cricket wakes up?" he whispered.

"Long enough," she whispered back.

In the days that followed, Letty found that Chase was insatiable. Not that she minded. In fact, she was thrilled that his need to make love to her was so great. Chase touched and held her often and each caress made her long for sundown. The nights were theirs.

Cricket usually went to bed early, tired out from the long day's activities. As always, Chase was endlessly patient with her, reading her bedtime stories and making up a few of his own, which he dutifully repeated for Letty.

Cricket taught him the game of blowing out the light that Letty had played with her from the time she was a toddler. Whenever she watched Chase with her daughter, Letty was quietly grateful. He was so good with Cricket, and the little girl adored him.

Letty had never been happier. Chase had never told her he loved her in so many words, but she was reassured of his devotion in a hundred different ways. He'd never communicated his feelings freely, and the years hadn't changed that. But the looks he gave her, the reverent way he touched her, his exuberant lovemaking, told her everything she needed to know.

The first week of September Cricket started kindergarten. On the opening day of school, Letty drove her into town and lingered after class had begun, talking to the other mothers for a few minutes. Then, feeling a little melancholy, she returned to the ranch. A new world was opening up for Cricket, and Letty's role in her daughter's life would change.

Letty parked the truck in the yard and walked into the kitchen. Chase wasn't due back at the house until eleven-thirty for lunch; Cricket would be coming home on the school bus, but that wasn't until early afternoon, so Letty's morning was free. She did some housework, but without much enthusiasm. After throwing a load of clothes in the washer, she decided to vacuum.

Once in the living room, she found herself drawn to the old upright piano. She stood over the keys and with one finger plinked out a couple of the songs she'd taught Cricket.

Before she knew it, she was sitting on the bench, running her fingers up and down the yellowing keys, playing a few familiar chords. Soon she was singing, and it felt wonderful, truly wonderful, to release some of the emotion she was experiencing in song.

She wasn't sure how long she'd been sitting there when she looked up and saw Chase watching her. His eyes were sad.

"Your voice is still as beautiful as it always was," he murmured.

"Thank you," she said, feeling shy. It had been months since she'd sat at the piano like this and sung.

"It's been a long time since I've heard you," he told her, his voice flat.

She slipped off the piano bench and closed the keyboard. She considered telling him she didn't do this often; she knew that, for some reason, her playing made him uncomfortable. That saddened Letty—even more so because she didn't understand his feelings.

An awkward silence passed.

"Chase," she said, realizing why he must be in the house. "I'm sorry. I didn't realize it was time for lunch already."

"It isn't," he said.

"Is something wrong?" she asked, feeling unnerved and not knowing why.

"No." The look in his eyes was one of tenderness… and fear? Pain? Either way, it made no sense to her.

Without a word, she slipped into his arms, hugging him close. He was tense and held himself stiffly, but she couldn't fathom why.

Tilting her head, Letty studied him. He glided his thumb over her lips and she captured it between her teeth. "Kiss me," she said. That was one sure way of comforting him.

He did, kissing her ravenously. Urgently. As if this was the last opportunity they'd have. When he ended the kiss, Letty finally felt him relax, and sighed in relief.

"I need you, Letty," he murmured.

Chase's mouth was buried in the hollow of her throat. She burrowed her fingers in his hair, needing to continue touching him.

He kissed her one more time, then drew back. "I want to have you in my arms and in my bed as often as I can before you go," he whispered, refusing to meet her gaze.

"Before I go?" she repeated in confusion. "I'm not going anywhere—Cricket's taking the bus home."

Chase shook his head. "When I married you, I accepted that sooner or later you'd leave," he said, his voice filled with resignation.

Letty was so stunned, so shocked, that for a second she couldn't believe what she was hearing. "Let me see if I understand you," she said slowly. "I married you, but you seem to think I had no intention of staying in the relationship and that sooner or later I'd fly the coop? Am I understanding you correctly?" It was an effort to disguise her sarcasm.

"You were facing a life-or-death situation. I offered you an alternative because of Cricket."

Chase spoke as if that explained everything. "I love you, Chase Brown. I loved you when I left Wyoming. I loved you when I came back.... I love you even more now."

He didn't look at her. "I never said I felt the same way about you."

The world seemed to skid to a halt; everything went

perfectly still except for her heart, which was ramming loudly against her chest.

"True," she began when she could find her voice. "You never *said* you did. But you *show* me every day how much you love me. I don't need the words, Chase. You can't hide what you feel for me."

He was making his way to the door when he turned back and snorted softly. "Don't confuse great sex with love, Letty."

She felt unbelievably hurt and fiercely angry.

"Do you *want* me to leave, Chase? Is that what you're saying?"

"I won't ask you to stay."

"In…in other words, I'm free to walk out of here anytime?"

He nodded. "You can go now, if that's what you want."

"Generous of you," she snapped.

He didn't respond.

"I get it," she cried sharply. "Everything's falling into place now. Every time I sit down at the piano, I can feel your displeasure. Why did you bring it here if it bothered you so much?"

"It wasn't my bright idea," he said curtly. "Joy thought it would help you recuperate. If I'd had my way, it would never have left Lonny's place."

"Take it back, then."

"I will once you're gone."

Letty pressed her hand against her forehead. "I can't believe we're having this conversation. I love you, Chase… I don't ever want to leave you."

"Whatever you decide is fine, Letty," he said, and again his voice was resigned. "That decision is yours."

He walked out of the house, letting the back door slam behind him.

For several minutes, Letty did nothing but lean against the living room wall. Chase's feigned indifference infuriated her. Hadn't the past few weeks meant *anything* to him? Obviously that was what he wanted her to think. He was pretending to be so damn smug... so condescending, that it demanded all her restraint not to haul out her suitcases that instant and walk away from him just to prove him right.

His words made a lie of all the happiness she'd found in her marriage. Angry tears scalded her eyes. For some reason she didn't grasp, Chase wanted her to think he was using her, and he'd paid a steep price for the privilege—he'd married her.

Letty sank down onto the floor and covered her face with her hands, feeling wretched to the marrow of her bones.

Like some romantic fool, she'd held on to the belief that everything between her and Chase was perfect now and would remain that way forever after. It was a blow to discover otherwise.

When she'd first come back to Wyoming, Letty had been afraid her life was nearly over and the only things awaiting her were pain and regret. Instead Chase had given her a glimpse of happiness. With him, she'd experienced an immeasurable sense of satisfaction and joy, an inner peace. She'd seen Chase as her future, seen the two of them as lifelong companions, a man and a woman in love, together for life.

Nearly blinded by her tears, she got up and grabbed her purse from the kitchen table. She had to get away to think, put order to her raging thoughts.

Chase was in the yard when she walked out the door. He paused, and out of the corner of her eye, Letty saw that he moved two steps toward her, then abruptly stopped. Apparently he'd changed his mind about whatever he was going to say or do. Which was just as well, since Letty wasn't in the mood to talk to him.

His gaze followed her as she walked toward the truck, as if he suspected she was leaving him right then and there.

Perhaps that was exactly what she should do.

Chapter 14

Letty had no idea where she was going. All she knew was that she had to get away. She considered driving to town and waiting for Cricket. But it was still a while before the kindergarten class was scheduled to be dismissed. In addition, Cricket was looking forward to riding the bus home; to her, that seemed the height of maturity. Letty didn't want to ruin that experience for her daughter.

As she drove aimlessly down the country road, Letty attempted to put the disturbing events of the morning in perspective. Leaving Chase, if only for a day or two, would be an overreaction, but she didn't know how else to deal with this situation. One moment she had everything a woman could want; the next it had all been taken away from her for reasons she couldn't understand or explain. The safe harbor she'd anchored in—her marriage to Chase—had been unexpectedly invaded by an enemy she couldn't even identify.

Without realizing where she'd driven, Letty noticed that the hillside where she'd so often sat with Chase was just over the next ridge. With an ironic smile, she stopped the truck. Maybe their hillside would give her the serenity and inner guidance she sought now.

With the autumn sun warm on her back, she strolled over to the crest of the hill and sat down on a soft patch of grass. She saw a few head of cattle resting under the shade of trees near the stream below, and watched them idly while her thoughts churned. How peaceful the animals seemed, how content. Actually, she was a little surprised to see them grazing there, since she'd heard Chase say that he was moving his herd in the opposite direction. But where he chose to let his cattle graze was the least of her worries.

A slow thirty minutes passed. What Letty found so disheartening about the confrontation with Chase was his conviction that she'd leave him and, worse, his acceptance of it. Why was he so certain she'd pack up and move away? Did he trust her so little?

To give up on their love, their marriage and all the happiness their lives together would bring was traumatic enough. For her and, she was convinced, for him. But the fact that he could do so with no more than a twinge of regret was almost more than Letty could bear. Chase's pride wouldn't let him tell her he loved her and that he wanted her to stay.

Yet he *did* love her and he loved Cricket. Despite his heartless words to the contrary, Letty could never doubt it.

Standing, Letty let her arms hang limply at her sides. She didn't know what she should do. Perhaps getting away for a day or two wasn't such a bad plan.

The idea started to gather momentum. It was as she turned to leave that Letty noticed one steer that had separated itself from the others. She paused, then stared at the brand, surprised it wasn't Chase's. Before she left Spring Valley she'd let Chase know that old man Wilber's cattle were on his property.

Chase was nowhere to be seen when Letty got back to the house. That was fine, since she'd be in and out within a matter of minutes. She threw a few things in a suitcase for herself and dragged it into the hallway. Then she rushed upstairs to grab some clothes for Cricket. Letty wasn't sure what she'd tell her daughter about this unexpected vacation, but she'd think of something later.

Chase was standing in the kitchen when she reached the bottom of the stairs. His eyes were cold and cruel in a way she hadn't seen since she'd first returned home. He picked up her suitcase and set it by the back door, as if eager for her to leave.

"I see you decided to go now," he said, leaning indolently against the kitchen counter.

His arms were folded over his chest in a gesture of stubborn indifference. If he'd revealed the least bit of remorse or indecision, Letty might have considered reasoning with him, but it was painfully apparent that he didn't feel anything except the dire satisfaction of being proven right.

"I thought I'd spend a few days with Lonny."

"Lonny," Chase repeated with a short, sarcastic laugh. "I bet he'll love that."

"He won't mind." A half-truth, but worth it if Chase believed her.

"You're sure of that?"

It was obvious from Chase's lack of concern that he

wasn't going to invite her to stay at the ranch so they could resolve their differences—which was what Letty had hoped he'd do.

"If Lonny *does* object, I'll simply find someplace in town."

"Do you have enough money?"

"Yes..." Letty said, striving to sound casual.

"I'll be happy to provide whatever you need."

Chase spoke with such a flippant air that it cut her to the quick. "I won't take any money from you."

Chase shrugged. "Fine."

Everything in Letty wanted to shout at him to give her some sign, anything, that would show her he wanted her to stay. It was the whole reason she was staging this. His nonchalant response was so painful, that not breaking down, not weeping, was all Letty could manage.

"Is this what you really want?" she asked in a small voice.

"Like I said before, if you're set on leaving, I'm not going to stop you."

Letty reached down for her suitcase, tightening her fingers around the handle. "I'll get Cricket at school. I'll think up some excuse to tell her." She made it all the way to the back door before Chase stopped her.

"Letty..."

She whirled around, her heart ringing with excitement until she saw the look in his eyes.

"Before you go, there's something I need to ask you," he said, his face drawn. "Is there any possibility you could be pregnant?"

His question seemed to echo against the walls.

"Letty?"

She met his gaze. Some of his arrogance was gone,

replaced with a tenderness that had been far too rare these past few hours. "No," she whispered, her voice hardly audible.

Chase's eyes closed, but she didn't know if he felt regret or relief. The way things had been going, she didn't want to know.

"I…went to the hillside," she said in a low voice that wavered slightly despite her effort to control it. She squared her shoulders, then continued. "There were several head of cattle there. The brand is Wilber's."

Chase clenched his jaw so tightly that the sides of his face went pale under his tan. "So you know," he said, his voice husky and filled with dread. His gaze skirted hers, fists at his sides.

Letty was baffled. Chase's first response to the fact that she'd seen his neighbor's cattle on his property made no sense. She had no idea why he'd react like that.

Then it struck her. "You sold those acres to Mr. Wilber, didn't you? Why?" That land had been in Chase's family for over three generations. Letty couldn't figure out what would be important enough for him to relinquish those acres. Not once in all the weeks they'd been married or before had he given her any indication that he was financially strapped.

"I don't understand," she said—and suddenly she did. "There wasn't any insurance money for my surgery, was there, Chase?"

She'd been so unsuspecting, so confident when he'd told her everything had been taken care of. She should've known—in fact, did know—that an insurance company wouldn't cover a preexisting condition without a lengthy waiting period.

"Chase?" She held his eyes with her own. Incredulous, shocked, she set the suitcase down and took one small step toward her husband. "Why did you lie to me about the insurance?"

He tunneled his fingers through his hair.

"Why would you do something like that? It doesn't make any sense." Very little of this day had. "Didn't you realize the state had already agreed to cover all the expenses?"

"You hated being a charity case. I saw the look in your eyes when I found your welfare check. It was killing you to accept that money."

"Of course I hated it, but I managed to swallow my pride. It was necessary. But what you did wasn't. Why would you sell your land? I just can't believe it." Chase loved every square inch of Spring Valley. Parting with a single acre would be painful, let alone the prime land near the creek. It would be akin to his cutting off one of his fingers.

Chase turned away from her and walked over to the sink. His shoulders jerked in a hard shrug as he braced his hands on the edge. "All right, if you must know. I did it because I wanted you to marry me."

"But you said the marriage was for Cricket's sake... in case anything happened to me.... Then you could raise her."

"That was an excuse." The words seemed to be wrenched from him. After a long pause, he added, "I love you, Letty." It was all the explanation he gave her.

"I love you, too... I always have," she whispered, awed by what he'd done and, more importantly, the reason behind it. "I told you only three hours ago how I felt about you, but you practically threw it back in my face.

If you love me so much," she murmured, "why couldn't you let me know it? Would that have been so wrong?"

"I didn't want you to feel trapped."

"Trapped?" How could Chase possibly view their marriage in such a light? He made it sound as if he'd taken her hostage!

"Sooner or later I realized you'd want to return to California. I knew that when I asked you to marry me. I accepted it."

"That's ridiculous!" Letty cried. "I don't ever want to go back. There's nothing for me there. Everything that's ever been good in my life is right here with you."

Chase turned to face her. "What about the fight you and Lonny had about your mother? You said—"

"I realized how wrong I was about Mom," she interrupted, gesturing with her hands. "My mother was a wonderful woman, but more significant than that, she was fulfilled as a person. I'm not going to say she had an easy life—we both know differently. But she loved the challenge here. She loved her art, too, and found ways to express her talent. I was just too blind to recognize it. I was so caught up in striving toward my dreams, I failed to see that my happiness was right here in Red Springs with you. The biggest mistake I ever made was leaving you. Do you honestly believe I'd do it again?"

A look of hope crept into Chase's eyes.

"Telling me I'm free to walk away from you is one thing," Letty said softly. "But you made it sound as if you wanted me gone—as if you couldn't wait to get me out of your life. You weren't even willing to give us a chance. That hurt more than anything."

"I was afraid to," he admitted, his voice low.

"Over and over again, you kept saying that you

wouldn't stop me from leaving. It was almost as if you'd been waiting for it to happen because I'd been such a disappointment to you."

"Letty, no, I swear that isn't true."

"Then why are you standing way over there—and I'm way over here?"

"Oh, Letty." He covered the space between them in three giant strides, wrapping his arms around her. When he lifted his head, their eyes melted together. "I love you, Letty, more than I thought it was possible to care about anyone. I haven't told you that, and I was wrong. You deserve to hear the words."

"Chase, you didn't need to say them for me to know how you feel. That's what was so confusing. I couldn't doubt you loved me, yet you made my leaving sound like some long-anticipated event."

"I couldn't let you know how much I was hurting."

"But I was hurting, too."

"I know, my love, I know."

He rained hot, urgent kisses down upon her face. She directed his mouth to hers, and his kiss intensified. Letty threaded her fingers through his hair, glorying in the closeness they shared. She was humbled by the sacrifice he'd made for her. He could have given her no greater proof of his love.

"Chase." His name was a broken cry on her lips. "The land…you sold… I can't bear to think of you losing it."

He caressed her face. "It's not as bad as it sounds. I have the option of buying it back at a future date, and I will."

"But—"

He silenced her with his mouth, kissing away her

objections and concerns. Then he tore his mouth from hers and brought it to the hollow of her throat, kissing her there. "I would gladly have sold all of Spring Valley if it had been necessary."

Letty felt tears gather in her eyes. Tears of gratitude and joy and need.

"You've given me so much," he whispered. "My life was so empty until you came back and brought Cricket with you. I love her, Letty, as if she were our own. I want to adopt her and give her my name."

Letty nodded through her tears, knowing that Cricket would want that, too.

Chase inhaled deeply, then exhaled a long, slow breath. "As much as I wanted you to stay, I couldn't let you know that. When I asked if you might be pregnant, it was a desperate attempt by a desperate man to find a way to keep you here, despite all my claims to the contrary. I think my heart dropped to my feet when you told me you weren't."

Letty wasn't sure she understood.

He stared down at her with a tender warmth. "I don't know if I can explain this, but when I mentioned the possibility of you being pregnant, I had a vision of two little boys."

Letty smiled. "Twins?"

"No," Chase said softly. "They were a year or so apart. I saw them clearly, standing beside each other, and somehow I knew that those two were going to be our sons. The day you had the surgery—I saw them then, too. I wanted those children so badly.... Today, when you were about to walk out the door, I didn't know if you'd ever come back. I knew if you left me, the emptiness would return, and I didn't think I could bear it. I tried to prepare myself for your going, but it didn't work."

"I couldn't have stayed away for long. My heart's here with you. You taught me to forgive myself for the past and cherish whatever the future holds."

His eyes drifted shut. "We have so much, Letty." He was about to say more when the kitchen door burst open and Cricket came rushing into the room.

Chase broke away from Letty just in time for the five-year-old to vault into his arms. "I have a new friend, and her name's Karen and she's got a pony, too. I like school a whole bunch, and Mrs. Webber let me hand out some papers and said I could be her helper every day."

Chase hugged the little girl. "I'm glad you like school so much, sweetheart." Then he put his hand on Letty's shoulder, pulling her to him.

Letty leaned into his strength and closed her eyes, savoring these few moments of contentment. She'd found her happiness in Chase. She'd come home, knowing she might die, and instead had discovered life in its most abundant form. Spring Valley was their future—here was where they'd thrive. Here was where their sons would be born.

Cricket came to her mother's side, and Letty drew her close. As she did, she looked out the kitchen window. The Wyoming sky had never seemed bluer. Or filled with greater promise.

* * * * *

Also available from RaeAnne Thayne

HQN Books

Visit the Author Profile page
at Harlequin.com for more titles.

A COLD CREEK REUNION

RaeAnne Thayne

To romance readers who, like me,
love happily ever afters.

Chapter 1

He loved these guys like his own brothers, but some-times Taft Bowman wanted to take a fire hose to his whole blasted volunteer fire department.

This was their second swift-water rescue training in a month—not to mention that he had been holding these regularly since he became battalion chief five years earlier—and they still struggled to toss a throw bag anywhere close to one of the three "victims" float-ing down Cold Creek in wet suits and helmets.

"You've got to keep in mind the flow of the water and toss it downstream enough that they ride the current to the rope," he instructed for about the six-hundredth time. One by one, the floaters—in reality, other volun-teer firefighters on his thirty-person crew—stopped at the catch line strung across the creek and began work-ing their way hand over hand to the bank.

Fortunately, even though the waters were plenty frigid this time of year, they were about a month away from the real intensity of spring runoff, which was why he was training his firefighters for water rescues now.

With its twists and turns and spectacular surroundings on the west slope of the Tetons, Cold Creek had started gaining popularity with kayakers. He enjoyed floating the river himself. But between the sometimes-inexperienced outdoor-fun seekers and the occasional Pine Gulch citizen who strayed too close to the edge of the fast-moving water, his department was called out on at least a handful of rescues each season and he wanted them to be ready.

"Okay, let's try it one more time. Terry, Charlie, Bates, you three take turns with the throw bag. Luke, Cody, Tom, stagger your jumps by about five minutes this time around to give us enough time on this end to rescue whoever is ahead of you."

He set the team in position and watched upstream as Luke Orosco, his second in command, took a running leap into the water, angling his body feetfirst into the current. "Okay, Terry. He's coming. Are you ready? Time it just right. One, two, three. Now!"

This time, the rope sailed into the water just downstream of the diver and Taft grinned. "That's it, that's it. Perfect. Now instruct him to attach the rope."

For once, the rescue went smoothly. He was watching for Cody Shepherd to jump in when the radio clipped to his belt suddenly crackled with static.

"Chief Bowman, copy."

The dispatcher sounded unusually flustered and Taft's instincts borne of fifteen years of firefighting and paramedic work instantly kicked in. "Yeah, I copy. What's up, Kelly?"

"I've got a report of a small structure fire at the inn, three hundred twenty Cold Creek Road."

He stared as the second rescue went off without a hitch. "Come again?" he couldn't help asking, adrenaline pulsing through him. Structure fires were a rarity in the quiet town of Pine Gulch. Really a rarity. The last time had been a creosote chimney fire four months ago that a single ladder-truck unit had put out in about five minutes.

"Yes, sir. The hotel is evacuating at this time."

He muttered an oath. Half his crew was currently in wet suits, but at least they were only a few hundred yards away from the station house, with the engines and the turnout gear.

"Shut it down," he roared through his megaphone. "We've got a structure fire at the Cold Creek Inn. Grab your gear. This is not a drill."

To their credit, his crew immediately caught the gravity of the situation. The last floater was quickly grabbed out of the water and everybody else rushed to the new fire station the town had finally voted to bond for two years earlier.

Less than four minutes later—still too long in his book but not bad for volunteers—he had a full crew headed toward the Cold Creek Inn on a ladder truck and more trained volunteers pouring in to hurriedly don their turnout gear.

The inn, a rambling wood structure with two single-story wings leading off a main two-story building, was on the edge of Pine Gulch's small downtown, about a mile away from the station. He quickly assessed the situation as they approached. He couldn't see flames yet, but he did see a thin plume of black smoke coming from a window on the far end of the building's east wing.

He noted a few guests milling around on the lawn and had just an instant to feel a pang of sympathy for the owner. Poor Mrs. Pendleton had enough trouble finding guests for her gracefully historic but undeniably run-down inn.

A fire and forced evacuation probably wouldn't do much to increase the appeal of the place.

"Luke, you take Pete and make sure everybody's out. Shep, come with me for the assessment. You all know the drill."

He and Cody Shepherd, a young guy in the last stages of his fire and paramedic training, headed into the door closest to where he had seen the smoke.

Somebody had already been in here with a fire extinguisher, he saw. The fire was mostly out but the charred curtains were still smoking, sending out that inky-black plume.

The room looked to be under renovation. It didn't have a bed and the carpet had been pulled up. Everything was wet and he realized the ancient sprinkler system must have come on and finished the job the fire extinguisher had started.

"Is that it?" Shep asked with a disgruntled look.

"Sorry, should have let you have the honors." He held the fire extinguisher out to the trainee. "Want a turn?"

Shep snorted but grabbed the fire extinguisher and sprayed another layer of completely unnecessary foam on the curtains.

"Not much excitement—but at least nobody was hurt. It's a wonder this place didn't go up years ago. We'll have to get the curtains out of here and have Engine Twenty come inside and check for hot spots."

He called in over his radio that the fire had been contained to one room and ordered in the team whose specialty was making sure the flames hadn't traveled inside the walls to silently spread to other rooms.

When he walked back outside, Luke headed over to him. "Not much going on, huh? Guess some of us should have stayed in the water."

"We'll do more swift-water work next week during training," he said. "Everybody else but Engine Twenty can go back to the station."

As he spoke to Luke, he spotted Jan Pendleton standing some distance away from the building. Even from here, he could see the distress on her plump, wrinkled features. She was holding a little dark-haired girl in her arms, probably a traumatized guest. Poor thing.

A younger woman stood beside her and from this distance he had only a strange impression, as if she was somehow standing on an island of calm amid the chaos of the scene, the flashing lights of the emergency vehicles, shouts between his crew members, the excited buzz of the crowd.

And then the woman turned and he just about tripped over a snaking fire hose somebody shouldn't have left there.

Laura.

He froze and for the first time in fifteen years as a firefighter, he forgot about the incident, his mission, just what the hell he was doing here.

Laura.

Ten years. He hadn't seen her in all that time, since the week before their wedding when she had given him back his ring and left town. Not just town. She had left the whole damn country, as if she couldn't run far enough to get away from him.

Some part of him desperately wanted to think he had made some kind of mistake. It couldn't be her. That was just some other slender woman with a long sweep of honey-blond hair and big blue, unforgettable eyes. But no, it was definitely Laura, standing next to her mother. Sweet and lovely.

Not his.

"Chief, we're not finding any hot spots." Luke approached him. Just like somebody turned back up the volume on his flat-screen, he jerked away from memories of pain and loss and aching regret.

"You're certain?"

"So far. The sprinkler system took a while to kick in and somebody with a fire extinguisher took care of the rest. Tom and Nate are still checking the integrity of the internal walls."

"Good. That's good. Excellent work."

His assistant chief gave him a wary look. "You okay, Chief? You look upset."

He huffed out a breath. "It's a fire, Luke. It could have been potentially disastrous. With the ancient wiring in this old building, it's a wonder the whole thing didn't go up."

"I was thinking the same thing," Luke said.

He was going to have to go over there and talk to Mrs. Pendleton—and by default, Laura. He didn't want to. He wanted to stand here and pretend he hadn't seen her. But he was the fire chief. He couldn't hide out just because he had a painful history with the daughter of the property owner.

Sometimes he hated his job.

He made his way toward the women, grimly aware of his heart pounding in his chest as if he had been the one diving into Cold Creek for training.

Laura stiffened as he approached but she didn't meet

his gaze. Her mother looked at him out of wide, frightened eyes and her arms tightened around the girl in her arms.

Despite everything, his most important job was calming her fears. "Mrs. Pendleton, you'll be happy to know the fire is under control."

"Of course it's under control." Laura finally faced him, her lovely features cool and impassive. "It was under control before your trucks ever showed up—ten minutes after we called the fire in, by the way."

Despite all the things he might have wanted to say to her, he had to first bristle at any implication that their response time might be less than adequate. "Seven, by my calculations. Would have been half that except we were in the middle of water rescue training when the call from dispatch came in."

"I guess you would have been ready, then, if any of our guests had decided to jump into Cold Creek to avoid the flames."

Funny, he didn't remember her being this tart when they had been engaged. He remembered sweetness and joy and light. Until he had destroyed all that.

"Chief Bowman, when will we be able to allow our guests to return to their rooms?" Jan Pendleton spoke up, her voice wobbling a little. The little girl in her arms—who shared Laura's eye color, he realized now, along with the distinctive features of someone born with Down syndrome—patted her cheek.

"Gram, don't cry."

Jan visibly collected herself and gave the girl a tired smile.

"They can return to get their belongings as long as they're not staying in the rooms adjacent to where the fire started. I'll have my guys stick around about an hour or so to keep an eye on some hot spots." He paused, wishing he didn't have to be the bearer of this particular bad news. "I'm going to leave the final decision up to you about your guests staying here overnight, but to be honest, I'm not sure it's completely safe for guests to stay here tonight. No matter how careful we are, sometimes embers can flare up again hours later."

"We have a dozen guests right now." Laura looked at him directly and he was almost sure he saw a hint of hostility there. Annoyance crawled under his skin. *She* dumped him, a week before their wedding. If anybody here had the right to be hostile, he ought to be the first one in line. "What are we supposed to do with them?"

Their past didn't matter right now, not when people in his town needed his help. "We can talk to the Red Cross about setting up a shelter, or we can check with some of the other lodgings in town, maybe the Cavazos' guest cabins, and see if they might have room to take a few."

Mrs. Pendleton closed her eyes. "This is a disaster."

"But a fixable one, Mom. We'll figure something out." She squeezed her mother's arm.

"Any idea what might have started the fire?" He had to ask.

Laura frowned and something that looked oddly like guilt shifted across her lovely features. "Not the *what* exactly, but most likely the *who*."

"Oh?"

"Alexandro Santiago. Come here, young man."

He followed her gaze and for the first time, he noticed a young dark-haired boy of about six or seven sitting on the curb, watching the activity at the scene with a sort of avid fascination in his huge dark brown eyes. The boy didn't have her blond, blue-eyed coloring, but he shared her wide, mobile mouth, slender nose and high cheekbones, and was undoubtedly her child.

The kid didn't budge from the curb for a long, drawn-out moment, but he finally rose slowly to his feet and headed toward them as if he were on his way to bury his dog in the backyard.

"Alex, tell the fireman what started the fire."

The boy shifted his stance, avoiding the gazes of both his mother and Taft. "Do I have to?"

"Yes," Laura said sternly.

The kid fidgeted a little more and finally sighed. "Okay. I found a lighter in one of the empty rooms. The ones being fixed up." He spoke with a very slight, barely discernible accent. "I never saw one before and I only wanted to see how it worked. I didn't mean to start a fire, *es la verdad.* But the curtains caught fire and I yelled and then *mi madre* came in with the fire extinguisher."

Under other circumstances he might have been amused at the no-nonsense way the kid told the story and how he manipulated events to make it seem as if everything had just sort of happened without any direct involvement on his part.

But this could have been a potentially serious situation, a crumbling old fire hazard like the inn.

He hated to come off hard-nosed and mean, but he had to make the kid understand the gravity. Education was a huge part of his job and a responsibility he took very seriously. "That was a very dangerous thing to do. People could have been seriously hurt. If your mother hadn't been able to get to the room fast enough with the fire extinguisher, the flames could have spread from room to room and burned down the whole hotel and everything in it."

To his credit, the boy met his gaze. Embarrassment and shame warred on his features. "I know. It was stupid. I'm really, really sorry."

"The worst part of it is, I have told you again and again not to play with matches or lighters or anything else that can cause a fire. We've talked about the dangers." Laura glowered at her son, who squirmed.

"I just wanted to see how it worked," he said, his voice small.

"You won't do it again, will you?" Taft said.

"Never. Never, ever."

"Good, because we're pretty strict about this kind of thing around here. Next time you'll have to go to jail."

The boy gave him a wide-eyed look, but then sighed with relief when he noticed Taft's half grin. "I won't do it again, I swear. Pinky promise."

"Excellent."

"Hey, Chief," Lee Randall called from the engine. "We're having a little trouble with the hose retractor again. Can you give us a hand?"

"Yeah. Be there in a sec," he called back, grateful for any excuse to escape the awkwardness of seeing her again.

"Excuse me, won't you?" he said to the Pendleton women and the children.

"Of course." Jan Pendleton gave him an earnest look. "Please tell your firefighters how very much we appreciate them, don't we, Laura?"

"Absolutely," she answered with a dutiful tone, but he noticed she pointedly avoided meeting his gaze.

"Bye, Chief." The darling little girl in Jan's arm

gave him a generous smile. Oh, she was a charmer, he thought.

"See you later."

The girl beamed at him and waved as he headed away, feeling as if somebody had wrapped a fire hose around his neck for the past ten minutes.

She was here. Really here. Blue eyes, cute kids and all.

Laura Pendleton, Santiago now. He had loved her with every bit of his young heart and she had walked away from him without a second glance.

Now she was here and he had no way to avoid her, not living in a small town like Pine Gulch that had only one grocery store, a couple of gas stations and a fire station only a few blocks from her family's hotel.

He was swamped with memories suddenly, memories he didn't want and didn't know what to do with.

She was back. And here he had been thinking lately how lucky he was to be fire chief of a small town with only six thousand people that rarely saw any disasters.

Taft Bowman.

Laura watched him head back into the action—which, really, wasn't much action at all, given that the fire had been extinguished before any of them arrived. He paused here and there in the parking lot to talk to his crew, snap out orders, adjust some kind of mechanical thing on the sleek red fire truck.

Seeing him in action was nothing new. When they had been dating, she sometimes went on ride-alongs, mostly because she couldn't bear to be separated from him. She remembered now how Taft had always seemed comfortable and in control of any situation, whether responding to a medical emergency or dealing with a grass fire.

Apparently that hadn't changed in the decade since she had seen him. He also still had that very sexy, lean-hipped walk, even under the layers of turnout gear. She watched him for just a moment, then forced herself to look away. This little tingle of remembered desire inside her was wrong on so many levels, completely twisted and messed up.

After all these years and all the pain, all those shards of crushed dreams she finally had to sweep up and throw away, how could he still have the power to affect her at all? She should be cool and impervious to him, completely untouched.

When she finally made the decision to come home after Javier's death, she had known she would inevitably run into Taft. Pine Gulch was a small town after all. No matter how much a person might wish to, it was generally tough to avoid someone forever.

When she thought about it—and she would be lying to herself if she said she *hadn't* thought about it—she had foolishly imagined she could greet him with only a polite smile and a *Nice to see you again,* remaining completely impervious to the man.

Their shared history was a long time ago. Another lifetime, it seemed. She had made the only possible choice back then and had completely moved on with her life, had married someone else, given birth to two children and put Pine Gulch far in her past.

As much as she had loved him once, Taft was really just a small chapter in her life. Or so she told herself anyway. She had been naively certain she had dealt with the hurt and betrayal and the deep sense of loss long ago.

Maybe she should have put a little more energy and effort into making certain of all that before she packed up her children and moved thousands of miles from the only home they had ever known.

If she'd had a little energy to spare, she might have given it more thought, but the past six months seemed like a whirlwind, first trying to deal with Javier's estate and the vast debts he had left behind, then that desperate scramble to juggle her dwindling bank account and two hungry children in expensive Madrid, and finally the grim realization that she couldn't do it by herself and had no choice but to move her little family across the world and back to her mother.

She had been focused on survival, on doing what she thought was right for her children. She supposed she really hadn't wanted to face the reality that moving back also meant dealing with Taft again—until it smacked her upside the head, thanks to her rascal of a son and his predilection for finding trouble wherever he could.

"What are we going to do?" Her mother fretted beside her. She set Maya down on the concrete sidewalk, and the girl immediately scampered beside Alex and stood holding her brother's hand while they watched the firefighters now cleaning up the scene and driving away. "This is going to ruin us!"

Laura put an arm around her mother's plump shoulders, guilt slicing through her. She should have been watching her son more carefully; she certainly knew better than to give him any free rein. She had allowed herself to become distracted checking in some guests—the young married couple on spring break from graduate school in Washington who had found more excitement than they had probably anticipated when their hotel caught fire before they had even seen their room.

While she was busy with them, Alex must have slipped out of the office and wandered to the wing of the hotel they were currently renovating. She still couldn't believe he had found a lighter somewhere. Maybe a previous guest had left it or one of the subcontractors who had been coming in and out the past week or so.

It really *was* a miracle her son hadn't been injured or burned the whole place down.

"You heard Chief Bowman. The fire and smoke damage was contained to only one room, so that's good news."

"How is any of this good news?" In the flash of the emergency vehicles as they pulled away, her mother's features looked older somehow and her hands shook as she pushed a stray lock of carefully colored hair away.

Despite Taft and all the memories that had suddenly been dredged up simply by exchanging a few words with the man, she didn't regret coming back to Pine Gulch. The irony was, she thought she was coming home because she needed her mother's help only to discover how very much Jan needed hers.

Care and upkeep on this crumbling twenty-room inn were obviously wearing on her mother. Jan had been deeply grateful to turn some of those responsibilities over to her only daughter.

"It could be much worse, Mom. We have to focus on that. No one was hurt. That's the important thing. And outdated as it is, the sprinkler system worked better than we might have expected. That's another plus.

Besides, look at it this way—now insurance will cover some of the repairs we already planned."

"I suppose. But what are we going to do with the guests?" Her mother seemed defeated, overwhelmed, all but wringing her hands.

Laura hugged her again. "Don't worry about anything. In fact, why don't you take the children back to the house? I think they've had enough excitement for one afternoon."

"Do you think Chief Bowman will consider it safe?"

Laura glanced over at the three-bedroom cottage behind the inn where she had spent her childhood. "It's far enough from the action. I can't see why it would be a problem. Meantime, I'll start making phone calls. We'll find places for everyone and for our reservations for the next few nights while the smoke damage clears out. We'll get through this just like everything else."

"I'm so glad you're here, my dear. I don't know what I would do without you."

If she *hadn't* been here—along with her daughter and her little firebug of a son—none of this would have happened.

"So am I, Mom," she answered. It was the truth, despite having to confront a certain very sexy fire chief with whom she shared a tangled history.

"Oh, I should go talk to poor Mr. Baktiri. He probably doesn't quite understand what's going on."

One of their long-term guests stood in the middle of the lawn, looking at the hectic scene with confusion. She remembered Mr. Baktiri from when she was a girl. He and his wife used to run the drive-in on the outskirts of town. Mrs. Baktiri had passed away and Mr. Baktiri had moved with his son to Idaho Falls, but he apparently hated it there. Once a month or so, he would escape back to Pine Gulch to visit his wife's graveside.

Her mother gave him substantially reduced rates on their smallest room, where he stayed for a week or two at a time until his son would come down from Idaho Falls to take him back home. It wasn't a very economically feasible operating procedure, but she couldn't fault her mother for her kindness.

She had the impression Mr. Baktiri might be suffering from mild dementia and she supposed familiar surroundings were a comfort to him.

"Mommy. Lights." Maya hugged her legs and looked up, the flashing emergency lights reflecting in her thick glasses.

"I know, sweetie. They're bright, aren't they?"

"Pretty."

"I suppose they are, in a way."

Trust Maya to find joy in any situation. It was her child's particular skill and she was deeply grateful for it.

She had a million things to do, most pressing to find somewhere for their guests to spend the night, but for now she gathered this precious child in her arms.

Out of the corner of her gaze, she saw Alex edge toward them somewhat warily.

"Come here, *niño,*" she murmured.

He sank into her embrace and she held both children close. This was the important thing. As she had told her mother, they would get through this minor setback. She was a survivor. She had survived a broken heart and broken engagement and then a disaster of a marriage.

She could get through a little thing like a minor fire with no problem.

Chapter 2

"Guess who I saw in town the other day."

Taft grabbed one of his sister's delicious dinner rolls from the basket being passed around his family's dining-room table and winked at Caidy. "Me, doing something awesome and heroic, probably. Fighting a fire. Saving someone's life. I don't know. Could be anything."

His niece, Destry, and Gabrielle Parsons, whose older sister was marrying Taft's twin brother, Trace, in a few months, both giggled—just as he had intended—but Caidy only rolled her eyes. "News flash. Not everything is about you, Taft. But oddly, in a way, this is."

"Who did you see?" he asked, though he was aware of a glimmer of uneasy trepidation, already expecting what was coming next.

"I didn't have a chance to talk to her. I just happened to see her while I was driving," Caidy said.

"Who?" he asked again, teetering on the brink of annoyance.

"Laura Pendleton," Caidy announced.

"Not Pendleton anymore," Ridge, their older brother and Destry's father, corrected.

"That's right," Trace chimed in from the other side of the table, where he was holding hands with Becca. How the heck did they manage to eat when they couldn't seem to keep their hands off each other? Taft wondered.

"She got married to some guy while she was living in Spain and they had a couple of kids," Trace went on. "I hear one of them was involved in all the excitement the other day at the inn."

Taft pictured her kid solemnly promising he wouldn't play with matches again. He'd picked up the definite vibe that the kid was a mischievous little rascal, but for all that, his sincerity had rung true.

"Yeah. Apparently her older kid, Alex, was a little too curious about a lighter he found in an empty room and caught some curtains on fire."

"And you had to ride to her rescue?" Caidy gave him a wide-eyed look. "Gosh, that must have been awkward for both of you."

Taft reached for more mashed potatoes, hoping the heat on his face could be attributed to the steaming bowl.

"Why would it be? Everything was fine," he muttered.

Okay, that was a lie, but his family didn't necessarily need to know he hadn't been able to stop thinking about Laura for the past few days. Every time he had a quiet moment, her blue eyes and delicate features would pop into his head and some other half-forgotten memory of their time together would emerge like the Tetons rising out of a low fog bank.

That he couldn't seem to stop them annoyed him. He had worked damn hard to forget her after she walked away. What was he supposed to do now that she was back in town and he couldn't escape her or her kids or the weight of all his mistakes?

"You'll have to catch me up here." Becca, Trace's fiancée, looked confused as she reached for her glass. "Who's Laura Pendleton? I'm taking a wild guess here that she must be related to Mrs. Pendleton at the inn somehow—a client of mine, by the way—but why would it be awkward to have Taft put out a fire at the inn?"

"No reason really." Caidy flashed him a quick look. "Just that Taft and Laura were engaged once."

He fidgeted with his mashed potatoes, drawing his fork in a neat little firebreak to keep the gravy from spreading while he avoided the collective gaze of his beloved family. Why, again, had he once enjoyed these Sunday dinners?

"Engaged? Taft?" He didn't need to look at his future sister-in-law to hear the surprise in her voice.

"I know," his twin brother said. "Hard to believe, right?"

He looked up just in time to see Becca quickly try to hide her shocked gaze. She was too kindhearted to let him see how stunning she found the news, which somehow bothered him even more.

Okay, maybe he had a bit of a reputation in town—most of it greatly exaggerated—as a bit of a player. Becca knew him by now. She should know how silly it all was.

"When was this?" she asked with interest. "Recently?"

"Years ago," Ridge said. "He and Laura dated just out of high school—"

"College," he muttered. "She was in college." Okay, she had been a freshman in college. But she wasn't in high school, damn it. That point seemed important somehow.

"They were inseparable," Trace interjected.

Ridge picked up where he'd left off. "And Taft proposed right around the time Laura graduated from the Montana State."

"What happened?" Becca asked.

He really didn't want to talk about this. What he wouldn't give for a good emergency call right now. Nothing big. No serious personal injury or major property damage. How about a shed fire or a kid stuck in a well or something?

"We called things off."

"The week before the wedding," Caidy added.

Oh, yes. Don't forget to add that little salacious detail.

"It was a mutual decision," he lied, repeating the blatant fiction that Laura had begged him to uphold. Mutual decision. Right. If by *mutual* he meant *Laura* and if by *decision* he meant *crush-the-life-out-of-a-guy blow*.

Laura had dumped him. That was the cold, hard truth. A week before their wedding, after all the plans and deposits and dress fittings, she had given him back his ring and told him she couldn't marry him.

"Why are we talking about ancient history?" he asked.

"Not so ancient anymore," Trace said. "Not if Laura's back in town."

He was very much afraid his brother was right. Whether he liked it or not, with her once more residing in Pine Gulch, their past together would be dredged up again—and not by just his family.

Questions would swirl around them. Everybody had to remember that they had been just a few days away from walking down the aisle of the little church in town when things ended and Laura and her mother sent out those regrets and made phone calls announcing the big celebration wasn't happening—while he had gone down to the Bandito and gotten drunk and stayed that way until about a month or two after the wedding day that didn't happen.

She was back now, which meant that, like it or not, he would have to deal with everything he had shoved down ten years ago, all the emotions he had pretended weren't important in order to get through the deep, aching loss of her.

He couldn't blame his family for their curiosity—not even Trace, his twin and best friend, knew the full story about everything that had happened between him and Laura. He had always considered it his private business.

His family had loved her. Who didn't? Laura had a knack for drawing people toward her, finding commonalities. She and his mother used to love discussing the art world and painting techniques. His mother had been an artist, only becoming renowned around the time of her murder. While Laura hadn't any particular skill in that direction, she had shared a genuine appreciation for his parents' extensive art collection.

His father had adored her, too, and had often told Taft that Laura was the best thing that would ever happen to him.

He looked up from the memory to find Becca's eyes filled with a compassion that made him squirm and lose whatever appetite he might have had left.

"I'm sorry," she murmured in that kind way she had. "Mutual decision or not, it still must have been painful. Is it hard for you to see her again?"

He faked a nonchalant look. "Hard? Why would it be hard? It was all a decade ago. She's moved on. I've moved on. No big deal."

Ridge gave what sounded like a fake cough and Trace had the same skeptical expression on his face he always wore when Taft was trying to talk him into living a little, doing something wild and adventurous for a change.

How was it possible to love his siblings and at the same time want to throw a few punches around the table, just on general principles?

Becca eyed him and then his brothers warily as if sensing his discomfort, then she quickly changed the subject. "How's the house coming?" she asked.

His brother wasn't nearly good enough for her, he decided, seizing the diversion. "Good. I've got only a couple more rooms to drywall. Should be done soon. After six months, the place is starting to look like a real house inside now."

"I stopped by the other day and peeked in the windows," Caidy confessed. "It's looking great."

"Give me a call next time and I can swing by and give you the tour, even if I'm at the fire station. You haven't been by in a month or so. You'll be surprised at how far along it is these days."

After years of renting a convenient but small apartment near the fire station, he had finally decided it was time to build a real house. The two-story log house was set on five acres near the mouth of Cold Creek Canyon.

"How about the barn and the pasture?" Ridge asked, rather predictably. Over the years, Taft had bred a couple mares to a stallion with excellent lines he had picked up for a steal from a rancher down on his luck up near Wood River. He had traded and sold the colts until he now had about six horses he'd been keeping at his family's ranch.

"The fence is in. I'd like to get the barn up before I move the horses over, if you don't mind keeping them a little longer."

"That's not what I meant. You know we've got plenty of room here. You can keep them here forever if you want."

Maybe if he had his horses closer he might actually ride them once in a while instead of only stopping by to visit when he came for these Sunday dinners.

"When do you think all the work will be done?" Becca asked.

"I'm hoping by mid-May. Depends on how much free time I can find to finish things up inside."

"If you need a hand, let me know," Ridge offered quietly.

"Same goes," Trace added.

Both of them had crazy-busy lives: Ridge running the ranch and raising Destry on his own and Trace as the overworked chief of police for an understaffed small-town force—in addition to planning his future together with Becca and Gabi. Their sincere offers to help touched him.

"I should be okay," he answered. "The hard work is done now and I only have the fun stuff to finish."

"I always thought there was something just a little crazy about you." Caidy shook her head. "I must be right, especially if you think finish work and painting are fun."

"I like to paint stuff," Destry said. "I can help you, Uncle Taft."

"Me, too!" Gabrielle exclaimed. "Oh, can we?"

Trouble followed the two of these girls around like one of Caidy's rescue dogs. He had visions of paint spread all over the woodwork he had been slaving over the past month. "Thanks, girls. That's really sweet of you. I'm sure Ridge can find something for you to touch up around here. That fence down by the creek was looking like it needed a new coat."

"There's always something that needs painting around here," Ridge answered. "As soon as the weather warms up a little at night, I can put you both to work."

"Will you pay us?" Gabrielle asked, always the opportunist.

Ridge chuckled. "We can negotiate terms with your attorney."

Caidy asked Becca—said attorney—a question about their upcoming June wedding and attention shifted away from Taft, much to his relief. He listened to the conversation of his family, aware of this low simmer of restlessness that had become a familiar companion.

Ever since Trace and Becca found each other and fell in love, he had been filled with this vague unease, as if something about his world had shifted a little. He loved his brother. More than that, he respected him. Trace was his best friend and Taft could never begrudge him the happiness he had found with Becca and Gabi, but ever since they announced their engagement, he felt weird and more than a little off-balance.

Seeing Laura and her kids the other day had only intensified that odd feeling.

He had never been a saint—he would be the first to admit that and his family would probably stand in line right behind him—but he tried to live a decent life. His general philosophy about the world ran parallel to the premier motto of every emergency medical worker as well as others in the medical field: Primum Non Nocere. First, Do No Harm.

He did his best. He was a firefighter and paramedic and he enjoyed helping people of his community and protecting property. If he didn't find great satisfaction in it, he would find something else to do. Maybe pounding nails for a living because he enjoyed that, too.

Despite his best efforts in the whole *do no harm* arena, he remembered each and every failure.

He had two big regrets in his life, and Laura Pendleton was involved in both of them.

He had hurt her. Those months leading up to her ultimate decision to break things off had been filled with one wound after another. He knew it. Hell, he had known it at the time, but that dark, angry man he had become after his parents' murder seemed like another creature who had emerged out of his skin to destroy everything good and right in his life.

He couldn't blame Laura for calling off their wedding. Not really. Even though it had hurt like the devil.

She had warned him she couldn't marry him unless he made serious changes, and he had stubbornly refused, giving her no choice but to stay true to her word. She had moved on, taken some exotic job in hotel management in Spain somewhere and a few years later married a man she met there.

The reminder of her marriage left him feeling petty and small. Yeah, he had hurt her, but his betrayal probably didn't hold a candle to everything else she had lost—her husband and the father of her children, whom he'd heard had drowned about six months earlier.

"Are you planning on eating any of that or just pushing it around your plate?"

He glanced up and, much to his shock, discovered Ridge was the only one left at the table. Everybody else had cleared off while he had been lost in thought, and he hadn't even noticed.

"Sorry. Been a long couple of days." He hoped his brother didn't notice the heat he could feel crawling over his features.

Ridge gave him a long look and Taft sighed, waiting for the inevitable words of advice from his brother.

As the oldest Bowman sibling left after their parents died, Ridge had taken custody of Caidy, who had been a teenager at the time. Even though Taft and Trace had both been in their early twenties, Ridge still tried to take over the role of father figure to them, too, whether they liked it or not—which they usually didn't.

Instead of a lecture, Ridge only sipped at his drink. "I was thinking about taking the girls for a ride up to check the fence line on the high pasture. Want to come along? A little mountain air might help clear your head."

He did love being on the back of a horse amid the pine and sage of the mountains overlooking the ranch, but he wasn't in the mood for more questions or sympathy from his family about Laura.

"To tell you the truth, I'm itching to get my hands

dirty. I think I'll head over to the house and put in a window frame or something."

Ridge nodded. "I know you've got plenty to do on your own place, but I figured this was worth mentioning, too. I heard the other day at the hardware store that Jan Pendleton is looking to hire somebody to help her with some renovations to the inn."

He snorted. As if Laura would ever let her mother hire him. He figured Ridge was joking but he didn't see any hint of humor in his brother's expression.

"Just saying. I thought you might be interested in helping Laura and her mother out a little."

Ah. Without actually offering a lecture, this must be Ridge's way of reminding Taft he owed Laura something. None of the rest of the family knew what had happened all those years ago, but he was pretty sure all of them blamed him.

And they were right.

Without answering, he shoved away from the table and grabbed his plate to carry it into the kitchen. First, do no harm. But once the harm had been done, a stand-up guy found some way to make it right. No matter how difficult.

Chapter 3

Laura stared at her mother, shock buzzing through her as if she had just bent down and licked an electrical outlet.

"Sorry, say that again. You did *what?*"

"I didn't think you'd mind, darling," her mother said, with a vague sort of smile as she continued stirring the chicken she was cooking for their dinner.

Are you completely mental? she wanted to yell. *How could you possibly think I wouldn't mind?*

She drew a deep, cleansing breath, clamping down on the words she wanted to blurt out. The children were, for once, staying out of trouble, driving cars around the floor of the living room and she watched them interact for a moment to calm herself.

Her mother was under a great deal of strain right now, financially and otherwise. She had to keep that in mind—not that stress alone could explain her mother making such an incomprehensible decision.

"Really, it was all your idea," Jan said calmly.

"*My* idea?" Impossible. Even in her most tangled nightmare, she never would have come up with this possible scenario.

"Yes. Weren't you just saying the other day how much it would help to have a carpenter on the staff to help with the repairs, especially now that we totally have to start from the ground up in the fire-damaged room?"

"I say a lot of things, Mom." *That doesn't mean I want you to rush out and enter into a deal with a particular devil named Taft Bowman.*

"I just thought you would appreciate the help, that's all. I know how much the fire has complicated your timeline for the renovation."

"Not really. Only one room was damaged and it was already on my schedule for renovations."

"Well, when Chief Bowman stopped by this morning to check on things after the excitement we had the other day—which I thought was a perfectly lovely gesture, by the way—he mentioned he could lend us a hand with any repairs in his free time. Honestly, darling, it seemed like the perfect solution."

Really? Having her daughter's ex-fiancé take an empty room at the inn for the next two weeks in exchange for a little skill with a miter saw was *perfect* in what possible alternative universe?

Her mother was as sharp as the proverbial tack. Jan Pendleton had been running the inn on her own since Laura's father died five years ago. While she didn't always agree with her mother's methods and might have run things differently if she had been home, Laura knew Jan had tried hard to keep the inn functioning all those years she had been living in Madrid.

But she still couldn't wrap her head around this one. "In theory, it is a good idea. A resident carpenter would come in very handy. But not Taft, for heaven's sake, Mom!"

Jan frowned in what appeared to be genuine confusion. "You mean because of your history together?"

"For a start. Seeing him again after all these years is more than a little awkward," she admitted.

Her mother continued to frown. "I'm sorry but I don't understand. What am I missing? You always insisted your breakup was a mutual decision. I distinctly remember you telling me over and over again you had both decided you were better off as friends."

Had she said that? She didn't remember much about that dark time other than her deep despair.

"You were so cool and calm after your engagement ended, making all those terrible phone calls, returning all those wedding presents. You acted like you didn't care at all. Honey, I honestly thought you wouldn't mind having Taft here now or I never would have taken him up on his suggestion."

Ah. Her lying little chickens were now coming home to roost. Laura fought the urge to bang her head on the old pine kitchen table a few dozen times.

Ten years ago, she had worked so hard to convince everyone involved that nobody's heart had been shattered by the implosion of their engagement. To her parents, she had put on a bright, happy face and pretended to be excited about the adventures awaiting her, knowing how crushed they would have been if they caught even a tiny glimmer of the truth—that inside her heart felt like a vast, empty wasteland.

How could she blame her mother for not seeing through her carefully constructed act to the stark and painful reality, especially when only a few years later, Laura was married to someone else and expecting Jan's first grandchild? It was unfair to be hurt, to wish Jan had somehow glimpsed the depth of her hidden heartache.

This, then, was her own fault. Well, hers and a certain opportunistic male who had always been very good at charming her mother—and every other female within a dozen miles of Pine Gulch.

"Okay, the carpentry work. I get that. Yes, we certainly need the help and Taft is very good with his hands." She refused to remember just *how* good those hands could be. "But did you have to offer him a room?"

Jan shrugged, adding a lemony sauce to the chicken that instantly started to burble, filling the kitchen with a delicious aroma. "That was his idea."

Oh, Laura was quite sure it *was* Taft's idea. The bigger question was *why?* What possible reason could he have for this sudden wish to stay at the inn? By the stunned look he had worn when he spotted her at the fire scene, she would have assumed he wanted to stay as far away from her as possible.

He had to find this whole situation as awkward and, yes, painful as she did.

Maybe it was all some twisted revenge plot. She had spurned him after all. Maybe he wanted to somehow punish her all these years later with shoddy carpentry work that would end up costing an arm and a leg to repair....

She sighed at her own ridiculous imaginings. Taft didn't work that way. Whatever his motive for making this arrangement with her mother, she had no doubt he would put his best effort into the job.

"Apparently his lease was up on the apartment where he's been living," Jan went on. "He's building a house in Cold Creek Canyon—which I've heard is perfectly lovely, by the way—but it won't be finished for a few more weeks. Think of how much you can save on paying for a carpenter, all in exchange only for letting him stay in a room that was likely to be empty anyway, the way our vacancy rate will be during the shoulder season until the summer tourist activity heats up. I honestly thought you would be happy about this. When Taft suggested it, the whole thing seemed like a good solution all the way around."

A good solution for everyone except *her!* How would she survive having him underfoot all the time, smiling at her out of those green eyes she had once adored so much, talking to her out of that delicious mouth she had tasted so many times?

She gave a tiny sigh and her mother sent her a careful look. "I can still tell him no. He was planning on bringing some of his things over in the morning, but I'll just give him a ring and tell him never mind. We can find someone else, honey, if having Taft here will make you too uncomfortable."

Her mother was completely sincere, she knew. Jan would call him in immediately if she had any idea how much Laura had grieved for the dreams they had once spun together.

For an instant, she was tempted to have her mother do exactly that, call and tell him the deal was off.

How could she, though? She knew just what Taft would think. He would guess, quite accurately, that she was the one who didn't want him here and would know she had dissuaded her mother from the plan.

Her shoulder blades itched at the thought. She didn't want him thinking she was uncomfortable having him around. Better that he continue to believe she was completely indifferent to the ramifications of being back in Pine Gulch with him.

She had done her very best to strike the proper tone the day of the fire, polite but cool, as if they were distant acquaintances instead of once having shared everything.

If she told her mother she didn't want to have Taft here, he would know her demeanor was all an act.

She was trapped. Well and truly trussed, just like one of the calves he used to rope in the high-school rodeo. It was a helpless, miserable feeling, one that felt all too familiar. She had lived with it every day of the past seven years, since her marriage to Javier Santiago. But unlike those calves in the rodeo ring, she had wandered willingly into the ropes that bound her to a man she didn't love.

Well, she hadn't been completely willing, she supposed. From the beginning she had known marrying him was a mistake and had tried every way she could think short of jilting him also to escape the ties binding them together. But unlike with Taft, this time she'd had a third life to consider. She had been four months pregnant with Alexandro. Javier—strangely old-fashioned about this, at least—wouldn't consider any other option but marriage.

She had tried hard to convince herself she was in love

with him. He was handsome and seductively charming and made her laugh with his extravagant pursuit of her, which had been the reason she had finally given in and begun to date him while she was working at the small, exclusive boutique hotel he owned in Madrid.

She had tried to be a good wife and had worked hard to convince herself she loved him, but it hadn't been enough. Not for him and not for her—but by then she had been thoroughly entangled in the piggin' rope, so to speak, by Alex and then by Maya, her sweet-natured and vulnerable daughter.

This, though, with Taft. She couldn't control what her mother had done, but she could certainly control her own response to it. She wouldn't allow herself to care if the man had suddenly invaded every inch of her personal space by moving into the hotel. It was only temporary and then he would be out of her life again.

"Do you want me to call him?" her mother asked again.

She forced herself to smile. "Not at all, Mama. I'm sorry. I was just…surprised, that's all. Everything should be fine. You're right—it's probably a great idea. Free labor is always a good thing, and like you said, the only thing we're giving up is a room that probably wouldn't have been booked anyway."

Maya wandered into the kitchen, apparently tired of playing, and gave her mother one of those generous hugs Laura had come to depend upon like oxygen and water. "Hungry, Mama."

"Gram is fixing us something delicious for dinner. Aren't we lucky to have her?"

Maya nodded with a broad smile to her grandmother. "Love you, Gram."

"I love you, too, sweetheart." Jan beamed back at her.

This—her daughter and Alex—was more important than her discomfort about Taft. She was trying her best to turn the hotel into something that could actually turn a profit instead of just provide a subsistence for her mother and now her and her children.

She had her chance to live her lifelong dream now and make the Cold Creek Inn into the warm and gracious facility she had always imagined, a place where families could feel comfortable to gather, where couples could find or rekindle romance, where the occasional business traveler could find a home away from home.

This was her moment to seize control of her life and make a new future for herself and her children. She couldn't let Taft ruin that for her.

All she had to do was remind herself that she hadn't loved him for ten years and she should be able to handle his presence here at the inn with calm aplomb.

No big deal whatsoever. Right?

If some part of him had hoped Laura might fall all over him with gratitude for stepping up to help with the inn renovations, Taft would have been doomed to disappointment.

Over the next few days, as he settled into his surprisingly comfortable room in the wing overlooking the creek, a few doors down from the fire-damaged room, he helped Mrs. Pendleton with the occasional carpentry job. A bathroom cabinet repair here, a countertop fix there. In that time, he barely saw Laura. Somehow she was always mysteriously absent whenever he stopped at the front desk.

The few times he did come close enough to talk to

her, she would exchange a quick, stiff word with him and then manufacture some excuse to take off at the earliest opportunity, as if she didn't want to risk some kind of contagion.

She had dumped *him,* not the other way around, but she was acting as if he was the biggest heel in the county. Still, he found her prickly, standoffish attitude more a challenge than an annoyance.

Truth was, he wasn't used to women ignoring him—and he certainly wasn't accustomed to *Laura* ignoring him.

They had been friends forever, even before that momentous summer after her freshman year of college when he finally woke up and realized how much he had come to care about her as much more than simply a friend. After she left, he had missed the woman he loved with a hollow ache he had never quite been able to fill, but he sometimes thought he missed his best friend just as much.

After three nights at the hotel with these frustrating, fleeting encounters, he was finally able to run her to ground early one morning. He had an early meeting at the fire station, and when he walked out of the side entrance near where he parked the vehicle he drove as fire chief—which was as much a mobile office as a mode of transportation—he spotted someone working in the scraggly flower beds that surrounded the inn.

The beds were mostly just a few tulips and some stubbly, rough-looking shrubs but it looked as if somebody was trying to make it more. Several flats of colorful blooms had been spaced with careful efficiency along the curvy sidewalk, ready to be transplanted into the flower beds.

At first, he assumed the gardener under the straw hat was someone from a landscaping service until he caught a glimpse of honey-blond hair.

He instantly switched direction. "Good morning," he called as he approached. She jumped and whirled around. When she spotted him, her instinctive look of surprise twisted into something that looked like dismay before she tucked it away and instead gave him a polite, impersonal smile.

"Oh. Hello."

If it didn't sting somewhere deep inside, he might have been amused at her cool tone.

"You do remember this is eastern Idaho, not Madrid, right? It's only April. We could have snow for another six weeks yet, easy."

"I remember," she answered stiffly. "These are all hardy early bloomers. They should be fine."

What he knew about gardening was, well, *nothing,* except how much he used to hate it when his mom would wake him and his brothers and Caidy up early to go out and weed her vegetable patch on summer mornings.

"If you say so. I would just hate to see you spend all this money on flowers and then wake up one morning to find a hard freeze has wiped them out overnight."

"I appreciate your concern for my wallet, but I've learned in thirty-one years on the earth that if you want to beautify the world around you a little bit, sometimes you have to take a few risks."

He could appreciate the wisdom in that, whether he was a gardener or not.

"I'm only working on the east-and south-facing beds for now, where there's less chance of frost kill. I might have been gone a few years, but I haven't quite forgotten the capricious weather we can see here in the Rockies."

What *had* she forgotten? She didn't seem to have too many warm memories of their time together, not if she could continue treating him with this annoyingly polite indifference.

He knew he needed to be heading to the station house for his meeting, but he couldn't resist lingering a moment with her to see if he could poke and prod more of a reaction out of her than this.

He looked around and had to point out the obvious. "No kids with you this morning?"

"They're inside fixing breakfast with my mother." She gestured to the small Craftsman-style cottage behind the inn where she had been raised. "I figured this was a good time to get something done before they come outside and my time will be spent trying to keep Alex from deciding he could dig a hole to China in the garden and Maya from picking every one of the pretty flowers."

He couldn't help smiling. Her kids were pretty darn cute—besides that, there was something so *right* about standing here with her while the morning sunlight glimmered in her hair and the cottonwood trees along the river sent out a few exploratory puffs on the sweet-smelling breeze.

"They're adorable kids."

She gave him a sidelong glance as if trying to gauge his sincerity. "When they're not starting fires, you mean?"

He laughed. "I'm going on the assumption that that was a fluke."

There. He saw it. The edges of her mouth quirked

up and she almost smiled, but she turned her face away and he missed it.

He still considered it a huge victory. He always used to love making her smile.

Something stirred inside him as he watched her pick up a cheerful yellow flower and set it in the small hole she had just dug. Attraction, yes. Most definitely. He had forgotten how much he liked the way she looked, fresh and bright and as pretty as those flowers. Somehow he had also forgotten over the years that air of quiet grace and sweetness.

She was just as lovely as ever. No, that wasn't quite true. She was even more beautiful than she had been a decade ago. While he wasn't so sure how life in general had treated her, the years had been physically kind to her. With those big eyes and her high cheekbones and that silky hair he used to love burying his hands in, she was still beautiful. Actually, when he considered it, her beauty had more depth now than it did when she had been a young woman, and he found it even more appealing.

Yeah, he was every bit as attracted to her as he'd been in those days when thoughts of her had consumed him like the wildfires he used to fight every summer. But he'd been attracted to plenty of women in the past decade. What he felt right now, standing in the morning sunshine with Laura, ran much more deeply through him.

Unsettled and more than a little rattled by the sudden hot ache in his gut, he took the coward's way out and opted for the one topic he knew she wouldn't want to discuss. "What happened to the kids' father?"

She dumped a trowel full of dirt on the seedling with

enough force to make him wince. "Remind me again why that's any of your business," she bit out.

"It's not. Only idle curiosity. You married him just a few years after you were going to marry me. You can't blame me for wondering about him."

She raised an eyebrow as if she didn't agree with that particular statement. "I'm sure you've heard the gory details," she answered, her voice terse. "Javier died six months ago. A boating accident off the coast of Barcelona. He and his mistress du jour were both killed. It was a great tragedy for everyone concerned."

Ah, hell. He knew her husband had died, but he hadn't heard the rest of it. He doubted anyone else in Pine Gulch had or the rumor would have certainly slithered its way toward him, given their history together.

She studiously refused to look at him. He knew her well enough to be certain she regretted saying anything and he couldn't help wondering why she had.

He also couldn't think of a proper response. How much pain did those simple words conceal?

"I'm sorry," he finally said, although it sounded lame and trite.

"About what? His death or the mistress?"

"Both."

Still avoiding his gaze, she picked up another flower start from the colorful flat. "He was a good father. Whatever else I could say about Javier, he loved his children. They both miss him very much."

"You don't?"

"Again, why is this your business?"

He sighed. "It's not. You're right. But we were best friends once, even before, well, everything, and I would still like to know about your life after you left here.

I never stopped caring about you just because you dumped me."

Again, she refused to look at him. "Don't go there, Taft. We both know I only broke our engagement because you didn't have the guts to do it."

Oh. Ouch. Direct hit. He almost took a step back, but he managed to catch himself just in time. "Jeez, Laura, why don't you say what you really mean?" he managed to get out past the guilt and pain.

She rose to her feet, spots of color on her high cheekbones. "Oh, don't pretend you don't know what I'm talking about. You completely checked out of our relationship after your parents were murdered. Every time I tried to talk to you, you brushed me off, told me you were fine, then merrily headed to the Bandito for another drink and to flirt with some hot young thing there. I suppose it shouldn't have come as a surprise to anyone that I married a man who was unfaithful. You know what they say about old patterns being hard to break."

Well, she was talking to him. *Be careful what you wish for, Bowman.*

"I was *never* unfaithful to you."

She made a disbelieving sound. "Maybe you didn't actually go that far with another woman, but you sure seemed to enjoy being with all the Bandito bar babes much more than you did me."

This wasn't going at all the way he had planned when he stopped to talk to her. Moving into the inn and taking the temporary carpenter job had been one of his crazier ideas. Really, he had only wanted to test the waters and see if there was any chance of finding their way past the ugliness and anger to regain the friendship they had once shared, the friendship that had once meant everything to him.

Those waters were still pretty damn frigid.

She let out a long breath and looked as if she regretted bringing up the past. "I knew you wanted out, Taft. *Everyone* knew you wanted out. You just didn't want to hurt me. I understand and appreciate that."

"That's not how it happened."

"I was there. I remember it well. You were grieving and angry about your parents' murder. Anyone would be. It's completely understandable, which is why, if you'll remember, I wanted to postpone the wedding until you were in a better place. You wouldn't hear of it. Every time I brought it up, you literally walked away from me. How could I have married you under those circumstances? We both would have ended up hating each other."

"You're right. This way is much better, with only you hating me."

Un-freaking-believable. She actually looked hurt at that. "Who said I hated you?"

"*Hate* might be too big a word. *Despise* might be a little more appropriate."

She drew in a sharp breath. "I don't feel either of those things. The truth is, Taft, what we had together was a long time ago. I don't feel anything at all for you other than maybe a little fond nostalgia for what we once shared."

Oh. Double ouch. Pain sliced through him, raw and sharp. That was certainly clear enough. He was very much afraid it wouldn't take long for him to discover he was just as crazy about her as he had always been and all she felt in return was "fond nostalgia."

Or so she said anyway.

He couldn't help searching her expression for any hint that she wasn't being completely truthful, but she only gazed back at him with that same cool look, her mouth set in that frustratingly polite smile.

Damn, but he hated that smile. He suddenly wanted to lean forward, yank her against him and kiss away that smile until it never showed up there again.

Just for the sake of fond nostalgia.

Instead, he forced himself to give her a polite smile of his own and took a step in the direction of his truck. He had a meeting and didn't want to be later than he already was.

"Good to know," he murmured. "I guess I had better let you get back to your gardening. My shift ends tonight at six and then I'm only on call for the next few days, so I should have a little more time to work on the rooms you're renovating. Leave me a list of jobs you would like me to do at the front desk. I'll try my best to stay out of your way."

There. That sounded cool and uninvolved.

If he slammed his truck door a little harder than strictly necessary, well, so what?

Chapter 4

When would she ever learn to keep her big mouth shut?

Long after Taft climbed into his pickup truck and drove away, Laura continued to yank weeds out of the sadly neglected garden beds with hands that shook while silently castigating herself for saying anything.

The moment she turned and found him walking toward her, she should have thrown down her trowel and headed back to the cottage.

Their conversation replayed over and over in her head. If her gardening gloves hadn't been covered in dirt, she would have groaned and buried her face in her hands.

First of all, why on earth had she told him about Javier and his infidelities? Taft was the *last* person in Pine Gulch with whom she should have shared that particular tidbit of juicy information.

Even her mother didn't know how difficult the last few years of her marriage had become, how she would have left in an instant if not for the children and their adoration for Javier. Yet she had blurted the gory details right out to Taft, gushing her private heartache like a leaky sprinkler pipe.

So much for wanting him to think she had moved onward and upward after she left Pine Gulch. All she had accomplished was to make herself an object of pity in his eyes—as if she hadn't done that a decade ago by throwing all her love at someone who wasn't willing or capable at the time of catching it.

And then she had been stupid enough to dredge up the past, something she vowed she wouldn't do. Talking about it again had to have made him wonder if she were *thinking* about it, which basically sabotaged her whole plan to appear cool and uninterested in Taft.

He could always manage to get her to confide things she shouldn't. She had often thought he should have been the police officer, not his twin brother, Trace.

When she was younger, she used to tell him everything. They had talked about the pressure her parents placed on her to excel in school. About a few of the mean girls in her grade who had excluded her from their social circle because of those grades, about her first crush—on a boy other than him, of course. She didn't tell him that until much later.

They had probably known each other clear back in grade school, but she didn't remember much about him other than maybe seeing him around in the lunchroom, this big, kind of tough-looking kid who had an identical twin and who always smiled at everyone. He had been two whole grades ahead of her after all, in an entirely different social stratosphere.

Her first real memory of him was middle school, which in Pine Gulch encompassed seventh through ninth grades. She had been in seventh grade, Taft in ninth. He had been an athletic kid and well-liked, always able to make anyone laugh. She, on the other hand, had been quiet and shy, much happier with a book in her hand than standing by her locker with her friends between classes, giggling over the cute boys.

She and Taft had ended up both taking a Spanish elective and had been seated next to each other on Señora Baker's incomprehensible seating chart.

Typically, guys that age—especially jocks—didn't want to have much to do with younger girls. Gawky, insecure, bookish girls might as well just forget it. But somehow while struggling over past participles and conjugating verbs, they had become friends. She had loved his sense of humor and he seemed to appreciate how easily she picked up Spanish.

They had arranged study groups together for every test, often before school because Taft couldn't do it afterward most of the time due to practice sessions for whatever school sport he was currently playing.

She could remember exactly the first moment she knew she was in love with him. She had been in the library waiting for him early one morning. Because she lived in town and could easily walk to school, she was often there first. He and his twin brother usually caught a ride with their older brother, Ridge, who was a senior in high school at the time and had a very cool pickup truck with big tires and a roll bar.

While she waited for him, she had been fine-tuning a history paper due in a few weeks when Ronnie Lowery showed up. Ronnie was a jerk and a bully in her grade who had seemed to have it in for her for the past few years.

She didn't understand it but thought his dislike might have something to do with the fact that Ronnie's single mother worked as a housekeeper at the inn. Why that should bother Ronnie, she had no idea. His mom wasn't a very good maid and often missed work because of her drinking, but she had overheard her mom and dad talking once in the office. Her mom had wanted to fire Mrs. Lowery, but her dad wouldn't allow it.

"She's got a kid at home. She needs the job," her dad had said, which was exactly what she would have expected her dad to say. He had a soft spot for people down on their luck and often opened the inn to people he knew could never pay their tab.

She suspected Ronnie's mom must have complained about her job at home, which was likely the reason Ronnie didn't like her. He had tripped her a couple of times going up the stairs at school and once he had cornered her in the girls' bathroom and tried to kiss her and touch her chest—what little chest she had—until she had smacked him upside the head with her heavy advanced-algebra textbook and told him to keep his filthy hands off her, with melodramatic but firm effectiveness.

She usually did her best to avoid him whenever she could, but that particular morning in seventh grade, she had been the only one in the school library. Even Mrs. Pitt, the plump and kind librarian who introduced her to Georgette Heyer books, seemed to have disappeared, she saw with great alarm.

Ronnie sat down. "Hey, Laura the whore-a."

"Shut up," she had said, very maturely, no doubt.

"Who's gonna make me?" he asked, looking around with exaggerated care. "I don't see anybody here at all."

"Leave me alone, Ronnie. I'm trying to study."

"Yeah, I don't think I will. Is that your history paper? You've got Mr. Olsen, right? Isn't that a coin-ki-dink? So do I. I bet we have the same assignment. I haven't started mine. Good thing, too, because now I don't have to."

He grabbed her paper, the one she had been working on every night for two weeks, and held it over his head.

"Give it back." She did her best not to cry.

"Forget it. You owe me for this. I had a bruise for two weeks after you hit me last month. I had to tell my mom I ran into the bleachers going after a foul ball in P.E."

"Want me to do it again?" she asked with much more bravado than true courage.

His beady gaze narrowed. "Try it, you little bitch, and I'll take more from you than just your freaking history paper."

"This history paper?"

At Taft's hard voice, all the tension coiled in her stomach like a rattlesnake immediately disappeared. Ronnie was big for a seventh grader, but compared to Taft, big and tough and menacing, he looked like just what he was—a punk who enjoyed preying on people smaller than he was.

"Yes, it's mine," she blurted out. "I would like it back."

Taft had smiled at her, plucked the paper out of Ronnie's greasy fingers and handed it back to Laura.

"Thanks," she had mumbled.

"You're Lowery, right?" he said to Ronnie. "I think you've got P.E. with my twin brother, Trace."

"Yeah," the kid had muttered, though with a tinge of defiance in his voice.

"I'm sorry, Lowery, but you're going to have to move. We're studying for a Spanish test here. Laura is my tutor and I don't know what I would do if something happened to her. All I can say is, I would *not* be happy. I doubt my brother would be, either."

Faced with the possibility of the combined wrath of the formidable Bowman brothers, Ronnie had slunk away like the coward he was, and in that moment, Laura had known she would love Taft for the rest of her life.

He had moved on to high school the next year, of course, while she had been left behind in middle school to pine for him. Over the next two years, she remembered going to J.V. football games at the high school to watch him, sitting on the sidelines and keeping her fingers crossed that he would see her and smile.

Oh, yes. She had been plenty stupid when it came to Taft Bowman.

Finally, she had been in tenth grade and they would once more be in the same school as he finished his senior year. She couldn't wait, that endless summer. To her eternal delight, when she showed up at her first hour, Spanish again, she had found Taft seated across the room.

She would never forget walking into the room and watching Taft's broad smile take over his face and how he had pulled his backpack off the chair next to him, as if he had been waiting just for her.

They hadn't dated that year. She had been too young and still in her awkward phase, and anyway, he had senior girls flocking around him all the time, but their friendship had picked up where it left off two years earlier.

He had confided his girl troubles to her and how he was trying to figure out whether to join the military like his brother planned to do, or go to college. Even though she had ached inside to tell him how she felt about him, she hadn't dared. Instead, she had listened and offered advice whenever he needed it.

He had ended up doing both, enrolling in college and joining the Army Reserve, and in the summers, he had left Pine Gulch to fight woodland fires. They maintained an email correspondence through it all and every time he came home, they would head to The Gulch to share a meal and catch up and it was as if they had never been apart.

And then everything changed.

Although a painfully late bloomer, she had finally developed breasts somewhere around the time she turned sixteen, and by the time she went to college, she had forced herself to reach outside her instinctive shyness. The summer after her freshman year of college when she had finally decided to go into hotel management, Taft had been fighting a fire in Oregon when he had been caught in a flare-up.

Everyone in town had been talking about it, how he had barely escaped with his life and had saved two other firefighters from certain death. The whole time, she had been consumed with worry for him.

Finally, he came back for a few weeks to catch up with his twin, who was back in Pine Gulch between military assignments, and she and Taft had gone for a late-evening horseback ride at the River Bow Ranch and he finally spilled out the story of the flare-up and how it was a miracle he was alive.

One minute he was talking to her about the fire, something she was quite certain he hadn't done with anyone else. The next—she still wasn't sure how it happened—he was kissing her like a starving man and she was a giant frosted cupcake.

They kissed for maybe ten minutes. She wasn't sure exactly how long, but she only knew they were the most glorious moments of her life. When he finally eased away from her, he had looked as horrified as if he had just accidentally stomped on a couple of kittens.

"I'm sorry, Laura. That was… Wow. I'm so sorry."

She remembered shaking her head, smiling at him, her heart aching with love. "What took you so blasted long, Taft Bowman?" she had murmured and reached out to kiss him again.

From that point on, they had been inseparable. She had been there to celebrate with him when he passed his EMT training, then paramedic training. He had visited her at school in Bozeman and made all her roommates swoon. When she came home for summers, they would spend every possible moment together.

On her twenty-first birthday, he proposed to her. Even though they were both crazy-young, she couldn't have imagined a future without him and had finally agreed. She missed those times, that wild flutter in her stomach every time he kissed her.

She sighed now and realized with a little start of surprise that while she had been woolgathering, she had weeded all the way around to the front of the building that lined Main Street.

Her mom would probably be more than ready for

her to come back and take care of the children. She stood and stretched, rubbing her cramped back, when she heard the rumble of a pickup truck pulling alongside her.

Oh, she hoped it wasn't Taft coming back. She was already off-balance enough from their encounter earlier and from remembering all those things she had purposely kept buried for years. When she turned, she saw a woman climbing out of the pickup and realized it was indeed a Bowman—his younger sister, Caidy.

"Hi, Laura! Remember me? Caidy Bowman."

"Of course I remember you," she exclaimed. Caidy rushed toward her, arms outstretched, and Laura just had time to shuck off her gardening gloves before she returned the other woman's embrace.

"How are you?" she asked.

Despite the six-year difference in their ages, they had been close friends and she had loved the idea of having Caidy for a sister when she married Taft.

Until their parents died, Caidy had been a fun, bright, openly loving teenager, secure in her position as the adored younger sister of the three older Bowman brothers. Everything changed after Caidy witnessed her parents' murder, Laura thought sadly.

"I'm good," Caidy finally answered. Laura hoped so. Those months after the murders had been rough on the girl. The trauma of witnessing the brutal deaths and being unable to do anything to stop them had left Caidy frightened to the point of helplessness. For several weeks, she refused to leave the ranch and had insisted on having one of her brothers present twenty-four hours a day.

Caidy and her grief had been another reason Laura

had tried to convince Taft to postpone their June wedding, just six months after the murders, but he had insisted his parents wouldn't have wanted them to change their plans.

Not that any of that mattered now. Caidy had become a beautiful woman, with dark hair like her brothers' and the same Bowman green eyes.

"You look fantastic," Laura exclaimed.

Caidy made a face but hugged her again. "Same to you. Gosh, I can't believe it's been so long."

"What are you up to these days? Did you ever make it to vet school?"

Something flickered in the depths of her eyes but Caidy only shrugged. "No, I went to a couple semesters of school but decided college wasn't really for me. Since then, I've mostly just stuck around the ranch, helping Ridge with his daughter. I do a little training on the side. Horses and dogs."

"That's terrific," she said, although some part of her felt a little sad for missed opportunities. Caidy had always adored animals and had an almost uncanny rapport with them. All she used to talk about as a teenager was becoming a veterinarian someday and coming back to Pine Gulch to work.

One pivotal moment had changed so many lives, she thought. The violent murder of the Bowmans in a daring robbery of their extensive American West art collection had shaken everyone in town really. That sort of thing just didn't happen in Pine Gulch. The last murder the town had seen prior to that had been clear back in the 1930s when two ranch hands had fought it out over a girl.

Each of the Bowman siblings had reacted in different

ways, she remembered. Ridge had thrown himself into the ranch and overseeing his younger siblings. Trace had grown even more serious and solemn. Caidy had withdrawn into herself, struggling with a completely natural fear of the world.

As for Taft, his answer had been to hide away his emotions and pretend everything was fine while inside he seethed with grief and anger and pushed away any of her attempts to comfort him.

"I'm looking for Taft," Caidy said now. "I had to make a run to the feed store this morning and thought I would stop and see if he wanted to head over to The Gulch for coffee and an omelet."

Oh, she loved The Gulch, the town's favorite diner. Why hadn't she been there since she returned to town? An image of the place formed clearly in her head—the tin-stamped ceiling, the round red swivel seats at the old-fashioned counter, the smell of frying bacon and coffee that had probably oozed into the paneling.

One of these mornings, she would have to take her children there.

"Taft isn't here. I'm sorry. He left about a half hour ago. I think he was heading to the fire station. He did say something about his shift ending at six."

"Oh. Okay. Thanks." Caidy paused a moment, tilting her head and giving Laura a long, inscrutable look very much like her brother would do. "I don't suppose you would like to go over to The Gulch with me and have breakfast, would you?"

She gazed at the other woman, as touched by the invitation as she was surprised. In all these years, Taft hadn't told his family that she had been the one to break their engagement? She knew he couldn't have. If Caidy knew, Laura had a feeling the other woman wouldn't be nearly as friendly.

The Bowmans tended to circle the wagons around their own.

That had been one of the hardest things about walking away from him. Her breakup with Taft had meant not only the loss of all her childish dreams but also the big, boisterous family she had always wanted as an only child of older parents who seemed absorbed with each other and their business.

For a moment, she was tempted to go to The Gulch with Caidy. Her mouth watered at the thought of Lou Archuleta's famous sweet rolls. Besides that, she would love the chance to catch up with Caidy. But before she could answer, her children came barreling out of the cottage, Maya in the lead for once but Alex close behind.

"Ma-ma! Gram made cakes. So good," Maya declared.

Alexandro caught up to his sister. "Pancakes, not cakes. You don't have cakes for breakfast, Maya. We're supposed to tell you to come in so you can wash up. Hurry! Grandma says I can flip the next one."

"Oh."

Caidy smiled at the children, clearly entranced by them.

"Caidy, this is my daughter, Maya, and my son, Alexandro. Children, this is my friend Caidy. She's Chief Bowman's sister."

"I like Chief Bowman," Alex declared. "He said if I start another fire, he's going to arrest me. Do you think he will?"

Caidy nodded solemnly. "Trust me, my brother never

says anything he doesn't mean. You'll have to be certain not to start any more fires, then, won't you?"

"I know. I know. I already heard it about a million times. Hey, Mom, can I go so I can turn the pancakes with Grandma?"

She nodded and Alex raced back for the cottage with his sister in close pursuit.

"They're beautiful, Laura. Truly."

"I think so." She smiled and thought she saw a hint of something like envy in the other woman's eyes. Why didn't Caidy have a family of her own? she wondered. Was she still living in fear?

On impulse, she gestured toward the cottage. "Unless you have your heart set on cinnamon rolls down at The Gulch, why don't you stay and have breakfast here? I'm sure my mother wouldn't mind setting another plate for you."

Caidy blinked. "Oh, I couldn't."

"Why not? My mother's pancakes are truly delicious. In fact, a week from now, we're going to start offering breakfast at the inn to our guests. The plan is to start with some of Mom's specialties like pancakes and French toast but also to begin ordering some things from outside sources to showcase local businesses. I've already talked to the Java Hut about serving their coffee here and the Archuletas about offering some of The Gulch pastries to our guests."

"What a great idea."

"You can be our guinea pig. Come and have breakfast with us. I'm sure my mother will enjoy the company."

She would, too, she thought. She missed having a friend besides her mother. Her best friend in high school, besides Taft, had moved to Texas for her husband's job and Laura hadn't had a chance to connect with anyone else.

Even though she still emailed back and forth with her dearest friends and support system in Madrid, it wasn't the same as sharing coffee and pancakes and stories with someone who had known her for so long.

"I would love that," Caidy exclaimed. "Thank you. I'm sure Taft can find his own breakfast partner if he's so inclined."

From the rumors Laura had heard about the man in the years since their engagement, she didn't doubt that for a moment.

Chapter 5

To her relief, her children were charming and sweet with Caidy over breakfast. As soon as he found out their guest lived on a real-life cattle ranch, Alex peppered her with questions about cowboys and horses and whether she had ever seen a real-life Indian.

Apparently she had to have a talk with her son about political correctness and how reality compared to the American Westerns he used to watch avidly with their gnarled old housekeeper in Madrid.

Maya had apparently decided Caidy was someone she could trust, which was something of a unique occurrence. She sat beside her and gifted Taft's sister with her sweet smile and half of the orange Laura peeled for her.

"Thank you, sweetheart," Caidy said, looking touched by the gesture.

Whenever someone new interacted with Maya, Laura

couldn't help a little clutch in her stomach, worry at how her daughter would be accepted.

She supposed that stemmed from Javier's initial reaction after her birth when the solemn-faced doctors told them Maya showed certain markers for Down syndrome and they were running genetic testing to be sure.

Her husband had been in denial for a long time and had pretended nothing was wrong. After all, how could he possibly have a child who wasn't perfect—by the world's standards anyway? Even after the testing revealed what Laura had already known in her heart, Javier has refused to discuss Maya's condition or possible outcomes.

Denial or not, he had still loved his daughter, though. She couldn't fault him for that. He was sometimes the only one who could calm the baby's crankiness and he had been infinitely calm with her.

Maya didn't quite understand that Javier was dead. She still had days when she asked over and over again where her papa was. During those rough patches, Laura would have to fight down deep-seated fury at her late husband.

Her children needed him and he had traded his future with them for the momentary pleasure he had found with his latest honey. Mingled with the anger and hurt was no small amount of guilt. If she had tried a little harder to open her heart to him and truly love him, maybe he wouldn't have needed to seek out other women.

She was doing her best, she reminded herself. Hadn't she traveled across the world to give them a home with family and stability?

"This was fun," Caidy said, drawing her back to the

conversation. "Thank you so much for inviting me, but I probably better start heading back to the ranch. I've got a buyer coming today to look at one of the border collies I've been training."

"You're going to sell your dog?" Alex, who dearly wanted a puppy, looked horrified at the very idea.

"Sue isn't really my dog," Caidy explained with a smile. "I rescued her when she was a puppy and I've been training her to help someone else at their ranch. We have plenty of dogs at the River Bow."

Alex didn't seem to quite understand the concept of breeding and training dogs. "Doesn't it make you sad to give away your dog?"

Caidy blinked a little, but after a pause she nodded. "Yes, I guess it does a little. She's a good dog and I'll miss her. But I promise I'll make sure whoever buys her will give her a really good home."

"We have a good home, don't we, Grandma?" Alex appealed to Jan, who smiled.

"Why, yes, I believe we do, son."

"We can't have a dog right now, Alex."

Laura tried to head him off before he started extolling the virtues of their family like a used-car salesman trying to close a deal. "We've talked about this. While we're settling in here in Pine Gulch and living with Grandma here at the inn, it's just not practical."

He stuck out his lower lip, looking very much like his father when he couldn't get his way. "That's what you always say. I still really, really, really want a dog."

"Not now, Alexandro. We're not getting a dog. Maybe in a year or so when things here are a little more settled."

"But I want one now!"

"I'm sorry," Caidy said quickly, "but I'm afraid Sue wouldn't be very happy here. You see, she's a working dog and her very favorite thing is telling the cattle on our ranch which way we want them to go. You don't look very much like a steer. Where are your horns?"

Alex looked as if he wanted to ramp up to a full-fledged tantrum, something new since his father died, but he allowed himself to be teased out of it. "I'm not a steer," he said, rolling his eyes. Then a moment later he asked, "What's a steer?"

Caidy laughed. "It's another name for the male version of cow."

"I thought that was a bull."

"Uh." Caidy gave Laura a helpless sort of look.

While Jan snickered, Laura shook her head. "You're right. There are two kinds of male bovines, which is another word for cow. One's a bull and one is a steer."

"What's the difference?" he asked.

"Steers sing soprano," Caidy said. "And on that lovely note, I'd better get back to the bulls *and* steers of the River Bow. Thanks for a great breakfast. Next time it's my turn."

"Alex, will you and Maya help Gram with clearing the table while I walk Caidy out? I'll do the dishes when I come back inside."

To her relief, her son allowed himself to be distracted when Jan asked him if he and Maya would like to go to the park later in the day.

"I'm sorry about the near-tantrum there," she said as they headed outside to Caidy's pickup truck. "We're working on them, but my son still likes his own way."

"Most kids do. My niece is almost ten and she still

thinks she should be crowned queen of the universe. I didn't mean to start something by talking about dogs."

"We've been having this argument for about three years now. His best friend in Madrid had this mangy old mutt, but Alex adored him and wanted one so badly. My husband would never allow it and for some reason Alex got it in his head after his father died that now there was no reason we couldn't get a dog."

"You're welcome to bring your kids out to the ranch sometime to enjoy my dogs vicariously. The kids might enjoy taking a ride, as well. We've got some pretty gentle ponies that would be perfect for them."

"That sounds fun. I'm sure they would both love it." She was quite certain this was one of those vague invitations that people said just to be polite, but to her surprise, Caidy didn't let the matter rest.

"How about next weekend?" she pressed. "I'm sure Ridge would be delighted to have you out."

Ridge was the Bowman sibling she had interacted with the least. At the time she was engaged to Taft, he and his parents weren't getting along, so he avoided the River Bow as much as possible. The few times she had met him, she had always thought him a little stern and humorless.

Still, he'd been nice enough to her—though the same couldn't have been said about his ex-wife, who had been rude and overbearing to just about everyone on the ranch.

"That's a lovely invitation, but I'm sure the last thing you need is to entertain a bunch of greenhorns."

"I would love it," Caidy assured her. "Your kids are just plain adorable and I can't tell you how thrilled I am that you're back in town. To tell you the truth, I'm a little desperate for some female conversation. At least something that doesn't revolve around cattle."

She should refuse. Her history with Taft had to make any interaction with the rest of the Bowmans more than a little awkward. But like Caidy, she welcomed any chance to resurrect their old friendship—and Alex and Maya *would* love the chance to ride horses and play with the ranch dogs.

"Yes, all right. The weekend would be lovely. Thank you."

"I'll call you Wednesday or Thursday to make some firm arrangements. This will be great!" Caidy beamed at her, looking fresh and pretty with her dark ponytail and sprinkling of freckles across the bridge of her nose.

The other woman climbed into her pickup truck and drove away with a wave and a smile and Laura watched after her for a moment, feeling much better about the morning than she had when the previous Bowman sibling had driven away from the inn.

Taft had visitors.

The whir of the belt sander didn't quite mask the giggles and little scurrying sounds from the doorway. He made a show of focusing on the window he was framing while still maintaining a careful eye on the little creatures who would occasionally peek around the corner of the doorway and then hide out of sight again.

He didn't want to let his guard down, not with all the power equipment in here. He could just imagine Laura's diatribe if one of her kids somehow got hurt. She would probably accuse him of letting her rambunctious older kid cut off his finger on purpose.

The game of peekaboo lasted for a few more minutes

until he shut off the belt sander. He ran a finger over the wood to be sure the frame was smooth before he headed over to the window to hold it up for size, keeping an eye on the door the whole time.

"Go on," he heard a whispered voice say, then giggles, and a moment later he was joined by Laura's daughter.

Maya. She was adorable, with that dusky skin, curly dark hair in pigtails and Laura's huge blue eyes, almond-shaped on Maya.

"Hola," she whispered with a shy smile.

"Hola, señorita," he answered. Apparently he still remembered a *little* of the high-school Spanish he had struggled so hard to master.

"What doing?" she asked.

"I'm going to put some new wood up around this window. See?" He held the board into the intended place to demonstrate, then returned it to the worktable.

"Why?" she asked, scratching her ear.

He glanced at the doorway where the boy peeked around, then hid again like a shadow.

"The old wood was rotting away. This way it will look much nicer. More like the rest of the room."

That face peeked around the doorway again and this time Taft caught him with an encouraging smile. After a pause, the boy sidled into the room.

"Loud," Maya said, pointing to the belt sander with fascination.

"It can be. I've got things to block your ears if you want them."

He wasn't sure she would understand, but she nodded vigorously, so he reached for his ear protectors on top of his toolbox. The adult-size red ear guards were huge on her—the bottom of the cups hit her at about shoulder height. He reached out to work the slide adjustment on top. They were still too big but at least they covered most of her ears.

She beamed at him, pleased as punch, and he had to chuckle. "Nice. You look great."

"I see," she said, and headed unerringly for the mirror hanging on the back of the bathroom door, where she turned her head this way and that, admiring her headgear as if he had given her a diamond tiara.

Oh, she was a heartbreaker, this one.

"Can I use some?" Alexandro asked, from about two feet away, apparently coaxed all the way into the room by what his sister was wearing.

"I'm afraid I've got only the one pair. I wasn't expecting company. Sorry. Next time I'll remember to pack a spare. I probably have regular earplugs in my toolbox."

Alex shrugged. "That's okay. I don't mind the noise. Maya freaks at loud noises, but I don't care."

"Why is that? Maya, I mean, and loud noises?"

The girl was wandering around the room, humming to herself loudly, apparently trying to hear herself through the ear protection.

The kid looked fairly protective himself, watching over his sister as she moved from window to window. "She just does. Mom says it's because she has so much going on inside her head she sometimes forgets the rest of us and loud noises startle her into remembering. Or something like that."

"You love your sister a lot, don't you?"

"She's my sister." He shrugged, looking suddenly much older than his six years. "I have to watch out for her and Mama now that our papa is gone."

Taft wanted to hug him, too, and he had to fight down a lump in his throat. He thought about his struggle when his parents had died. He had been twenty-four years old. Alex was just a kid and had already lost his father, but he seemed to be handling it with stoic grace. "I bet you do a great job, protecting them both."

The boy looked guilty. "Sometimes. I didn't on the day of the fire."

"We've decided that was an accident, right? It's over and you're not going to do it again. Take it from me, kid. Don't beat yourself up over past mistakes. Just move on and try to do better next time."

Alex didn't look as if he quite understood. Why should he? Taft rolled his eyes at himself. Philosophy and six-year-old boys didn't mix all that well.

"Want to try your hand with the sander?" he asked.

Alex's blue eyes lit up. "Really? Is it okay?"

"Sure. Why not? Every guy needs to know how to run a belt sander."

Before beginning the lesson, Taft thought it wise to move toward Maya, who was sitting on the floor some distance away, drawing her finger through the sawdust mess he hadn't had time to clear up yet. Her mom would probably love that, but because she was already covered, he decided he would clean her up when they were done.

He lifted one of the ear protectors away from her ear so he could talk to her. "Maya, we're going to turn on the sander, okay?"

"Loud."

"It won't be when you have this on. I promise."

She narrowed her gaze as if she were trying to figure out whether to believe him, then she nodded and returned to the sawdust. He gazed at the back of her head, tiny compared to the big ear guards, and was completely bowled over by her ready trust.

Now he had to live up to it.

He turned on the sander, hoping the too-big ear protectors would still do their job. Maya looked up, a look of complete astonishment on her cute little face. She pulled one ear cup away, testing to see if the sander was on, but quickly returned it to the original position. After a minute, she pulled it away again and then replaced it, a look of wonder on her face at the magic of safety wear.

He chuckled and turned back to Alex, waiting eagerly by the belt sander.

"Okay, the most important thing here is that we don't sand your fingers off. I'm not sure your mom would appreciate that."

"She wouldn't," Alex assured him with a solemn expression.

Taft had to fight his grin. "We'll have to be careful, then. Okay. Now you always start up the belt sander before you touch it to the wood so you don't leave gouges. Right here is the switch. Now keep your hands on top of mine and we can do it together. That's it."

For the next few minutes, they worked the piece of wood until he was happy with the way it looked and felt. He always preferred to finish sanding his jobs the old-fashioned way, by hand, but a belt sander was a handy tool for covering a large surface quickly and efficiently.

When they finished, he carefully turned off the belt sander and set it aside, then returned to the board and the boy. "Okay, now here's the second most important part, after not cutting your fingers off. We have to blow off the sawdust. Like this."

He demonstrated with a puff of air, then handed the

board to the boy, who puckered up and blew as if he were the big, bad wolf after the three little pigs.

"Perfect," Taft said with a grin. "Feel how smooth that is now?"

The boy ran his finger along the wood grain. "Wow! I did that?"

"Absolutely. Good job. Now every time you come into this room, you can look out through the window and remember you helped frame it up."

"Cool! Why do you have to sand the wood?"

"When the wood is smooth, it looks better and you get better results with whatever paint or varnish you want to use on it."

"How does the sander thingy work?"

"The belt is made of sandpaper. See? Because it's rough, when you rub it on the wood, it works away the uneven surface."

"Can you sand other things besides wood?" he asked.

Taft had to laugh at the third degree. "You probably can but it's made for wood. It would ruin other things. Most tools have a specific purpose and when you use them for something else, you can cause more problems."

"Me," an abnormally loud voice interrupted before Alex could ask any more questions. With the ear protectors, Maya obviously couldn't judge the decibel level of her own voice. "I go now."

"Okay, okay. You don't need to yell about it," Alex said, rolling his eyes in a conspiratorial way toward Taft.

Just like that, both of these kids slid their way under his skin, straight to his heart, partly because they were Laura's, but mostly because they were just plain adorable.

"Can I?" she asked, still speaking loudly.

He lifted one of the ear protectors so she could hear him. "Sure thing, sweetheart. I've got another board that needs sanding. Come on."

Alex looked disgruntled, but he backed away to give his sister room. Taft was even more careful with Maya, keeping his hands firmly wrapped around hers on the belt sander as they worked the wood.

When they finished, he removed her earwear completely. "Okay, now, like I told your brother, this is the most important part. I need you to blow off the sawdust."

She puckered comically and puffed for all she was worth and he helped her along. "There. Now feel what we did."

"Ooh. Soft." She smiled broadly at him and he returned her smile, just as he heard their names.

"Alex? Maya? Where are you?"

Laura's voice rang out from down the hall, sounding harried and a little hoarse, as if she had been calling for a while.

The two children exchanged looks, as if they were bracing themselves for trouble.

"That's our mama," Alex said unnecessarily.

"Yeah, I heard."

"Alex? Maya? Come out this instant."

"They're in here," he called out, although some part of him really didn't want to take on more trouble. He thought of their encounter a few days earlier when she had looked so fresh and pretty while she worked on the inn's flower gardens—and had cut into his heart more effectively than if she had used her trowel.

She charged into the room, every inch the concerned

mother. "What's going on? Why didn't you two answer me? I've been calling through the whole hotel."

Taft decided to take one for the team. "I'm afraid that's my fault. We had the sander going. We couldn't hear much up here."

"Look, Mama. Soft." Maya held up the piece of wood she had helped him sand. "Feel!"

Laura stepped closer, reluctance in her gaze. He was immediately assailed by the scent of her, of flowers and springtime.

She ran a hand along the wood, much as her daughter had. "Wow. That's great."

"I did it," Maya declared.

Laura arched an eyebrow. She managed to look huffy and disapproving at him for just a moment before turning back to her daughter with what she quickly transformed into an interested expression. "Did you, now? With the power sander and everything?"

"I figured I would let them run the circular saw next," he said. "Really, what's the worst that can happen?"

She narrowed her gaze at him as if trying to figure out if he was teasing. Whatever happened to her sense of humor? he wondered. Had he robbed her of that or had it been her philandering jackass of a husband?

"I'm kidding," he said. "I was helping them the whole way. Maya even wore ear protection, didn't you? Show your mom."

The girl put on her headgear and started singing some made-up song loudly, pulling the ear guards away at random intervals.

"Oh, that looks like great fun," Laura said, taking the ear protectors off her daughter and handing them to Taft. Their hands brushed as he took them from her and a little charge of electricity arced between them, sizzling right to his gut.

She pulled her hands away quickly and didn't meet his gaze. "You shouldn't be up here bothering Chief Bowman. I told you to stay away when he's working."

And why would she think she had to do that? he wondered, annoyed. Did she think he couldn't be trusted with her kids? He was the Pine Gulch fire chief, for heaven's sake, and a trained paramedic to boot. Public safety was sort of his thing.

"It was fun," Alex declared. "I got to use the sander first. Feel my board now, Mama."

She appeared to have no choice but to comply. "Nice job. But next time you need to listen to me and not bother Chief Bowman while he's working."

"I didn't mind," Taft said. "They're fun company."

"You're busy. I wouldn't want them to be a bother."

"What if they're not?"

She didn't look convinced. "Come on, you two. Tell Chief Bowman thank-you for letting you try out the dangerous power tools, after you promise him you'll never touch any of them on your own."

"We promise," Alex said dutifully.

"Promise," his sister echoed.

"Thanks for showing me how to use a sander," Alex said. "I need one of those."

Now *there* was a disaster in the making. But because the kid wasn't his responsibility, as his mother had made quite clear, he would let Laura deal with it.

"Thanks for helping me," he said. "I couldn't have finished without you two lending a hand."

"Can I help you again sometime?" the boy asked eagerly.

Laura tensed beside him and he knew she wanted him to say no. It annoyed the heck out of him and he wanted to agree, just to be contrary, but he couldn't bring himself to blatantly go against her wishes.

Instead, he offered the standard adult cop-out even though it grated. "We'll have to see, kiddo," he answered.

"Okay, now that you've had a chance with the power tools, take your sister and go straight down to the front desk to your grandmother. No detours, Alex. Got it?"

His stubborn little chin jutted out. "But we were having fun."

"Chief Bowman is trying to get some work done. He's not here to babysit."

"I'm not a baby," Alex grumbled.

Laura bit back what Taft was almost certain was a smile. "I know you're not. It's just a word, *mi hijo*. Either way, you need to take your sister straight down to the lobby to find your grandmother."

With extreme reluctance in every step, Alex took his little sister's hand and led her out the door and down the hall, leaving Laura alone with him.

Even though he could tell she wasn't thrilled to have found her children there with him and some part of him braced himself to deal with her displeasure, another, louder part of him was just so damn happy to see her again.

Ridiculous, he knew, but he couldn't seem to help it.

How had he forgotten that little spark of happiness that always seemed to jump in his chest when he saw her after an absence of just about any duration?

Even with her hair in a ponytail and an oversize shirt and faded jeans, she was beautiful, and he wanted to stand here amid the sawdust and clutter and just savor the sight of her.

As he might have expected, she didn't give him much of a chance. "Sorry about the children," she said stiffly. "I thought they were watching *SpongeBob* in the bedroom of Room Twelve while I cleaned the bathroom grout. I came out of the bathroom and they were gone, which is, unfortunately, not all that uncommon with my particular kids."

"Next time maybe you should use the security chain to keep them contained," he suggested, only half-serious.

Even as he spoke, he was aware of a completely inappropriate urge to wrap her in his arms and absorb all her cares and worries about wandering children and tile grout and anything else weighing on her.

"A great idea, but unfortunately I've already tried that. Within about a half hour, Alex figured out how to lift his sister up and have her work the chain free. They figured out the dead bolt in about half that time. I just have to remember I can't take my eyes off them for a second. I'll try to do a better job of keeping them out of your way."

"I told you, I don't mind them. Why would I? They're great kids." He meant the words, even though his previous experience with kids, other than the annual fire-safety lecture he gave at the elementary school, was mostly his niece, Destry, Ridge's daughter.

"I think they're pretty great," she answered.

"That Alex is a curious little guy with a million questions."

She gave a rueful sigh and tucked a strand of hair behind her delicate ear. She used to love it when he kissed her neck, just there, he remembered, then wished the memory had stayed hidden as heat suddenly surged through him.

"Yes, I'm quite familiar with my son's interrogation technique," Laura said, oblivious to his reaction, thank heavens. "He's had six years to hone them well."

"I don't mind the questions. Trace and I were both the same way when we were kids. My mom used to say that between the two of us, we didn't give her a second to even catch a breath between questions."

She trailed her fingers along the wood trim and he remembered how she used to trail them across his stomach....

"I remember some of the stories your mother used to tell me about you and Trace and the trouble you could get into. To be honest with you, I have great sympathy with your mother. I can't imagine having two of Alex."

He dragged his mind away from these unfortunate memories that suddenly crowded out rational thought. "He's a good boy, just has a lot of energy. And that Maya. She's a heartbreaker."

She pulled her hand away from the wood, her expression suddenly cold. "Don't you dare pity her."

"Why on earth would I do that?" he asked, genuinely shocked.

She frowned. "Because of her Down syndrome. Many people do."

"Then you shouldn't waste your time with them. Down syndrome or not, she's about the sweetest thing I've ever seen. You should have seen her work the belt sander, all serious and determined, chewing on her lip in concentration—just like you used to do when you were studying."

"Don't."

He blinked, startled at her low, vehement tone. "Don't what?"

"Try to charm me by acting all sweet and concerned. It might work on your average bimbo down at the Bandito, but I'm not that stupid."

Where did *that* come from? "Are you kidding? You're about the smartest person I know. I never thought you were stupid."

"That makes one of us," she muttered, then looked as if she regretted the words.

More than anything, he wanted to go back in time ten years and make things right again with her. He had hurt her by closing her out of his pain, trying to deal with the grief and guilt in his own way.

But then, she had hurt him, too. If only she had given him a little more time and trusted that he would work things through, he would have figured everything out eventually. Instead, she had gone away to Spain and met her jerk of a husband—and had two of the cutest kids he had ever met.

"Laura—" he began, not sure what he intended to say, but she shook her head briskly.

"I'm sorry my children bothered you. I won't let it happen again."

"I told you, I don't mind them."

"I mind. I don't want them getting attached to you when you'll be in their lives for only a brief moment."

He hadn't even known her kids a week ago. So why did the idea of not seeing them again make his chest ache? Uneasy with the reaction, he gave her a long look.

"For someone who claims not to hate me, you do a pretty good impression of it. You don't even want me around your kids, like I'll contaminate them somehow."

"You're exaggerating. You're virtually a stranger to me after all this time. I don't hate you. I feel nothing at all for you. Less than nothing."

He moved closer to her, inhaling the springtime scent of her shampoo. "Liar."

The single word was a low hush in the room and he saw her shiver as if he had trailed his finger down her cheek.

She started to take a step back, then checked the motion. "Oh, get over yourself," she snapped. "Yes, you broke my heart. I was young and foolish enough to think you meant what you said, that you loved me and wanted forever with me. We were supposed to take vows about being with each other in good times and bad, but you wouldn't share the bad with me. Instead, you started drinking and hanging out at the Bandito and pretending nothing was wrong. I was devastated. I won't make a secret of that. I thought I wouldn't survive the pain."

"I'm sorry," he said.

She made a dismissive gesture. "I should really thank you, Taft. If not for that heartbreak, I would have been only a weak, silly girl who would probably have become a weak, silly woman. Instead, I became stronger. I took my broken heart and turned it into a grand adventure in Europe, where I matured and experienced the world a little bit instead of just Pine Gulch, and now I have two beautiful children to show for it."

"Why did you give up on us so easily?"

Her mouth tightened with anger. "You know, you're right. I should have gone ahead with the wedding and then just waited around wringing my hands until you decided to pull your head out of whatever crevice you jammed it into. Although from the sound of it, I might still have been waiting, ten years later."

"I'm sorry for hurting you," he said, wishing again that he could go back and change everything. "More sorry than I can ever say."

"Ten years too late," she said tersely. "I told you, it doesn't matter."

"It obviously does or you wouldn't bristle like a porcupine every time you're near me."

"I don't—" she started to say, but he cut her off.

"I don't blame you. I was an ass to you. I'll be the first to admit it."

"The second," she said tartly.

If this conversation didn't seem so very pivotal, he might have smiled, but he had the feeling he had the chance to turn things around between them right here and now, and he wanted that with a fierce and powerful need.

"Probably. For what it's worth, my family would fill out the rest of the top five there, waiting in line to call me names."

She almost smiled but she hid it quickly. What would it take for him to squeeze a real smile out of her and keep it there? he wondered.

"I know we can't go back and change things," he said slowly. "But what are the chances that we can at least be civil to each other? We were good friends once, before we became more. I miss that."

She was quiet for several moments and he was aware of the random sounds of the old inn. The shifting of old wood, the creak of a floorboard somewhere, a tree branch that needed to be pruned back rattling against the thin glass of the window.

When she spoke, her voice was low. "I miss it, too," she said, in the tone of someone confessing a rather shameful secret.

Something inside him seemed to uncoil at her words. He gazed at her so-familiar features that he had once known as well as his own.

The high cheekbones, the cute little nose, those blue eyes that always reminded him of his favorite columbines that grew above the ranch. He wanted to kiss her, with a raw ferocity that shocked him to his toes. To sink into her and not climb out again.

He managed, just barely, to restrain himself and was grateful for it when she spoke again, her voice just above a whisper.

"We can't go back, Taft."

"No, but we can go forward. That's better anyway, isn't it? The reality is, we're both living in the same small town. Right now we're living at the same address, for Pete's sake. We can't avoid each other. But that doesn't mean we need to go on with this awkwardness between us, does it? I would really like to see if together we can find some way to move past it. What do you say?"

She gazed at him for a long moment, uncertainty in those eyes he loved so much. Finally she seemed to come to some internal decision.

"Sure. We can try to be friends again." She gave him a tentative smile. A real one this time, not that polite thing he had come to hate, and his chest felt tight and achy all over again.

"I need to get back to work. I'll see you later."

"Goodbye, Laura," he said.

She gave him one more little smile before hurrying out of the room. He watched her go, more off-balance by the encounter with Laura and her children than he wanted to admit. As he turned back to his work, he was also aware of a vague sense of melancholy that made no sense. This was progress, right? Friendship was a good place to start—hadn't their relationship begun out of friendship from the beginning?

He picked up another board from the pile. He knew the source of his discontent. He wanted more than friendship with Laura. He wanted what they used to have, laughter and joy and that contentment that seemed to seep through him every time he was with her.

Baby steps, he told himself. He could start with friendship and then gradually build on that, see how things progressed. Nothing wrong with a little patience once in a while.

Her hands were still shaking as Laura walked out of the room and down the hall. She headed for the lobby, with the curving old stairs and the classic light fixtures that had probably been installed when Pine Gulch finally hit the electrical grid.

Only when she was certain she was completely out of sight of Taft did she lean against the delicately flowered wallpaper and press a hand to her stomach.

What an idiot she was, as weak as a baby lamb around him. She always had been. Even if she had hours of other more urgent homework, if Taft called her and needed help with Spanish, she would drop everything to rush to his aid.

It didn't help matters that the man was positively dangerous when he decided to throw out the charm.

Oh, it would be so easy to give in, to let all that seductive charm slide around and through her until she forgot all the reasons she needed to resist him.

He asked if they could find a way to friendship again. She didn't have the first idea how to answer that. She wanted to believe her heart had scarred over from the disappointment and heartache, the loss of those dreams for the future, but she was more than a little afraid to peek past the scars to see if it had truly healed.

She was tough and resilient. Hadn't she survived a bad marriage and then losing the husband she had tried to love? She could surely carry on a civil conversation with Taft on the rare occasions they met in Pine Gulch.

What was the harm in it? For heaven's sake, re-establishing a friendly relationship with the man didn't mean she was automatically destined to tumble head-long back into love with him.

Life in Pine Gulch would be much easier all the way around if she didn't feel jumpy and off-balance every time she was around him.

She eased away from the wallpaper and straightened her shirt that had bunched up. This was all ridiculous anyway. What did it matter if she was weak around him? She likely wouldn't ever have the opportunity to test out her willpower. From the rumors she heard, Taft probably had enough young, hot bar babes at the Bandito that he probably couldn't be bothered with a thirty-two-year-old widow with two children, one of whom with a disability that would require lifelong care.

She wasn't the same woman she had been ten years ago. She had given birth to two kids and had the body to show for it. Her hair was always messy and falling out of whatever clip she had shoved it in that morning, half the time she didn't have time to put on makeup until she had been up for hours and, between the kids and the inn, she was perpetually stressed.

Why on earth would a man like Taft, gorgeous and masculine, want anything *but* friendship with her these days?

She wasn't quite sure why that thought depressed her and made her feel like that gawky seventh grader with braces crushing on a ninth-grade athlete who was nice to her.

Surely she didn't *want* to have to resist Taft Bowman. It was better all around if he saw her merely as that frumpy mother.

She knew that was probably true, even as some secret, silly little part of her wanted to at least have the *chance* to test her willpower around him.

Chapter 6

"Hurry, Mama." Alex practically jumped out of his booster seat the moment she turned off the engine at the River Bow Ranch on Saturday. "I want to see the dogs!"

"Dogs!" Maya squealed after him, wiggling and tugging against the car-seat straps. The only reason she didn't rush to join her brother outside the car was her inability to undo the straps on her own, much to her constant frustration.

"Hang on, you two." Their excitement made her smile, despite the host of emotions churning through her at visiting the River Bow again for the first time in a decade. "The way you're acting, somebody might think you'd never seen a dog before."

"I have, too, seen a dog before," Alex said. "But this isn't just *one* dog. Miss Bowman said she had a *lot* of dogs. And horses, too. Can I really ride one?"

"That's the plan for now, but we'll have to see how things go." She was loath to make promises about things that were out of her control. Probably a fallback to her marriage, those frequent times when the children would be so disappointed if their father missed dinner or a school performance or some special outing.

"I hope I *can* ride a horse. Oh, I hope so." Alex practically danced around the used SUV she had purchased with the last of her savings when she arrived back in the States. She had to smile at his enthusiasm as she unstrapped Maya and lifted her out of the vehicle.

Maya threw her chubby little arms around Laura's neck before she could set her on the ground.

"Love you," her daughter said.

The spontaneously affectionate gesture turned her insides to warm mush, something her sweet Maya so often did. "Oh, I love you, too, darling. More than the moon and the stars and the sea."

"Me, too," Alex said.

She hugged him with the arm not holding Maya. "I love you both. Aren't I the luckiest mom in the world to have two wonderful kiddos to love?"

"Yes, you are," he said, with a total lack of vanity that made her smile.

She supposed she couldn't be a completely terrible mother if she was raising her children with such solid assurance of their place in her heart.

At the sound of scrabbling paws and panting breaths, she raised her head from her children. "Guess what? Here come the dogs."

Alex whirled around in time to see Caidy approaching them with three dogs shadowing her. Laura identified two of them as border collies, mostly black with white patches on their faces and necks, quizzical ears and eerily intelligent expressions. The third was either a breed she didn't recognize or some kind of mutt of undetermined origin, with reddish fur and a German shepherd–like face.

Maya stiffened nervously, not at all experienced around dogs, and tightened her arms around Laura's neck. Alex, on the other hand, started to rush toward the dogs, but Laura checked him with a hand on his shoulder.

"Wait until Caidy says it's safe," she ordered her son, who would run directly into a lion's enclosure if he thought he might have a chance of petting the creature.

"Perfectly safe," Caidy assured them.

Taft's sister wore jeans and a bright yellow T-shirt along with boots and a straw cowboy hat, her dark hair braided down her back. She looked fresh and pretty as she gave them all a welcoming smile. "The only danger from my dogs is being licked to death—or maybe getting knocked over by a wagging tail."

Alex giggled and Caidy looked delighted at the sound.

"Your mother is right, though," she said. "You should never approach any strange animal without permission until you know it's safe."

"Can I pet one?"

"Sure thing. King. Forward."

One of the lean black-and-white border collies obeyed and sidled toward them, sniffing eagerly at Alex's legs. The boy giggled and began to pet the dog with sheer joy.

"This was such a great idea," Laura said, smiling as

she watched her son. "Thank you so much for the invitation, Caidy."

"You're welcome. Believe me, it will be a fun break for me from normal ranch stuff. Spring is always crazy on the ranch and I've been looking forward to this all week as a great respite."

She paused. "I have to tell you, I'm really glad you're still willing to have anything to do with the Bowmans after the way things ended with Taft."

She really didn't want to talk about Taft. This was what she had worried about after Caidy extended the invitation, that things might be awkward between them because of the past.

"Why wouldn't I? Taft and I are still friendly." And that's all they ever *would* be, she reminded herself. "Just because he and I didn't end up the way we thought we would doesn't mean I should shun his family. I loved your family. I'm only sorry I haven't stayed in touch all these years. I see no reason we can't be friends now, unless you're too uncomfortable because of…everything?"

"Not at all!" Caidy exclaimed. Laura had the impression she wanted to say something else, but Alex interrupted before she could.

"He licked me. It tickles!"

Caidy grinned down at the boy's obvious enjoyment of the dogs. He now had all three dogs clustered around him and was petting them in turns.

"We've got puppies. Would you like to see them?" Caidy asked.

"Puppies!" Maya squealed, still in her arms, while Alex clasped his hands together, a reverential look on his face.

"Puppies! Oh, Mama, can we?"

She had to laugh at his flair for drama. "Sure. Why not? As long as it's all right with Caidy."

"They're in the barn. I was just checking on the little family a few minutes ago and it looks like a few of the pups are awake and might just be in the mood to play."

"Oh, yay!" Alex exclaimed and Caidy grinned at him.

They followed her into the barn. For Laura, it was like walking back in time. The barn smelled of hay and leather and animals, and the familiar scent mix seemed to trigger an avalanche of memories. They tumbled free of whatever place she'd stowed them after she walked away from Pine Gulch, jostling and shoving their way through her mind before she had a chance to block them out.

She used to come out to the ranch often to ride horses with Taft and their rides always started here, in the barn, where he would teach her about the different kinds of tack and how each was used, then patiently give her lessons on how to tack up a horse.

One wintry January afternoon, she suddenly remembered, she had helped him and his father deliver a foal. She could still vividly picture her astonishment at the gangly, awkward miracle of the creature.

Unbidden, she also remembered that the relative privacy of the barn compared to other places on the ranch had been one of their favorite places to kiss. Sultry, long, intense kisses that would leave them both hungry for more....

She absolutely did not need to remember *those* particular memories, full of heat and discovery and that all-consuming love that used to burn inside her for Taft. With great effort, she struggled to wrestle them back into the corner of her mind and slam the door to them so she could focus on her children and Caidy and new puppies.

The puppies' home was an empty stall at the end of the row. An old russet saddle blanket took up one corner and the mother dog, a lovely black-and-white heeler, was lying on her side taking a rest and watching her puppies wrestle around the straw-covered floor of the stall. She looked up when Caidy approached and her tail slapped a greeting.

"Hey, Betsy, here I am again. How's my best girl? I brought some company to entertain your pups for a while."

Laura could swear she saw understanding and even relief in the dog's brown eyes as Caidy unlatched the door of the stall and swung it out. She could relate to that look—every night when her children finally closed their eyes, she would collapse onto the sofa with probably that same sort of look.

"Are you sure it's okay?" Alex asked, standing outside the stall, barely containing his nervous energy.

"Perfectly sure," Caidy answered. "I promise, they love company."

He headed inside and—just as she might have predicted—Maya wriggled to get down. "Me, too," she insisted.

"Of course, darling," Laura said. She set her on her feet and the girl headed inside the stall to stand beside her brother.

"Here, sit down and I'll bring you a puppy each," Caidy said, gesturing to a low bench inside the stall, really just a plank stretched across a couple of overturned oats buckets.

She picked up a fat, waddling black-and-white puppy from the writhing, yipping mass and set it on Alex's lap, then reached into the pile again for a smaller one, mostly black this time.

Now she had some very different but infinitely precious memories of this barn to add to her collection, Laura thought a few moments later. The children were enthralled with the puppies. Children and puppies just seemed to go together like peanut butter and jelly. Alex and Maya giggled as the puppies squirmed around on their laps, licking and sniffing. Maya hugged hers as enthusiastically as she had hugged her mother a few minutes earlier.

"Thank you for this," she said to Caidy as the two of them smiled at the children and puppies. "You've thrilled them to their socks."

"I'm afraid the pups are a little dirty and don't smell the greatest. They're a little young for baths yet."

"I don't worry about a little dirt," Laura said. "I've always figured if my kids don't get dirty sometimes, I'm doing something wrong."

"I don't think you're doing *anything* wrong," Caidy assured her. "They seem like great kids."

"Thank you."

"It can't be easy, especially now that you're on your own."

As much as Javier had loved the children, she had always felt very much on her own in Madrid. He was always busy with the hotel and his friends and, of course, his other women. Bad enough she had shared that with Taft. She certainly wasn't about to share that information with his sister.

"I have my mother to help me now. She's been a lifesaver."

Coming home had been the right decision. As much as she had struggled with taking her children away from half of their heritage probably forever, Javier's family had never been very welcoming to her. They had become even less so after Maya was born, as if Laura were to blame somehow for the genetic abnormality.

"I'm just going to come out and say this, okay?" Caidy said after a moment. "I really wish you had married Taft so we could have been sisters."

"Thank you," she said, touched by the words.

"I mean it. You were the best thing that ever happened to him. We all thought so. Compared to the women he... Well, compared to anybody else he's dated, you're a million times better. I still can't believe any brother of mine was stupid enough to let you slip through his fingers. Don't think I haven't told him so, too."

She didn't know quite how to answer—or why she had this sudden urge to protect him. Taft hadn't been stupid, only hurt and lost and not at all ready for marriage.

She hadn't been ready, either, although it had taken her a few years to admit that to herself. At twenty-one, she had been foolish enough to think her love should have been enough to help him heal from the pain and anger of losing his parents in such a violent way, when he hadn't even had the resolution of the murderers being caught and brought to justice.

An idealistic, romantic young woman and an angry, bitter young man would have made a terrible combination, she thought as she sat here in this quiet barn while the puppies wriggled around with her children and a horse stamped and snorted somewhere nearby.

"I also have a confession." Caidy shifted beside her at the stall door.

She raised an eyebrow. "Do I really want to hear this?"

"Please don't be mad, okay?"

For some reason, Laura was strongly reminded of Caidy as she had known her a decade ago, the light-hearted, mischievous teenager who thought she could tease and cajole her way out of any situation.

"Tell me. What did you do?" she asked, amusement fighting the sudden apprehension curling through her.

Before the other woman could answer, a male voice rang out through the barn. "Caidy? Are you in here?"

Her stomach dropped and the little flutters of apprehension became wild-winged flaps of anxiety.

Caidy winced. "Um, I may have casually mentioned to Taft that you and the children were coming out to the ranch today and that we might be going up on the Aspen Leaf Trail, if he wanted to tag along."

So much for her master plan of escaping the inn today so she could keep her children—and herself—out from underfoot while he was working on the other renovations.

"Are you mad?" Caidy asked.

She forced a smile when she really wanted to sit right down on the straw-covered floor of the stall and cry.

Yes, when she decided to return to Pine Gulch, she had known seeing him again was inevitable. She just hadn't expected to bump into the dratted man every flipping time she turned around.

"Why would I be mad? Your brother and I are

friends." Or at least she was working hard at pretending they could be. Anyway, this was his family's ranch. Some part of her had known when she accepted Caidy's invitation to come out for a visit that there was a chance he might be here.

"Oh, good. I was worried things might be weird between the two of you."

But you invited him along anyway? she wanted to ask, but decided that sounded rude. "No. It's perfectly fine," she lied.

"I thought he could lend a hand with the children. He's really patient with them. In fact, he's the one who taught Gabi to ride. Gabi is the daughter of Becca, Trace's fiancée. Anyway, it's always good to have another experienced rider on hand when you've got kids who haven't been on a horse before."

"Caidy?" he called again.

"Back here, with the puppies," she returned.

A moment later, Taft rounded the corner of a support beam. At the sight of him, everything inside her seemed to shiver.

Okay, really? This was getting ridiculous. She huffed. So far since she had been back in town, she had seen the man in full firefighter turnout gear when he and his crew responded to the inn fire, wearing a low-slung construction belt while he worked on the renovations at the inn, and now he was dressed in worn jeans, cowboy boots and a tan Stetson that made him look dark and dangerous.

Was he purposely trying to look as if he just stepped off every single page of a beefcake calendar?

Taft Bowman—doing his part to fulfill any woman's fantasy.

"Here you are," he said with that irresistible smile.

She couldn't breathe suddenly as the dust motes floating on the air inside the barn seemed to choke her lungs. This wasn't really fair. Why hadn't his hair started to thin a little in the past decade or his gut started to paunch?

He was so blasted gorgeous and she was completely weak around him.

He leaned in to kiss his sister on the cheek. After a little awkward hesitation, much to her dismay he leaned in to kiss her on the cheek, as well. She could do nothing but endure the brush of his mouth on her skin as the familiar scent of him, outdoorsy and male, filled her senses, unleashing another flood of memories.

Before she could make her brain cooperate and think of something to say, her children noticed him for the first time.

"Hi!" Maya beamed with delight.

"Hey, pumpkin. How are things?"

"Look! Puppies!"

She thrust the endlessly patient black puppy at him and Taft graciously accepted the dog. "He's a cute one. What's his name, Caid?"

"Puppy Number Five," she answered. "I don't name them when I sell them as pups without training. I let their new owners do it."

"Look at this one." Alex pushed past his sister to hold up his own chubby little canine friend.

"Nice," Taft said. He knelt right there in the straw and was soon covered in puppies and kids. Even the tired-looking mother dog came over to him for affection.

"Hey, Betsy. How are you holding up with this brood?"

he asked, rubbing the dog between the ears and earning a besotted look that Laura found completely exasperating.

"Thanks for coming out," Caidy said.

"Not a problem. I can think of few things I enjoy more than going on a spring ride into the mountains."

"Not too far into the mountains," she assured Laura. "We can't go very far this time of year anyway. Too much snow, at least for a good month or so."

"Aspen Leaf is open, though, isn't it?"

"Yes. Destry and I checked it the other day. She was disappointed to miss the ride today, by the way," Caidy told Laura. "Becca was taking her and Gabi into Idaho Falls for fittings for their flower-girl dresses."

"And you missed out on all that girly fun?" Taft asked, climbing to his feet and coming to stand beside his sister and Laura. Suddenly she felt crowded by his heat and size and…maleness.

"Are you kidding? This will be much more enjoyable. If you haven't heard, Trace is getting hitched in June," she said to Laura.

"To Pine Gulch's newest attorney, if you can believe that," Taft added.

She *had* heard and she was happy for Trace. He had always been very kind to her. Trace, the Pine Gulch police chief, had always struck her as much more serious than Taft, the kind of person who liked to think things through before he spoke.

For being identical twins, Taft and Trace had two very unique personalities, and even though they were closer than most brothers, they had also actively cultivated friendships beyond each other, probably because of their mother's wise influence.

She did find it interesting that both of them had chosen professions in the public-safety sector, although Trace had taken a route through the military to becoming a policeman while Taft had gravitated toward fire safety and becoming a paramedic.

"Why don't we give the kids another few minutes with the puppies?" Caidy said. "I've already saddled a couple of horses I thought would be a good fit."

"Do I need to saddle Joe?"

"Nope. He's ready for you."

Taft grinned. "You mean all I had to do today was show up?"

"That's the story of your life, isn't it?" Caidy said with a disgruntled sort of affection. "If you want to, I'll let you unsaddle everybody when we're done and groom all the horses. Will that make you feel better?"

"Much. Thanks."

The puppy on Maya's lap wriggled through her fingers and waddled over to squat in the straw.

"Look," she exclaimed with an inordinate degree of delight. "Puppy pee!"

Taft chuckled at that. "I think all the puppies are ready for a snack and a nap. Why don't we go see if the horses are ready for us?"

"Yes!" Maya beamed and scampered eagerly toward Taft, where she reached up to grab his hand. After a stunned sort of moment, he smiled at her and folded her hand more securely in his much bigger one.

Alex rose reluctantly and set the puppy he had been playing with down in the straw. "Bye," he whispered, a look of naked longing clear for all to see.

"I hear the kid wants a dog. You know you're going to have to cave, don't you?" Taft spoke in a low voice.

Laura sighed through her own dismay. "You don't think I'm tough enough to resist a six-year-old?"

"I'm not sure a hardened criminal could resist *that* particular six-year-old."

He was right, darn it. She was pretty sure she would have to give in and let her son have a dog. Not a border collie, certainly, because they were active dogs and needed work to do, but she would find something.

As they walked outside the barn toward the horse pasture, she saw Alex's eyes light up at the sight of four horses saddled and waiting. Great. Now he would probably start begging her for a horse, too.

She had to admit, a little burst of excitement kicked through her, too, as they approached the animals. She loved horses and she actually had Taft to thank for that. Unlike many of her schoolmates in the sprawling Pine Gulch school district, which encompassed miles of ranch land, she was a city girl who walked or rode her bike to school instead of taking the bus. Even though she had loved horses from the time she was young— didn't most girls?—her parents had patiently explained they didn't have room for one of their own at their home adjacent to the inn.

She had enjoyed riding with friends who lived outside of town, but had very much considered herself a greenhorn until she became friends with Taft. Even before they started dating, she would often come out to the ranch and ride with him and sometimes Caidy into the mountains.

This would be rather like old times—which, come to think of it, wasn't necessarily a good thing.

Since moving away from Pine Gulch, she hadn't been

on a horse one single time, she realized with shock. Even more reason for this little thrum of anticipation.

"Wow, they're really big," Alex said in a soft voice. Maya seemed nervous as well, clinging tightly to Taft's hand.

"Big doesn't have to mean scary," Taft assured him. "These are really gentle horses. None of them will hurt you. I promise. Old Pete, the horse you're going to ride, is so lazy, you'll be lucky to make it around the barn before he decides to stop and take a nap."

Alex giggled but it had a nervous edge to it and Taft gave him a closer look.

"Do you want to meet him?"

Her son toed the dirt with the shiny new cowboy boots she had picked up at the farm-implement store before they drove out to the ranch. "I guess. You sure they don't bite?"

"Some horses do. Not any of the River Bow horses. I swear it."

He picked Maya up in his arms and reached for Alex's hand, leading them both over to the smallest of the horses, a gray with a calm, rather sweet face.

"This is Pete," Taft said. "He's just about the gentlest horse we've ever had here at River Bow. He'll treat you right, kid."

As she watched from the sidelines, the horse bent his head down and lipped Alex's shoulder. Alex froze, eyes wide and slightly terrified, but Taft set a reassuring hand on his other shoulder. "Don't worry. He's just looking for a treat."

"I don't have a treat." Alex's voice quavered a bit. These uncharacteristic moments of fear from her usually bold, mischievous son always seemed to take her by surprise, although she knew they were perfectly normal from a developmental standpoint.

Taft reached into his pocket and pulled out a handful of small red apples. "You're in luck. I always carry a supply of crab apples for old Pete. They're his favorite, probably because I can let him have only a few at a time. It's probably like you eating pizza. A little is great, but too much would make you sick. Same for Pete and crab apples."

"Where on earth do you find crab apples in April?" Laura couldn't resist asking.

"That's my secret."

Caidy snorted. "Not much of a secret," she said. "Every year, my crazy brother gathers up two or three bushels from the tree on the side of the house and stores them down in the root cellar. Nobody else will touch the things—they're too bitter even for pies unless you pour in cup after cup of sugar—but old Pete loves them. Every year Taft puts up a supply so he's got something to bring the old codger."

She shouldn't find it so endearing to imagine him picking crab apples to give to an old, worn-out horse—or to watch his ears turn as red as the apples under his cowboy hat.

He handed one of the pieces of sour fruit to her son and showed him the correct way to feed the horse. Alex held his hand out flat and old Pete lapped it up.

"It tickles like the dog," Alex exclaimed.

"But it doesn't hurt, right?" Taft asked.

The boy shook his head with a grin. "Nope. Just tickles. Hi, Pete."

The horse seemed quite pleased to make his acquaintance, especially after he produced a few more crab apples for the horse, handed to him by Taft.

"Ready to hop up there now?" Taft asked. When the boy nodded, Caidy stepped up with a pair of riding helmets waiting on the fence.

"We're going to swap that fancy cowboy hat for a helmet, okay?"

"I like my cowboy hat, though. I just got it."

"And you can wear it again when we get back. But when you're just learning to ride, wearing a helmet is safer."

"Just like at home when you have to wear your bicycle helmet," Laura told him.

"No helmet, no horse," Taft said sternly.

Her son gave them all a grudging look, but he removed his cowboy hat and handed it to his mother, then allowed Caidy to fasten on the safety helmet. Caidy took Maya from Taft and put one on her, as well, which eased Laura's safety worries considerably.

Finally Taft picked up Alex and hefted him easily into the saddle. The glee on her son's face filled her with a funny mix of happiness and apprehension. He was growing up, embracing risks, and she wasn't sure she was ready for that.

Caidy stepped up to adjust the stirrups to the boy's height. "There you go, cowboy. That should be better."

"What do I do now?" Alex asked with an eager look up into the mountains as if he were ready to go join a posse and hunt for outlaws right this minute.

"Well, the great thing about Pete is how easygoing he is," Taft assured him. "He's happy to just follow along behind the other horses. That's kind of his specialty and what makes him a perfect horse for somebody just beginning. I'll hold his lead line so you won't even have to worry about turning him or making him slow down or anything. Next time you come out to the ranch we'll work on those other things, but this time is just for fun."

Next time? She frowned, annoyed that he would give Alex the impression there would be another time—and that Taft would be part of it, if she ever did bring the kids out to River Bow again. Children didn't forget things like that. Alex would hold him to it and be gravely disappointed if a return trip never materialized.

This was not going at all like she'd planned. She and Caidy were supposed to be taking the children for an easy ride. Instead Taft seemed to have taken over, in typical fashion, while Caidy answered her cell phone a short distance away from the group.

After a moment, Maya grew impatient and tugged on his jeans. "My horse?" she asked, looking around at the animals. She looked so earnest and adorable that it was tough for Laura to stay annoyed at anything.

He smiled down at her with such gentleness that her chest ached. "I was thinking you could just ride with me on my old friend Joe. What do you say, pumpkin? We'll try a pony for you another day, okay?"

She appeared to consider this, looking first at the big black gelding he pointed at, then back at Taft. Finally she gave him that brilliant, wide heartbreaker of a smile. "Okay."

Taft Bowman may have met his match for sheer charm, she thought.

"I guess that just leaves me," she said, eyeing the two remaining horses. Something told her the dappled gray-and-black mare was Caidy's, which left the bay for her.

"Do you need a crab apple to break the ice, too?"

Taft asked with a teasing smile so appealing she had to turn away.

"I think I'll manage," she said more tersely than she intended. She modified her tone to be a little warmer. "What's her name?"

"Lacey," he answered.

"Hi, Lacey." She stroked the horse's neck and was rewarded with an equine raspberry sound that made Alex laugh.

"That sounded like her mouth farted!" he exclaimed.

"That's just her way of saying hi." Taft's gaze met hers, laughter brimming in his green eyes, and Laura wanted to sink into those eyes.

Darn the man.

She stiffened her shoulders and resolve and shoved her boot in the stirrup, then swung into the saddle and tried not to groan at the pull of muscles she hadn't used in a long time.

Taft pulled the horse's reins off the tether and handed them to her. Their hands brushed again, a slight touch of skin against skin, and she quickly pulled the reins to the other side and jerked her attention away from her reaction to Taft and back to the thousand-pound animal beneath her.

Oh, she had missed this, she thought, loosely holding the reins and reacquainting herself to the unique feel of being on a horse. She had missed all of it. The stretch of her muscles, the heat of the sun on her bare head, the vast peaks of the Tetons in the distance.

"You ready, sweetie?" he asked Maya, who nodded, although the girl suddenly looked a little shy.

"Everything will be just fine," he assured her. "I won't let go. I promise."

He loosed his horse's reins from the hitch as well as the lead line for old Pete before setting Maya in the saddle. Her daughter looked small and vulnerable at such a height, even under her safety helmet, but she had to trust that Taft would take care of her.

"While I mount up, you hold on right there. It's called the saddle horn. Got it?"

"Got it," she mimicked. "Horn."

"Excellent. Hang on, now. I'll keep one hand on you."

Laura watched anxiously, afraid Maya would slide off at the inevitable jostling of the saddle, but she needn't have worried. He swung effortlessly into the saddle, then scooped an arm around the girl.

"Caid? You coming?" Taft called.

She glanced over and saw Caidy finish her phone conversation and tuck her cell into her pocket, then walk toward them, her features tight with concern. "We've got a problem."

"What's wrong?"

"That was Ridge. A speeder just hit a dog a quarter mile or so from the front ranch gates. Ridge was right behind the idiot and saw the whole thing happen."

"One of yours?" Taft asked.

Her braid swung as she shook her head. "No. I think it's a little stray I've seen around the last few weeks. I've been trying to coax him to come closer to the house but he's pretty skittish. Looks like he's got a broken leg and Ridge isn't sure what to do with him."

"Can't he take him to the vet?"

"He can't reach Doc Harris. I guess he's been trying to find the backup vet but he's in the middle of equine surgery up at Cold Creek Ranch. I should go help. Poor guy."

"Ridge or the stray?"

"Both. Ridge is a little out of his element with dogs. He can handle horses and cattle, but anything smaller than a calf throws him off his game." She paused and sent a guilty look toward Laura. "I'm sorry to do this after I invited you out and all, but do you think you'll be okay with only my brother as a guide while I go help with this injured dog?"

If not for the look in Caidy's eyes, Laura might have thought she had manufactured the whole thing as an elaborate ruse to throw her and Taft together. But either Caidy was an excellent actress or her distress was genuine.

"Of course. Don't worry about a thing. Do you need our help?"

The other woman shook her head again. "I doubt it. To be honest, I'm not sure there's anything *I* can do, but I have to try, right? I'm just sorry to invite you out here and then ditch you."

"No worries. We should be fine. We're not going far, are we?"

Taft shook his head. "Up the hill about a mile. There's a nice place to stop and have the picnic Caidy packed."

She did *not* feel like having a picnic with him but could think of no graceful way to extricate herself and her children from it, especially when Alex and Maya appeared to be having the time of their lives.

"Thanks for being understanding," Caidy said, with a harried look, unsaddling the other horse at lightning speed. "I'll make it up to you."

"No need," Laura said as her horse took a step or two sideways, anxious to go. "Take care of the stray for us."

"I'll do my best. Maybe I'll try to catch up with you. If I don't make it, though, I'll probably see you later after you come back down."

She glanced up at the sky. "Looks like a few clouds gathering up on the mountain peaks. I hope it doesn't rain on you."

"They're pretty high. We should be fine for a few hours," Taft said. "Good luck with the dog. Shall we, guys?"

Leaving Caidy behind to deal with a crisis felt rude and selfish, but Laura didn't know what else to do. The children would be terribly disappointed if she backed out of the ride, and Caidy was right. What could they do to help her with the injured dog?

She sighed. And of course this also meant she and the children would have to be alone with Taft.

She supposed it was a very good thing Taft had no reason to be romantically interested in her anymore. She had a feeling she would be even more weak than normal on a horseback ride with him into the mountains, especially when she had so many memories of other times and other rides that usually ended with them making out somewhere on the ranch.

"Yes," she finally said. "Let's go."

The sooner they could be on their way, the quicker they could return and she and her children could go back to the way things were before Taft burst so insistently back into her life.

Chapter 7

With Maya perched in front of him, Taft led the way and held the lead line for Alex's horse while Laura brought up the rear. A light breeze danced in her hair as they traveled through verdant pastureland on their way to a trailhead just above the ranch.

The afternoon seemed eerily familiar, a definite déjà vu moment. It took her a moment to realize why—she used to fantasize about a day exactly like this when she had been young and full of dreams. She used to imagine the two of them spending a lovely spring afternoon together on horseback along with their children, laughing and talking, pausing here and there for some of those kisses she had once been so addicted to.

Okay, they had the horses and the kids here and definitely the lovely spring afternoon, but the rest of it wasn't going to happen. Not on her watch.

She focused on the trail, listening to Alex jabber a mile a minute about everything he saw, from the double-trunked pine tree alongside the trail, to one of Caidy's dogs that had come along with them, to about how much he loved old Pete. The gist, as she fully expected, was that he now wanted a horse *and* a dog of his own.

The air here smelled delicious: sharp, citrusy pine, the tart, evocative scent of sagebrush, woodsy earth and new growth.

She had missed the scent of the mountains. Madrid had its own distinctive smells, flowers and spices and baking bread, but this, this was home.

They rode for perhaps forty minutes until Alex's chatter started to die away. It was hard work staying atop a horse. Even if the rest of him wasn't sore, she imagined his jaw muscles must be aching.

The deceptively easy grade led one to think they weren't gaining much in altitude, but finally they reached a clearing where the pines and aspens opened up and she could look down on the ranch and see its eponymous river bow, a spot where the river's course made a horseshoe bend, almost folding in on itself. The water glimmered in the afternoon sunlight, reflecting the mountains and trees around it.

She admired the sight from atop her horse, grateful that Taft had stopped, then realized he was dismounting with Maya still in his arms.

"I imagine your rear end could use a little rest," he said to Alex, earning a giggle.

"Sí," he said, reverting to the Spanish he sometimes still used. "My bum hurts and I need to pee," he said.

"We can take care of that. Maya, you sit here while I help your brother." He set the girl atop a couch-size boulder, then returned to the horses and lifted Alex down, then turned to Laura again. "What about you? Need a hand?"

"I've got it," she answered, quite certain it wouldn't be a good idea for him to help her dismount.

Her muscles were stiff, even after such a short time on the horse, and she welcomed the chance to stretch her legs a little. "Come on, Alex. I'll take you over to the bushes. Maya, do you need to go?"

She shook her head, busy picking flowers.

"I'll keep an eye on her," Taft said. "Unless you need me on tree duty?"

She shook her head, amused despite herself, at the term. "I've got it."

As she walked away, she didn't want to think about what a good team they made or how very similar this was to those fantasies she used to weave.

Alex thought it was quite a novel thing to take care of his business against a tree and didn't even complain when she whipped the hand sanitizer out of her pocket and made him use it afterward.

The moment they returned to the others, Caidy's dog King brought a stick over and dropped it at Alex's feet, apparently knowing an easy mark when he saw one. Alex picked up the stick and chucked it for the dog as far as his little arm could go and the dog bounded after it while Maya clapped her hands with excitement.

"Me next," she said.

The two were perfectly content to play with the dog and Laura was just as content to lean against a sun-warmed granite boulder and watch them while she listened to a meadowlark's familiar song.

Idaho is a pretty little place. That's what her mother

always used to say the birds were trilling. The memory made her smile.

"I can picture you just like that when you were younger. Your hair was longer, but you haven't changed much at all."

He had leaned his hip against the boulder where she sat and her body responded instantly to his proximity, to the familiar scent of him. She edged away so their shoulders wouldn't brush and wondered if he noticed.

"I'm afraid that's where you're wrong. I'm a very different person. Who doesn't change in ten years?"

"Yeah, you're right. I'm not the same man I was a decade ago. I like to think I'm smarter these days about holding on to what's important."

"Do you ride often?" she asked.

A glint in his eye told her he knew very well she didn't want to tug on that particular conversational line, but he went along with the obvious change of topic. "Not as much as I would like. My niece, Destry, loves to ride and now Gabi has caught the bug. As often as they can manage it, they do their best to persuade one of us to take them for a ride. I haven't been up for a few months, though."

He obviously loved his niece. She had already noticed that soft note in his voice when he talked about the girl. She would have expected it. The Bowmans had always been a close, loving family before their parents' brutal murder. She expected they would welcome Becca and her sister into the family's embrace, as well.

"Too busy with your social life?"

The little niggle of envy under her skin turned her tone more caustic than she intended, but he didn't seem offended.

He even chuckled. "Sure. If by *social life* you mean the house I'm building on the edge of town that's filled all my waking hours for the last six months. I haven't had much room for other things."

"You're building it yourself?"

"Most of it. I've had help here and there. Plumbing. HVAC. That sort of thing. I don't have the patience for good drywall work, so I paid somebody else to do that, too. But I've done all the carpentry and most of the electrical. I can give you some good names of subcontractors I trust if you decide to do more on the inn."

"Why a house?"

He appeared to be giving her question serious thought as he watched the children playing with the dog, with the grand sprawl of the ranch below them. "I guess I was tired of throwing away rent money and living in a little apartment where I didn't have room to stretch out. I've had this land for a long time. I don't know. Seemed like it was time."

"You're building a house. That's pretty permanent. Does that mean you're planning to stay in Pine Gulch?"

He shrugged, and despite her efforts to keep as much distance as possible between them, his big shoulder still brushed hers. "Where else would I go? Maybe I should have taken off for somewhere exotic when I had the chance. What do they pay firefighters in Madrid?"

"I'm afraid I have no idea. I have friends I can ask, though." He would fit in well there, she thought, and the *madrileñas*—the women of Madrid—would go crazy for his green eyes and teasing smile.

Which he utilized to full effect on her now. "That eager to get rid of me?"

She had no answer to that, so she again changed the subject. "Where did you say your house was?"

"A couple of miles from here, near the mouth of Cold Creek Canyon. I've got about five acres there in the trees. Enough room to move over some of my own horses eventually."

He paused, an oddly intent look in his green eyes. "You ought to come see it sometime. I would even let Alex pound a couple of nails if he wanted."

She couldn't afford to spend more time with him, not when he seemed already to be sneaking past all her careful defenses. "I'm sure we've got all the nails Alex could wish to pound at the inn."

"Sure. Yeah. Of course." He nodded, appearing nonchalant, but she had the impression she had hurt him somehow.

She wanted to make it right, tell him she would love to come see his house under construction anytime he wanted them to, but she caught the ridiculous words before she could blurt them out.

Taft picked up an early-spring wildflower—she thought it might be some kind of phlox—and twirled it between his fingers, his gaze on the children playing with the dog. This time he was the one who picked another subject. "How are the kids settling into Pine Gulch?"

"So far they're loving it, especially having their grandmother around."

"What about you?"

She looked out over the ranch and at the mountains in the distance. "It's good. There are a lot of things I love about being home, things I missed more than I realized while I was in Spain. Those mountains, for instance. I had forgotten how truly quiet and peaceful it could be here."

"This is one of my favorite places on the ranch."

"I remember."

Her soft words hung between them and she heartily wished she could yank them back. Tension suddenly seethed between them and she saw that he also remembered the significance of this place.

Right here in this flower-strewn meadow was where they had kissed that first time when he had returned after the dangerous flashover. She had always considered it their place, and every time she came here after that, she remembered the sheer joy bursting through her as he finally—finally!—saw her as more than just his friend.

They had come here often after that. He had proposed, right here, while they were stretched out on a blanket in the meadow grass.

She suddenly knew it was no accident he had stopped the horses here. Anger pumped through her, hot and fierce, that he would dredge up all these hopes and dreams and emotions she had buried after she left Pine Gulch.

With jerky motions, she climbed off the boulder. "We should probably be heading back."

His mouth tightened and he looked as if he wanted to say something else but he seemed to change his mind. "Yeah, you're right. That sky is looking a little ominous."

She looked up to find dark clouds smearing the sky, a perfect match to her mood, as if she had conjured them. "Where did those come from? A minute ago it was perfectly sunny."

"It's springtime in Idaho, where you can enjoy all four seasons in a single afternoon. Caidy warned us about possible rain. I should have been paying more attention. You ready, kids?" he called. "We've got to go."

Alex frowned from where he and Maya were flopped in the dirt petting the dog. "Do we have to?"

"Unless you want to get drenched and have to ride down on a mud slide all the way to the ranch."

"Can we?" Alex asked eagerly.

Taft laughed, although it sounded strained around the edges. "Not this time. It's up to us to make sure the ladies make it back in one piece. Think you're up to it?"

If she hadn't been so annoyed with Taft, she might have laughed at the way Alex puffed out his little chest. "Yes, sir," he answered.

"Up you go, then, son." He lifted the boy up onto the saddle and adjusted his helmet before he turned back to Maya.

"What about you, Maya, my girl? Are you ready?"

Her daughter beamed and scampered toward him. Watching them all only hardened Laura's intention to fortify her defenses around Taft.

One person in her family needed to resist the man. By the looks of things, she was the only one up for the job.

Maybe.

They nearly made it.

About a quarter mile from the ranch, the clouds finally let loose, unleashing a torrent of rain in one of those spring showers that come on so fast, so cold and merciless that they had no time to really prepare themselves.

By the time they reached the barn, Alex was shivering, Laura's hair was bedraggled and Taft was kicking himself for not hurrying them down the hill a little faster. At least Maya stayed warm and dry, wrapped in the spare raincoat he pulled out of his saddlebag.

He took them straight to the house instead of the barn. After he climbed quickly down from his horse, he set Laura's little girl on the porch, then quickly returned to the horses to help Alex dismount.

"Head on up to the porch with your sister," he ordered. After making sure the boy complied, he reached up without waiting for permission and lifted Laura down, as well. He winced as her slight frame trembled when he set her onto solid ground again.

"I'm sorry," he said. "I should have been paying better attention to the weather. That storm took me by surprise."

Her teeth chattered and her lips had a blue tinge to them he didn't like at all. "It's okay. My SUV has a good heater. We'll warm up soon enough."

"Forget it. You're not going home in wet clothes. Come inside and we'll find something you and the kids can change into."

"It's fine. We'll be home in fifteen minutes."

"If I let you go home cold and wet, I would never hear the end of it from Caidy. Trust me—the wrath of Caidy is a fearful thing and she would shoot me if I let you get sick. Come on. The horses can wait out here for a minute."

He scooped both kids into his arms, much to their giggly enjoyment, and carried them into the ranch house to cut off any further argument. That they could still laugh under such cold and miserable conditions touched something deep inside him.

He loved these kids already. How had that happened? Alex, with his million questions, Maya with her loving spirit and eager smile. Somehow when he wasn't looking, they had tiptoed straight into his heart and he had a powerful feeling he wasn't going to be able to shoo them out again anytime soon.

He wanted more afternoons like this one, full of fun and laughter and this sense of belonging. Hell, he wasn't picky. He would take mornings or evenings or any time he could have with Laura and her kids.

Yet Laura seemed quite determined to keep adding bricks to the wall between them. Every time he felt as if he was maybe making a little progress, she built up another layer and he didn't know what the hell to do about it.

"Here's the plan," he said when she trailed reluctantly inside after him. "You get the kids out of their wet clothes and wrapped in warm blankets. We've got a gas fireplace in the TV room that will warm you up in a second. Meanwhile, I'll see what I can do about finding something for you to wear."

"This is ridiculous. Honestly, Taft, we can be home and changed into our own clothes in the time it's going to take you to find something here."

He aimed a stern look at her. "Forget it. I'm not letting you leave this ranch until you're dry, and that's the end of it. I'm a paramedic, trained in public safety. How would it look if the Pine Gulch fire chief stood around twiddling his thumbs while his town's newest citizens got hypothermia?"

"Oh, stop exaggerating. We're not going to get hypothermia," she muttered, but she still followed him to the media room of the ranch house, a big, comfortable space with multiple sofas and recliners.

This happened to be one of his favorite rooms at River Bow Ranch, a place where he and his brothers often gathered to watch college football and NBA basketball.

He flipped the switch for the fireplace. The blower immediately came on, throwing welcome heat into the room while he grabbed a couple of blankets from behind one of the leather sofas for the kids.

"Here you go. You guys shuck your duds and wrap up in these blankets."

"Really?" Alex looked wide-eyed. "Can we, Mama?"

"Just for a few minutes, while we throw our clothes in the dryer."

"I'll be back in a second with something of Caidy's for you," he told her.

He headed into his sister's room and quickly found a pair of sweats and a hooded sweatshirt in the immaculately organized walk-in closet.

By the time he returned to the TV room, the children were bundled in blankets and cuddled up on the couch. He set the small pile of clothes on the edge of the sofa.

"Here you go. I know Caidy won't mind if you borrow them. The only thing in this situation that would make her angry would be if I *didn't* give you dry clothes."

Even though her mouth tightened as if she wanted to argue, she only nodded. The wet locks of hair hanging loosely around her face somehow made her even more beautiful to him. She seemed delicate and vulnerable here in the flickering firelight, and he wanted to tuck her up against him and keep her safe forever.

Yeah, he probably should keep that particular desire to himself for the moment.

"Give me a few minutes to take care of the horses and then I can throw your clothes in the dryer."

"I think I can probably manage to find the laundry room by myself," she murmured. "I'll just toss everything in there together after I change."

"Okay. I'll be back in a few minutes."

Caring for the horses took longer than he'd hoped. He was out of practice, he guessed, plus he had three horses to unsaddle.

When he finally finished up in the barn about half an hour later, the rain was still pouring in sheets that slanted sideways from the wind. Harsh, punishing drops cut into him as he headed back up the porch steps and into the entryway.

Caidy wouldn't be happy about him dripping all over her floor but she would probably forgive him, especially because he had done his best to take good care of the horses—and her guests. That would go a long way toward keeping him out of the doghouse.

He headed into Ridge's room to swipe a dry pair of jeans and a soft green henley. After quickly changing, he walked through the house in his bare feet to the TV room to check on Laura and her kids.

When he opened the door, she pressed a finger to her mouth and gestured to one of the sofas. He followed her gaze and found both Alex and Maya asleep, wrapped in blankets and nestled together like Caidy's puppies while a cartoon on the television murmured softly in the background.

"Wow, that was fast," he whispered. "How did *that* happen?"

She rose with a sidelong look at her sleeping children and led the way back into the hall. She had changed into Caidy's clothes, he could see, and pulled her damp hair back into a ponytail. In the too-big hoodie, she looked young and sweet and very much like the girl he had fallen in love with.

"It's been a big afternoon for them, full of much more excitement than they're used to, and Maya, at least, missed her nap. Of course, Alex insists he's too old for a nap, but every once in a while he still falls asleep in front of the TV."

"Yeah, I have that problem, too, sometimes."

"Really? With all that company I've heard you keep? That must be so disappointing for them."

He frowned. "I don't know what you've heard, but the rumors about my social life are greatly exaggerated."

"Are they?"

He didn't want to talk about this now. What he wanted to do was wrap his arms around her, press her up against that wall and kiss her for the next five or six hours. Because he couldn't do that, he figured he should at least try to set the record straight.

"After you broke things off and left for Spain, I... went a little crazy, I'll admit." He had mostly been trying to forget her and the aching emptiness she left behind, but he wasn't quite ready to confess that much to her. A few years later when he found out she had married another man in Madrid and was expecting a baby, he hadn't seen any reason for restraint.

"I did a lot more drinking and partying than I should

have. I'm not particularly proud of who I was back then. The thing is, a guy gets a reputation around Pine Gulch and that's how people tend to see him forever. I haven't been that wild in a long time."

"You don't have to explain yourself to me, Taft," she said, rather stiffly.

"I don't want you to think I'm the Cold Creek Casanova people seem to think."

"What does it matter what I think?"

"It matters," he said simply and couldn't resist taking her hand. Her fingers were still cold and he wrapped his bigger hands around hers. "Brrr. Let me warm up your hands. I'm sorry I didn't keep a better eye on the weather. I should have at least provided gloves for you."

"It's fine. I'm not really cold anymore." She met his gaze, then quickly looked away, and her fingers trembled slightly inside his. "Anyway, I don't think the children minded the rain that much. To them, it was all part of the adventure. Alex already told me he pretended he was a Texas marshal trying to track a bad guy. Rain and all, the whole day will be a cherished memory for them both."

Tenderness for this woman—and her children— washed through him just like that rain, carving rivulets and channels through all the places inside him that had been parched for far too long. "You're amazing at that."

A faint blush soaked her cheeks. "At what?"

"Finding the good in every situation. You always used to do that. Somehow I'd forgotten it. If you had a flat tire, you would say you appreciated the chance to slow down for a minute and enjoy your surroundings. If you broke a nail, you would just say you now had a good excuse to give yourself a manicure."

"Annoying, isn't it? How do people stand me?"

Her laugh sounded embarrassed and she tried to tug her hands away, but he held them fast, squeezing her fingers.

"No, I think it's wonderful. I didn't realize until right this moment how much I've missed that about you."

She gazed up at him, her eyes that lovely columbine-blue and her mouth slightly parted. Her fingers trembled again in his and he was aware of the scent of her, flowery and sweet, and of the sudden tension tightening between them.

He wanted to kiss her as he couldn't remember wanting anything in his life, except maybe the first time he had kissed her on the mountainside so many years ago.

If he followed through on the fierce hunger curling through him, she would just think he was being the player the whole town seemed to think he was, taking advantage of a situation just because he could.

Right now she didn't even like him very much. Better to just bide his time, give her a chance to come to know him again and trust him.

Yeah, that would be the wise, cautious thing to do. But as her hands trembled in his, he knew with a grim sort of resignation that he couldn't be wise or cautious. Not when it came to Laura.

As everything inside him tightened with anticipation, he tugged her toward him and lowered his mouth to hers.

Magic. Simply delicious. She had the softest, sweetest mouth and he couldn't believe he had forgotten how perfectly she fit against him.

Oh, he had missed her, missed this.

For about ten seconds, she didn't move anything except her fingers, now curled in his, while his mouth touched and tasted hers. For those ten seconds, he waited for her to push him away. She remained still except for her hands, and then, as if she had come to some internal decision—or maybe just resisted as long as she could—she returned the kiss, her mouth warm and soft and willing.

That was all the signal he needed to deepen the kiss. In an instant, need thundered through him and he released her hands and wrapped his arms around her, pulling her closer, intoxicated by her body pressed against him.

She felt wonderfully familiar but not quite the same, perhaps a little curvier than she'd been back when she had been his. He supposed two children and a decade could do that. He tightened his arms around her, very much appreciating the difference as her curves brushed against his chest.

She made a low sound in her throat and her arms slipped around his neck and he did what he had imagined earlier, pressed her back against the wall.

She kissed him back and he knew he didn't imagine the hitch in her breathing, the rapid heartbeat he could feel beneath his fingers.

This. This was what he wanted. Laura, right here.

All the aimless wandering of the past ten years had finally found a purpose, here in the arms of this woman. He wanted her and her children in his life. No, it was more than just a whim. He *needed* them. He pictured laughter and joy, rides into the mountains, winter nights spent cuddling by the fireplace of the log home he was building.

For her. He was building it for her and he had never

realized it until this moment. Every fixture, every detail had been aimed at creating the home they had always talked about building together.

That didn't make sense. It was completely crazy. Yeah, he'd heard her husband died some months back and had grieved for the pain she must have been feeling, but he hadn't even known she was coming home until he showed up to fight the fire at the inn and found her there.

He had thought he was just building the house he wanted, but now he could see just how perfectly she and her children would fit there.

Okay, slow down, Bowman, he told himself. One kiss did not equal happy ever after. He had hurt her deeply by pushing her away so readily after his parents died and it was going take more than just a few heated embraces to work past that.

He didn't care. He had always craved a challenge, whether that was climbing a mountain, kayaking rapids or conquering an out-of-control wildfire. He had been stupid enough to let her go once. He damn well wasn't going to do it again.

She made another low sound in her throat and he remembered how very sexy he used to find those little noises she made. Her tongue slid along his, erotic and inviting, and heat scorched through him, raw and hungry.

He was just trying to figure out how to move this somewhere a little more comfortable than against the wall of the hallway when the sound of the door opening suddenly pierced his subconscious.

A moment later, he heard his sister's voice from the entry at the other side of the house.

"We've got to go look for them." Caidy sounded stressed and almost frantic. "I can't believe Taft didn't make it back before the rain hit. What if something's happened to them?"

"He'll take care of them. Don't worry about it," Ridge replied in that calm way of his.

They would be here any second, he realized. Even though it was just about the toughest thing he'd ever done—besides standing by and letting her walk out of his life ten years ago—he eased away from her.

She looked flustered, pink, aroused. Beautiful.

He cleared his throat. "Laura," he started to say, but whatever thoughts jumbled around in his head didn't make it to words before his siblings walked down the hall and the moment was gone.

"Oh!" Caidy pedaled to a stop when she saw them. Her gaze swiveled between him and Laura and then back to him. Her eyes narrowed and he squirmed at the accusatory look in them, as if he was some sort of feudal lord having his way with the prettiest peasant. Yeah, he had kissed her, but she hadn't exactly put up any objections.

"You made it back safely."

"Yes."

Laura's voice came out husky, thready. She cleared it. Her cheeks were rosy and she refused to meet his gaze. "Yes. Safe but not quite dry. On our way down, we were caught in the first few minutes of the rainstorm. Taft loaned me some of your clothes. I hope you don't mind."

"Oh, of course! You can keep them, for heaven's sake. What about the kids? Are they okay?"

"More than okay." Her smile seemed strained, but he wasn't sure anyone but him could tell. "This was the most exciting thing that has happened to them since we've been back in Pine Gulch—and that's saying something, considering Alex started a fire that had four ladder trucks responding. They were so thrilled by the whole day that they were both exhausted and fell asleep watching cartoons while we have been waiting for our clothes to run through the dryer—which is silly, by the way. We could have been home in fifteen minutes, but Taft wouldn't let us leave in our wet gear."

"Wise man." Ridge spoke up for the first time. His brother gave him a searching look very much like Caidy's before turning back to her. "Great to see you again, Laura."

Ridge stepped forward and pulled her into a hug, and she responded with a warm smile she still hadn't given *Taft*.

"Welcome back to Pine Gulch. How are you settling in?"

"Good. Being home again is…an adventure."

"How's the dog?" Taft asked.

"Lucky. Looks like only a broken leg," Caidy said. "Doc Harris hurried back from a meeting in Pocatello so he could set it. He's keeping him overnight for observation."

"Good man, that Doc Harris."

"I know. I don't know what we're all going to do when he finally retires."

"You'll have to find another vet to keep on speed dial," Taft teased.

Caidy made a face at him, then turned back to Laura. "You and the kids will stay for dinner, won't you? I can throw soup and biscuits on and have it ready in half an hour."

As much as he wanted her to agree, he knew—even before she said the words—exactly how she would answer.

"Thank you for the invitation, but I'm afraid I'm covering the front-desk shift this evening. I'm sorry. In fact, I should really be going. I'm sure our clothes are dry by now. Perhaps another time?"

"Yes, definitely. Let me go check on your clothes."

"I can do it," Laura protested, but Caidy was faster, probably because she had grown up in a family of boys where you had to move quick if you wanted the last piece of pie or a second helping of potato salad.

Ridge and Laura talked about the inn and her plans for renovating it for the few moments it took for Caidy to return from the laundry room off the kitchen with her arms full of clothing.

"Here you go. Nice and dry."

"Great. I'll go wake up my kids and then we can get out of your way."

"You're not in our way. I promise. I'm so glad you could come out to the ranch. I'm only sorry I wasn't here for the ride, since I was the one who invited you. I'm not usually so rude."

"It wasn't rude," Laura protested. "You were helping a wounded dog. That's more important than a little ride we could have done anytime."

Caidy opened the door to the media room. Laura gave him one more emotion-charged look before following his sister, leaving Taft alone with Ridge.

His brother studied him for a long moment, reminding Taft uncomfortably of their father when he and Trace found themselves in some scrape or other.

"Be careful there, brother," Ridge finally said.

He was thirty-four years old and wasn't at all in the mood for a lecture from an older brother who tended to think he was the boss of the world. "About?"

"I've got eyes. I can tell when a woman's just been kissed."

He was *really* not in the mood to talk about Laura with Ridge. As much as he respected his brother for stepping up and taking care of both Caidy and the ranch after their parents died, Ridge was *not* their father and he didn't have to answer to the man.

"What's your point?" he asked, more belligerently than he probably should have.

Ridge frowned. "You sure you know what you're doing, dredging everything up again with Laura?"

If I figure that out, I'll be sure to let you know. "All I did was take her and her kids for a horseback ride."

Ridge was silent for a long moment. "I don't know what happened between the two of you all those years ago, why you didn't end up walking down the aisle when everybody could tell the two of you were crazy in love."

"Does it matter? It's ancient history."

"Not that ancient. Ten years. And take it from an expert, the choices we make in the past can haunt us for the rest of our lives."

Ridge should definitely know that. He had married a woman completely unsuitable for ranch life who had ended up making everybody around her miserable, too.

"Given your track record with women in the years since," Ridge went on, "I'm willing to bet you're the one who ended things. You didn't waste much time being heartbroken over the end of your engagement."

That shows what you know, he thought. "It was a mutual decision," he lied for the umpteenth time.

"If I remember right, you picked up with that Turner woman just a week or two after Laura left town. And then Sonia Gallegos a few weeks after that."

Yeah, he remembered those bleak days after she left, the gaping emptiness he had tried—and failed—to fill, when he had wanted nothing but to chase after her, drag her home and keep her where she belonged, with him.

"What's your point, Ridge?"

"This goes without saying—"

"Yet you're going to say it anyway."

"Damn straight. Laura isn't one of your Bandito bimbos. She's a decent person with a couple of kids, including one with challenges. Keep in mind she lost her husband recently. The last thing she probably needs is you messing with her head and heart again when she's trying to build a life here."

Like his favorite fishing knife, his brother's words seemed to slice right to the bone.

He wanted her fiercely—but just because he wanted something didn't mean he automatically deserved it. He'd learned that lesson young when his mother used to make him and Trace take out the garbage or change out a load of laundry if they wanted an extra cookie before dinner.

If he wanted another chance with her after the way he had treated her—and damn it, he *did*—he was going to have to earn his way back. He didn't know how yet. He only knew he planned to work like hell to become the kind of man he should have been ten years ago.

Chapter 8

Laura was going to kill him. Severely.

Five days after going riding with her and her kids above River Bow, Taft set down the big bag of supplies his sister had given him onto the concrete, then shifted the bundle into his left arm so he could use his right arm to wield his key card, the only way after hours to enter the side door of the inn closest to his room.

"Almost there, buddy," he said when the bundle whimpered.

He swiped the card, waiting for the little light to turn green, but it stayed stubbornly red. Too fast? Too slow? He hated these things. He tried it again, but the blasted light still didn't budge off red.

Apparently either the key code wasn't working any-more or his card had somehow become demagnetized.

Shoot. Of all the nights to have trouble, when he lit-erally had his hands full.

"Sorry, buddy. Hang on a bit more and we'll get you settled inside. I promise."

The little brown-and-black corgi-beagle mix perked his ginormous ears at him and gave him a quizzical look.

He tried a couple more times in the vain hope that five or six times was the charm, then gave up, accepting the inevitable trip to the lobby. He glanced at his watch. Eleven thirty-five. The front desk closed at midnight. Barring an unforeseen catastrophe between here and the front door, he should be okay.

He shoved the dog food and mat away from the door in case somebody else had better luck with their key card and needed to get through, then carried the dog around the side of the darkened inn.

The night was cool, as spring nights tended to be in the mountains, and he tucked the little dog under his jacket. The air was sweet with the scent of the flowers Laura had planted and new growth on the trees that lined the Cold Creek here.

On the way, he passed the sign he had noticed before that said Pets Welcome.

Yeah. He really, really hoped they meant it.

The property was quiet, as he might have expected. Judging by the few cars behind him in the parking lot, only about half the rooms at the inn were occupied. He hadn't seen any other guests for a couple of days in his wing of the hotel, which he could only consider a good thing, given the circumstances—though he doubted Laura would agree.

At least his room was close to the side door in case he had to make any emergency trips outside with the injured dog his sister had somehow conned him into babysitting. He had to consider that another thing to add to the win column.

Was Laura working the front desk? She did sometimes, probably after her children were asleep. In the few weeks he'd been living at the inn, most of the time one of the college students Mrs. Pendleton hired was working the front desk on the late shift, usually a flirtatious coed he tried really hard to discourage.

He wasn't sure whether he hoped to find Laura working or would prefer to avoid her a little longer. Not that he'd been avoiding her on purpose. He had been working crazy hours the past few days and hadn't been around the inn much.

He hadn't seen her since the other afternoon, when she had melted in his arms, although she hadn't been far from his mind. Discovering he wanted her back in his life had been more than a little unsettling.

The lobby of the inn had seen major changes in the few weeks since Laura arrived. Through the front windows he could see that the froufrou couches and chairs that used to form a conversation pit of sorts had been replaced by a half-dozen tables and chairs, probably for the breakfast service he'd been hearing about.

Fresh flower arrangements gave a bright, springlike feeling to the place—probably Laura's doing, as well.

When he opened the front door, he immediately spotted a honey-blond head bent over a computer and warmth seeped through him. He had missed her. Silly, when it had been only four days, but there it was.

The dog in his arms whimpered a little. Deciding discretion was the better part of valor and all that, he wrapped his coat a little more snugly around the dog. No sense riling her before she needed to be riled.

He wasn't technically doing anything wrong—pets *were* welcome after all, at least according to the sign, but somehow he had a feeling normal inn rules didn't apply to him.

He warily approached her and as she sensed him, she looked up from the computer with a ready smile. At the sight of him, her smile slid away and he felt a pang in his gut.

"Oh. Hi."

He shifted Lucky Lou a little lower in his arm. "Uh, hi. Sorry to bug you, but either my key card isn't working or the side door lock is having trouble. I tried to come in that way, but I couldn't get the green light."

"No problem. I can reprogram your card."

Her voice was stiff, formal. Had that stunning kiss ruined even the friendship he had been trying to rekindle?

"I like the furniture," he said.

"Thanks. It was just delivered today. I'm pleased with the colors. We should be ready to start serving breakfast by early next week."

"That will be a nice touch for your guests."

"I think so."

He hated that they had reverted back to polite small talk. They used to share everything with each other and he missed it.

The bundle under his jacket squirmed a little and she eyed him with curiosity.

"Uh, here's my key," he said, handing it over.

She slid it across the little doohickey card reader and handed it back to him. "That should work now, but let me know if you have more trouble."

"Okay. Thanks. Good night."

"Same to you," she answered. He started to turn and leave just as Lou gave a small, polite yip and peeked his head out of the jacket, his mega-size ears cocked with interest.

She blinked, clearly startled. "Is that…"

"Oh, this? Oh. Yeah. You probably need to add him to your list of guests. This is Lucky Lou."

At his newly christened name, the dog peeked all the way out. With those big corgi ears, he looked like a cross between a lemur and some kind of alien creature.

"Oh, he's adorable."

He blinked. Okay, she wasn't yelling. That was a good sign. "Yeah, pretty cute, I guess. Not exactly the most manly of dogs, but he's okay."

"Is this the dog that was hit by a car the other day?"

"This is the one."

To his great surprise, she walked around the side of the lobby desk for a closer look. He obliged by unwrapping the blanket, revealing the cast on the dog's leg.

"Oh, he's darling," she exclaimed and reached out to run a hand down the animal's fur. The dog responded just as Taft wanted to do, by nudging his head closer to her hand. So far, so good. Maybe she wasn't going to kill him after all.

"How is he?" she asked.

"Lucky. Hence the name."

She laughed softly and the sound curled through him, sweet and appealing.

He cleared his throat. "Somehow he came through with just a broken leg. It should heal up in a few weeks, but he needs to be watched closely during that time to make sure he doesn't reinjure himself. He especially can't be around the other dogs at the ranch because they tend to play rough, which poses a bit of a problem."

"What kind of problem?"

"It's a crazy-busy time at the ranch, with spring planting and all, not to mention Trace's wedding. Caidy was looking for somebody who could keep an eye on Lou here and I sort of got roped into it."

He didn't add that his sister basically blackmailed him to take on the responsibility, claiming he owed her this because she told him about the planned horseback ride with Laura and her children in the first place.

"I guess I should ask whether you mind if I keep him here at the inn with me. Most of the time he'll be at the station house or in my truck with me, but he'll be here on the nights I'm not working there."

She cupped the dog's face in her hand. "I would have to be the most hardhearted woman on the planet to say no to that face."

Okay, now he owed his sister big-time. Who knew the way to reach Laura's heart was through an injured mongrel?

As if she suddenly realized how close she was standing, Laura eased away from him. The dog whimpered a little and Taft wanted to join him.

"Our policy does allow for pets," she said. "Usually we charge a hundred-dollar deposit in case of damages, but given the circumstances I'm sure we can waive that."

"I'll try to keep him quiet. He seems to be a well-behaved little guy. Makes me wonder what happened. How he ended up homeless."

"Maybe he ran away."

"Yeah, that's the logical explanation, but he didn't have a collar. Caidy checked with animal control and the vet and everybody else she could think of. Nobody in the county has reported a lost pet matching his description. I wonder if somebody just dropped him off and abandoned him."

"What's going to happen to him? Eventually, I mean, after he heals?" she asked.

"Caidy has a reputation for taking in strays. Her plan is to nurse him back to health and then look for a good placement somewhere for the little guy. Meantime I'm just the dogsitter for a few days."

"And you can take him to the fire station with you?"

"I'm the fire chief, remember? Who's going to tell me I can't?"

She raised an eyebrow. "Oh, I don't know. Maybe the mayor or the city council."

He laughed, trying to imagine any of the local politicians making a big deal about a dog at the fire station. "This is Pine Gulch," he answered. "We're pretty casual about things like that. Anyway, it's only for a few days. We can always call him our unofficial mascot. Lucky Lou, Fire Dog."

The dog's big ears perked forward, as if eager to take on the new challenge.

"You like the sound of that, do you?" He scratched the dog's ears and earned an adoring look from his new best friend. He looked up to find Laura watching him, an arrested look in her eyes. When his gaze collided with hers, she turned a delicate shade of pink and looked away from him.

"Like I said, he doesn't seem to be much of a barker. I'll try to keep him quiet when I'm here so he doesn't disturb the other guests."

"Thank you, I appreciate that. Not that you have that many guests around you to be disturbed."

The discouragement in her voice made him want to hold her close, dog and all, and take away her worries. "Things will pick up come summer," he assured her.

"I hope so. The inn hasn't had the greatest reputation over the years. My mom did her best after my dad died, but I'm afraid things went downhill."

He knew this to be an unfortunate fact. Most people in town steered their relatives and friends to other establishments. A couple new B and Bs had sprung up recently and there were some nice guest ranches in the canyon. None had the advantage of Cold Creek Inn's location and beautiful setting, though, and with Laura spearheading changes, he didn't doubt the inn would be back on track in no time.

"Give it time. You've been home only a few weeks."

She sighed. "I know. But when I think about all the work it's going to require to counteract that reputation, I just want to cry."

He could certainly relate to that. He knew just how tough it was to convince people to look beyond the past. "If anybody can do it, you're perfect for the job. A degree in hotel management, all those years of international hotel experience. This will be a snap for you."

She gave him a rueful smile—but a smile nonetheless. He drew in a breath, wishing he could set the dog down and pull Laura into his arms instead. He might have considered it, but Lucky made a sound as if warning him against that particular course of action.

"What you need is a dog," he said suddenly. "A *lucky* dog."

"Oh, no, you don't," she exclaimed on a laugh. "Forget that right now, Taft Bowman. I'm too smart to let myself be swayed by an adorable face."

"Mine or the dog's?" he teased.

This smile looked definitely genuine, but she shook

her head. "Go to bed, Taft. And take your lucky dog with you."

I'd rather take you.

The words simmered between them, unsaid, but she blushed anyway, as if she sensed the thoughts in his head.

"Good night, then," he said with great reluctance. "I really don't mind paying the security deposit for the dog."

"No need. Consider it my way of helping in Lucky Lou's recovery."

"Thanks, then. I'll try to be sure you don't regret it."

He hitched the dog into a better position, picked up the key card from the counter and headed down the hall.

He had enough regrets for the both of them.

Her children were in love.

"He's the cutest dog *ever,*" Alex gushed, his dark eyes bright with excitement. "And so nice, too. I petted him and petted him and all he did was lick me."

"Lou tickles," Maya added, her face earnest and sweet.

"Lucky Lou. That's his name, Chief Bowman says."

Alex was perched on the counter, pulling items out of grocery bags, theoretically "helping" her put them away, but mostly just jumbling them up on the counter. Still, she wasn't about to discourage any act of spontaneous help from her children.

"And where was your grandmother while Chief Bowman was letting you play with his dog?" she asked.

The plan had been for Jan to watch the children while Laura went to the grocery store for her mother, but it sounded very much as if they had been wandering through the hotel, bothering Taft.

"She had a phone call in the office. We were coloring at a new table in the lobby, just like Grandma told us to. I promise we didn't go anywhere like upstairs. I was coloring a picture of a horse and Maya was just scribbling. She's not a very good colorer."

"She's working on it, aren't you, *mi hija?*"

Maya giggled at the favorite words and the everyday tension and stress of grocery shopping and counting coupons and loading bags into her car in a rainstorm seemed to fade away.

She was working hard to give her family a good life here. Maybe it wasn't perfect yet, but it was definitely better than what they would have known if she'd stayed in Madrid.

"So you were coloring and…" she prompted.

"And Chief Bowman came in and he was carrying the dog. He has great big ears. They're like donkey ears!"

She had to smile at the exaggeration. The dog had big ears but nothing that unusual for a corgi.

"Really?" she teased. "I've never noticed that about Chief Bowman."

Alex giggled. "The dog, silly! The *dog* has big ears. His name is Lucky Lou and he has a broken leg. Did you know that? He got hit by a car! That's sad, huh?"

"Terribly sad," she agreed.

"Chief Bowman says he has to wear a cast for another week and he can't run around with the other dogs."

"That's too bad."

"I know, huh? He can only sit quiet and be petted, but Chief Bowman says I can do it anytime I want to."

"That's very kind of Chief Bowman," she answered, quite sure her six-year-old probably wouldn't notice the caustic edge to her tone. She knew just what Taft was after—a sucker who would take the dog off his hands.

"He's super nice."

"The dog?"

"No! Chief Bowman! He says I can come visit Lou whenever I want, and when his cast comes off, I can maybe take him for a walk."

The decided note of hero-worship she heard in Alex's voice greatly worried her. Her son was desperate for a strong male influence in his life. She understood that.

But Taft wasn't going to be staying at the inn forever. Eventually his house would be finished and he would move out, taking his little dog with him.

The thought depressed her, although she knew darn well it was dangerous to allow herself to care what Taft Bowman did.

"And guess what else?" Alex pressed, his tone suddenly cagey.

"What?"

"Chief Bowman said Lucky Lou is going to need a new home once he recovers!"

Oh, here we go, she thought. It didn't take a child-behavior specialist to guess what would be coming next.

Sure enough, Alex tilted his head and gave her a deceptively casual look. "So I was thinking maybe *we* could give him a new home."

You're always thinking, aren't you, kiddo? she thought with resignation, gearing up for the arguments she could sense would follow that declaration.

"He's a super-nice dog and he didn't bark one single time. I know I could take care of him, Mama. I just *know* it."

"I know it," Maya said in stout agreement, although Laura had doubts as to whether her daughter had even been paying attention to the conversation as she played with a stack of plastic cups at the kitchen table.

How was she going to get out of this one without seeming like the meanest mom in the world? The dog *was* adorable. She couldn't deny it. With those big ears and the beagle coloring and his inquisitive little face, he was a definite charmer.

Maybe in a few months she would be in a better position to get a pet, but she was barely holding on here, working eighteen-hour days around caring for her children so she could help her mother rehabilitate this crumbling old inn and bring it back to the graceful accommodations it once had been.

She had to make the inn a success no matter how hard she had to work to do it. She couldn't stomach another failure. First her engagement to Taft, then her marriage. Seeing the inn deteriorate further would be the last straw.

A dog, especially a somewhat fragile one, would complicate *everything*.

"I would really, really love a dog," Alex persisted.

"Dog. Me, too," Maya said.

Drat Taft for placing her in this position. He had to have known her children would come back brimming over with enthusiasm for the dog, pressing her to add him to her family.

Movement outside the kitchen window caught her gaze and through the rain she saw Taft walking toward the little grassy area set aside for dogs. He was wearing a hooded raincoat and carrying an umbrella. At the dog-walking area, he set Lucky Lou down onto the grass and she saw the dog's cast had been wrapped in plastic.

She watched as Taft held the umbrella over the little corgi-beagle mix while the dog took care of business.

The sight of this big, tough firefighter showing such care for a little injured dog touched something deep inside her. Tenderness rippled and swelled inside her and she drew in a sharp breath. She didn't want to let him inside her heart again. She couldn't do it.

This was Taft Bowman. He was a womanizer, just as Javier had been. The more the merrier. That was apparently his mantra when it came to women. She had been through this before and she refused to do it again.

From his vantage point on top of the counter, Alex had a clear view out the window. "See?" he said with a pleading look. "Isn't he a great dog? Chief Bowman says he doesn't even poop in the house or anything."

She sighed and took her son's small hand in hers, trying to soften the difficulty of her words. "Honey, I don't know if this is the best time for us to get a dog. I'm sorry. I can't tell you yes or no right now. I'm going to have to think hard about this before I can make any decision. Don't get your hopes up, okay?"

Even as she said the words, she knew they were useless. By the adoration on his face as he looked out the rain-streaked window at the little dog, she could plainly tell Alex already had his heart set on making a home for Lou.

She supposed things could be worse. The dog was apparently potty-trained, friendly and not likely to grow much bigger. It wasn't as if he was an English sheep-dog, the kind of pet who shed enough fur it could be knitted into a sweater.

But then, this was Taft Bowman's specialty, convincing people to do things they otherwise wouldn't even consider.

She was too smart to fall for it all over again. Or at least that's what she told herself.

Chapter 9

Nearly a week later, Laura spread the new duvet across
the bed in the once-fire-damaged room, then stepped
back to survey her work.

Not bad, if she did say so herself. She was especially proud of the new walls, which she had painted
herself, glazing with a darker earth tone over the tan
to create a textured, layered effect, almost like a Tus-
can farmhouse.

Hiring someone else to paint would have saved a
great deal of time and trouble, of course. The idea of all
the rooms yet to paint daunted her, made her back ache
just thinking about it. On the other hand, this renovation had been *her* idea to breathe life into the old hotel,
and the budget was sparse, even with the in-kind labor
Taft had done for them over the past few weeks.

It might take her a month to finish all the other

rooms, but she would still save several thousand dollars that could be put into upgrading the amenities offered by the inn.

She intended to make each room at the inn charming and unique. This was a brilliant start. The room looked warm and inviting and she couldn't wait to start renting it out. She smoothed a hand over the wood trim around the windows, noting the tightness of the joints and the fine grain that showed beautifully through the finish.

"Wow, it looks fantastic in here."

She turned at the voice from the open doorway and found Taft leaning against the doorjamb. He looked tired, she thought, with a day's growth of whiskers on his cheeks and new smudges under his eyes. Not tired, precisely. Weary and worn, as if he had stopped here because he couldn't move another step down the hall toward his own room.

"Amazing the difference a coat of paint and a little love can do, isn't it?" she answered, worried for him.

"Absolutely. I would stay here in a heartbeat."

"You *are* staying here. Okay, not *here* precisely, in this particular room, but at the inn."

"If this room is any indication, the rest of this place will be beautiful by the time you're finished. People will be fighting over themselves to get a room."

"I hope so," she answered with a smile. This was what she wanted. The chance to make this historic property come to life.

"Do you ever sleep?" he asked.

"I could ask the same question. You look tired."

"Yeah, it's been a rough one."

She found the weary darkness in his gaze disconcerting. Taft was teasing and fun, with a smile and a lighthearted comment for everyone. She rarely saw him serious and quiet. "What's happened?"

He sank down onto the new sofa, messing up the throw pillows she had only just arranged. She didn't mind. He looked like a man who needed somewhere comfortable to rest for a moment.

"Car accident on High Creek Road. Idiot tourist took one of those sharp turns up there too fast. The car went off the road and rolled about thirty feet down the slope."

"Is he okay?"

"The driver just had scrapes and bruises and a broken arm." He scratched at a spot at the knee of his jeans. "His ten-year-old kid wasn't so lucky. We did CPR for about twenty minutes while we waited for the medevac helicopter and were able to bring him back. Last I heard, he survived the flight to the children's hospital in Salt Lake City, but he's in for a long, hard fight."

Her heart ached for the child and for his parents. "Oh, no."

"I hate incidents with kids involved." His mouth was tight. "Makes me want to tell every parent I know to hug their children and not let go. You just never know what could happen on any given day. If I didn't know Ridge would shoot me for it, I'd drive over to the ranch and wake up Destry right now, just so I could give her a big hug and tell her I love her."

His love for his niece warmed her heart. He was a man with a huge capacity to love and he must have deep compassion if he could be so upset by the day's events. Hadn't he learned how to keep a safe distance between his emotions and the emergency calls he had to respond to as a firefighter and paramedic?

"I'm sorry you had to go through that today."

He shrugged. "It's part of the job description, I guess. Sometimes I think my life would have been a hell of a lot easier if I'd stuck to raising cattle with Ridge."

These moments always took her by surprise when she realized anew that Taft was more than just the light-hearted, laughing guy he pretended to be. He felt things deeply. She had always known that, she supposed, but it was sometimes easy to forget when he worked so hard to be a charming flirt.

After weighing the wisdom of being in too close proximity to him against her need to offer comfort, she finally sank onto the sofa beside him.

"I'm sure you did everything you could."

"That's what we tell ourselves to help us sleep at night. Yet we always wonder."

He had been driving back to the ranch after being with her that terrible December night his parents were killed, when a terrified Caidy had called 9-1-1, she remembered now. Taft had heard the report go out on the radio in his truck just as he'd been turning into the gates of the ranch and had rushed inside to find his father shot dead and his mother bleeding out on the floor.

Not that he ever talked about this with her, but one of the responding paramedics had told her about finding a blood-covered Taft desperately trying to do CPR on his mother. He wouldn't stop, even after the rescue crews arrived.

His failure to revive his mother had eaten away at him, she was quite certain. If he had arrived five minutes earlier, he might have been able to save her.

She suspected, though of course he blocked this part of his life from her, that some part of him had even blamed Caidy for not calling for rescue earlier. Caidy had been home, as well, and had hidden in a closet in terror for several moments after her parents were shot, not sure whether the thieves—who had come to what they thought was an empty ranch to steal the Bowmans' art collection and been surprised into murder—might still actually be in the house.

After Laura left Pine Gulch, she had wondered if he blocked out his emotions after the murders in an effort to protect himself from that guilt at not being able to do enough to save his parents.

Even though he pretended he was fine, the grief and loss had simmered inside him. If only he had agreed to postpone the wedding, perhaps time would have helped him reach a better place so they could have married without that cloud over them.

None of that mattered now. He was hurting and she was compelled by her very nature to help ease that pain if she could. "What you do is important, Taft, no matter how hard it sometimes must feel. Think of it this way— if not for you and the other rescuers, that boy wouldn't have any chance at all. He wouldn't have made it long enough for the medical helicopter. And he's only one of hundreds, maybe thousands, of people you've helped. You make a real difference here in Pine Gulch. How many people can say that about their vocation?"

He didn't say anything for a long time and she couldn't read the emotion in his gaze. "There you go again. Always looking for the good in a situation."

"It seems better than focusing on all the misery and despair around me."

"Yeah, but sometimes life sucks and you can't gloss over the smoke damage with a coat of paint and a couple new pictures on the wall."

His words stung more than they should have, piercing unerringly under an old, half-healed scar.

Javier used to call her *dulce y inocente.* Sweet and innocent. He treated her like a silly girl, keeping away all their financial troubles, his difficulties with the hotel, the other women he slept with, as if she were too fragile to deal with the harsh realities of life.

"I'm not a child, Taft. Believe me, I know just how harsh and ugly the world can be. I don't think it makes me silly or naive simply because I prefer to focus on the hope that with a little effort, people can make a difference in each other's lives. We can always make tomorrow a little better than today, can't we? What's the point of life if you focus only on the negative, on what's dark or difficult instead of all the joy waiting to be embraced with each new day?"

She probably sounded like a soppy greeting card, but at that moment she didn't care.

"I never said you were silly." He gave her a probing look that made her flush. "Who did?"

She wanted to ignore the question. What business was it of his? But the old inn was quiet around them and there was an odd sort of intimacy in this pretty, comfortable room.

"My husband. He treated me like I was too delicate to cope with the realities of life. It was one of the many points of contention between us. He wanted to put a nice shiny gloss over everything, pretend all was fine."

He studied her for a long moment, then sighed. "I suppose that's not so different from what I did to you after my parents died."

"Yes," she answered through her surprise that he would actually bring up this subject and admit to his behavior. "If not for our…history, I guess you could say, it might not have bothered me so much when Javier insisted on that shiny gloss. But I had been through it all before. I didn't want to be that fragile child."

Before she realized what he intended, he covered her hand with his there on the sofa between them. His hand was large and warm, his fingers rough from years of both working on the ranch and putting his life on the line to help the residents of Pine Gulch, and for one crazy moment, she wanted to turn her hand over, grab tightly to his strength and never let go.

"I'm so sorry I hurt you, Laura. It was selfish and wrong of me. I should have postponed the wedding until I was in a better place."

"Why didn't you? A few months—that might have made all the difference, Taft."

"Then I would have had to admit I was still struggling to cope, six months later, when I thought I should have been fine and over things. I was a tough firefighter, Laura. I faced wildfires. I ran into burning buildings. I did whatever I had to. I guess I didn't want to show any signs of weakness. It was…tough for me to accept that my parents' murders threw me for a loop, so I pretended I was fine, too selfish and immature a decade ago to consider that you might have been right, that I needed more time."

She closed her eyes, wondering how her life might have been different if she had gone ahead with the wedding, despite all her misgivings. If she had been a little more certain he would come through his anger and grief, if she had married him anyway, perhaps they could have worked through it.

On the other hand, even though she had loved him

with all her heart, she would have been miserable in a marriage where he refused to share important pieces of himself with her. They probably would have ended up divorced, hating each other, with a couple of messed-up kids trapped in the middle.

He squeezed her fingers and his gaze met hers. Something glimmered in the depths of those green eyes, emotions she couldn't identify and wasn't sure she wanted to see.

"For the record," he murmured, "nothing was right after you left. It hasn't been right all this time. I've missed you, Laura."

She stared at him, blood suddenly pulsing through her. She didn't want to hear this. All her protective instincts were urging her to jump up from this sofa and escape, but she couldn't seem to make herself move.

"I should have come after you," he said. "But by the time I straightened out my head enough to do it, you were married and expecting a baby and I figured I had lost my chance."

"Taft—" Her voice sounded husky and low and she couldn't seem to collect her thoughts enough to add anything more. It wouldn't have mattered if she had. He didn't give her a chance to say a word before he leaned in, his eyes an intense, rich green, and lowered his mouth to hers.

His mouth was warm and tasted of coffee and something else she couldn't identify. Some part of her knew she should move now, while she still had the will, but she couldn't seem to make any of her limbs cooperate, too lost in the sheer, familiar joy of being in his arms again.

He kissed her softly, not demanding anything, only

tasting, savoring, as if her mouth were some sort of rare and precious wine. She was helpless to do anything but try to remember to breathe while her insides twisted and curled with longing.

"I missed you, Laura," he murmured once more, this time against her mouth.

I missed you, too. So much.

The words echoed through her mind but she couldn't say them. Not now. Not yet.

She could do nothing now but soak in the stunning tenderness of his kiss and let it drift around and through her, resurrecting all those feelings she had shoved so deeply down inside her psyche.

Finally, when she couldn't think or feel past the thick flow of emotions, he deepened the kiss. Now. Now was the time she should pull away, before things progressed too far. Her mind knew it, but again, the rest of her was weak and she responded instinctively, as she had done to him so many times before, and pressed her mouth to his.

For long moments, nothing else existed but his strength and his heat, his mouth firm and determined on hers, his arms holding her tightly, his muscles surrounding her. She wasn't sure exactly how he managed it without her realizing, but he shifted and turned her so she was resting back against the armrest of the sofa while he half covered her with his body until she was lost in memories of making love with him, tangled bodies and hearts.

She was still in love with him.

The realization slowly seeped through her consciousness, like water finding a weakness in a seam and dripping through.

She was still in love with Taft and probably had been all this time.

The discovery left her reeling, disoriented. She had loved her husband. *Of course* she had. She never would have married him if she hadn't believed they could make a happy life together. Yes, she had discovered she was unexpectedly pregnant after their brief affair, but she hadn't married him for that, despite the intense pressure he applied to make their relationship legal.

Her love for Javier hadn't been the deep, rich, consuming love she had known with Taft, but she had cared deeply for the man—at first anyway, until his repeated betrayals and his casual attitude about them had eaten away most of her affection for him.

Even so, she realized now, throughout the seven years of her marriage, some part of her heart had always belonged to Taft.

"We were always so good together. Do you remember?"

The low words thrummed through her and images of exactly how things had been between them flashing through her head. From the very first, they had been perfectly compatible. He had always known just how to kiss, just where to touch.

"Yes, I remember," she said hoarsely. All the passion, all the heat, all the heartbreak. She remembered all of it. The memories of her despair and abject loneliness after leaving Pine Gulch washed over her like a cold surf, dousing her hunger with cruel effectiveness.

She couldn't do this. Not again. Not with Taft.

She might still love him, but that was even more reason she shouldn't be here on this sofa with him with their mouths entwined. She froze, needing distance and space to breathe and think, to remind herself of all the many reasons she couldn't go through this all over again.

"I remember everything," she said coldly. "I'm not the one whose memory might have been blurred by the scores of other people I've been with in the meantime."

He jerked his head back as if she had just slapped him. "I told you, reputation isn't necessarily the truth."

"But it has some basis in truth. You can't deny that."

Even as she snapped the words, she knew this wasn't the core of the problem. She was afraid. That was the bare truth.

She still loved him as much as she ever had, maybe more now that she was coming to know the man he had become over the past decade, but she had given her heart to him once and he had chosen his grief and anger over all she had wanted to give him.

If she only had herself to consider, she might be willing to take the risk. But she had two children to think about. Alex and Maya were already coming to care for Taft. What if he decided he preferred his partying life again and chose that over her and the children? He had done it once before.

Her late husband had done the same thing, chosen his own selfish pursuits over his family, time and again, and she had to remember she wouldn't be the only one devastated if Taft decided he didn't want a family. Her children had already been through the pain of losing their father. At all costs, she had to protect them and the life she was trying to create for them.

"I don't want this. I don't want *you,*" she said firmly, sliding away from him. Despite her resolve, her hands trembled and she shoved them into the pocket of her sweater and drew a deep breath for strength as she stood.

"Like apparently half the women in town, I'm weak when it comes to you, so I'm appealing to your better nature. Don't kiss me again. I mean it, Taft. Leave me and my children alone. We can be polite and friendly when we see each other in town, but I can't go through this again. I won't. The children and I are finally in a good place, somewhere we can be happy and build a future. I can't bear it if you bounce in and out again and break our hearts all over again. Please, Taft, don't make me beg. Go back to the life you had before and leave us alone."

Her words seemed to gouge and claw at his heart.
I don't want this. I don't want you.

That was clear enough. He couldn't possibly mis-understand.

The children and I are finally in a good place, some-where we can be happy and build a future. I can't bear it if you bounce in and out again and break our hearts all over again.

As she had done mere days before their wedding, she had looked at him and found him somehow want-ing. Again.

He sucked in a ragged breath, everything inside him achy and sore. This was too much after the misery of the day he had just been through, and left him feeling as battered as if he'd free-floated down several miles of level-five rapids.

In that moment, as he gazed at her standing slim and lovely in this graceful, comfortable room, he realized the truth. He loved her. Laura and her family were his life, his heart. He wanted forever with them—while *she* only wanted him gone.

The loss raced over him like a firestorm, like the sudden flashover he had once experienced as a wildlands firefighter in his early twenties. The pain was just like that fire, hot and raw and wild. He couldn't outrun it; he could only hunker down in his shelter and wait for it to pass over.

He wanted to yell at her—to argue and curse and tell her she was being completely unreasonable. He wasn't the same man he'd been a decade ago. Couldn't she see that? He had been twenty-four years old, just a stupid kid, when she left.

Yeah, it might have taken ten years to figure things out, but now he finally knew what he wanted out of life. He was ready to commit everything to her and her children. He wanted what Trace had found with Becca. Once he had held exactly that gift in his hands and he had let it slip away and the loss of it had never hurt as keenly as it did right in this moment.

What did it matter that he might have changed? She didn't want to risk being hurt again by him and he didn't know how to argue with that.

She was right, he had turned away from the warmth of her love at a time in his life when he had needed it most. He couldn't argue with that and he couldn't change things.

He didn't know how to demonstrate to her that *he* had changed, though, that he needed her now to help him become the kind of man he wanted to be. He would be willing to sacrifice anything to take care of her and her children now, and he had no idea how to prove that to her.

"Laura—" he began, but she shook her head.

"I'm sorry. I'm just… I'm not strong enough to go through this all over again."

The misery in her features broke his heart, especially because he knew he had put it there—now and ten years ago.

She gave him one last searching look, then rushed out of this bright, cheerily decorated room, leaving him alone.

He stood there for a long time in the middle of the floor, trying to absorb the loss of her all over again in this room that now seemed cold and lifeless.

What now? He couldn't stay here at the inn anymore. She obviously didn't want him here and he wasn't sure he could linger on the edges of her life, having to content himself with polite greetings at the front desk and the occasional wave in the hallway.

He had finished the carpentry work Jan asked of him in this room and the other six in this wing that had needed the most repair. Because his house was ready for occupancy, with only a few minor things left to finish, he had no real excuse for hanging around.

She hadn't wanted him here in the first place, had only tolerated his presence because her mother had arranged things. He would give her what she wanted. He needed to move out, although the thought of leaving her and Alex and Maya left him feeling grimly empty.

Losing her ten years ago had devastated him. He had a very strong suspicion the pain of their broken engagement would pale compared to the loss of her now.

Chapter 10

"So how's the house?"

Taft barely heard his brother's question, too busy watching a little kid about Alex's age eating one of The Gulch's famous hamburgers and chattering away a mile a minute while his parents listened with slightly glazed expressions on their faces.

Tourists, he figured, because he didn't recognize them and he knew most of the people in his town, at least by sight. It was a little early for the full tourism season to hit—still only mid-May, with springtime in full bloom—but maybe they were visiting family for the Mother's Day weekend.

Where were they staying? he wondered. Would it be weird if he dropped over at their booth and casually mentioned Cold Creek Inn and the new breakfast service people were raving about? Yeah, probably. Trace, at least, would never let him hear the end of it.

Anyway, if they asked him about the quality of the food, he would have to admit he had no idea. He had moved out of his room at the inn and into his new house the day before Laura started the breakfast service.

But then, he wasn't going to think about Laura right now. He had already met his self-imposed daily limit about ten minutes after midnight while he had been answering a call for a minor fender bender, a couple of kids who wouldn't be borrowing their dad's new sedan again anytime soon.

And then exceeded his thinking-about-Laura quota about 1:00 a.m. and 2:00 a.m. and 3:00 a.m. And so on and so on.

He was a cute kid, Taft thought now as he watched the kid take a sip of his soda. Not as adorable as Alex, of course, but then, he was a little biased.

"The house?" Trace asked again and Taft had to jerk his attention back to his brother.

"It's been okay," he answered.

"Just okay? Can't you drum up a little more excitement than that? You've been working on this all winter long."

"I'm happy to be done," he answered, not in the mood for an interrogation.

If his brother kept this up, he was going to think twice next time about inviting Trace for a late lunch after a long shift. It had been a crazy idea anyway. He and his twin used to get together often for meals at The Gulch, but since Trace's engagement, his brother's free time away from Becca and Gabi had become sparse, as it should be.

He hadn't been quite ready to go home for a solitary TV dinner after work, so had persuaded Trace to take a break and meet him. They could usually manage to talk enough about the general public safety of Pine Gulch for it to technically be considered a working lunch.

Except now, when the police chief appeared to have other things on his mind.

"I can tell when somebody's lying to me," Trace said with a solemn look. "I'm a trained officer of the law, remember? Besides that, I'm your brother. I know you pretty well after sharing this world for thirty-four years. You're not happy and you haven't been for a couple of weeks now. Even Becca commented on it. What's going on?"

He couldn't very well tell his brother he felt as if Laura had made beef jerky out of his heart. He ached with loneliness for her and for Maya and Alex. Right now, he would give anything to be sitting across the table from them while Maya grinned at him and Alex jabbered his ear off. Even if he could find the words to explain away his lousy mood, he wasn't sure he was ready to share all of that with Trace.

"Maybe I'm tired of the same-old, same-old," he finally said, when Trace continued to give him the Bowman interrogation look: *Talk or you will be sorry.*

"I've been doing the same job for nearly six years, with years fighting wildland fires and doing EMT work before I made chief. Maybe it's time for me to think about taking a job somewhere else."

"Where?"

He shrugged. "Don't know. I've had offers here and there. Nevada. Oregon. Alaska, even. A change could be good. Get out of Pine Gulch, you know?"

Trace lifted an eyebrow and looked at him skeptically. "You just finished your new house a week ago.

And now you're thinking about leaving it? After all that work you put into it?"

He had come to the grim realization some nights ago during another sleepless episode that it would be torture continuing to live here in Pine Gulch, knowing she was so close but forever out of reach. He missed her. A hundred times a day he wanted to run over to the hotel claiming fire-code enforcement checks or something ridiculous like that just for the chance to see her and the children again.

Being without her had been far easier when she was half a world away in Spain. He was afraid the idea of weeks and months—and possibly *years*—of having her this close but always just out of his reach was more than he could endure.

Maybe it was his turn to leave this time.

"It's just an idea. Something I'm kicking around. I haven't actually *done* anything about it."

Before Trace could answer, Donna Archuleta, who owned The Gulch with her husband, brought over their order.

"Here you go, Chief Bowman." She set down Trace's plate, his favorite roast-beef sandwich with green peppers and onions. "And for the other Chief Bowman," she said in her gravelly ex-smoker voice, delivering Taft's lunch of meat loaf and mashed potatoes, a particular specialty of Lou's.

"Thanks, Donna."

"You're welcome. How are the wedding plans coming along?" she asked Trace.

His brother scratched his cheek. "Well, I'll admit I'm mostly staying out of it. You'll have to ask Becca that one."

"I would if she would ever come around. I guess now she's opened that fancy attorney-at-law office and doesn't have to wait tables anymore, she must be too busy for us these days."

Trace shook his head with a smile at the cantankerous old woman. "I'll bring her and Gabi in for breakfast over the weekend. How would that be?"

"I guess that'll do. You two enjoy your lunch."

She headed away amid the familiar diner sounds of rattling plates and conversation.

He had hoped the distraction would derail Trace's train of thought but apparently not. "If you think taking a job somewhere and moving away from Pine Gulch is what you want and need right now, I say go for it," his brother said, picking up right where he had left off. "You know the family will support you in whatever you decide. We'll miss you but we will all understand."

"Thank you, I appreciate that."

He considered it one of his life's greatest blessings that he had three siblings who loved him and would back him up whenever he needed it.

"We'll understand," Trace repeated. "As long as you leave for the right reasons. Be damn careful you're running *to* something and not just running away."

Lou must be having an off day. The meat loaf suddenly tasted like fire-extinguisher chemicals. "Running away from *what?*"

Trace took a bite of his sandwich and chewed and swallowed before he answered, leaving Taft plenty of time to squirm under the sympathy in his gaze. "Maybe a certain innkeeper and her kids, who shall remain nameless."

How did his brother do that? He hadn't said a single

word to him about Laura, but Trace had guessed the depth of his feelings anyway, maybe before he did. It was one of those weird twin things, he supposed. He had known the first time he met Becca, here in this diner, that Trace was already crazy about her.

The only thing he could do was fake his way out of it. "What? Laura? We were done with each other ten years ago."

"You sure about that?"

He forced a laugh. "Yeah, pretty darn sure. You might have noticed we didn't actually get married a decade ago."

"Yeah, I did pick up on that. I'm a fairly observant guy." Trace gave him a probing look. "And speaking of observant, I've also got an active network of confidential informants. Word is you haven't been to the Bandito for the greater part of a month, which coincidentally happens to be right around the time Laura Santiago showed up back in town with her kids."

"Checking up on me?"

"Nope. More like vetting questions from certain segments of the female society in Pine Gulch about where the hell you've been lately. Inquiring minds and all that."

He took a forkful of mashed potatoes, but found them every bit as unappealing as the meat loaf. "I've been busy."

"So I hear. Working on renovations at the inn, from what I understand."

"Not anymore. That's done now."

He had no more excuses to hang around Cold Creek Inn. No more reason to help Alex learn how to use power tools, to listen to Maya jabber at him, half in a language he didn't understand, or to watch Laura make the inn blossom as she had dreamed about doing most of her life.

Yeah, he wasn't sure he could stick around town and watch as Laura settled happily into Pine Gulch, working on the inn, making friends, moving on.

All without him.

"When I heard from Caidy that you'd moved into the inn and were helping Laura and her mother with some carpentry work, I thought for sure you and she were starting something up again. Guess I was wrong, huh?"

Another reason he should leave town. His family and half the town were probably watching and waiting for just that, to see if the two of them would pick up where they left off a decade and an almost-wedding later.

"Laura isn't interested in rekindling anything. Give her a break, Trace. I mean, it hasn't even been a year since she lost her husband. She and the kids are trying to settle into Pine Gulch again. She's got big plans for the inn, and right now that and her children are where her focus needs to be."

Some of his despair, the things he thought he had been so careful not to say, must have filtered through his voice anyway. His brother studied him for a long moment, compassion in his green eyes Taft didn't want to see.

He opened his mouth to deflect that terrible sympathy with some kind of stupid joke, but before he could come up with one, his radio and Trace's both squawked at the same moment.

"All officers in the vicinity. I've got a report of a Ten Fifty-Seven. Two missing juveniles in the area of Cold Creek Inn. Possible drowning."

Everything inside him froze to ice, crackly and fragile.
Missing juveniles. Cold Creek Inn. Possible drowning.

Alex and Maya.

He didn't know how he knew so completely, but his heart cramped with agony and bile rose in his throat for a split second before he shoved everything aside. Not now. There would be time later, but right now he needed to focus on what was important.

He and Trace didn't even look at each other. They both raced out of the restaurant to their vehicles parked beside each other and squealed out of the parking lot.

He picked up his radio. "Maria, this is Fire Chief Bowman. I want every single damn man on the fire department to start combing the river."

"Yes, sir," she answered.

His heart pounding in his chest, he sped through the short three blocks to Cold Creek Inn, every light flashing and every siren blaring away as he drove with a cold ball of dread in his gut. He couldn't go through this. Not with her. Everything inside him wanted to run away from what he knew would be deep, wrenching pain, but he forced himself to push it all out of his head.

He beat Trace to the scene by a heartbeat and didn't even bother to turn off his truck, just raced to where he saw a group of people standing beside the fast-moving creek.

Laura was being restrained by two people, her mother and a stranger, he realized. She was crying and fighting them in a wild effort to jump into the water herself.

"Laura, what's happened?"

She gazed blankly at him for a moment, her eyes

wide and shocky, then her features collapsed with raw relief.

"Taft, my children," she sobbed and it was the most heartrending sound he had ever heard. "I have to go after them. Why won't anyone let me go after them?"

Jan, still holding her, was also in tears and appeared even more hysterical, her face blotchy and red. He wouldn't be able to get much information out of either of them.

Beyond them, he could see the water running fast and high and Lucky Lou running back and forth along the bank, barking frantically.

"Laura, honey, I need you to calm down for just a moment." While everything inside him was screaming urgency, he forced himself to use a soothing, measured tone, aware it might be his only chance to get through to her.

"Please, sweetheart, this is important. Why do you think they're in the river? What happened?"

She inhaled a ragged breath, visibly struggling to calm herself down to answer his question—and he had never loved her more than in that single moment of stark courage.

"They were just here. Right here. Playing with Lucky. They know they're not to go near the creek. I've told them a hundred times. I was out here with them, planting flowers, and kept my eye on them the whole time. I walked around the corner of the inn for another flat and was gone maybe thirty seconds. That's all. When I came back Lucky was running along the bank and they were g-gone." She said the last word on a wailing sob that made everything inside him ache.

"How long ago?"

The stranger, who must have restrained her from jumping in after them, spoke. "Three minutes. Maybe four. Not long. I pulled into the parking lot just in time to see her running down the bank screaming something about her kids. I stopped her from jumping in after them and called 9-1-1. I don't know if that was right."

He would shake the guy's hand later and pay for his whole damn stay, but right now he didn't have even a second to spare.

"You did exactly right. Laura, stay here. Promise me," he ordered. "You won't find them by jumping in and you'll just complicate everything. The water is moving too fast for you to catch up. Stay here and I will bring them back to you. Promise me."

Her eyes were filled with a terrified anguish. He wanted to comfort her, but damn it, he didn't have time.

"Promise me," he ordered again.

She sagged against the stranger and Jan and nodded, then collapsed to her knees in the dirt, holding on to her mother.

He raced back to his truck, shouting orders into his radio the whole time as he set up a search perimeter and called in the technical rescue team. Even as one part of his mind was busy dealing with the logistics of the search and setting up his second in command to run the grid, the other part was gauging the depth of the water, velocity of the current, the creek's route.

Given that the incident happened five minutes ago now, he tried to calculate how far the children might have floated. It was all guesswork without a meter to give him exact stream flow, but he had lived along Cold Creek all his life and knew its moods and its whims. He and Trace and their friends used to spend summers fishing for native rainbows, and as he grew older, he had kayaked the waters innumerable times, even during high runoff.

Something urged him to head toward Saddleback Road. Inspiration? Some kind of guardian angel? Just a semi-educated guess? He didn't know, but a picture formed itself clearly in his head, of a certain spot where the creek slowed slightly at another natural bow and split into two channels before rejoining. Somehow he knew *that* was the spot where he needed to be right now.

He could be totally off the mark but he could only hope and pray he wasn't.

"Battalion Twenty, what's your status?" he heard over the radio. Trace.

"Almost to Saddleback," he said, his voice hoarse. "I'm starting here. Send a team to the road a quarter mile past that. What is that? Barrelwood?"

"Copy. Don't be stupid, Chief."

One of the hazards of working with his brother—but he didn't care about that now, when he had reached the spot that seemed imprinted in his mind, for all those reasons he couldn't have logically explained.

He jerked the wheel to the side of the road and jumped out, stopping only long enough to grab the water-rescue line in its throw bag in one of the compartments in the back of his truck. He raced to the water's edge, scanning up and down for any sign of movement. This time of year, mid-May, the runoff was fast and cold coming out of the mountains, but he thanked God the peak flow, when it was a churning, furious mess, was still another few weeks away as the weather warmed further.

Had he overshot them or had they already moved

past him? Damn it, he had no way of knowing. Go down or up? He screwed his eyes shut and again that picture formed in his head of the side channel that was upstream about twenty yards. He was crazy to follow such a vague impression but it was all he had right now.

He raced up the bank, listening to the reports of the search on his radio as he ran.

Finally he saw the marshy island in the middle of the two channels. A couple of sturdy pine trees grew there, blocking a good part of his view, but he strained his eyes.

There!

Was that a flash of pink?

He moved a little farther upstream for a different vantage point. The instant he could see around the pines, everything inside him turned to that crackly ice again.

Two small dark heads bobbed and jerked, snagged in the deadfall of a tree that was half-submerged in the water. The tree was caught between two boulders in the side channel. From here, he couldn't tell if the kids were actually actively holding on or had just been caught there by the current.

He grabbed his radio, talking as he moved as close as he could. "Battalion Twenty. I've got a sighting twenty yards east of where my truck is parked on Saddleback Road. I need the tech team and Ambulance Thirty-Six here now."

He knew, even as he issued the order, that no way in hell was he going to stand here and do nothing during the ten minutes or so it might take to assemble the team and get them here. Ten minutes was the difference between life and death. Anything could happen in those ten minutes. He didn't know if the children were breathing—and didn't even want to think about any other alternative—but if they weren't, ten minutes could be critical to starting CPR.

Besides that, the water could be a capricious, vengeful thing. The relentless current could tug them farther downstream and away from him. He wasn't about to take that chance.

This was totally against protocol, everything he had trained his own people *not* to do. Single-man water rescues were potentially fatal and significantly increased the dangers for everybody concerned.

Screw protocol.

He needed to reach Laura's children. Now.

This would be much more comfortable in a wet suit but he wasn't about to take the time to pull his on. He raced upstream another ten yards to a small bridge formed by another fallen tree. On the other side of the creek, the children were only a dozen feet away. He called out and thought he saw one of the dark heads move.

"Alex! Maya! Can you hear me?"

He thought he saw the head move again but he couldn't be sure. No way could they catch the throw bag. He was going to have to go after them, which he had known from the moment he spotted that flash of pink.

If he calculated just right and entered at the correct place upstream, the current would float him right to them, but he would have to aim just right so the first boulder blocked his movement and his weight didn't dislodge the logjam, sending the children farther downstream.

He knew the swift-water safety algorithm. Talk. Reach. Wade. Throw. Helo. Go. Row. Tow. The only thing he could do here was reach them and get them the hell out.

He tied the rescue rope around the sturdy trunk of a cottonwood, then around his waist, then plunged into the water that came up to his chest. The icy water was agony and he felt his muscles cramp instantly, but he waded his way toward the deadfall, fighting the current as hard as he could. It was useless. After only a few steps, the rushing water swept his feet out from under him, as he expected.

It took every ounce of strength he could muster to keep his feet pointed downstream so they could take the brunt of any impact with any boulders or snags in the water. The last thing he needed here was a head injury.

He must have misjudged the current because he ended up slightly to the left of the boulder. He jammed his numb feet on the second boulder to stop his momentum. A branch of the dead tree gouged the skin of his forehead like a bony claw, but he ignored it, fighting his way hand over hand toward the children, praying the whole time he wouldn't dislodge the trunk.

"Alex, Maya. It's Chief Bowman. Come on, you guys." He kept up a nonstop dialogue with them but was grimly aware that only Alex stirred. The boy opened one eye as Taft approached, then closed it again, looking as if he were utterly exhausted.

The boy's arm was around his sister, but Maya was facedown in the water. He used all his strength to fight the current as he turned her and his gut clenched when he saw her eyes staring blankly and her sweet features still and lifeless.

He gave her a quick rescue breath. She didn't respond, but he kept up the rescue breaths to her and Alex while he worked as quickly as he could, tying them both to him with hands that he could barely feel, wondering as he worked and breathed for all three of them how much time had passed and what the hell was taking his tech rescue crew so long.

This was going to be the toughest part, getting them all out of the water safely, but with sheer muscle, determination—and probably some help from those guardian angels he was quite certain had to be looking after these two kids—he fought the current and began pulling himself hand over hand along the tree trunk, wet and slippery with moss and algae, pausing every ten seconds to give them both rudimentary rescue breaths.

Just as he reached the bank, completely exhausted by the effort of fighting the current, he heard shouts and cries and felt arms lifting him out and untying the kids.

"Chief! How the hell did you find them clear over here?" Luke Orosco, his second in command, looked stunned as he took in the scene.

He had no idea how to explain the process that had led him here. Miracle or intuition, it didn't matter, not when both children were now unresponsive, although it appeared Alex was at least breathing on his own.

Satisfied that his crew was working with Alex, he immediately turned to the boy's sister and took command. He was the only trained paramedic in this group, though everyone else had basic EMT training. "Maya? Come on, Maya, honey. You've got to breathe, sweetheart."

He bent over the girl and turned her into recovery position, on her side, nearly on her stomach, her knee up to drain as much water from her lungs as he could. He could hear Alex coughing up water, but Maya remained still.

"Come on, Maya."

He turned her and started doing CPR, forcing himself to lock away his emotions, the knowledge that Laura would be destroyed if he couldn't bring back her daughter. He continued, shaking off other crew members who wanted to take over.

Some part of him was afraid all this work was for nothing—she had been in the water too long—but then, when despair began to grip him colder than the water, he felt something change. A stirring, a movement, a heartbeat. And then she gave a choking cough and he turned her to her side just in time as she vomited what seemed like gallons of Cold Creek all over the place.

Pink color began to spread through her, another miracle, then she gave a hoarse, raspy cry. He turned her again to let more water drain, then wrapped her in a blanket one of his crew handed over.

"Oxygen," he called. Maya continued to cry softly and he couldn't bring himself to let her go.

"Good job, Chief!"

He was vaguely aware of the guys clapping him and themselves on the back and the air of exultation that always followed a successful rescue, but right now he couldn't focus on anything but Maya.

"You ready for us to load her up?" Ron asked.

He didn't want to let her go, but he knew she needed more than the triage treatment they could offer here. There was still a chance she had been without oxygen long enough for brain damage, but he had to hope the cold water might help ease that possibility.

"Yeah, we'd better get her into the ambulance," he answered. When the EMTs loaded her onto the stretcher, he finally turned to find Alex being loaded onto another stretcher nearby. The boy was conscious and watching the activity around him. When Taft approached, his mouth twisted into a weary smile.

"Chief." The kid's voice sounded hoarse, raw. "You saved us. I knew you would."

He gripped the boy's hand, humbled and over-whelmed at that steady trust. "What happened, Alex? You know you're not supposed to be near the water."

"I know. We always stay away from it. *Always.* But Lucky ran that way and Maya followed him. I chased after her to take her back to Mama and she thought it was a game. She laughed and ran and then slipped and went in the creek. I didn't know what to do. I thought… I thought I could get her. I had swimming lessons last year. But the water was so *fast.*"

The boy started to cry and he gathered him up there on the stretcher as he had done Maya. What a great kid he was, desperately trying to protect his little sister. Taft felt tears threaten, too, from emotion or delayed reaction, he didn't know, but he was deeply grateful for any guardian angels who had been on his rescue squad for this one.

"You're safe now. You'll be okay."

"Is Maya gonna be okay?" Alex asked.

He still wasn't sure he knew the answer to that. "My best guys are just about to put her in the ambulance. You get to take a ride, too."

Before Alex could respond to that, Taft saw a Pine Gulch P.D. SUV pull up to the scene. His brother's vehicle. The thought barely registered before the passenger door was shoved open and a figure climbed out.

Laura.

She stood outside the patrol vehicle for just a moment as if not quite believing this could be real and then she rushed toward them. In a second she scooped Alex into her arms and hugged him.

"Oh, baby. Sweetheart," she sobbed. "You're okay. You're really okay? And Maya?" Still carrying Alex, she rushed over to Maya and pulled her into her other arm.

"I'm sorry, ma'am, but we need to transport both of the children to the clinic in town." Ron looked compassionate but determined. "They're in shock and need to be treated for possible hypothermia."

"Oh. Of course." Her strained features paled a little at this further evidence that while the children were out of the water, they still required treatment.

"They're going to be okay, Laura," Taft said. He hoped anyway, though he knew Maya wasn't out of the woods.

She glanced over at him and seemed to have noticed him for the first time. "You're bleeding."

Was he? Probably from that branch that had caught him just as he was reaching the children. He hadn't even noticed it in the rush of adrenaline but now he could feel the sting. "Just a little cut. No big deal."

"And you're soaking wet."

"Chief Bowman pulled us out of the water, Mama," Alex announced, his voice still hoarse. "He tied a rope to a tree and jumped in and got us both. That's what *I* should have done to get Maya."

She gazed at her son and then at Taft, then at the roaring current and the rope still tied to the tree.

"You saved them."

"I told you I would find them."

"You did."

He flushed, embarrassed by the shock and gratitude in her eyes. Did she really think he would let the kids drown? He loved them. He would have gone after them no matter what the circumstances.

"And broke about a dozen rules for safe rescue in the process," Luke Orosco chimed in, and he wanted to pound the guy for opening his big mouth.

"I don't care," she said. "Oh, thank you. Taft, thank you!"

She grabbed him and hugged him, Alex still in her arms, and his arms came around her with a deep shudder. He couldn't bear thinking about what might have happened. If he had overshot the river and missed them. If he hadn't been so close, just at The Gulch, when the call came in. A hundred small tender mercies had combined to make this moment possible.

Finally Luke cleared his throat. "Uh, Doc Dalton is waiting for us at the clinic."

She stepped away from him and he saw her eyes were bright with tears, her cheeks flushed. "Yes, we should go."

"We should be able to take you and both kids all in one ambulance," Luke offered.

"Perfect. Thank you so much."

She didn't look at him again as the crews loaded the two kids into their biggest ambulance. There wasn't room for him in there, although he supposed as battalion chief he could have pulled rank and insisted he wanted to be one of the EMTs assisting them on the way to the hospital.

But Laura and her children were a family unit that didn't have room for him. She had made that plain enough. He would have to remain forever on the outside of their lives. That was the way Laura wanted things and he didn't know how to change her mind.

He watched the doors close on the ambulance with finality, then Cody Shepherd climb behind the wheel and pull away from the scene. As he watched them drive away, he was vaguely aware of Trace moving to stand beside him. His brother placed a hand on his shoulder, offering understanding without words.

Another one of those twin things, he supposed. Trace must have picked up on his yearning as he watched the family he wanted drive away from him.

"Good save," Trace said quietly. "But it's a damn miracle all three of you didn't go under."

"I know." The adrenaline rush of the rescue was fading fast, leaving him battered and embarrassingly weak-kneed.

"For the record, you ever pull a stunt like that again, trying a single-man water rescue, Ridge and I will drag what's left of you behind one of the River Bow horses."

"What choice did I have? I knew the deadfall wasn't going to hold them for long, the way the current was pushing at them. Any minute, they were going to break free and float downstream and I wouldn't have had a second chance. Think if it was Destry or Gabi out there. You would have done the same thing."

Taft was silent for a moment. "Yeah, probably. That still doesn't make it right."

Terry McNeil, one of his more seasoned EMTs,

approached the two of them with his emergency kit. "Chief, your turn."

He probably needed a stitch or two, judging by the amount of blood, but he wasn't in the mood to go to the clinic and face Laura again, to be reminded once more of everything he couldn't have. "I'll take care of it myself."

"You sure? That cut looks deep."

He gave Terry a long look, not saying anything, and the guy finally shrugged. "Your call. You'll need to clean it well. Who knows what kind of bacteria is floating in that water."

"I'm heading home to change anyway. I'll clean it up there."

He knew he should be jubilant after a successful rescue. Some part of him was, of course. The alternative didn't bear thinking about, but he was also crashing now after an all-nighter at the fire station combined with exhaustion from the rescue. Right now, all he wanted to do was go home and sleep.

"Don't be an idiot," Terry advised him, an echo of what his brother had said earlier.

He wanted to tell both of them it was too late for that. He had been nothing short of an idiot ten years ago when he let Laura walk away from him. Once, he had held happiness in his hands and had blown it away just like those cottonwood puffs floating on the breeze.

She might be back but she wouldn't ever be his, and the pain of that hurt far worse than being battered by the boulders and snags and raging current of Cold Creek.

Chapter 11

So close. She had been a heartbeat away from losing everything.

Hours after the miracle of her children's rescue, Laura still felt jittery, her insides achy and tight with reaction. She couldn't bear to contemplate what might have been.

If not for Taft and his insane heroics, she might have been preparing for two funerals right now instead of sitting at the side of her bed, watching her children sleep. Maya was sucking her thumb, something she hadn't done in a long time, while Alex slept with his arm around his beloved dog, who slept on his side with his short little legs sticking straight out.

So much for her one hard-and-fast rule when she had given in to Alex's determined campaign and allowed the adoption of Lucky Lou.

No dogs on the bed, she had told her son firmly,

again and again, but she decided this was a night that warranted exceptions.

She hadn't wanted to let either of them out of her sight, even at bedtime. Because she couldn't watch them both in their separate beds, she had decided to lump everyone together in here, just this once. She wasn't sure where she would sleep, perhaps stretched across the foot of the bed, but she knew sleep would be a long time coming anyway.

She should be exhausted. The day had been draining. Even after the rescue, they had spent several hours at the clinic, until Dr. Dalton and his wife, Maggie, had been confident the children appeared healthy enough to return home.

Dr. Dalton had actually wanted to send them to the hospital in Idaho Falls for overnight observation, but after a few hours, Maya was bouncing around the bed in her room like a wild monkey and Alex had been jabbering a mile a minute with his still-raspy voice.

"You can take them home," Dr. Dalton had reluctantly agreed, his handsome features concerned but kind, "as long as they remain under strict observation. Call me at once if you notice any change in breathing pattern or behavior."

She was so grateful to have her children with her safe and sound that she would have agreed to anything by that point. Every time she thought about what might have happened if Taft hadn't been able to find the children, her stomach rolled with remembered fear and she had to fold her arms around it and huddle for a few moments until she regained control.

She would never forget that moment she climbed out of his brother's patrol vehicle and had seen Taft there, bloodied and soaking wet, holding her son close. Something significant had shifted inside her in that moment, something so profound and vital that she shied away from examining it yet.

She was almost relieved when a crack of light through the doorway heralded her mother's approach. Jan pushed the door open and joined her beside the bed. Her mother looked older than she had that morning, Laura reflected. The lines fanning out from her eyes and bracketing her mouth seemed to have been etched a little deeper by the events of the day.

"They look so peaceful when they're sleeping, don't they?" Jan murmured, gazing down at her only grandchildren.

Laura was suddenly awash with love for her mother, as well. Jan had been a source of steady support during her marriage. Even though Laura hadn't revealed any of the tumult of living with Javier—she still couldn't—she had always known she could call or email her mother and her spirits would lift.

Her mother hadn't had an easy life. She had suffered three miscarriages before Laura was born and two after. When Laura was a teenager, she had often felt the pressure of that keenly, knowing she was the only one of six potential siblings who had survived. She could only hope she was the kind of daughter her mother wanted.

"They do look peaceful," she finally answered, pitching her voice low so she didn't wake the children, although she had a feeling even the high-school marching band would have a tough time rousing them after their exhausting day. "Hard to believe, looking at them now, what kind of trouble they can get into during daylight hours, isn't it?"

"I should have fenced off the river a long time ago." Weary guilt dragged down the edges of her mother's mouth.

Laura shook her head. "Mom, none of this was your fault. I should have remembered not to take my eyes off them for a second. They're just too good at finding their way to trouble."

"If Taft hadn't been there..."

She reached out and squeezed her mother's hand, still strong and capable at seventy. "I know. But he *was* there." And showed incredible bravery to climb into the water by himself instead of waiting for a support team. The EMTs couldn't seem to stop talking about the rescue during the ambulance ride to the clinic.

"Everyone is okay," she went on. "No lasting effects, Dr. Dalton said, except possibly intestinal bugs from swallowing all that creek water. We'll have to keep an eye out for stomachaches, that sort of thing."

"That's a small thing. They're here. That's all that matters." Her mother gazed at the children for a long moment, then back at Laura, her eyes troubled. "You're probably wondering why you ever came home. With all the trouble we've had since you arrived—fires and near-drownings and everything—I bet you're thinking you would have been better off to have stayed in Madrid."

"I wouldn't want to be anywhere else right now, Mom. I still think coming home was the right thing for us."

"Even though it's meant you've had to deal with Taft again?"

She squirmed under her mother's probing look. "Why should that bother me?"

"I don't know. Your history together, I guess."

"That history didn't seem to stop you from inviting the man to live at the inn for weeks!"

"Don't think I didn't notice during that time how you went out of your way to avoid him whenever you could. You told me things ended amicably between you, but I'm not so sure about that. You still have feelings for him, don't you?"

She started to give her standard answer. *The past was a long time ago. We're different people now and have both moved on.*

Perhaps because the day had been so very monumental, so very profound, she couldn't bring herself to lie to her mother.

"Yes," she murmured. "I've loved him since I was a silly girl. It's hard to shut that off."

"Why do you need to? That man still cares about you, my dear. I could tell that first day when he came to talk to me about helping with the inn renovations. He jumped into the river and risked his life to save your children. That ought to tell you something about the depth of his feelings."

She thought of the dozens of reasons she had employed to convince herself not to let Taft into her life again. None of them seemed very important right now—or anything she wanted to share with her mother. "It's complicated."

"Life is complicated, honey, and hard and stressful and exhausting. And *wonderful*. More so if you have a good man to share it with."

Laura thought of her father, one of the best men she had ever known. He had been kind and compassionate, funny and generous. The kind of man who often opened the doors of his inn for a pittance—or sometimes nothing—to people who had nowhere else to go.

In that moment, she would have given anything if he could be there with them, watching over her children with them.

Perhaps he had been, she thought with a little shiver.

By rights, her children should have died today in the swollen waters of Cold Creek. That they survived was nothing short of a miracle and she had to think they had help somehow.

She missed her father deeply in that moment. He had loved Taft and had considered him the son he had always wanted. Both of her parents had been crushed by the end of her engagement, but her father had never pressed her to know the reasons.

"While you were busy at the clinic this afternoon," Jan said after a moment, "I was feeling restless and at loose ends and needed to stay busy while I waited for you. I had to do something so I made a caramel-apple pie. You might not remember but that was always Taft's favorite."

He did have a sweet tooth for pastries, she remembered.

"It's small enough payment for giving me back my grandchildren, but it will have to do for now, until I can think of something better. I was just about to take it to him…unless you would like to."

Laura gazed at her sleeping children and then at her mother, who was trying her best to be casual and non-chalant instead of eagerly coy. She knew just what Jan was trying to do—push her and Taft back together, which was probably exactly the reason she agreed to let him move into the inn under the guise of trading carpentry work for a room.

Jan was sneaky that way. Laura couldn't guess at her motives—perhaps her mother was looking for any way she could to bind Laura and her children to Pine Gulch. Or perhaps she was matchmaking simply because she had guessed, despite Laura's attempts to put on a bright facade, that her marriage had not been a happy one and she wanted to see a different future for her daughter.

Or perhaps Jan simply adored Taft, because most mothers did.

Whatever the reason, Laura had a pivotal decision to make: Take the pie to him herself as a small token of their vast gratitude or thwart her mother's matchmaking plans and insist on staying here with the children?

Her instincts urged her to avoid seeing him again just now. With these heavy emotions churning inside her, she was afraid seeing him now would be too dangerous. Her defenses were probably at the lowest point they had been since coming home to Pine Gulch. If he kissed her again, she wasn't at all certain she would have the strength to resist him.

But that was cowardly. She needed to see him again, if for no other reason than to express, now that she was more calm and rational than she had been on that riverbank, her deep and endless gratitude to him for giving her back these two dear children.

"I'll go, Mom."

"Are you sure? I don't mind."

"I need to do this. You're right. Will you watch the children for me?"

"I won't budge," her mother promised. "I'll sit right here and work on my crocheting the entire time. I promise."

"You don't have to literally watch them. You may certainly sit in the living room and check on them at various intervals."

"I'm not moving from this spot," Jan said. "Between Lou and me, we should be able to keep them safe."

The evening was lovely, unusually warm for mid-May. She drove through town with her window down, savoring the sights and sounds of Pine Gulch settling down for the night. Because it was Friday, the drive-in on the edge of the business district was crowded with cars. Teenagers hanging out, anxious for the end of the school year, young families grabbing a burger on payday, senior citizens treating their grandchildren to an ice-cream cone.

The flowers were beginning to bloom in some of the sidewalk planters along Main Street and everything was greening up beautifully. May was a beautiful time of year in eastern Idaho after the inevitable harshness of winter, brimming with life, rebirth, hope.

As she was right now.

She had heard about people suffering near-death encounters who claimed the experience gave them a new respect and appreciation for their life and the beauty of the world around them. That's how she felt right now. Even though it was her children who had nearly died, Laura knew she would have died right along with them if they hadn't been rescued.

She had Alex and Maya back now, along with a new appreciation for those flowers in carefully tended gardens, the mountains looming strong and steady over the town, the sense of home that permeated this place.

She drove toward those mountains now, to Cold Creek Canyon, where the creek flowed out of the high country and down through the valley. Her mother had given her directions to Taft's new house and she followed them, turning onto Cold Creek Road.

She found it no surprise that Jan knew Taft's address. Jan and her wide circle of friends somehow managed to keep their collective finger on the pulse of everything going on in town.

The area here along the creek was heavily wooded

with Douglas fir and aspen trees and it took her a moment to find the mailbox with his house number. She peered through the trees but couldn't see anything of his house except a dark green metal roof that just about matched the trees in the fading light.

A bridge spanned the creek here and as she drove over it, she couldn't resist looking down at the silvery ribbon of water, darting over boulders and around fallen logs. Her children had been in that icy water, she thought, chilled all over again at how close she had come to losing everything.

She couldn't let it paralyze her. When the runoff eased a little, she needed to take Alex and Maya fishing in the river to help all of them overcome their fear of the water.

She stayed on the bridge for several moments, watching lightning-fast dippers crisscross the water for insects and a belted kingfisher perching on a branch without moving for long moments before he swooped into the water and nabbed a hapless hatchling trout.

As much as she enjoyed the serenity of the place, she finally gathered her strength and started her SUV again, following the winding driveway through the pines. She had to admit, she was curious to see his house. He had asked her to come see it, she suddenly remembered, and she had deflected the question and changed the subject, not wanting to intertwine their lives any further. She was sorry now that she hadn't come out while it was under construction.

The trees finally opened up into a small clearing and she caught her breath. His house was gorgeous: two stories of honey-colored pine logs and river rock with windows dominating the front and a porch that wrapped around the entire house so that he could enjoy the view of mountains and creek in every direction.

She loved it instantly, from the river-rock chimney rising out of the center to the single Adirondack chair on the porch, angled to look out at the mountains. She couldn't have explained it but she sensed warmth and welcome here.

Her heart pounded strangely in her ears as she parked the SUV and climbed out. She saw a light inside the house but she also heard a rhythmic hammering coming from somewhere behind the structure.

That would be Taft. Somehow she knew it. She reached in for the pie her mother had made—why hadn't she thought of doing something like this for him?—and headed in the direction of the sound.

She found him in another clearing behind the house, framing up a building she assumed would be an outbuilding for the horses he had talked about. He had taken off his shirt to work the nail gun, and that leather tool belt he had used while he was working at the inn— not that she had noticed or anything—hung low over his hips. Muscles rippled in the gathering darkness and her stomach shivered.

Here was yet another image that could go in her own mental Taft Bowman beefcake calendar.

She huffed out a little breath, sternly reminding herself that standing and salivating over the man was *not* why she was here, and forced herself to move forward. Even though she wasn't trying to use stealth, he must not have heard her approach over the sound of the nail gun and the compressor used to power it, even when she was almost on top of him. He didn't turn around or respond in any way and she finally realized why when she saw white earbuds dangling down, tethered to a player in the back pocket of his jeans.

She had no idea what finally tipped him off to her presence, but the steady motion of the nail gun stopped, he paused for just a heartbeat and then he jerked his head around. In that instant, she saw myriad emotions cross his features—surprise, delight, resignation and something that looked very much like yearning before he shuttered his expression.

"Laura, hi."

"Hello."

"Just a second."

He pulled the earbuds out and tucked them away, then crossed to the compressor and turned off the low churning sound. The only sound to break the abrupt silence was the moaning of the wind in the treetops. Taft quickly grabbed a T-shirt slung over a nearby sawhorse and pulled it over his head, and she couldn't help the little pang of disappointment.

"I brought you a pie. My mother made it for you." She held out it, suddenly feeling slightly ridiculous at the meagerness of the offering.

"A pie?"

"I know, it's a small thing. Not at all commensurate with everything you did, but…well, it's something."

"Thank you. I love pie. And I haven't had anything to eat yet, so this should be great. I might just have pie for dinner."

He had a square bandage just under his hairline that made him look rather rakish, a startling white contrast to his dark hair and sun-warmed features.

"Your head. You were hurt during the rescue, weren't you?"

He shrugged. "No big deal. Just a little cut."

Out of nowhere, she felt the hot sting of tears threaten. "I'm sorry."

"Are you kidding? This is nothing. I would have gladly broken every limb, as long as it meant I could still get to the kids."

She stared at him there in the twilight, looking big and solid and dearly familiar, and a huge wave of love washed over her. This was Taft. Her best friend. The man she had loved forever, who could always make her laugh, who made her feel strong and powerful and able to accomplish anything she wanted.

Everything she had been trying to block out since she arrived back in Pine Gulch seemed to break through some invisible dam and she was filled, consumed, by her love for him.

Those tears burned harder and she knew she had to leave or she would completely embarrass herself by losing her slippery hold on control and sobbing all over him.

She drew in a shuddering breath. "I… I just wanted to say thank-you. Again, I mean. It's not enough. It will never be enough, but thank you. I owe you…everything."

"No, you don't. You owe me nothing. I was only doing my job."

"Only your job? Really?"

He gazed at her for a long moment and she prayed he couldn't see the emotions she could feel nearly choking her. "Okay, no," he finally said. "If I had been doing my job and following procedure, I would have waited for the swift-water tech team to come help me extri-cate them. I would have done everything by the book. I spend seventy percent of my time training my volunteers in the fire department *not* to do what I did today. This wasn't a job. It was much, much more."

A tear slipped free but she ignored it. She could barely make out his expression now in the twilight and had to hope the reverse was also true. She had to leave. Now, before she made a complete fool of herself.

"Well... I'm in your debt. You've got a room anytime you want at the inn."

"Thanks, I appreciate that."

She released a breath and nodded. "Well, thank you again. Enjoy the pie. I'll, uh, see you later."

She turned so swiftly that she nearly stumbled but caught herself and began to hurry back to her SUV while the tears she had struggled to contain broke free and trickled down her cheeks. She didn't know exactly why she was crying. Probably not a single reason. The stress of nearly losing her children, the joy of having them returned to her. And the sudden knowledge that she loved Taft Bowman far more than she ever had as a silly twenty-one-year-old girl.

"Laura, wait."

She shook her head, unable to turn around and reveal so much of her heart to him. As she should have expected, she only made it a few more steps before he caught up with her and turned her to face him.

He gazed down at her and she knew she must look horrible, blotchy-faced and red, with tears dripping everywhere.

"Laura," he murmured. Just that. And then with a groan he folded her into his arms, wrapping her in his heat and his strength. She shuddered again and could no longer stop the deluge. He held her as she sobbed out everything that suddenly seemed too huge and heavy for her to contain.

"I could have lost them."

"I know. I know." His arms tightened and his cheek rested on her hair, and she realized this was exactly where she belonged. Nothing else mattered. She loved Taft Bowman, had always loved him, and more than that, she trusted him.

He was her hero in every possible way.

"And you." She sniffled. "You risked your life to go after them. You could have been carried away just as easily."

"I wasn't, though. All three of us made it through."

She tightened her arms around him and they stood that way for a long time with the creek rumbling over rocks nearby while the wind sighed in the trees and an owl hooted softly somewhere close and the crickets chirped for their mates.

Something changed between them in those moments. It reminded her very much of the first time he had kissed her, on that boulder overlooking River Bow Ranch, when she somehow knew that the world had shifted in some fundamental way and nothing would ever be the same.

After several moments, he moved his hands from around her and framed her face, his eyes reflecting the stars, then he kissed her with a tenderness that made her want to weep all over again.

It was a perfect moment, standing here with him as night descended, and she never wanted it to end. She wanted to savor everything—the soft cotton of his shirt, the leashed muscles beneath, his mouth, so firm and determined on hers.

She spread her palms on his back, pressing him closer, and he made a low sound in his throat, tightening his arms around her and deepening the kiss. She opened her mouth for him and slid her tongue out to dance with his while she pressed against those solid muscles, needing more.

His hand slipped beneath her shirt to the bare skin at her waist and she remembered just how he had always known how to touch her and taste her until she was crazy with need. She shivered, just a slight motion, but it was enough that he pulled his mouth away from hers, his breathing ragged and his eyes dazed.

He gazed down at her and she watched awareness return to his features like storm clouds crossing the moon, then he slid his hands away and took a step back.

"You asked me not to kiss you again. I'm sorry, Laura. I tried. I swear I tried."

She blinked, trying to force her brain to work. After a moment, she remembered the last time he had kissed her, in the room she had just finished decorating. She remembered her confusion and fear, remembered being so certain he would hurt her all over again if she let him.

That all seemed another lifetime ago. Had she really let her fears rule her common sense?

This was Taft, the man she had loved since she was twelve years old. He loved her and he loved her children. When she had climbed out of his brother's police vehicle and seen him there by the stretcher with his arms around Alex—and more, when she had seen that rope still tied to the tree and the churning, dangerous waters he had risked to save both of her children—she had known he was a man she could count on. He had been willing to break any rule, to give up everything to save her children.

I would have gladly broken every limb, as long as it meant I could still get to the kids.

He had risked his life. How much was she willing to risk?

Everything.

She gave him a solemn look, her heart jumping inside her chest, feeling very much as if *she* was the one about to leap into Cold Creek. "Technically, *I* could still kiss you, though, right?"

He stared at her and she saw his eyes darken with confusion and a wary sort of hope. That little glimmer was all she needed to step forward into the space between them and grab his strong, wonderful hands. She tugged him toward her and stood on tiptoe and pressed her mouth to the corner of his mouth.

He didn't seem to know how to respond for a moment and then he angled his mouth and she kissed him fully, with all the joy and love in her heart.

Much to her shock, he eased away again, his expression raw and almost despairing. "I can't do this back-and-forth thing, Laura. You have to decide. I love you. I never stopped, all this time. I think some part of me has just been biding my time, waiting for you to come home."

He pulled his hands away. "I know I hurt you ten years ago. I can't change that. If I could figure out how, I would in a heartbeat."

At that, she had to shake her head. "I wouldn't change anything," she said. "If things had been different, I wouldn't have Alex and Maya."

He released a breath. "I can tell you, I realized right after you left what a fool I had been, too stubborn and proud to admit I was hurting and not dealing with it well. And then I compounded my stupidity by not coming after you like I wanted to."

"I waited for you. I didn't date anyone for two years, even though I heard all the stories about…well, the Bandito and everything. If you had called or emailed or anything, I would have come home in an instant."

"I'm a different man than I was then. I want to think I've become a *better* man, but I've still probably picked up a few more nicks and bruises than I had then."

"Haven't we all?" she murmured.

"I need to tell you, I want everything, Laura. I want a home, family. I want those things with you, the same things I wanted a decade ago."

Joy burst through her. When he reached for her hand, she curled her fingers inside his, wondering how it was possible to go from the depths of hell to this brilliant happiness in the course of one day.

"I hope you know I love your children, too. Alex is such a great kid. I can think of a hundred things I would love to show him. How to ride a two-wheeler, how to throw a spitball, how to saddle his own horse. I think I could be a good father to him."

He brought their intertwined fingers to his heart. "And Maya. She's a priceless gift, Laura. I don't know exactly what she's going to need out of life, but I can promise you, right now, that I would spend the rest of my life doing whatever it takes to give it to her. I swear to you, I would watch over her, keep her safe, give her every chance she has to stretch her wings as far as she can. I want to give her a place she can grow. A place where she knows, every single minute, that she's loved."

If she hadn't already been crazy in love with this man, his words alone and his love for her fragile, vulnerable daughter would have done the trick. She gazed up at him and felt tears of joy trickle out.

"I didn't mean to make you cry," he murmured, his own eyes wet. The significance of that did not escape her. The old Taft never would have allowed that sign of emotion.

"I love you, Taft. I love you so very much."

Words seemed wholly inadequate, like offering a caramel-apple pie in exchange for saving two precious lives, so she did the only thing she could. She kissed him again, holding him tightly to her. Could he feel the joy pulsing through her, powerful, strong, delicious?

After long, wonderful moments, he eased away again and she saw that he had been as moved as she by the embrace.

"Will you come see the house now?" he asked.

Was this his subtle way of taking her inside to make love? She wasn't quite sure she was ready to add one more earthshaking experience on this most tumultuous of days, but she did want to see his house. Besides that, she trusted him completely. If she asked him to wait, he would do it without question.

"Yes," she answered. He grinned and grabbed her hand and together they walked through the trees toward his house. He guided her up the stairs at the side of the house that led first to the wide uncovered porch and then inside to the great room with the huge windows.

She saw some similarities to the River Bow ranch house in the size of the two-story great room and the wall of windows, but there were differences, too. A balcony ringed the great room and she could see rooms leading off it.

How many bedrooms were in this place? she wondered. And why would a bachelor build this house that seemed made for a family?

The layout seemed oddly familiar to her and some of the details, as well. The smooth river-rock fireplace, the open floor plan, the random use of knobby, bulging, uniquely shaped logs as accents.

Only after he took her into the kitchen and she looked around at the gleaming appliances did all the details come together in her head.

"This is my house," she exclaimed.

"Our house," he corrected. "Remember how you used to buy log-home books and magazines and pore over them? I started building this house six months ago. It wasn't until you came back to Pine Gulch that I realized how I must have absorbed all those dreams inside me. I guess when I was planning the house, some of them must have soaked through my subconscious and onto the blueprints. I didn't even think about it until I saw you again."

It was a house that seemed built for love, for laughter, for children to climb over the furniture and dangle toys off the balcony.

"Do you like it?" he asked, and she saw that wariness in his eyes again that never failed to charm her far more than a teasing grin and lighthearted comment.

"I love everything about it, Taft. It's perfect. Beyond perfect."

He pulled her close again and as he held her there in the house he had built, she realized that love wasn't always a linear journey. Sometimes it took unexpected dips and curves and occasional sheer dropoffs. Yet somehow, despite the pain of their past, she and Taft had found their way together again.

This time, she knew, they were here to stay.

Epilogue

His bride was late.

Taft stood in the entryway of the little Pine Gulch chapel under one of the many archways decorated with ribbons and flowers of red and bronze and deep green, greeting a few latecomers and trying his best not to fidget. He glanced at his watch. Ten minutes and counting when he was supposed to be tying the knot, and so far Laura was a no-show.

"She'll go through with it this time. The woman is crazy about you. Relax."

He glanced over at Trace, dressed in his best-man's Western-cut tuxedo. His brother looked disgustingly calm and Taft wanted to punch him.

"I know," he answered. For all his nerves, he didn't doubt that for a moment. Over the past six months, their love had only deepened, become more rich and beautiful like the autumn colors around them. He had no worries about her pulling out of the wedding at the last minute.

He glanced through the doors of the chapel as if he could make her appear there. "I'm just hoping she's not having trouble somewhere. You don't have your radio on you, do you?"

Trace raised an eyebrow. "Uh, no. It's a wedding, in case you forgot. I don't need to have my radio squawking in the middle of the ceremony. I figured I could do without it for a few hours."

"Probably a good idea. You don't think she's been in an accident or something?"

Trace gave him a compassionate look. One of the hazards of working in public safety was this constant awareness of all the things that could go wrong in a person's life, but usually didn't. He was sure Trace worried about Becca and Gabi just as much as he fretted for Laura and the children.

"No. I'm sure there's a reasonable explanation. Why don't we check in with Caidy?"

That would probably be the logical course of action before he went off in a panic, since as maid of honor, she should be with Laura. "Yeah. Right. Good idea. Give me your phone."

"I can do it. That's what a best man is for, right?"

"Just give me your phone. Please?" he added, when Trace looked reluctant.

Trace reached into the inside pocket of his black suit jacket for his phone. "Hold on. I'll have to turn it back on. Wouldn't want any phones going off as you're taking your vows, either."

He waited impatiently, and after an eternity, his brother handed the activated phone over. Before he could find Caidy's number in the address book, the phone buzzed.

"Where are you?" he answered when he saw her name on the display.

"Taft? Why do you have Trace's phone?"

"I was just about to call you. What's wrong? Is Laura okay?"

"We're just pulling up to the church. I was calling to give you the heads-up that we might need a few more minutes. Maya woke up with a stomachache, apparently. She threw up before we left the cottage and then again on our way, all over her dress. We had to run back to the inn to find something else for her to wear."

"Is she all right now?"

"Eh. Okay, but not great. She's still pretty fretful. Laura's trying to soothe her. Have the organist keep playing, and as soon as we get there, we'll try to fix Maya up and calm her down a little more, then we can get this show on the road. Here we are now."

He saw the limo he had hired from Jackson Hole pulling up to the side door of the church, near the room set aside for the bridal party. "I see you. Thanks for calling."

He hung up the phone and handed it back to Trace. Ridge had joined them, he saw, and wore a little furrow of concern between his eyes.

"The girls okay?" Ridge asked.

"Maya's got a stomachache. Can you stall for a few more minutes?"

"Sure. How about a roping demonstration or something? I think I've got a lasso in the pickup."

He had to look closely at his older brother to see that Ridge was teasing, probably trying to ease the tension.

Yeah, it wasn't really working. "I think a few more songs should be sufficient. I'm going to go check on Maya."

"What about the whole superstition about not seeing the bride before the wedding?" Trace asked. "As I recall, you and Ridge practically hog-tied me to keep me away from Becca before ours."

"These are special circumstances. You want to try to stop me, you're more than welcome. Good luck with that."

Neither brother seemed inclined to interfere, so Taft made his way through the church to the bridal-party room. Outside the door, he could hear the low hush of women's voices and then a little whimper. That tiny sound took away any remaining hesitation and he pushed open the door.

His gaze instinctively went to Laura. She was stunning in a cream-colored mid-length lace confection, her silky golden hair pulled up in an intricate style that made her look elegant and vulnerable at the same time. Maya huddled in her lap, wearing only a white slip. Caidy and Jan stood by, looking helpless.

When Maya spotted him, she sniffed loudly. "Chief," she whimpered.

He headed over to the two females he loved with everything inside him and picked her up, heedless of his rented tux.

"What's the matter, little bug?"

"Tummy hurts."

She didn't seem to have a fever, from what he could tell.

"Do you think it's the giardiasis?" Jan asked.

He thought of the girl's abdominal troubles after her

near-drowning, the parasite she had picked up from swallowing half the Cold Creek. "I wouldn't think so. She's been healthy for three months. Doc Dalton said she didn't need any more medicine."

His knees still felt weak whenever he thought of the miraculous rescue of the children. He knew he had been guided to them somehow. He found it equally miraculous that Alex had emerged unscathed from the ordeal and Maya's only lingering effect was the giardia bug she'd picked up.

She sure didn't look very happy right now, though. He wondered if he ought to call in Jake Dalton from the congregation to check on her, when he suddenly remembered a little tidbit of information that had slipped his mind in the joy-filled chaos leading up to the wedding.

"Maya, how many pieces of cake did you have last night at the rehearsal dinner?"

Two separate times he'd seen her with a plate of dessert but hadn't thought much about it until right now.

She shrugged, though he thought she looked a little guilty as she held up two fingers.

"Are you sure?"

She looked at her mother, then back at him, then used her other hand to lift up two more fingers.

Laura groaned. "No wonder she's sick this morning. I should have thought of that. We were all so distracted, I guess we must not have realized she made so many trips to the dessert table."

"I like cake," Maya announced.

He had to smile. "I do too, bug, but you should probably go easy on the wedding cake at the reception later."

"Okay."

He hugged her. "Feel better now?"

She nodded and wiped a fist at a few stray tears on her cheeks. She was completely adorable, and he still couldn't believe he had been handed this other miraculous gift, the chance to step in and be the father figure to this precious child and her equally precious brother.

"My dress is icky."

"You won't be able to wear your flower-girl dress with the fluffy skirt," Jan agreed. "We're going to have to wash it. It will probably be dry by the reception tonight, though. And look! I bought this red one for you for Christmas. We'll use that one at the wedding now and you'll look beautiful."

"You're a genius, Mom," Laura murmured.

"I have my moments," Jan said. She took her granddaughter from his arms to help her into the dress and fix her hair again.

"Crisis averted?" he asked Laura while Jan and Caidy fussed around Maya.

"I think so." She gave him a grateful smile and his heart wanted to burst with love for her, especially when she stepped closer to him and slipped her arms around his waist. "Are you sure you're ready to take on all this fun and excitement?"

He wrapped his arms around her, thinking how perfectly she fit there, how she filled up all the empty places that had been waiting all these years just for her. He kissed her forehead, careful not to mess up her pretty curls. "I've never been more sure of anything. I hope you know that."

"I do," she murmured.

He desperately wanted to kiss her, but had a feeling his sister and her mother wouldn't appreciate it in the middle of their crisis.

The door behind them opened and Alex burst through, simmering with the energy field that always seemed to surround him except when he was sleeping. "When is the wedding going to start? I'm tired of waiting."

"I know what you mean, kid," Taft said with a grin, stepping away from Laura a little so he could pull Alex over for a quick hug.

His family. He had waited more than ten years for this, and he didn't know if he had the patience to stand another minute's delay before all his half-buried dreams became reality.

"Okay. I think we're good here," Caidy said, as Jan adjusted the ribbon in the girl's brown hair.

"Doesn't she look great?"

"Stunning," he claimed.

Maya beamed at him and slipped her hand in his. "Marry now."

"That's a great idea, sweetheart." He turned to Laura. "Are you ready?"

She smiled at him, and as he gazed at this woman he had known for half his life and loved for most of that time, he saw the rest of their lives ahead of them, bright and beautiful, and filled with joy and laughter and love.

"I finally am," she said, reaching for his hand, and together they walked toward their future.

* * * * *

We hope you enjoyed reading

DENIM AND DIAMONDS

by *New York Times* bestselling author

DEBBIE MACOMBER

and

A COLD CREEK REUNION

by *New York Times* bestselling author

RAEANNE THAYNE

Both were originally
Harlequin® Special Edition series stories!

Discover more heartfelt tales of family, friendship and love from the **Harlequin® Special Edition** series. Romance is for life, and these stories show that every chapter in a relationship has its challenges and delights, and that love can be renewed with each turn of the page.

♦HARLEQUIN®

SPECIAL EDITION

Life, Love and Family

Look for six *new* romances every month
from **Harlequin Special Edition!**

Available wherever books are sold.

SPECIAL EXCERPT FROM

H HARLEQUIN®

SPECIAL EDITION

Zoe Robinson refuses to believe she's a secret Fortune, but she can't deny the truth—she's falling for Joaquin Mendoza! But can this Prince Charming convince his Cinderella to find happily-ever-after with him once he uncovers his own family secrets?

Read on for a sneak preview of
FORTUNE'S PRINCE CHARMING,
the latest installment in
THE FORTUNES OF TEXAS:
ALL FORTUNE'S CHILDREN*.*

Joaquin nodded. "It was interesting. I saw a side of your father I'd never seen before. I have acquired a brand-new appreciation for him."

"That makes me so happy. You don't even know. I wish everyone could see him the way you do."

"Thanks for having him invite me."

Zoe held up her hand. "Actually, all I did was ask him if you were coming tonight, and he's the one who decided to invite you. He really likes you, Joaquin. And so do I."

He was silent for a moment, just looking at her in a way that she couldn't read. For a second, she was afraid he was going to friend-zone her again.

"I like you, too, Zoe. You know what I like most about you?"

She shook her head.

"You always see the best in everyone, even in me. I know I haven't been the easiest person to get to know."

Zoe laughed. Even if he was hard to get to know, Joaquin obviously had no idea what a great guy he was.

"I wish I could claim that as a heroic quality," she said. "But it's not hard to see the good in you. I mean, good grief, half the women in the office are in love with you."

He made a face that said he didn't believe her.

"But I don't want to share you."

He answered her by lowering his head and covering her mouth with his. It was a kiss that she felt all the way down to her curled toes.

When they finally came up for air, he said, "In case you're wondering, I just made a move on you."

Don't miss
FORTUNE'S PRINCE CHARMING
by Nancy Robards Thompson,
available May 2016 wherever
Harlequin® Special Edition books and ebooks are sold.

www.Harlequin.com

HSEEXP0416

H HARLEQUIN®
™

SPECIAL EDITION

Life, Love and Family

Use this coupon to save

$1.00

on the purchase of any
Harlequin® Special Edition book.

Available wherever books are sold, including
most bookstores, supermarkets, drugstores
and discount stores.

Save $1.00

on the purchase of any Harlequin® Special Edition book.

Coupon valid until June 27, 2016.
Redeemable at participating outlets in the U.S. and Canada only.
Not redeemable at Barnes & Noble stores. Limit one coupon per customer.

52613614

5 65373 00076 2   (8100)0 12153

THE WORLD IS BETTER
WITH
Romance

Harlequin has everything from contemporary, passionate and heartwarming to suspenseful and inspirational stories.

Whatever your mood,
we have a romance just for you!

Connect with us to find your next great read, special offers and more.

f /HarlequinBooks

🐦 @HarlequinBooks

www.HarlequinBlog.com

www.Harlequin.com/Newsletters

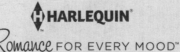

⬦ HARLEQUIN®

A *Romance* FOR EVERY MOOD™

www.Harlequin.com